FIC ALEXAND HA Solemn
Alexander, Hannah.
Solemn oath /

D0204561

AUG 0 5 2011

# SOLEMN OATH

# HANNAH ALEXANDER

# SOLEMN OATH

**BETHANY HOUSE PUBLISHERS**
MINNEAPOLIS, MINNESOTA 55438

*Solemn Oath*
Copyright © 2000
Hannah Alexander

Cover by Lookout Design Group, Inc.

All rights reserved. No part of this publication may be reproduced, stored in a retrieval system, or transmitted in any form or by any means—electronic, mechanical, photocopying, recording, or otherwise—without the prior written permission of the publisher and copyright owners.

Published by Bethany House Publishers
A Ministry of Bethany Fellowship International
11400 Hampshire Avenue South
Minneapolis, Minnesota 55438
www.bethanyhouse.com

Printed in the United States of America by
Bethany Press International, Minneapolis, Minnesota 55438

Library of Congress Cataloging-in-Publication Data

Alexander, Hannah.
    Solemn oath / by Hannah Alexander.
        p. cm.
    Sequel to: Sacred trust.
    ISBN 0-7642-2348-8
    1. Physicians—Fiction.  I. Title.
PS3551.L3558 S65 2000
813'.54—dc21                                                         99-050972

Now to him who is able to do
immeasurably more than all we ask or imagine,
according to his power that is at work within us,
to him be glory in the church and in Christ Jesus
throughout all generations, for ever and ever! Amen.

(EPHESIANS 3:20–21, NIV)

———

In memory of Vickie Ann Mills,

July 26, 1954, to January 23, 2000,

a dear friend and co-laborer in Christ
who is now enjoying a miraculous reward.
Vickie has left a spirit of kindness as her legacy.
Her favorite verse was Jeremiah 29:11:
" 'For I know the plans I have for you,' declares the Lord,
'plans to prosper you and not to harm you,
plans to give you hope and a future . . .' "

HANNAH ALEXANDER is a pseudonym for the writing team of Cheryl and Melvin Hodde. Their previous fiction includes *The Healing Promise* and *Ozark Sunrise*. When not assisting Cheryl in the writing process, Melvin practices emergency medicine in a Missouri hospital.

Books by
# Hannah Alexander
FROM BETHANY HOUSE PUBLISHERS

*Sacred Trust*

*Solemn Oath*

# ACKNOWLEDGMENTS

Again, thanks to David Horton, Senior Editor at Bethany House, for continued support, advice, and patience with us as we learn and grow (we hope). We also owe Terry McDowell and Jeremy Greenhouse on the staff our gratitude for the time spent on research and personal encouragement in addition to editing duties—Terry, you'll never know how much we appreciate the pep talks. We are blessed by the dedication of the Bethany House staff.

Thanks to Mom, Lorene Cook, for serving as first draft editor, sounding board, local publicity manager, and anything else that needs to be done. Thanks, also, to Mom and Stepdad, Vera and Ray Overall, for constant encouragement and PR.

For the input on arson and fire safety, we are indebted to our friend and former fireman and writer Gregg Mercer, and to uncle Fred Baugher, retired Battalion Chief of Ventura County Fire Department. The blame for any discrepancies in this book belongs solely to the authors, not to the experts.

Thanks, again, to cousin Mark Patterson for the lovable pattern you have given us for Clarence's character and struggles. Thanks to Jack and Mary Clotfelter for an intimate view of Arthur and Alma's pain, and their ability to forgive. And thanks to Jack and Marty Frost for the giving spirit displayed by Theo's boss down at Jack's Print Shop.

Thanks to Barbara Warren, who is never too busy for a good manuscript slashing. Thanks to Jackie Bolton, whose attention to detail and willingness to drop everything helped us a great deal with galley proofs.

We appreciate Murray Bishoff, editor of the *Monett Times*, who gave us such a good write-up in our hometown paper, and serves as an excellent contrast to the poor diplomacy skills of Harvey at the *Knolls Review*.

Thanks to Dr. Dennis Hensley, Jack Cavanaugh, and Gayle Roper for many insights into the writing life. We have been uplifted by your sharing spirits.

Thanks to all those who helped this story come about. May God bless you.

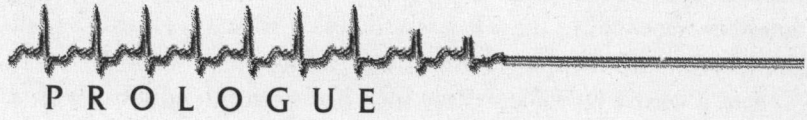

# PROLOGUE

Leonardo the lion lay cold in his cage. Splotches of rusty red-brown stained his coat around a bullet wound in his right side, and a grown man's sobs echoed against the concrete wall that protected Leonardo's inner sanctum.

Cowboy Casey knelt beside his pet, forehead pressed against the stained velvet shoulder, tears dampening the tawny fur. "My friend . . . why?"

With callused fingers, he tested the stiffness of the lion's well-fed ribs. Rigor mortis. The killer had probably struck before dawn, when Cowboy was taking his autumn load of exotic animals to the station for shipment.

"Who would do a thing like this? What kind of a cruel . . ." Cowboy knew the answer before the question completely formed in his mind. The muscles in his jaw hardened, and his teeth ground together as he fought against a sudden, overwhelming rage. "Berring!"

He exhaled an angry gush of air and jerked to his feet to pace across the cage. Of course Berring. Two weeks after that madman had moved into the neighboring farm this summer, a gaping hole mysteriously appeared in the bison pasture fence. Thank goodness for three brave buddies with herding skills.

Berring had also called the sheriff out twice in the past month with some wild-haired story about Leonardo roaming the woods at night. The sheriff knew better, and so did every farmer in Knolls County. Cowboy had never put his neighbors in danger of the powerful animals he raised on his ranch.

He pivoted and walked across to hunker down once more beside the big cat. Leonardo had been his most faithful pal for the past four years, in spite of the roughhousing that had gone too far a couple of times and sent him to the ER a few times. It wasn't Leonardo's fault he had jaws with the impact of a backhoe.

And it wasn't his fault a crazy man had been turned loose with a gun.

"He won't get away with it, my friend," Cowboy said as he grabbed up his hat and strode from the cage.

---

Off-duty fireman Buck Oppenheimer stepped through the front entrance of his favorite convenience store, the Pride of Knolls. He unfolded a ten-dollar bill to pay for his gasoline, looking around for Roxie, the regular weekday clerk. The place was deserted.

"Hey, Rox!" His voice carried over the tops of tightly packed shelves toward the back of the store. "Put your cigarette out and get back to work. Break's over!"

He grinned to himself, waiting for her usual sharp comeback. He and Roxie had an ongoing rivalry about who could give the best insult. Roxie usually won, because Buck had been raised to treat all women like ladies. And Roxie was no lady.

There was no reply, but sure enough, he did smell smoke. He always smelled smoke in here. All the old farmers ignored the signs plastered by management on the windows and the front of the counter, and Roxie was the worst offender of the bunch. She always stated proudly that she'd been smoking two packs a day for fifty years, and management could fire her if they wanted. She'd been here for the past ten years. Truth was, management was scared of her.

But sixty-year-old Roxie didn't come plunging through the squeaky swinging doors from the back the way she always did. Buck listened for the sound of a toilet flushing or of Roxie shuffling boxes around in the back. Could be she hadn't heard him come in.

"Roxie?" He sniffed again and noticed that the smoke was stronger.

And different . . . sharper.

"Roxie!"

A faint popping, rushing, cracking sound reached him, then a heavy thump . . . and a muffled cry that sounded like a tomcat meowing.

A wisp of smoke slithered into the shopping area between the twin stock room doors.

"Help!" came the tomcat's voice again. It was Roxie.

Buck ran out the door and the few feet back to his truck. He radioed for backup, then grabbed his fire-resistant jacket and his ax and raced back in through the swinging doors into the storage area. Bright tongues of flame raced along a stack of cardboard boxes that surrounded a smoking barbeque grill in the far corner.

"Roxie, where are you?" he shouted, covering the lower part of his face with his arm to protect his lungs from the heat and smoke.

"Help me! I'm in here with the fire extinguisher!" The thumps came from his right, on the other side of a solid wooden door that led to a smaller storage room. "This door's stuck again, and it's getting smoky in here! Hurry!"

"Stand back, Rox, I'm going to force it open."

"Who's out there?" she demanded. "Buck, that you?"

"Yes, stand back!"

He knew there wasn't a whole lot of room in there to move around, much less stand back. He rammed his shoulder against the door and bounced hard against it. "Is it unlocked?"

"Of course!"

He shoved again, this time putting his full muscle-builder's weight against it, but he bounced from the wood once more as a slice of pain streaked down his right arm. He coughed at the thickening smoke.

The fire quickened with sudden life. Snapping heat puckered his flesh, and the smoke twisted and bunched around him as if it were alive. He struggled not to breathe too much of the dark thickness. He stood back from the door, raised his ax, and slammed the blade into the wood above the knob. Roxie squealed. When he plunged forward with his shoulder this time, the door splintered and gave way with him and he tumbled in.

"Hurry!" Roxie shouted. "There's a barbeque grill that could—"

A loud sound like the boom of a cannon reached them, and the wall beside them imploded. Sudden, sharp pain pierced Buck's chest just before he grabbed Roxie, threw her beneath him, and fell over her. A shelf of paper towels toppled onto them as another blast hit.

Through the blackness and heat and smothering smoke, he heard the welcome sound of a siren. His friends would come through.

————

Downtown Knolls, Missouri, held the picturesque quality of one of those postcards they sold in the ancient Ben Franklin store on the northeast corner of the square. Early autumn barely touched the lush growth of maple and oak trees with kisses of gold and rust. The three-story brick courthouse in the center of the square rose up from its broad landscape of green grass and evergreen hedge like a graceful sculpture. Across the street Arthur and Alma Collins stepped out of Little Mary's Barbeque with their sandwiches and home fries.

"I never could figure out how they can say the food is homemade when the café isn't home to anybody," Alma chattered to Arthur, her dark gold, naturally wavy hair reflecting the sun's warm rays. Her eyes held the same golden glow, highlighted by a gleam of anticipation as they ambled across the street toward the courthouse lawn. Their destination was a group of picnic tables settled deeply beneath the shade of the trees, where the rest of their tour group gathered.

"I mean, they make the buns at the café, don't they?" Alma stepped over the curb, taking care to walk on the sidewalk and not the grass. "Not at home in their own kitchens. They should say 'made from scratch' or somethin'. I tried to explain that to a waitress while you were orderin', but I don't think she appreciated it." The deep, warm tones of Alma's voice betrayed the southern heritage of her parents and mingled in an interesting way with the Spanish accent she and Arthur had both picked up during their years of missionary service in Mexico.

Arthur couldn't suppress a grin at his wife. This tour was a rare treat for both of them, but especially for Alma. Where they lived there were no antique stores, no modern grocery stores, no medical care. They didn't even have electricity in the small village where they'd been building a new church for the past year. Alma had worked hard alongside him, loving the people who struggled just to feed their children, teaching them safer cooking habits and hygiene as she told them about the new life they could find in Christ.

"Where do you want to go after we eat?" he asked. "We have a whole afternoon to explore before we load onto the vans again."

Alma's smile broadened. She laid a hand on Arthur's arm. "There's an antique shop down a block from the secondhand bookstore, and I know Phyllis and Shirley wanted to see if they—"

A squeal of tires from the street behind her cut off her words. Her eyes widened in alarm as she spun around, instinctively reaching for her husband.

Arthur gasped at the sight of a big black Plymouth careening around the corner of the square, going clockwise on the one-way, counterclockwise street. The car hit the curb and jumped it with a squeal of springs, rumbling toward them with evil intent.

"Oh my goodness . . . Arthur, look out!"

Arthur grabbed Alma's shoulders and jerked her toward him.

He caught sight of a dark head slumped over the steering wheel just before the front tires dug into the lawn. Alma screamed as the heavy bumper slammed into the backs of her legs and thrust her against Arthur. A confusion of tearing pain and terrified cries collided with jumbled bits of sky and ground. Picnic tables and people scattered across the broad lawn.

Everything ended abruptly with the crash of metal against concrete.

------

Cowboy saw the gleam of dark steel from the barrel of the .22 rifle just before it exploded with fire and sound, ripping into his right upper arm and shoving him sideways with the force of its blast. He cried out with pain and surprise as his body slammed against the front porch railing.

Berring, greasy haired and scowling, slung the screen door wide open and followed the gun out onto the porch. "Get off my property or I'll blow that arm off next time!" he growled in a voice that could cut tin cans in two with its gritty depth.

Blood oozed out between Cowboy's fingers as he gripped the bullet wound. He gaped at the man. Cold shock washed through him as he stared at Leonardo's murderer—and maybe his own.

Sharp, angry pain raced through his arm and shoulder. He stumbled backward down the steps of the porch. Berring raised his gun, took aim again, and fired a booming shot that sent a bullet whizzing past Cowboy's left ear.

Cowboy pivoted and plunged into the thicket of woods beside the littered front yard. This was crazy! Things like this didn't happen in Knolls. He stumbled over roots and limbs, twisted his foot in a hole but caught himself and kept running.

Berring's voice came closer. "How does it feel, zoo keeper?" The machine gun fire of laughter followed. "How does it feel to be afraid? Why don't you turn around and face me like a man?"

Another shot rang out, along with the wicked thud of tearing wood and the crackle of footsteps through briars and poison ivy. Cowboy tripped through a thicket of gooseberry bushes and danced across oak tree roots to keep from falling on his face. A bullet whisked barely an inch over his head before he could straighten again. For a desperate second he considered turning and facing his attacker and trying to wrestle the rifle from him, but the sudden sound of a John Deere tractor echoed through the trees.

Yes! He remembered! Old Mr. Gibson was plowing his south twenty today.

Cowboy plunged from the protective stand of forest and ran across the unbroken ground, waving his good arm. Mr. Gibson caught sight of him and casually waved back, then frowned and stopped his tractor as Cowboy drew nearer.

"What happened this time, Jacob?" the old farmer called out. "That lion try to eat you again, or did one of those ostriches finally get a kick at you?"

"Berring shot me." Barely breaking stride, Cowboy leaped onto the tow bar behind the big back wheels of the small farm tractor. "Can you get me to the hospital? And we'd better call the sheriff. That man's dangerous!"

Mr. Gibson blinked at Cowboy, then something caught his attention from the edge of the woods. Cowboy cast a panicked glance over his shoulder and saw the maniac run out of the forest shadow and stop to stand at the edge of the field, glaring at them, rifle tucked beneath his left arm.

Mr. Gibson didn't ask any questions, just pulled back the clutch and steered the tractor out of the field. "Guess the plowin' can wait."

# CHAPTER 1

Knolls Community Hospital, settled within the autumn-dusted elegance of a Knolls residential section, gave new arrivals the impression of serenity with its pink granite two-story structure and thick evergreen landscaping. The emergency and outpatient areas formed a wing jutting out from the building westward, looking like an arm reaching out to welcome patients in. Two hundred fifty health-care personnel, food service and housekeeping providers, and office workers earned their living here. They gave quality care to up to sixty patients on the floor. Family physicians' offices clustered close, circling the main structure in a large section of acreage. The hospital administrator, Mrs. Estelle Pinkley, ruled with the firm hand of a hardheaded, hard-nosed grandmother, who almost everyone in the county knew and loved.

Dr. Lukas Bower, the unwilling temporary director of Knolls Emergency Department, depended on Mrs. Pinkley to help him handle staff and make executive decisions. In the meantime he took every opportunity to convince her that he was a doctor, not an administrator. If the future of Knolls Community Hospital depended on his interdepartmental skills, the jobs of two hundred fifty people stood in the shadow of death.

Today, however, the third Monday in September, Lukas gave even less thought than usual to paper work and verbal sparring. The ambulance radio had just blared out the news of a bad accident involving a car and a tour group down on the square. At least five people, including the driver of the car, were being brought in, several of them serious.

Lukas released the switch that had sent his voice over the radio to the paramedic on scene and turned with growing restlessness to locate his staff. Judy, the slender secretary with short salt-and-pepper hair, sat at the computer and spoke on the telephone to a patient who had been treated and released last night.

Lukas picked up his own phone at his workstation at the large oblong central ER control counter and dialed Surgery. He told the nurse to keep a surgery suite open until he knew for sure if it would be needed. He hung up and turned around to find Lauren McCaffrey, RN, stepping back into the ER from an early lunch break. Good. He needed her.

Lauren stopped to joke with one of the housekeepers, peered over Judy's shoulder to see what was on the computer screen, then glanced over at Lukas. She caught sight of his expression, and her characteristic smile disappeared.

"What's up, Dr. Bower?" She hurriedly stashed her purse beneath the desk and tied her long blond hair back into the ponytail she wore for work.

"Accident coming in," he said. "Several injuries. Apparently a group of pedestrians took on a car with a drunk driver."

She nodded. "Why does stuff like this always happen at lunch-time? I'll go make sure the trauma rooms are ready, and I'll break out the gear for the staff."

"Thanks, Lauren. Has Claudia gone to lunch?"

"Yes, but she may be back in the break room. I think she brought her lunch today." Lauren smiled and shook her head as she turned and walked toward the trauma rooms. "Mrs. Pinkley's a smart lady," she called over her shoulder. "I bet she knew double nursing coverage would increase business."

Lukas looked over to find the secretary off the phone. "Judy, would you please call upstairs for an extra nurse, and then contact Dr. Richmond. She's medical backup for today, and I need her."

"You sure?" Judy asked, peering at him over her reading glasses. "I talked to her secretary a few minutes ago, and they're up to their eyeballs in walk-ins over there at the clinic."

"Tell her I'm sorry, but it looks like we have some bad ones coming in." He turned toward the trauma rooms to make sure Lauren had all the gear the staff would need.

He knew Mercy Richmond's practice was doing well, and he was glad for her. She had worked hard for it, she was a caring doctor, and she deserved a break after long years of struggle. He hated to overwhelm her today. A busy Monday could keep her occupied long after clinic hours were over.

Times like this were why Lukas needed to hire more help, and he needed to do it as soon as possible. The growth of this progressive Ozark town of ten thousand would be reflected in the use of the hospital. They had to be prepared, and like it or not, the ER was his responsibility. The problem was, he'd never hired anyone before. Thanks to Mrs. Pinkley's erroneous faith in him, he was jumping into the directorship with both feet. He might drown.

So far Lukas was the first and only full-time physician in this department. The family practice docs affiliated with the hospital picked up hours on nights and weekends, but they were getting tired of the extra load, especially as the opportunities dwindled for sleep during night shifts. Lukas knew that firsthand, because when someone didn't come in, he usually got stuck with the extra shift. Last night was a case in point, and today was a bad day to be sleep deprived.

"Dr. Bower, I have a call for you," yelled Judy from the central desk.

When he turned to look at her, she pointed toward his workstation and motioned for him to pick up his phone. He groaned. It was probably Dorothy Wild again. She got a power rush as director of the quality assurance program, and she flaunted it at every opportunity. Once, she had even gone so far as to coordinate a disaster drill just to test Lukas. This time she was probably calling to complain because he hadn't okayed the stack of charts she'd given him last week. Or maybe Medical Records was calling to scream at him because he hadn't written a diagnosis on a patient *before* ordering lab tests.

Medicare and Medicaid and health plans were making it harder to practice medicine with the good of the patient in mind instead of the glorified buck. Health-care providers often found themselves in a Catch 22 situation. Doctors and hospitals were under increasing pressure to eliminate "unnecessary" tests, yet were provided no protection from litigation if omission of one of these "unnecessary" tests resulted in a missed diagnosis. It was crazy. And medical costs were still on the rise. If Lukas were in charge of the insurance programs, he wasn't sure what he would do about it.

He picked up the receiver. "Yes." His voice was clipped as he imagined Dorothy Wild on the other end of the line.

"Doctor?" It was an unfamiliar woman's voice, shaky with tears, and Lukas immediately regretted his curt tone. "You've got to help us. Our little boy just swallowed some stuff, and I don't know how much"—her words tumbled over themselves, threatening to spiral out of control—"and we don't know what to do, and we're too far away to—"

"Hold it, wait, calm down." Lukas kept his own voice low and calm. He glanced toward the entrance to see if the ambulance had arrived yet. The bay was still clear. He turned back. "What did your little boy swallow?"

He heard the muffled sound of a hand over the receiver, heard the woman's panicky voice, and then the sound cleared as the hand was removed.

A man's voice, high-pitched with near panic, as well, came across the line. "Hello? This is Craig Chapman. My wife's not doing too well right now." He stopped and took a breath. "I was winterizing the car out in the garage, and our three-year-old drank some of the antifreeze while my back was turned. It was dripping from his chin when I caught him."

Some of Mr. Chapman's tension transferred itself to Lukas. This could be bad. "Do you have any idea about how much he swallowed?"

"No. I hadn't used the stuff for a few months, and I didn't pay any attention. I tried to get him to throw it up, but nothing worked."

"Where do you live?" Lukas asked.

"We're out by Old Well. You're the closest hospital."

Lukas grimaced. Old Well was almost an hour's drive into the hills over rocky dirt roads.

"What can we do?" Mr. Chapman asked, panic once more filling his voice. "Will this stuff hurt him?"

"It depends on how much he drank, Mr. Chapman. I need you and your wife to stay calm so we can discuss this and help your son as quickly as possible." Old Well . . . what was it Lukas remembered about that place? "Do you have any liquor in the house?"

"No, we don't drink."

"How about your neighbors? Are you close to a liquor store?"

"We don't know our neighbors around here yet. We just moved in from Kansas." The man's voice grew tighter and higher. "Tell me what to do!"

"Do you have any cooking extracts? Any vanilla?" If there was enough, vanilla extract could save the child's eyesight due to the high percentage of alcohol. It could even save his life.

He heard the man put the phone down and ask his wife, heard her frantic reply and a small clatter of bottles, and then suddenly remembered who else lived near Old Well. Yes!

Chapman came back on the line. "We've just got half of a little bottle of vanilla, Doctor. Is that enough? Will that help?"

"Give it to him, but you'll need more."

"He's not showing any symptoms yet. He isn't acting sick."

"The symptoms won't show up for twelve to twenty-four hours." And then it would be too late. "Mr. Chapman, do you know Emmet and Ruby Taylor? They live out in the hills near you at the edge of Mark Twain National Forest, about two miles from the cemetery by the church at Old Well." He should know. Ruby Taylor had almost died of lead poisoning from her still a few months ago. The still had been destroyed since then, but Lukas knew Ruby. "Take your son over to their place. Tell them I sent you, and ask for a bottle of their best. They'll have liquor somewhere." He prayed that the Taylors were there. They usually were, with their teenaged boys and dairy farm, pigs and chickens, and rusted-out tireless cars sitting in the front yard.

"You want me to get my little boy drunk?" Chapman asked, a hint of indignation in his voice, as if it had suddenly dawned on him what Lukas was saying.

"I want you to get enough grain alcohol down him to counteract the effects of the antifreeze," Lukas said. "About three tablespoons of Ruby's stuff ought to do it, but you don't want to underdose him, especially since we don't know how much he's ingested. Mix some orange juice or something with it so he'll drink it. Maybe some sugar will kill the taste. Then get him here as fast as you can."

"Won't the alcohol interfere with the antidote?"

"In this case, the alcohol *is* the antidote. Mr. Chapman, the effects can kill him if you don't treat." He didn't want to be cruel, but the man needed to be aware of the serious risks. The sound of a siren echoed through the doors, then the reflection of ambulance lights bounced against the bay entrance. "Are you okay with that?"

"Yeah, Doctor. We'll get him there."

"Good. I'll see you then."

Lukas hung up and got up to walk out to the ambulance bay just as the EMT threw open the back doors of the van. He stepped over to the foot of the first cot that was pulled out.

The patient was a female in a nonrebreather mask, fully immobilized on a long spine backboard with head blocks. She had a large bore IV in her right arm, and blood splattered her clothing. Blood also concentrated in a dark, thick stain that had seeped through a bandage over her right lower leg, where her jeans had been cut free, and a Harris long traction splint held firm.

"Is this the worst?" Lukas asked.

"Sure is. She looks pretty bad." The EMT gestured to the other patient, who was still inside the van. "That's her husband in there."

Lukas didn't like the looks of the patient's right foot—almost white from lack of circulation. She moaned, but her eyes remained closed.

The paramedic stepped out of the back of the van. Connie was a muscular, seasoned professional with short boy-cut blond hair and a chronically serious expression. "Hi, Dr. Bower. This is Alma Collins, forty-five years old. First responders had to free her from between the car and the concrete balustrade of the courthouse." Her voice remained monotone, a habit she practiced when she worked with patients to keep from alarming them. "She was unconscious on scene, but she's been coming around since we've been en route, and she's in a lot of pain. She has an obvious open tib-fib fracture, badly mangled leg, no pulse on the foot. Vitals initially on scene, heart rate 115, BP 90 over 60, respiratory rate rapid, with slight improvement following a liter bag of normal saline wide open. She's received 700 cc's so far. A lot of bleeding on scene from right lower extremity, but we managed to control it some after we placed the splint."

"What about the other patient?" Lukas gestured toward the cot still in the van.

"That's Arthur Collins, the husband," Connie said. "He has a deep scalp laceration, and it looks like he may have a dislocated or broken right shoulder. He lost a lot of blood from the scalp, but it's been controlled by direct pressure."

Lukas reached forward to check Alma more thoroughly while he continued to talk to Connie. "What else is coming?"

"Two more are on their way in the BLS ambulance, and one's coming in by private car."

Lukas placed his hands over the sides of Alma's hips and gave a gentle but firm squeeze. There was no reaction of pain. Good. He would get a film on it, but if she didn't have a pelvic fracture, it would be a lot easier for her. As Connie continued with the report, Lukas helped her rush the patient through the doors and into the first trauma room, leaving the EMT and ER tech to handle Alma's injured husband.

"Judy, get a chopper on standby," he called over his shoulder as he and Connie transferred Alma to the exam bed. "And let Lab know we've got stat blood work for them." He turned to Lauren, who had come in behind them. "Start another IV, and draw blood for a stat trauma panel."

Alma's pupils reacted briskly, and her breathing, though a little fast, was even. Her eyes remained open after he checked them. She moaned again, and Lukas bent toward her. "Mrs. Collins, I'm Dr. Bower, the ER physician here." Because Connie's businesslike manner could sometimes make a patient feel cut off from human support, he injected even more tenderness than usual into his own voice. "Can you hear me?"

Physical pain etched itself in the lines of the woman's face. Her eyes filled with tears. "Yes . . . hurts bad . . . can you help me?"

"Yes. I'm sorry, but I need to do a quick check and ask you some questions. Do you have any drug allergies?"

She attempted to shake her head.

"Please don't move your head or neck until we know how badly you're hurt. Just tell me yes or no."

"No." Her voice shook with the effort to control her reactions.

"Good. I know your right leg hurts. Do you have pain anywhere else?"

"My head." Her chin quivered. "I think I hit my head."

"Were you knocked out?"

"I think so. Arthur?" She stretched out the fingers of her right hand as if to free herself, but she was constricted by the backboard. "Where's Arthur? Is he okay?"

"I haven't checked him, but he seems to be doing okay. Do you hurt anywhere else?"

"I can't tell." She grimaced. "My leg hurts so bad. Please!"

Lukas turned to find Lauren securing the second IV tube with tape. "Get me a pressure, and if that's okay, give Mrs. Collins 2 milligrams of morphine, slow IV push. And add 12.5 milligrams of Phenergan. I don't want to risk the morphine nauseating her." He looked at the open tib-fib fracture just below the knee, then moved down to look at Alma's right foot. He still didn't like what he saw. It was cool to the touch, white, and when he checked for a pulse on top of the foot, he found none. The capillary refill was very sluggish. He had to get this woman to a vascular surgeon fast if he wanted to save her leg.

*Lord, guide me. Touch her through me. Give her the comfort I can't.*

He stepped to the hallway and called, "Judy, launch that chopper, then order me a c-spine, chest, pelvis, and right tib-fib and ankle x-rays. Have you heard from Dr. Richmond yet?"

"Yes, she'll be here shortly. She said she had to finish with a really sick patient."

Lauren straightened from Alma's bedside. "Dr. Bower, the pressure's good. Want me to do the morphine?"

"Yes. Run the second IV at 200 cc's per hour. I want her kidneys well hydrated to prevent damage. I'll be back in a moment. I need to go check on her husband." He called out to Claudia to help him and stepped into the next room, where the techs and Connie were transferring Arthur from cot to bed.

Arthur, too, was on a long spine board, with a c-collar and head blocks to keep him as immobile as possible. Blood had seeped through the gauze and Ace bandage the attendants had used to stop the bleeding from an obvious scalp laceration.

Claudia, chunky and motherly and expert with patients, stepped into the room behind Lukas and immediately began her assessment while Lukas talked to the attendants.

"Connie, you said there was a lot of blood loss. How much would you estimate?"

"At least a unit, maybe two" came the paramedic's monotone again. "The first responders said he wasn't answering their questions, but when we arrived he was alert and oriented and asking about his wife. He grew very agitated when he saw her leg. His pressure was a little low, but it came up with a fluid bolus."

Claudia turned from her assessment and nodded. "BP's 122 over 79, heart rate's 110."

Lukas nodded. Not bad. "Okay, get me a second IV." He stepped to the head of the bed and introduced himself to Arthur Collins.

"How's Alma?" the man asked. "My wife . . . she looks so bad. She's—"

"She's very worried about you," Lukas said. "We've given her morphine to help control her pain, and we're running tests now to assess her injuries. How about you, Mr. Collins? Where do you hurt?"

The man closed his eyes for a moment, as if trying to focus for a few seconds on his own symptoms. "Call me Arthur. We're Arthur and Alma. My right shoulder and my scalp took a beating, but please take care of Alma first. Her leg looks so bad, Dr. Bower. Can you help her?"

"We're going to fly her to Springfield for vascular and orthopedic surgeons to take care of her. I've already ordered an Air Care helicopter." Lukas took out his penlight. "I'm going to check your pupils right now." He shone the light into the man's worried eyes. "Are you having any trouble with blurred vision?"

"No."

"Nausea or vomiting?"

"No. When will the helicopter be here?"

Lukas turned off the light and put it in his pocket. "Shouldn't be too long, less than thirty minutes. Arthur, it's very important that I know if you're having any nausea. We have you strapped down and on your back, and that can spell trouble if you're sick. We don't want to risk letting you develop aspiration pneumonia."

"I had a little trouble before I got here, but I'm fine now."

Lukas studied the man's expression for a moment, trying to decide if he was just trying to divert help and attention back to his wife. "Have you eaten?"

"No, Alma and I didn't get a chance. Where are you taking her in Springfield?"

"Cox South, unless you have a preference."

"Cox is fine. Is there room for me in that helicopter?"

"I'm sorry, Arthur, but we'll need to keep you here for a while."

Lukas turned to Claudia and ordered blood work and x-rays. "Are the other patients here yet?"

"Yes, they came in just a couple of minutes ago. Lauren didn't want to leave Alma, so a nurse from upstairs is doing the new assessments. They don't look too bad." She leaned toward the patient and placed a hand on his uninjured shoulder. "Mr. Collins, the people from your tour group are here, and they asked us to tell you they're holding a prayer service out in the waiting room."

Some of the tension left Arthur's face, and he sent her a grateful half smile. "Thank you. Will you tell Alma? And, Dr. Bower, will you let her know I'm fine? She worries about me so much."

"Apparently the feeling is mutual. I'll reassure her." Lukas squeezed Arthur's arm, then went back into trauma one to find the x-ray tech setting up films, and Lauren taking Alma's blood pressure again.

"She's doing better, Dr. Bower." Lauren glanced at the clear plastic bag hanging from the IV pole. "But she's still in a lot of pain. Her blood pressure is okay, and she's responsive. The liter of fluid is almost in."

"Cut her rate down to 50 cc's per hour—just enough to keep the IV open. That'll hold her until she gets to Springfield. Keep the second IV at 200 cc's per hour."

The x-ray tech slid a cartridge into the Stryker bed, which was a newly purchased, state-of-the-art setup for the trauma room. "Dr. Bower, I'm ready to shoot."

Lukas and Lauren stepped out of the room while the tech shot the films, and from the hallway they could see the bustle and activity of a suddenly full waiting room and ambulance bay. As Claudia had said, a group of casually dressed people stood in a circle in the corner of the waiting room and held hands, heads bowed.

The EMT from the Collinses' ambulance passed by them in the broad hallway, saw Lukas, and stopped. "They brought in the drunk driver who hit everybody, Dr. Bower. He's crying, talking to everybody who walks by, but nobody knows what he's saying. Sounds like he's speaking Spanish. The police are here, and they're itching to haul him in. They're really ticked."

Lukas shook his head. "They can't have him until we've checked him out, and that'll be a few minutes. We'll need an interpreter. I'll ask Judy to call one in." He turned to Lauren. "Repeat Alma's morphine dose, two milligrams every five minutes, and let me know if her pressure drops or if she develops depressed respirations. And tell her Arthur is okay."

Lauren nodded. "I'll reassure her."

The tech left the room, pushing the portable x-ray machine.

As Lauren went back in to recheck Alma, Lukas walked to the central desk. "Judy, would you please call a Spanish interpreter?"

"Did it already," Judy said without looking up from her keyboard.

He reached into a drawer and drew out a consent form for Arthur to sign so they could transfer Alma. "Has the chopper called yet?"

Judy's fingers still didn't break stride. "No, but I should hear from them anytime."

"When they call, let them know her vitals are stable, but she has a class-one limb threat to her right lower extremity."

No answer. The sound of the clattering keyboard stilled suddenly.

He glanced up to find the secretary staring toward the entrance, and when he looked, he saw Jacob Casey—Cowboy to most of the citizens of Knolls—come stumbling through the glass doors, aided by an older man in bib overalls. Somewhere, Cowboy had lost his hat.

"Oh no, not again," Judy said softly.

Lanky, weathered Cowboy was such a frequent visitor in this ER, Lukas wondered how the forty-three-year-old man had survived his occupation. He'd been kicked, gouged, bitten, and knocked senseless on that exotic animal ranch of his—he believed in personal contact with his bison, zebras, lions, and whatever else he raised on his three hundred acres of reinforced paddocks. Scars on several areas of his hard-bodied frame attested to his dedication.

Today blood covered Cowboy's upper right arm and splattered his chest and back. The left arm of his long-sleeved denim shirt had been ripped off and tied over his upper right arm in a crude attempt at a pressure dressing.

Lukas pushed back from the desk and got up to help. "Cowboy, what happened this time?" He took a closer look at what appeared, surprisingly, to be a bullet wound. "Has Leonardo started bearing arms?" Everybody knew the rancher wouldn't touch a gun.

Cowboy shook his head as he allowed his helper to transfer his leaning weight to Lukas.

"The neighbor shot him," the farmer said. "He chased Cowboy clear out of the woods into my field with a rifle. I saw it myself. Didn't take the time to call the sheriff. Guess we oughta call him now, huh, Doc?"

"No need, the police are already here doing an accident report. Would you please go tell them about this? They'll want to check it out and take your statement."

The man nodded, then patted Cowboy on his bare good arm. "Don't you worry, Jake, I'll take care of it."

Lukas helped Cowboy to exam room five. "How many times did the guy shoot you?"

"Once." Cowboy grunted as Lukas lowered him to sit on the bed. "Lost some blood. The guy's crazy."

"Is that the one who moved onto that farm next to yours, then started complaining about the smell of the animals? I heard about him." Lukas removed his patient's shirt and then helped him lie back. "How much blood do you think you lost?"

"Maybe a pint." Cowboy's deep voice thickened with pain as the shirt came off. "No time to measure."

Lukas stepped out into the hallway and called for a nurse, then returned to the bedside. He made a quick check of airway, breathing, and circulation, then listened to Cowboy's heart. Not bad, a little fast, but understandable under the circumstances. The left wrist had a strong pulse, and the fingers were warm and healthy.

When the relief nurse from upstairs stepped into the room, Lukas gave immediate orders for an IV and a trauma panel, then repeated his check on Cowboy, this time on the arm that had been shot. To his relief, it looked good. "Okay, Jake, I'll regret this, but give my hand a firm squeeze." He braced himself for the man's well-known iron grip, but it didn't come.

Cowboy grimaced again, the lines of his face deepening as his color faded. "Hurts to squeeze. Is it bad?"

"Not as bad as it could have been." Lukas pulled on a pair of sterile gloves and reached for a packet of 4x4s. He removed the make-shift bandage and saw no active bleeding. He found the entrance and exit wounds. "What did he shoot you with?"

"Looked like a .22 rifle, almost point-blank. Just up and shot me in cold blood, the same way he did—"

A young steel-faced policeman pulled back the curtain and stepped into the room. "Dr. Bower? Do you mind if we interrupt? The sooner we talk to Cowboy, the faster we'll be on the guy's trail."

Judy came in behind the policeman. "Dr. Bower, we just got a call from the fire department. They're bringing in two more patients."

Lukas shook his head in frustration. The day was exploding like popcorn in a microwave. Why did everything have to happen at once?

The secretary continued. "The nurse with Air Care just radioed us, and they'll be here in a few minutes to pick up Mrs. Collins."

"Thanks, Judy." Lukas ripped open one of the sterile packs of 4x4s and a roll of elastic gauze, then regloved and dressed the wound. He looked over at the policeman. "Officer, you can do your interview now. Looks like I'll have my hands full." He turned and followed the secretary out of the room. "Judy, I need a right shoulder x-ray in five, and he's going to need a surgical consult. Is Dr. Wong on call? He usually is when Cowboy gets hurt."

"Yes, Dr. Wong's the lucky guy today." Judy grinned at him. "Cowboy won't want a surgeon, he never does. Dr. Mercy will be here soon." Her expression turned serious. "One of the patients they're bringing in is our part-time EMT, Buck Oppenheimer. He got hurt in a fire."

"Buck! How bad?"

"Haven't heard yet. There was an explosion at the Quick Stop out by P Highway, and his buddies are bringing him in so he won't have to wait for an ambulance. I sure hope he's okay, and I hope his wife doesn't kill him when she finds out he played hero again."

Lukas nodded, then went in to check on Alma again and read her x-rays. There were no pneumo-thorax or rib or pelvis fractures, but the x-ray of her right tib-fib confirmed his worst fears. Both bones of the lower leg were shattered. If the blood vessels and nerves were as badly damaged as the bone, they would be doing an amputation in Springfield instead of a vascular and orthopedic repair.

Someone cried out in Spanish in one of the rooms, and Lukas hoped the interpreter would arrive soon. That patient was the one who reportedly drove the car into Arthur and Alma's tour group.

One of the most frustrating things in emergency medicine was treating those responsible for the pain and suffering of others—and one of the most difficult things to do was to have compassion for everyone involved.

*Lord, give me strength and wisdom. Give Alma and Arthur your peace, and use me as a vessel of healing. And, Lord, would you please slow things down a little?*

# CHAPTER 2

If this was another disaster drill, Mercy Richmond was going to make someone pay dearly. She kept her white lab coat on to protect the pink-and-blue bunny scrubs she wore underneath—her family practice consisted mostly of women and children. After apologizing to the six long-suffering patients in her waiting room, she marched out the front door and down the block toward the hospital.

Mercy's stomach growled. Monday afternoon was the worst time to get called out. There'd been no time for lunch. Everyone in this town of ten thousand must have developed strep, flu, or pneumonia over the weekend. She shouldn't have agreed to be ER backup today. Her patient volume had increased to the point that she was going to have to stop seeing new patients or start keeping the office open an extra day a week.

This spring she might have considered that possibility, but she'd won custody of her eleven-year-old daughter a few months ago, and she wanted to spend more time at home with Tedi. Since she no longer had to make two house payments, two car payments, and cover the bills her ex-husband had run up, she didn't need the income she made from ER shifts. She hoped Theo never got out of that detox unit in Springfield. Her life was going so well with him out of the way . . . and with Dr. Lukas Bower taking more of an interest in her and in Tedi. Everything was looking good.

As she stepped across the parking lot curb and strode toward the ER entrance, the distant, thrusting rhythm of a helicopter in flight reached her for the first time. She noticed that the landing pad on the parking lot had been cleared of cars.

Okay, so this time it probably wasn't a drill.

She looked down. That probably wasn't fake blood on the concrete, either. In the back rooms of her clinic, she had never been able to hear the ambulances when they pulled into the ER. Always before, she had considered that to be a good thing. Today, though, she could have used a little warning.

She rushed through the sliding glass doors to find the waiting room filled with people in various stages of fluster. A patient with a splinted arm was being helped inside by a friend. The buzz of voices and the aura of worry greeted her like a familiar co-worker. A group of three middle-aged women and two elderly men stood in the west corner by the vending machines with their hands clasped, praying.

That happened a lot around here. It didn't matter what you thought about God the rest of the time, when you faced life and death in the emergency room, you begged Him to give you another chance. Mercy had done it herself when her own daughter nearly died from a life-threatening allergic reaction to a beesting—she who had always prided herself on her self-reliance. She'd even considered herself an agnostic until Lukas Bower exploded into her life last spring with his gentle humor, strong compassion for others, and his vibrant faith. Nothing in her life had been the same since.

A moan and a tormented shout reached her from one of the exam rooms, but she couldn't understand the words. The mingled scents of antiseptic, body odor, and diesel exhaust from the ambulance bay drifted through the room.

"Thank goodness, Dr. Mercy," Judy called from the emergency desk. She pulled off her reading glasses and picked up a clipboard with a T-sheet already attached. Her short salt-and-pepper hair spiked out on the right side, where she'd been keeping her ink pen tucked behind her ear. "Dr. Bower's in trauma one trying to save the leg of a lady who got hit by a car. Her husband's in trauma two in stable condition, and the guy who hit everybody is in exam room three." She shoved the clipboard across the desk. "There's lots more, but Dr. Bower wanted you to see about the man in two. Name's Arthur Collins, and he's really upset about his wife. They just took him off the backboard. Nice guy. Never complains about his own pain.

Wish my husband treated me like that."

Mercy took the chart, then paused as the patient in three—or so she presumed—shouted something again. The words were slurred, and they sounded Hispanic. She raised a brow at Judy. "Who did you say that was?"

Judy waved a dismissing hand. "That's the drunk driver who hit them. He drove right up onto the courthouse lawn and mowed over a bunch of people from a tour group. He doesn't even speak English."

"Has he been checked?"

"Dr. Bower ordered some tests and a trauma panel, but they've been busy with the other patients, and nobody's gotten to him yet except to put him on oxygen."

"Get to him."

Judy shrugged. "Okay, but I hope we can find somebody who can speak Spanish. So far the translator hasn't come in."

The thumping of the helicopter rotors grew louder as the Air Care helicopter descended to the landing spot outside, the loud *whomp-whomp-whomp* of the rotors vibrating the windows.

"Oh, good, they're here for Alma Collins," Judy said.

"How many patients do we have, and how many more are coming?" Mercy asked, glancing at the T-sheet.

"We've got six in and two more coming that I know about, but Dr. Wong's on his way over to take care of our favorite exotic animal rancher."

"Cowboy's hurt again?"

"He sure is. His neighbor shot him."

Mercy wasn't sure she heard the secretary correctly. *"Shot him!"*

Judy shook her head. "Nobody's going to tell me human beings aren't meaner than any other mammal. Looks like we'll all be busy for a while."

Mercy suppressed a sigh. "Call my office, then. Tell Josie to do a triage and find out who really needs to see me today. Let her know what's going on here. She'll have to send some people home."

"Don't worry, Dr. Mercy. They'll come in here looking for you if they have to."

Mercy carried her clipboard into trauma room two, where Claudia Zebert, a stout fifty-year-old RN with twenty-five years of ER experience, took the blood pressure of a slender forty-seven-year-old man in a pressure turban. The view box on the wall held two shots of a dislocated right shoulder. Not broken. That made things a lot easier.

Mercy stepped up to the exam bed. "Mr. Collins? I'm Dr. Mercy Richmond. My patients call me Dr. Mercy, and you just became one of my patients."

He looked up at her with troubled hazel eyes. "Dr. Mercy . . . that's a good name for a doctor."

"My father was a physician, and he named me. When I got my license, our shared last name confused patients, so we both started using our first names. We were Dr. Cliff and Dr. Mercy." *Were*. Dad was dead now.

"You can call me Arthur. You'll have to excuse me. I'm so worried about my wife that I'm not very good company."

"I understand, Arthur. Your wife is in good hands. Dr. Bower is one of the best."

Claudia reached down and squeezed his left arm. "See there, Arthur, I told you Dr. Bower will take good care of Alma." The nurse's brisk, familiar manner almost always calmed frightened patients. She gestured toward the turban. "We need to get this fixed up and get that shoulder back in shape so you can be there for Alma. The helicopter's here now to pick her up and take her to the trauma center in Springfield."

Arthur caught his breath and reached up toward the side of the bed, as if he might try to get out. "I don't want her to go alone."

"There's no room in the helicopter for any passengers, but she won't be alone once she gets up there," Claudia soothed. "I saw half your tour group climbing into one of the vans to drive up and meet her there. The rest are staying here to pray for you. They seem like good people." She squeezed his arm once more before leaving the room to check another patient.

Mercy read Claudia's notes on Arthur, then did her own assessment. He was a little tachycardic from blood loss, but IV fluids were already running into his uninjured left arm, and his pressure was already rising. Good sign. His heart would slow down naturally.

Another shout reached them from the next room, and Arthur laid his head back against his pillow and sighed. "That poor man's sure hurting. Can you do something for him?"

Mercy frowned. She had heard the drunk driver had no obvious injuries. "Someone will be getting to him as soon as possible."

"He's not drunk, you know."

Mercy looked up from her chart and studied Arthur's green-gold eyes. "How can you tell?"

"I speak Spanish. Alma and I are missionaries in Mexico. He's making some sense. He's saying over and over again how sorry he is, and that he doesn't drink, doesn't do drugs."

Mercy didn't comment. She'd heard that a lot.

"He's also confused and hurting," Arthur added.

"Isn't he the man who hit you and your wife?"

Arthur nodded, then worry marred the fine features of his face once again. "My wife . . . I wish I could be with her."

A light, warm baritone voice reached them from the doorway. "I came over to give you an update, Arthur."

Mercy silently caught her breath and let the calm strength of that familiar voice settle over her like a blanket. She and Arthur both looked up at the same time to see Lukas Bower walking in to join them, his trauma shield in place over his gray framed glasses. His short brown hair was disheveled as usual. Lukas stood a couple of inches taller than Mercy's five feet eight. In her eyes he had grown at least a foot since she had first met him last spring. Her gaze met his, and she smiled. The smile he returned was only for her, and the brilliance of it heated her cheeks. One of the nurses had told her once that when she entered the ER, Dr. Bower's face looked as if he'd just received a special gift.

He stepped up to the bed, his blue eyes calm and reassuring behind the glare of glasses and shield. "Arthur, your wife is awake and talking, and she's worried about you. I told her you'd be fine."

Arthur raised a hand toward him. "Will you let me see her before they take her away? Please. I want to talk to her a second. I just want to tell her I love her."

Lukas looked at Mercy, then looked back at Arthur and nodded. "I think we can do that. They'll be wheeling her out in just a moment, and we'll roll you into the hallway and let you rendezvous with her there. No, don't try to get up. We don't want you bleeding on us again before Dr. Mercy can get you stitched and get that shoulder fixed." He gestured to Mercy and laid a hand on her arm briefly. She released the brake on the exam bed, and together they rolled the bed out into the open space as the flight nurse and paramedic wheeled Alma past.

At the sight of Alma's bandaged and IV tubed body, Arthur's eyes filled with tears once again. He reached out and touched her shoulder. "Hi, sweetheart. I love you. I'll be with you as soon as I can."

"Oh, Arthur," she cried softly, "I can't believe this is happenin'. I'm just so glad you're alive. For a while, I thought . . ."

The flight nurse placed a gentle hand on Alma's shoulder. "Mrs. Collins, we need to get you into the helicopter now."

Alma nodded. Arthur drew his hand back, then kissed his fingertips and reached out and touched Alma's cheek with his hand. "I'll be praying with every breath."

Mercy allowed Lukas to help her push Arthur's bed back into the room. "Thanks, Lukas." She laid a hand on his arm, as she had found herself doing often lately without even thinking about it, as if a physical connection to him might anchor their friendship more securely. "Lukas, Arthur doesn't think the man who hit them is drunk. He also says the man's in pain."

Lukas turned his attention to Arthur. "What kind of pain? Where? We're waiting for the interpreter to arrive, and we can't communicate with him. My college Spanish died of disuse."

Arthur wiped leftover tears from his face. "I speak Spanish. Why don't you let me try to talk to him? I can—"

"We need to take care of you," Mercy said. "We'll get an interpreter."

Arthur looked up at her and sighed. "Give him a chance, Dr. Mercy. What if he's hurt worse than I am?" He raised his voice enough to be heard over the din of the ER and spoke a few phrases in Spanish, then winced, as if the extra exertion and sound hurt his head.

There was no reply.

He repeated the phrases, and seconds later he received an answer. He looked back at Mercy. "It's his mouth."

Mercy glanced sharply at Lukas. "A fracture from impact?"

Lukas shrugged, his attention focused on their patient. "Arthur, we aren't going to hold you liable as an interpreter, but will you please ask him if he had the pain before the wreck?"

Arthur did so, and they all understood part of the answer. "Sí." Lukas and Mercy did not, however, understand the remainder of the words, but the expression on Arthur's face told them it was significant.

"Does toothache medicine make you drunk?" Arthur asked them.

"How much toothache medicine?" Mercy asked.

Arthur asked the man, then interpreted. "He's used a bottle today."

Mercy caught her breath and turned to Lukas. "That could be—"

"Dangerous." Lukas spun out of the room. "Judy," he called to the secretary, "I need a stat ABG in exam room three." He rushed to the next room. "Lauren, would you help me?"

"Is the man in trouble, then?"Arthur asked Mercy. "Can't you just push my bed into his room the way you took me out to see Alma?"

"No need." Mercy stepped out the door, saw Claudia at the desk, and motioned to her before turning back to her patient. "Dr. Bower knows what tests to give, what drugs to use." She studied Arthur's expression. He had shown no resentment toward the person who had injured him and his wife. "We need to take care of you now." She pulled on some sterile gloves and a face shield. "Claudia," she said as the nurse walked into the room, "I need 2 milligrams of Versed and 25 of Demerol, slow IV push. Then have X-ray bring over some wrist weights. Arthur, we're going to try to reduce your shoulder dislocation with the prone method. We'll give you some medication for the pain, then we'll turn you over on your stomach and drop your right arm over the side of the bed with some weight on your wrist." She unwrapped the Ace bandage while Claudia carried out her orders, collecting and administering drugs and ordering the weights.

The wound in Arthur's scalp was deep and star-shaped with no active bleeding. Mercy cleaned it with some peroxide. "How did you get this, Arthur? Do you remember?"

"I think I hit the corner of a concrete balustrade, but I don't remember actually doing that, just waking up beside it."

She probed the wound with her gloved finger, felt him jerk. "Sorry, Arthur. I'm checking for any rough surfaces, making sure there are no obvious deformities. I don't feel any, but I'll get a CT later." She cleaned it a little more, then stepped back to allow Claudia to prep the site.

Five minutes later the weights arrived and Claudia had the wound ready for stitching. Arthur was groggy, feeling a lot less pain than he had been before. He groaned a couple of times when Mercy and Claudia turned him over and placed the padded weights on his wrist as his arm hung down over the side of the bed.

Mercy watched his profile as she prepared to anesthetize the wound site. "How long have you and Alma been married?"

He barely winced when the needle first touched his flesh. "Twenty-seven years. We got married as soon as Alma graduated from high school." His voice was only slightly muffled, since Mercy had taken the pillow out from under his head to keep his neck from stretching backward too far. "We knew what we wanted to do from the time we were in junior high, so we couldn't see any reason to wait."

"You mean to tell me you and your wife knew you wanted to be missionaries to Mexico from the time you were in junior high?" Mercy could tell when the local anesthesia began to work, because he no longer tensed when she touched him.

"Yes, we did. God was calling us there as surely as I'm lying here."

Mercy took her first stitch. "I don't suppose you could be involved in medical missions? Somehow you knew that man wasn't drunk. That was a good call."

"No, I'm not medical. Sadly, I've just seen a lot of drunks."

"Yeah, so have I," she murmured. "You obviously have some good friends out in the waiting room."

"They're from a group of churches in the state that support our work. We're here on furlough for three months." He grew silent for a moment. "Now I wonder if we'll be returning."

"Try not to think about that right now. How's the pain?" Mercy asked. "Do you need more medication?"

"I'm fine. A little woozy. Makes it hard to keep my prayers in focus. It's a good thing God knows my heart."

"You and your wife seem to have a very good relationship." Mercy had found that when she could keep her patients talking about something that really interested them, she didn't have to use nearly as many pain meds, and everything went smoother.

"That's because of Alma's sweet nature. She still treats me with the same consideration and patience she's always shown. It's just the kind of person she is."

"And you make it obvious you adore her."

From the side of his face, she saw him smile. What a handsome man, even cut and bruised as he was.

And what a rare thing—a happy marriage. The only other person she knew with a happy marriage was her nurse, Josie. Funny, Josie had the same last name, but Collins was a common name. And Mercy knew it wasn't a shared last name that made the difference. Josie, too, was a devoted Christian. So was Lukas. Lately, as Mercy grew to know him better, she wouldn't try to deny the fact that there was a noticeable difference between him and every other male she had ever met. And she felt more of an attraction to him than to any other male she'd ever met. She found herself wanting to spend more and more time with him, and being more and more disappointed when their busy work schedules prevented that.

Arthur's smile wavered and disappeared. "I wonder how Alma's doing. How long does it take them to fly a helicopter to Springfield?"

"About thirty minutes when the weather's good and the wind is right." Mercy laid a hand on his uninjured shoulder. "Don't worry, Arthur, she's in good hands. I know the flight nurse, and she's one of the best. She took care of my daughter this spring when we had to fly her out for emergency surgery."

"Your daughter?" Arthur's voice grew more slurred. "Sh-she okay now?"

"She's fine." Physically.

"How old is sh-she?"

"Eleven going on fifty. Sometimes I wonder which of us does the most mothering and worrying. Tell me about your mission in Mexico."

He talked for several moments while Mercy finished her two-layer closure. He had thick wavy red hair that was already showing a lot of gray, and the lines around his eyes revealed that he'd spent a lot of time in the sun and that he spent a lot of time smiling.

Mercy checked his arm, then rechecked the wound. "Arthur, we're almost finished with your head except for the CT. I'm hoping your shoulder will slip into place without much pain."

He paused for a moment, and Mercy could see his eyes tear up. He was thinking about Alma again.

"Would you pray with me?" The words were soft, but not hesitant.

Mercy blinked. This one hadn't ever come up in medical school. It hadn't come up afterward, either. "Well . . . I'm not sure. . . ." How was she supposed to turn him down? And yet, how was she supposed to pray when most of the time she refused to even acknowledge the presence—

"I'll do the talking," he said.

She heard the pleading in his voice, and she thought about his love for his wife. What could it hurt? Mercy had watched Lukas pray and watched her mother pray. All she had to do was bow her head. The only time she'd actually prayed was when Tedi nearly died, and then it had only been a "Please, God, please, God, please, God" out of desperation.

She nodded and bent her head.

"Thank you," Arthur whispered to her. "Dear Lord, we can't know what's going to happen to us next, and we're frightened and in pain. Please, God, please go with Alma. Give her comfort and peace that only you can give her. And help me depend on your strength. Help us, through this tragedy, to keep our witness pure for you, and hold our hearts firmly in your sheltering arms. We praise you for your constant presence and for the assurance that we will go through nothing without you. Lay your special blessing on Dr. Mercy today, and thank you for sending her to us as one of your ministering angels. Fill her with your special Spirit, dear Lord, in a way that will last. In our Lord Jesus' name, amen."

He opened his eyes and looked at Mercy. "Thank you." He gave a relaxed sigh. They heard a gentle pop. The shoulder was back in place.

---

Lukas finished assessing the lady with the broken arm, looked in quickly on Cowboy, then checked on Mercy's progress. He was relieved to find her and Arthur chattering about children and mission work and the beauty of the Missouri Ozarks while Claudia bandaged the wound and removed the weights from Arthur's wrist.

The quiet alto tone of Mercy's voice drew Lukas like a symphony. He allowed his gaze to rest, just for a moment, on the strong, feminine lines of her face. He felt himself drawn into the glowing depths of her coffee-colored eyes as she chuckled at something Arthur said. Her long black hair was drawn back in a clasp, and several tendrils had come loose, giving the impression that she was always too busy reaching out to others to check a mirror during the day.

Mercy had a talent for mothering patients. She was good at helping them through difficult and painful procedures with a minimum of panic or pain medication. Her self-deprecating sense of humor put everyone around her at ease, including the staff. Including Lukas. He found himself watching her when she worked in the same room, and he felt himself drawn to her in a way he'd never been before.

She looked up at him questioningly. He smiled and opened his mouth to speak, but the ER doors jerked open and in stumbled a trio of dirty firemen—two extremely young trainees carrying singed and blackened veteran fire fighter Buck Oppenheimer between them.

Actually, Buck wasn't being carried, but was trying valiantly to wrestle out of the clutches of his overeager charges, his soot-covered face filled with annoyance.

"Doc!" he called out to Lukas in frustration. "Would you please tell these kids I'm not dying?"

Lukas stifled a relieved grin. Buck worked a few shifts a month with the ambulance service as an EMT, and he was a first responder with the fire department, which meant Lukas and Buck saw a lot of each other. Buck's down-home hillbilly charm—complete with butch haircut and ears that could paddle a canoe—belied a sharp wit and a deep compassion for others. Unfortunately for him, his leadership abilities had landed him the added responsibility of overseeing two eighteen-year-old members of an Explorer group throughout their training period. He'd grumbled about it to Lukas ever since the kids arrived the week before.

Lukas led the way into exam room six and instructed the young men to help Buck onto the bed. "Ease him down gently, guys. No telling what he's gotten into this time."

"An explosion, that's what!" Skinny Kyle Alder, whose hair was as long and curly as Buck's was short and straight, kept a death grip on Buck's arm as he and his buddy eased their grubby, smoke-stained patient onto the clean sheet. "Saved a gal's life and almost died. Threw himself on top of her!"

"Oh?" Lukas stepped out into the hallway and caught Lauren's attention from her workstation at the central desk. He motioned for her to join him in the exam room, then returned to Buck's side. "And where is the victim?"

Buck fought off his overeager charges at last and started unbuttoning his shirt, still sitting up. "Roxie refused to come in, and believe me, I fought to get her in the ambulance. Should've just wrapped her in a straightjacket and shoved her in the back. You know how cantankerous she can be sometimes."

Lukas looked at Buck in alarm. "Wouldn't she let you check her out?"

"Barely. I listened to her chest and took her vitals. She sounded okay. She said she's fine except for the ribs I broke pouncing on her like that."

"What?"

Buck shook his head and frowned. "I think she was kidding, although with her it's hard to tell. After all I went through to get to her, she asked what took us so long, because she'd called ten minutes before I got there. That's the thanks I get for risking my life to—" He winced and bent forward. "I wasn't even on duty. I didn't know about any call."

"I told you that you oughta have that looked at," Kyle said.

"I'm having it looked at now," Buck snapped.

"It's his chest, Dr. Bower," Kyle explained. "It's been hurting him since the explosion. He says it's just a scrape, but . . ." His attention refocused with sudden interest as blond-haired, green-eyed Lauren walked into the room and began her assessment.

"Let's get a c-collar on him before you start that, Lauren." Lukas reached out and felt the back of Buck's neck for any step-off deformity. "Does this hurt, Buck?"

The fireman did not move his head. "Nope."

"Good. We'll go ahead and do a collar until we get the x-rays, just to be safe."

"Oh, come on, Dr. Bower, I'll be good. My neck doesn't hurt."

"You know it's protocol." Lukas leaned forward to take a look at Buck's exposed back and felt hot air hitting his own neck. He glanced around to find Kyle and his partner, Alex, hovering over him, eyes wide, jaws slack.

"Why don't you two go out into the waiting room," Lukas suggested. "The police are around somewhere, and they might want to question you about the fire."

With a look of sudden eagerness, the young men left, and Buck exhaled with relief. "Thanks. You can lay that collar on me now. Those kids couldn't find a fire hose with their—"

"Okay, here you go." Lauren positioned the stiff neck collar with Velcro, fastened it firmly, and resumed her assessment.

"They chattered like monkeys all the way here," Buck complained. "They went on and on about how I was a hero, and they would pay better attention next time I tried to teach them something."

"They're just kids," Lauren said. "Give them a chance."

"I did the other day, and, boy, was I sorry." Buck reached up and tugged at the collar. "Isn't this a little tight?"

Lauren leaned over and checked it. "It's perfect. What did you do the other day?"

"I got my model airplane stuff out of my locker and let the boys help me with it—or try to. Kyle spilled the glue, and Alex broke a wing tip, so it took us longer than I thought it would. My shift ended, but I couldn't leave them there with everything spread out all over the table, so I stayed and worked with them a couple more hours."

"Did you call Kendra?" Lauren asked, placing the blood pressure cuff around his thick upper arm.

"No, and I sure heard about it when I got home. She just about took my head off."

"Would you have left if you'd gotten called out for a fire?" Lauren asked, pumping the blood pressure cuff.

"Well, sure, but . . . hey, careful with that thing. Don't squeeze my arm off. I apologized and told her I'd never do that again."

Lauren let the pressure drop and watched the numbers, then wrote them down. "That's what you said after you let yourself be talked into feeding Leonardo for Cowboy."

Buck reached up as if to scratch at the small wound on his chest but stopped himself before he could touch it. "Hey, this was different . . . and worse. At least Leonardo couldn't follow me out of his cage. I haven't been able to get those kids off my tail ever since. Kyle, especially. I trip over him everywhere I go."

"He seems nice enough to me," Lauren said.

"So is a puppy, but I don't want one making runs with me. I think it's dangerous to take kids like that into a fire situation."

"But how else will they learn?" Lauren asked. "You know, Buck, all of us had to get a break somewhere. You've got to be more patient. Maybe that's why the chief put you in charge of these boys, so you could learn some mentoring skills."

Buck scowled at her. "I don't even know what that word means."

"It means you have some finely honed instincts you could use to train others, and you can't let all that go to waste just because you don't want to spend time with those—"

"Uh, Lauren," Lukas interrupted. "Quiet for a moment, please." He saw the sudden relief in Buck's expression and stifled a grin. Lauren was a great nurse, very caring, but when she slipped into chatterbox mode she could shut down traffic.

Lukas placed his stethoscope on Buck's back and chest, listened to breath sounds, and was satisfied. "Where's the pain Kyle's so concerned about?"

Buck gestured to the upper left area of his chest. "Just a little cut. I can't understand why it hurt so much, but, boy, Kyle grabbed me there when they helped me get up, and I nearly tore his head off."

Lukas found a very small wound just above Buck's left nipple. With a peroxide-soaked 4x4, he wiped off some of the blood.

Buck jerked. "Ow! Watch it, Dr. Bower. I did get knocked around a little, you know."

"Is that where your pain is located? Don't tell me you weren't wearing your jacket again."

"Yes, I was. I grabbed it before I went back inside."

Lukas frowned and checked the wound a little more closely. It wasn't even a centimeter in length, but there was no telling how deep it might be. "Tell me about the explosion."

"I was grabbing for Roxie when it hit. The manager keeps a barbeque grill back there in the storeroom to cook hot dogs and hamburgers to sell up front, and it runs on propane. It's big enough to take out a wall if it explodes, and that's what happened. Roxie told me she was cooking some stuff on it and had to go up front to answer the phone. When she hung up and turned around, she said she saw a lot of smoke coming in from the back. She says one of the new delivery guys placed some boxes too close to the fire, and Roxie couldn't move them."

"Did you feel anything hit you? How much smoke did you inhale?"

"I don't really think I got much smoke, but I couldn't tell you if anything hit me. I hit a lot of things, like Roxie, the wall, and then some shelves fell on top of us. I tried to brace myself on my elbows to keep from squashing Roxie. Do you think I could've pulled a muscle or something?"

"A pulled muscle doesn't break the skin." Lukas helped him lie down while he gave instructions to Lauren for routine trauma x-ray series with two-view chest. "What's the $O_2$ sat?"

"Good. Ninety-six," Lauren said.

Judy stepped to the doorway. "Dr. Bower, we have a drunk three-year-old in room seven. It's the Chapmans, who called you earlier."

Lukas glanced at his watch. "They made great time. Get Claudia to meet me there and I'll be right out." He ordered serum alcohol and poison levels for the child. "I hate to do it, but get Respiratory to draw a blood gas on him." Invasive procedures were a part of his job he had never enjoyed, especially when it involved causing pain for little children who were too young to even understand what was happening to them. Big needles that stuck deep and hurt were always traumatic, and this one needed an artery.

"Go on and see about the kid, Doc," Buck said. "I'll be fine as long as you can keep my young buddies from pestering me to death."

Lukas grinned. "It comes with being a hero."

"I don't want to be a hero. I just want to do a good job. This mentoring is new for me."

"It always helps to learn from the best."

"I'm not the best. The chief just didn't want to do it himself this time." Buck lowered his voice and glanced toward the doorway. "I don't want to be a jerk, but they're not going to get a good review from me."

"Come on, Buck, you were young once. In fact, you're still young."

Mercy walked into the room, greeted Buck as if she were used to seeing his burnt-to-a-crisp appearance every day, and held the clipboards for two more patients for Lukas to see. "Want me to do these for you while I'm here? I called Josie, and she's done a triage and sent some of my patients home."

Lukas shot her a grateful smile. "Thank you, Mercy."

"It'll cost you a dinner."

"Great. I'll cook."

"Hey! I'm doing you a favor here. Don't threaten me."

Lukas left Lauren to run his orders on Buck and walked out into the hallway with Mercy. He reached up instinctively to touch her shoulder, then hesitated and let his hand fall back to his side. He was already getting teased by the staff about his relationship with her.

"How's Arthur doing?" he asked.

"I'm releasing him to his friends." Mercy stopped outside the door, shook her head, frowned. "I didn't want to do it, but he didn't want to be so far from his wife. His CT's fine." She lowered her voice. "He's something else. I don't think I've met anybody quite like him." She looked into Lukas's eyes, then away. "Except maybe for you." She turned and walked into another exam room.

Lukas was glad she didn't see him blush.

The drunken child, three-year-old Jared Chapman, had a good serum alcohol level, which would counteract the effects of the antifreeze. The ethylene glycol and methanol levels were low enough that Jared wouldn't need dialysis, so they could just watch him closely in the telemetry unit overnight on an alcohol drip. The parents were relieved and happy, and so was Lukas. Even with the needle for the blood gas, Jared was feeling a minimum amount of pain. The poor little boy would probably have treatment for a hangover in the morning.

The pharmacist was the only one who complained. When Lukas personally ordered the alcohol drip, the man replied, "You know you guys can't be drinking on the job."

# CHAPTER 3

Eleven-year-old Tedi Zimmerman answered the final question on her test paper as the bell rang for afternoon recess. Yes! She pushed the page to the top of her desk and looked up at Mr. Walters to see if he noticed. He nodded and smiled. He'd been watching.

She got up and started toward the door, but Abby Cuendet—her worst enemy last year, her best friend this year—grabbed her arm and stopped her.

Tedi turned back around. "Hey, what're you doing?"

Abby pushed straight brown bangs out of her eyes, glanced out the window, then back at Tedi. "I thought you said your dad was locked up."

"He is. He's in detox up in Springfield."

Abby scrunched up her face, pushed her glasses back up onto the bridge of her nose, and turned to point out the window. "That sure looks like him to me."

Tedi caught her breath and stiffened, refusing to look. "That's not funny." Mom and Grandma both said Dad was supposed to be locked up for a long time.

"So who's that?"

Feeling the darkness of an old nightmare, Tedi turned slowly and looked in the direction Abby pointed. A man stood in the shade beneath the trees that surrounded the playground. His hands were in his pockets. With his head bent forward and his shoulders slumped, he didn't look as tall as Dad, and his clothes weren't silk and wool with ties and dress shoes. But the shape of his head and the line of his face, even at this distance, were too familiar. Abby's mom said Dad looked like a blond Pierce Brosnan, but Tedi had seen pictures of Pierce Brosnan, and he looked a lot nicer. He didn't look like the kind of man who would try to kill his own daughter.

For a minute Tedi thought she was going to throw up. She tightened her hands into fists and took some deep breaths. It couldn't be. Was she having another bad dream? She couldn't take her gaze from the intruder as he watched the kids spill out of the school building onto the grass. When they quit coming, he turned and looked directly toward the windows of Tedi's classroom, as if he knew she was there.

She gasped and stepped back. "What's he *doing* here?" Her voice shook. Her whole body shook. "He's not supposed to be out of—"

"Girls?" Mr. Walters called. "Aren't you finished with your papers?"

Tedi turned and looked hard at her teacher, at his wide middle and thick shoulders. "Yes, we're finished." He looked safe and calm as he gathered up papers and stacked them and turned to erase something from the chalkboard. One time he had stepped between a kid and an attacking dog and saved the kid from being bitten. He wasn't going to let anyone hurt his students. "Go out and enjoy the sunshine while you can," he called over his shoulder. "The rest of the week is supposed to be cloudy." Which was another way of saying he wanted some time to de-stress and straighten the room. He'd told Tedi that once when she stayed behind to help him collect papers.

Tedi almost asked if she could stay and help him with papers again, but Abby nudged her. "Why don't you just go and find out what your dad wants, dummy?"

Tedi shoved her friend's arm away. "Why should I? If he wants to talk to me he can go see the principal first. He's not even supposed to be here. No strangers on the playground, remember?"

"He's not a stranger. He's your dad. Come on, let's at least get out of here." She nudged Tedi again.

Tedi allowed herself to be pushed out the door and into the wide hallway. Together they walked to the side exit, where both of the double doors stood open to let in the cool late September air. Maybe he would be gone when they got outside . . . or maybe it wasn't even him. It just looked like him.

But when they stepped around the corner of the building in view of the broad, grassy playground, he was still in the same place in the shadows, hands in his pockets, head bent.

Tedi felt her heart pound, the way it did that night when he shouted at her and raised his hand and hit her so hard it knocked her out.

"Don't you want to find out what he's doing here?" Abby demanded, nudging Tedi again with her elbow.

Tedi jerked away. "Stop it!"

"Gosh, Tedi, it's no big deal. Just go talk to him."

"You don't know anything about it. You never saw him drunk."

"He's been in detox, hasn't he? He won't be drunk." Eyes flashing with curiosity behind shiny lenses, Abby nudged her again. "Go on and find out what he wants. I'll watch from here, and if he looks like he's going to get close to you, I'll run back in and get Mr. Walters."

"Oh sure, and what's Mr. Walters going to do, sit on him and crush him to death?"

Abby fell silent, giving Tedi her most stern look of reproach. Tedi stared back, hands on hips.

"Chicken," Abby muttered.

"Shut up. I am not. I'm just not stupid."

"Don't you trust me, Tedi? I won't let him hurt you."

Tedi snorted. "Oh yeah? What are you going to do if he grabs me and runs?"

"Chase him down and kick his rear. Maybe throw a rock and hit him in the head, and you know I can do it, too."

Tedi held her friend's steady gaze for another few seconds. Abby had given Graham Kutz a black eye the other day for picking on her little brother and sister. She could also throw a ball better than anybody in the school. And she was a loyal friend, even if she was pushy and had a big mouth.

Tedi sighed, and Abby grinned triumphantly. "Knew you'd go. I'll watch from here. Don't worry."

For a moment, Tedi couldn't get her feet to work. She did not want to go talk to her father. She didn't even want to think of him as her father. But she wanted to know what he was doing here, what he was up to. It would be better to do it now, with Abby standing by, ready to conk him in the head with a rock, than to wait for him to catch her when she wasn't expecting him.

When Abby pushed her again, she went, walking slowly, as if sneaking up on a dangerous animal. And he *was* dangerous. Tedi reached up and fingered the fading scar on her neck where the surgeon had cut into her throat to save her life after Dad had damaged an artery in his drunken rage. He'd also embezzled money where he worked. Everybody in town knew about him. Tedi knew the kids at school talked about her behind her back, and she hated it. She hated what he did to Mom and the way he'd threatened to ruin Mom's practice again if she tried to get custody of her. And the only reason he wanted custody was because Mom had to pay so much child support. Tedi would never go back to live with him. She would rather die first.

Her heart was beating so fast now she could barely hear the sound of wind flipping the leaves around on the trees. Breathing hard, yet trying not to make noise, she stopped about ten feet from where he stood, and she studied him.

He looked different. Of course, he wasn't drunk now, but he looked different from the way he did this spring even when he was sober. He looked smaller somehow. His blond hair looked more gray. He had more creases in his face.

"What are you doing here?" She said it, then held her breath, arms straight at her sides, anger and fear mingling within her. If he moved toward her, she would turn and run.

He swung around, and his pale blue eyes widened, his lips parted slightly in surprise. "Tedi." He breathed the name. He did not move a muscle, but stood staring at her as if she were a bird he was afraid would fly away.

Her gaze darted toward the kids on the playground, and at the teachers refereeing, and at Abby watching from the door of the school building, hands clenched at her sides, gaze fierce, as though she were getting ready to thwack a baseball.

"I'm sorry, Tedi. I didn't come here to scare you." Dad's voice drew Tedi's attention back to him, and his blue gaze held her, roving over her face, as if he was studying it. "I wasn't even going to let you know I was here. I just wanted to see you again. I thought you'd be out on the playground with the rest of the kids." He sounded hoarse, as if he hadn't been talking much lately and wasn't used to it.

He wouldn't stop looking at her.

"But why are you out?" she demanded.

"The judge released me."

Tedi felt a fresh surge of anger and fear. What kind of a judge would release a man who'd almost killed his own kid? "Why?"

"I dried out, no booze since . . . none all summer."

"Oh, sure. How can you get to the booze when you're locked up? That doesn't prove anything."

"That's what I asked them. I was afraid to leave. I didn't trust myself because I can't forget what I did to you." He slowly took his hands out of his pockets and spread them, taking care not to get close to her. "The judge assigned a new, young attorney to my case, and the guy got me out on bail because I had a good record at the detox center, and I'd never been in trouble with the police before, and—"

"But I almost died!" Tedi crossed her arms over her chest. How could they just let him go like that? "Mom said you couldn't get out to hurt me again."

He bent his head and winced, as if someone had slugged him. A muscle tightened in his jaw. "I won't hurt you again." Now he seemed to study the ground as closely as he had been studying her. "I'm sorry. I shouldn't have come here. I just wanted to see you, see for myself how you were doing . . . I guess I had to make sure you were really alive, really okay. I was so scared that night . . . so sure that . . . and the police took me in while you were being flown out for surgery." He looked up then, and his gaze pinpointed the scar at her throat. "I did that and so many other things. All these months in detox I've realized how much I did to destroy what I had with you, and . . . and I was the one who destroyed the relationship I had with your mother. I've been forced to admit so much this summer, so much I didn't want to see, but that I can't afford to forget."

Tedi watched his face and listened to his voice. He'd apologized before. Maybe he'd meant it when he said it, but what good had it done?

His gaze drifted again to her throat, and she knew he was looking at the scar, then he closed his eyes for a moment, squeezing them tightly shut, as if he were afraid they would burn out if he kept them open any longer. He looked old. He was the same age as Mom, but he looked a lot older than she did. His eyes looked wrinkled, and they turned down at the corners, the way his mouth did.

"I'm sorry," he said softly, and he raised his head and gazed into her eyes again. "I can't ever make it up to you, Tedi, and I'm so sorry." He took a deep breath. "But I'm going to try, anyway. Tedi, I'm not supposed to be here, but I want to get permission to try to see you again. Before I do that, though, I want to know if it's okay with you. If not, I'll wait."

She didn't move, didn't speak. She was too shocked, not by his words, but by the fact that she realized she didn't hate him totally. Mostly, but not totally.

"I'd like a chance to talk with you, Tedi. Your mother would have to be there with us."

She narrowed her eyes at him. "You're talking to me *now*."

"What I mean is that I want to start seeing you again, regularly, like the kind of visitation you had with your mom when you lived with me."

She took a step forward, feeling braver. "Mom would never let you take me away from her again. Never! And I will never go back."

He sighed and held her gaze steadily. "I wouldn't try to get you back. If I got to visit with you, I wouldn't even touch you. I promise. I just want to find out if it would be okay with you before I ask for permission from your mother." His light blue eyes filled with tears, and he looked away for a moment. "It's going to take a long time to become friends again, but I have to try."

Friends? Ha! A friend didn't try to kill a friend. And a friend didn't try to keep a friend from her mother or try to ruin her mother's name in town just out of spite. "I don't want to be your friend."

He reached up with the back of his hand and brushed his tears away. "Of course you don't. I've been talking with my counselor about it, and he said it would be unreasonable for me to expect that. I just felt like I had to make contact."

So now he'd made contact. What else would he want? When Dad was nice, it was always because he wanted something. Why was she even listening to him? Why was she talking to him and thinking about what it might be like to see him again? She should hate him for what he had done to her and Mom. She shouldn't've even come out here.

But what if he'd really changed?

"You'll have to ask Mom yourself," she said at last. "I'm not going to be your messenger this time."

Dad blinked a couple of times and looked back at her. "You'd meet with me?" Some of the sadness left his face. The bell rang, and he stiffened. He reached out as if to touch her and then drew his hand back. "Tedi, I want to prove to you—and maybe to myself—that people can change, that they don't have to be stuck in the rut they dig for themselves."

For a moment, she couldn't help hoping. Then she thought of something Grandma always said, and she knew Dad needed to hear it. "Grandma Ivy says nobody can do that without God's help."

Instead of sneering at her and laughing the way he used to do when she quoted Grandma, he cocked his head to the side. "How's your grandma doing?"

Tedi heard her name being called and glanced toward the building to find Abby gesturing for her to hurry. "I've got to go." She turned to leave.

"Okay. I'll talk to your mom, Tedi. Today. I'm going to walk to her office right now."

She paused and looked back and felt suddenly angry again. "Don't you hurt her. Don't scare her, and don't fight with her."

"I won't."

"If you do, I'll never talk to you again."

He closed his eyes and sighed, and the muscle flexed at the side of his jaw again. "I won't hurt her, Tedi. I promise."

———

Lukas slipped past the curtain in exam room five and greeted Jacob Cascy, who lay on the bed beneath a thin sheet, his wounded upper arm covered in a sterile dressing. "Well, Cowboy, I've got a lot of good news and a little bad news. The good news is that I see no vital damage to your arm, and you won't have to leave Knolls to have the wound repaired. The bullet exited with no bone involvement. The bad news is that I want a surgeon to have a look at you, and he'll probably want to keep you overnight."

He expected an argument but got no reaction. Cowboy lay watching him listlessly.

Lukas frowned. "It won't leave as much of a scar as the lion bite did this spring." He waited for one of the quick, witty replies Cowboy was known for during his many trips to the ER, but to his amazement the rugged forty-three-year-old man's eyes filled with sudden tears. For a moment Lukas wondered if maybe he should recheck Cowboy's vitals and see if someone had slipped him some pain medication by mistake, then the man cleared his throat and wiped his eyes.

"The police didn't tell you, did they?" Cowboy said, his voice husky. "The man who shot me also shot and killed Leonardo."

Lukas stared at Cowboy and felt his jaw go slack. "Oh no." Not Leonardo. That cat had become a legend around Knolls, and everybody knew Cowboy loved him fiercely. "I'm sorry, Jake. I didn't know. I had to see about some other patients when the police showed up to get your statement, and since you were stable—"

"Did you ever lose somebody you depended on, Doc?" Cowboy kept his voice low, obviously unwilling for anyone outside the exam room to hear him.

Lukas nodded. "My mother died three years ago."

Cowboy shook his head and grunted in shared sympathy. He was silent for a moment, then he said, "That lion was my best friend, and Berring just walked onto my ranch and shot him while I was gone. Killed him! I call it murder. How could he get away with that? He's crazy!"

"Nobody really gets away with anything," Lukas said. "Not in the end. But I came to tell you something about that, Cowboy. We received word that Berring has been picked up by the police, and they checked his records. He was released from state prison about six months ago after a fifteen-year stint for armed robbery and attempted murder. He's being held."

Cowboy stared at him for a moment, then shook his head and lay back. "I'm glad they got him. It doesn't bring Leonardo back, though."

"No, it doesn't. I'm sorry."

Someone knocked at the threshold, then swept inside the curtain without waiting. In stepped tall, redheaded Beverly, off-duty ER nurse and Cowboy's girlfriend for the past four months. In fact, the two had met right here in the emergency department when Cowboy came in with a "love bite" from Leonardo.

"Hey, pardner," Cowboy greeted Beverly, his voice suddenly back to its usual bass depth, all evidence of grief gone except for the telltale redness in his eyes. "Come to see if I'd died and left that Mustang to you in my will?"

Beverly did not smile. Her usually pale skin flushed with anger as she crossed her arms over her chest. Beverly's quick temper was even hotter than the color of her hair, which was no surprise to Lukas. He'd borne the brunt of her anger a few months ago. He wondered if he should leave and allow Cowboy to handle it alone.

"You didn't even call me!" she snapped at Cowboy. "I had to hear about it through the grapevine." She glanced at Lukas, then lowered her gaze, as if embarrassed. "Hello, Dr. Bower."

"Hello, Beverly."

She was silent for a moment, as if wishing Lukas would leave. Or maybe she was too acutely aware of the fact that legally she should not have been called unless Cowboy had requested it, and Cowboy was not the type to ask for emotional support. Someone—probably softhearted, bigmouthed Lauren—had called out of consideration for Beverly, breaking patient confidentiality.

"Jacob Casey," Beverly said, "do you know what the word 'macho' means? It's not flattering. I don't appreciate it that half the town knew about this thing"—she gestured toward the gauze-covered wound—"before I did."

"Oh, don't go and get all worked up." Cowboy reached up with his left hand and patted her arm. "I've been hurt worse than this lots of times."

"What happened to Leonardo?"

Cowboy froze for a moment, the muscles in his jaw clenching and unclenching. "He didn't fare too well."

Beverly studied his face, her forest-colored eyes showing compassion and just a hint of frustration. Some of the high color eased from her face. "I'm sorry, Jake." She glanced at her watch. "The kids will be home in about an hour. I'll get them and go out to the ranch—"

"Nope."

She paused. "There you go again. You're not going to stop me this ti—"

"I don't want the kids to see him like that, Bev. Call the vet. You know his number." His voice wobbled just a little. He stopped, swallowed, took a breath. "They've got a key to the cage. They'll take care of him."

"But I can meet them out there. Let me help—"

Lukas quietly slipped out of the room as their voices continued in gentle argument. Cowboy needed to realize he had other friends besides Leonardo. In the short time they had known each other, Beverly already seemed to be a staunch supporter. Funny how some men could inspire loyalty and some could not, even in the workplace. Maybe that was why, at thirty-five, Lukas remained unmarried.

But could Beverly be trusted to continue her loyalty during Cowboy's grieving period? She had refused to support Lukas last spring with the treatment of one of their ER patients. All he'd wanted her to do was follow accepted hospital protocol when he refused to give narcotics to a drug-seeking patient.

She was supposed to fill out an AMA form stating that the patient, Dwayne Little, had left against medical advice when he realized he wasn't going to get the narcotic he wanted. Her refusal resulted in a pending lawsuit against Lukas by Dwayne's father, Bailey Little, president of the hospital board. If not for Mrs. Pinkley, the hospital administrator, Lukas would no longer be working here.

Lukas sighed and went in to check on his other patients.

———

With the sound of mechanical beeps filling the room behind her, Mercy stood blocking the entrance, her arms crossed over her chest as she glared at a policeman trying to get past her to Ramón Martínez, who was on a nonrebreather oxygen mask and a cardiac monitor.

"This man is not drunk, Bill," she said. "We've proven that. The alcohol you smelled on his breath came from the toothache medicine he was taking. He accidentally overdosed. He's sick and he's in pain. How can you do this to him right now?"

"Dr. Mercy, you know I still have to give him a ticket. People were hurt. I'm required—"

"If you give it to him now, he won't even understand what's going on. The interpreter called and canceled on us."

Bill sighed, tugging at the too-tight collar of his uniform. "I know enough Spanish to explain it to him."

Mercy felt the tingle of anger work its way up her spine. "You know Spanish, and you didn't volunteer to interpret when we needed help with him?"

Bill shifted uncomfortably. "Come on, Dr. Mercy. I don't know that much. Look, I'm not the bad guy here. I'm just trying to do my job. I'm not gonna beat him up or anything. I'll just give him the ticket and leave you alone."

Mercy wanted to argue further, but she knew it wouldn't do any good. It would probably make things worse for Ramón. If Bill didn't give the ticket now, someone else might do it later, and there were a couple of people on the Knolls police force that Mercy wouldn't trust to haul a dead dog to the pound. Bill was a good guy, just a little too legalistic.

Mercy nodded her consent, gestured for Claudia to stay in the room, and stepped down the hallway to Arthur's room, where she found Lukas and Lauren assisting Arthur into a wheelchair.

"Going somewhere?" she asked, ignoring the sight of Lukas and Lauren with their heads so close together.

"Your walls aren't soundproof," Arthur said. "I heard you need an interpreter."

"But your friends are getting ready to take you to Springfield," Mercy protested. "I know how badly you want to be with Alma."

"I'm going soon. Alma would want me to help Mr. Martínez." He settled back into the chair with a groan. His head was cleanly bandaged, and his arm was in a sling. His voice was still just a little slurred from the effects of the Demerol as he asked Lukas questions about Mr. Martínez.

"I admire your ability to forgive, Arthur," Mercy said softly.

He looked up at her in surprise. "Forgiveness has nothing to do with it, Dr. Mercy. What happened to us was an accident. There's no one to blame."

Mercy shook her head and stood back to let Lukas wheel Arthur out of the room. Was this guy for real? As if unable to help herself, she followed the entourage from the exam room into the hallway.

"I know a man near here who speaks Spanish," Arthur was telling Lauren. "If you'll ask my friends to call him, he can come in and interpret when I leave." When he entered Ramón's room, he spoke without hesitation, interpreting for the policeman giving the ticket, then more softly, with words of comfort, when Ramón buried his face in his hands.

Mercy stood beside Lukas at the doorway watching the scene. Even high on drugs and obviously still in some pain when he moved too fast, Arthur seemed to have an aura of compassion that surrounded him. She only knew one other person with that kind of presence. She looked at Lukas and found him watching her.

She did not want to look away. What she saw in his gaze as he looked at her was a combination of concern and admiration and something warmer, deeper, an emotion she didn't dare try to identify.

He touched her shoulder. "Thanks for coming over, Mercy," he said softly. "I don't know what I'd have done without you. I know other docs who wouldn't have come."

"You're welcome. Now, why don't you let me finish taking care of this one? You're still swamped."

He smiled and nodded. "I do have a date with a broken arm."

Mercy watched Lukas and Lauren leave, along with the policeman, then she pulled her stethoscope from around her neck and listened to Ramón's labored breathing. Through Arthur, she explained to Ramón that he had overdosed on the pain medication for his tooth, and that kept the oxygen from carrying well through his body.

"Tell him this is serious, Arthur, and the drug they are giving him will take care of that, but I need to keep him overnight in the hospital on the telemetry unit."

She checked the monitor, and it looked good. Ramón still had some shortness of breath, but no chest pain. She checked his painful tooth and had Claudia begin the dosage of methylene blue through an IV to counteract the effects of the drug overdose.

While Arthur translated, Mercy checked Ramón's neck, belly, squeezed his hips and legs, listened again to his breathing. It could have been a lot worse, but he had a strong constitution. He also seemed to have a strong sense of guilt, and Mercy was glad for Arthur's attitude of compassion.

She looked at Arthur once more, who continued to talk in soothing tones while she worked. Alma Collins was a lucky woman.

# CHAPTER 4

Lukas studied the small image of shrapnel that showed clearly on Buck's chest x-ray, then looked back at Buck. "Sorry, pal, it's surgeon's territory."

Buck groaned and laid his head back. "Surgery? I have a shift tomorrow."

"Get a replacement."

"I can't. We've got the competition for the Explorers. I have to be there. Can't you just fish in there and pull it out?"

Lukas held the x-ray out and showed him, pointing to the image of metal. "It's deep in the muscle, Buck. I don't have any concerns about it being in the heart or lung, but I'm not going to go slicing through all that thick body-builder's muscle and tissue of yours to find something that's going to play hide-and-seek with a scalpel. Don't worry. You won't even have to leave Knolls. In fact, Dr. Wong is in the ER right now treating another patient, and I can have him give you a look while he's here."

"Will he do it here in the ER?"

"Probably."

"Then I'll get out today?"

"Barring complications."

Buck motioned for Lukas to lean closer. "Will you tell Kyle and Alex to go on back to the station? I'm not on duty today, and they're not my responsibility. And don't tell Lauren I said that, or she'll give me another lecture."

Lukas grinned. "I'll head everybody off except your wife. She should be here any time."

Buck's expression relaxed into a smile at last. "Kendra's the only one I want to see."

———

Mercy had been gone from her office for over two hours, and it was time to get back, if she had anybody left to treat. She felt bad for leaving them for so long. They depended on her. She knew they were loyal, but that wasn't what concerned her about this.

A little over five years ago she'd lost custody of her daughter, and she'd lost the majority of her practice, all because of rumors and public opinion—and the fact that she'd been forcibly committed to a psych ward for a ninety-six-hour stay. Her ex-husband, Theodore Zimmerman, had coerced a physician buddy of his to pull the double cross on her during a very high-profile custody case for their daughter, Tedi.

Those patients who came to her now most likely knew about her past, about the rumors, and they came to her anyway. They'd given her their loyalty, and she hated to let them down.

She stepped into the nearest call room, prepared to do dictation on Arthur, when a newly familiar sense of suffocating heat and slight nausea accosted her. She inhaled with sharp impatience, as if to will away the attack as it began its languid travel outward from the core of her body. She hated this feeling! There wasn't time for it now.

She stepped into the private bathroom and splashed some cold water on her face and neck, then took deep breaths in through her nose and out through her mouth to try to relax. Stress. It had to be stress. Her life was so full right now that she constantly felt tense, even irritable. She wasn't sleeping well at night, and she refused to try the sleeping pills she sometimes prescribed for her patients. She splashed water again on her face, then pulled off her lab coat and fanned herself with some paper towels. It would pass in a moment, as it had before. Some ice cubes would be nice, but—

"Mercy? You in there?" came Lukas Bower's voice from the call room entrance.

Dabbing moisture from her face and neck, she stepped out of the bathroom and waved him through the open doorway, then slumped onto the side of the bed in the corner beside the desk. She had to get back to the clinic. People were waiting. Who knew what state the office was in. But she was still perspiring heavily, and she didn't feel like getting up right now.

Lukas strolled in and sat down in the desk chair, releasing a sigh. "Thanks for coming in. I don't know what I'd've done without you. And thanks for taking such good care of Arthur." He quirked a brow at her, and his clear blue eyes filled with gentle humor. "He got to you, didn't he? I heard him asking you to pray with him."

Mercy took a couple more deep breaths. She knew her face was flushed. She probably looked like she'd been running a race.

Finally Lukas noticed. "Mercy? Are you okay? You don't look too hot."

Mercy sighed and rolled her eyes. Wonderful choice of words. Typically Lukas. "I'll be fine." Sometimes, when she became especially irritable, his tenderness and concern could calm her like nothing else. He blurted whatever he thought, and you never had to worry about where you stood with him. His soft brown hair, bespectacled face, and compact build disguised a powerhouse of character and intellect that she admired. In fact, she felt much more than admiration for him. But she wasn't ready to discuss the hot flashes with him or anybody else.

"I saw Beverly in with Cowboy today," she said, making a show of examining the few exposed parts of his flesh. "I don't see any scratch marks, and I didn't hear any raised voices. Did she see you?"

"She saw me."

"You know she's still feeling guilty."

"Why would she feel guilty? She swears I was the one in the wrong." Lukas shrugged, but Mercy knew him well enough to know the continued disagreement with Beverly bothered him.

Everyone knew the nurse was afraid she would lose her job if she filed the report to support Lukas. Bailey Little had a lot of power, and he used it to get what he wanted.

"She still tries to schedule her shifts to keep from working with me," Lukas said. "She's civil when she gets stuck with me, but it isn't a comfortable situation. I've been praying about it. Lauren says she's praying, too. She's even tried to talk to Beverly about it."

Mercy tensed against her will at the mention of Lauren's name. "And did our little supernurse get anywhere with her?" She cringed at the sound of her own jealousy.

Lukas blinked at her, and his forehead wrinkled in concern. "No, but at least Beverly's still speaking to her. Mercy? Are you sure you're okay?"

This time the heat that flushed her face was shame, and she couldn't hold his gaze. During all the time she'd spent with Lukas, she hadn't been able to get out of her mind the fact that Lauren McCaffrey had a lot more in common with him. She was a Christian, as he was. She was his age, and like him, she had never been married. She was kind and outgoing to everyone. Her constant chatter sometimes got on Mercy's nerves, but she had a good heart. Funny how jealousy could tinge someone's outlook.

"I've got to dictate this chart and get back to my patients," Mercy said at last, still not looking at him. "How about a date Thursday night? Jarvis George has a lady friend who is giving him a 'getting well' party at his house."

Lukas frowned at her. "You're kidding, right? Do you think that's a good idea? Don't you think my presence will be detrimental to his recovery?"

Mercy picked up the phone. "Don't be paranoid. He was so out of his mind last spring he probably doesn't even remember you—or the extent to which he went to get rid of you." She knew Lukas wouldn't buy that. Sixty-five-year-old Jarvis George, the Knolls Community ER director, had opposed Mrs. Pinkley when she first hired Lukas. It hadn't helped the situation when Jarvis, distracted by Lukas in an exam room, had accidentally stuck himself with a suture needle. The needle had been infected by a patient with undiagnosed tuberculosis.

"He remembers," Lukas said. "I bet he still blames me."

"Oh, come on, Lukas, it wasn't your—"

"Not to mention the fact that the TB encephalitis couldn't have kicked in until at least a couple of weeks later, during which time he used all the influence he could muster—"

"He was being manipulated by Bailey Little," Mercy said. Everyone knew about the ER visit when Lukas had refused to give morphine to Bailey's drug-seeking son, Dwayne. "Both men have lost a lot of points in this community," she continued. "Especially Jarvis." He had not only given the requested morphine but had allowed

Dwayne to drive away high on the drug. As a result, Dwayne had been in a fatal automobile accident.

"So how about it, Lukas?" Mercy asked. "You're off Thursday. I checked the schedule."

"I guess I could try, but if Jarvis starts shooting the moment I walk in the door, I refuse to stay past the obligatory thirty minutes."

"Wear your bulletproof vest, just in case." Mercy held his gaze a little longer than necessary, simply because she loved having that connection with him. Then she dragged her mind away from what could have been if they weren't both so busy. She punched her entry buttons and started dictation.

———

Lukas stood watching Mercy dictate her additional comments about Arthur. They had incorporated the "T-system" charting now, which did away with extensive dictation or handwritten notes, but the T-sheets didn't cover everything. Lukas liked the fact that Mercy didn't try to pigeonhole or computerize human beings. She often added extra notes to her files. She always did the extras for her patients, making them feel more like human beings and less like parts on an assembly line.

Lukas knew she was that way with every relationship in her life. She made him feel as if he was important to her, that their friendship was something special. Up to now it had been just that—a sharing friendship. He enjoyed her company so much . . . maybe a little too much? They had a lot of interesting discussions about life and about their pasts, and about his faith in God. But that was the catch. It was only *his* faith, not Mercy's. How could he enjoy her company so much when she couldn't even understand the most important foundation of his life?

But he kept telling himself she was getting closer.

She reached up to catch a strand of her long dark hair that had fallen from its clasp and caught sight of him still standing there. She gave him a questioning "do you need something?" glance.

He shook his head, waved, and turned to walk out of the room, and nearly bulldozed into Mrs. Estelle Pinkley, hospital administrator. He caught himself just in time, with the aid of a few spur-of-the-moment dance steps.

"Oh, good, Dr. Bower, I'm glad I found you." The tall silver-haired lady took his arm as if to steady him. "Are you too busy to step into the break room with me for a moment?"

"Uh, no, not at all. Is something wrong?" By habit he studied her features and gave her regal seventy-year-old frame a cursory glance up and down as they walked the few feet into the empty ER staff break room. Those slender shoulders held a lot of responsibility, and some-times, when the ER was slow and she was having back problems, she would "impose" upon him for a spinal adjustment. As a doctor of osteopathy, Lukas was knowledgeable about spinal manipulation.

"You could say that." She eased down onto the chair at the far west end of the circular table, massaging her fingers. "We're being investigated by COBRA."

She said it too calmly, and for a moment the words didn't register. Lukas stared at her.

"We could be in for a rough ride, Lukas."

The impact hit him. "COBRA?" He caught his breath, then pulled back a chair beside her and sank down into it, stunned. The federal watchdog agency had the power, if they searched enough re-cords and found enough infractions, to shut down any hospital or medical center in the country. Every hospital had infractions. Nobody was perfect all of the time, especially when they were the victims of a witch-hunt.

"Have you spoken with Beverly lately?" Mrs. Pinkley asked.

"She avoids me as much as possible."

"She needs to fill out that AMA form, Lukas. It's been over three months." She leaned forward and spread her hands across the table. "This is ridiculous! One conniving man should not have this much power over this many people. He's got Beverly so browbeaten she's terrified to tell the truth."

"That conniving man is a grieving father," Lukas reminded her. "He's still reacting." Attorney Bailey Little was also president of the hospital board, a dangerous situation for a doctor employed by that hospital. Bailey had promised vengeance several months ago when Lukas refused to give morphine to Dwayne. Bailey had furthermore used his influence to sway public and patient opinion against Lukas. The plan had failed miserably upon Dwayne's tragic death, but Bailey's influence still beleaguered Mrs. Pinkley and her plans for the hospital.

"I find it outrageous that you're the one being investigated." Mrs. Pinkley's voice dropped even deeper than usual in an unaccustomed show of anger. "You know Bailey's behind this."

"When does the investigation start?"

She fixed him with her cool gray gaze, all traces of anger suddenly gone, as if she were slipping into her attorney mode. "The investigator is scheduled to arrive in two weeks. Don't worry, we'll handle this together." She placed her hands on the table to push herself up, then shook her head and sighed. "I wish Bailey didn't hold such a strategic position." She stood with a suppressed groan. "The weather's changing. We're in for a big storm."

"Is your back bothering you again?"

She smiled at Lukas, patted his arm, and straightened her spine. "Nothing a little exercise and a couple of aspirin won't take care of. Oh, by the way, I do have some good news. That doctor you wanted to have checked out, Cherra Garcias? She's got good references. I set her up for an interview Thursday. I hope you don't mind. You were too busy to talk when she called."

"No, that's great."

"You'll have trouble if you hire her, you know. She's obviously Hispanic. The folks around here might be slightly skeptical."

"Are you saying I should allow public prejudice to sway my decision?"

"No, I just want you to be prepared for ungrounded complaints about her, just as I received complaints about you, and you're from right here in Missouri."

"I'm glad you ignored them."

"You had good references. Of course, I get lots of complaints about your directorship, mostly from you, so the sooner you can hire someone to help you out with shifts, the happier we'll both be."

Lukas grinned. "No one will be happier than I will. I don't suppose you'd consider looking for a new director?"

She smiled and patted his arm. "Hang in there, and I'll make an administrative person out of you yet."

"But I don't—"

"Lukas, I can't in good conscience replace Jarvis George while he's still suffering from the effects of tuberculin encephalitis." She lowered her voice. "Just between us, I'm hoping he'll retire and I won't have to make the decision, because I don't want him back here causing me trouble and complaining about every tiny decision I make for this hospital. Still, I want to be fair to him. You are the perfect choice as interim director because you're the only full-time ER physician, and you don't want the directorship, which means I won't have a fight on my hands if he comes back."

"What if he tries to fire me again?"

Her smile returned, and it held a hint of mischief in the fine, powdered lines of her face. "Then I'll have a valid reason to get rid of him for good."

After she left, Lukas couldn't help glancing into the call room where Mercy had been. She was gone. When he stepped into the exam room where Cowboy had been, he found that he had already been taken into surgery. A couple of rooms down, where Buck also awaited a surgeon's check, Buck's raised voice burst from behind the trauma room curtain.

"No! Kendra, you can't do this. Not now. Not here!"

Lukas frowned and stepped forward, but something stopped him from pulling the curtain back. Buck's voice wasn't betraying physical pain.

Then came Kendra's light soprano voice. "I warned you before about this, but did you ever listen? No. You were always too busy playin' hero, always bargin' in to save the day, whether it's a dangerous pet or a woman in a burnin' buildin', no matter whether you needed to or not. I'm sick of it, Buck, I mean it." In the silence, Lukas heard soft sniffles. "I'm sorry, but I can't take it no more."

Buck's deep voice came more gently. "Kendra, honey, this is about your father, not me. Don't—"

"And everybody loves Buck Oppenheimer. The good ol' boys slap you on the back when we go out anywhere and tell you what a great guy you are. Do they ever look at me? Do they ever think about what I go through when I'm at home, wonderin' if my husband's going to live through the next fire? I'm no hero. To them I'm just a whinin' female."

"Nobody's ever said that about you. They know what you've been through."

"No, they don't. They don't care! I can tell what they're thinkin' by the look in their eyes. How dare I gripe when my husband comes home late from savin' people from their own fires? You're just a fireman, Buck, not a husband." There was a quiet sob. "I can't take it no more. I'm sorry, but I'm done with this marriage. I'm just not hero material."

Lukas stood out in the hallway in shocked silence while Kendra continued to sniff.

"Honey, you're worked up right now because of this scare," Buck said with an unsteady voice, "but I'm going to be okay, really. You can ask Dr. Bower. Kendra, don't leave me, please! Not like—"

The curtain swished back, and a very pretty woman who looked like a young Michelle Pfeiffer swept out, her face contorted with tears. She didn't glance up, didn't even notice Lukas standing there, staring in stunned disbelief.

Before Lukas could do anything, however, the human chatterbox, Lauren McCaffrey, swept past him as if she'd been hovering nearby, eavesdropping on every word as shamelessly as Lukas had been. She walked up to the bedside of the shocked man and laid a hand on his muscled arm, her kind green eyes sympathetic.

"Now, don't you worry, Buck. You know why Kendra's upset. She'll come out of this in a while and be begging you to forgive her and forget what she just said, and you two will be all giggles and kisses again in no time. I've seen it too many times before. She's got her head on straight most of the time. She'll come out of it. Come on, I've got to take your blood pressure again, especially after that little display."

Now both Buck and Lukas stared at Lauren. She ignored them and continued with her job. Buck turned dazed eyes toward Lukas.

"You heard that, Doc?"

"Yes, Buck. I'm sorry."

"But what am I supposed to do? I'm no hero. I'm just a fireman. And now she's saying she doesn't want to be married to me? I don't take risks, not like—"

"Settle down," Lauren warned. "I can't get a good reading if you get all worked up, and it's not going to help your recovery any, either.

Come on, Buck, you're a fireman. You can handle a stressful situation. You know your wife better than that, and you know she's going to be fine. You two have had your spats before, and it just makes your marriage stronger. She knows better than to let go of a hunk like you." She checked his arm to take another reading.

"Lauren, do you have to get a reading right now?" Buck asked, jerking his arm away. "This is my marriage we're talking about." He looked at Lukas. "What am I supposed to do?"

Lauren, as always, was the one who answered. "Well, Buck, you pray about it, and you wait a while, then you call Kendra on the telephone and tell her how much you love her. Then arrange for her to pick you up when you're released, and she will have gotten over it. Isn't that right, Dr. Bower?"

Lukas quirked an eyebrow at her. "Why are you asking me? I've never been married. And neither have you. What makes you think—"

"Ever been dumped, Doc?" Buck asked.

"You haven't been dumped," Lauren insisted. "You know she's just scared. She's still—"

"Yeah, well, I'll feel better when I'm back home in my own bed, and I don't feel Kendra's foot shoving me out the door."

———

Mercy walked into a surprisingly calm waiting room. Josie had sent home most of the patients who could reschedule, and there were only a few scattered around in comfortable chairs, reading the well-stocked library of periodicals with resigned expressions. They perked up when they saw her walk through. She waved and greeted them and apologized without breaking stride as she marched toward her office.

Josie saw her first and scrambled over to her side. "Dr. Mercy, before you go into your office you need—"

"I know, I'll hurry. I'm sorry—"

"No, you don't understand—"

"Just let me change lab coats. I got some blood on this one, and it's all—" She threw open the door to her office, then gasped aloud at the sight of her ex-husband, Theodore Zimmerman, sitting in the straight-backed chair in front of her desk.

"Dr. Mercy, I tried to tell you," Josie said, stumbling in to stand behind her. "He insisted he had to see you today because he'd made a promise, and I didn't want to leave him sitting out in the waiting room so you'd have witnesses when you killed him."

Mercy stared at the man with five years worth of loathing. "Get out of this office. How dare you come in here like this?" She turned to Josie. "Start showing the patients to the exam rooms. This won't take long. I'm going to call the police and let them know he's here." She picked up the telephone, almost expecting him to jump up and knock the receiver from her grasp and start shouting obscenities at her—his usual code of conduct.

He didn't move. "Please don't, not yet," he said quietly. "They released me."

"I'm supposed to believe that?" She stood staring at the man she had hated for so long she couldn't remember feeling any other way about him. At times she'd dreamed of killing him—actually dreamed it. And they had been good dreams. Mom would be horrified at some of the thoughts that went through her mind. So would Lukas. So would Tedi. "What are you doing here?"

"I came to tell you how sorry I am." He said the words quickly, as if afraid she would shut him up before he could get them all out.

Mercy had heard that one lots of times before. Her hand tightened on the telephone receiver. What if he was lying about being released? What if he'd escaped?

"And I want to find out what it would take for me to see Tedi again."

A stab of fear chilled the anger momentarily. One of Mercy's worst nightmares was that he would be able to come back into their lives and take Tedi away from her again. She would die before that would happen.

"I don't mean I want to see her alone," he said quickly. "I wouldn't ask that. You would be there, and Ivy, and anybody else you wanted. I'd be willing to talk to her through the bars of a jail cell if I could just talk to her."

"Which reminds me, why aren't you *in* jail?" She still could not believe she was standing here talking to him and actually listening to anything he had to say.

Strangely, however, he had said nothing accusatory or threatening, and he hadn't even tried to twist her words around to use them against her—a favorite of his. She couldn't smell any alcohol on his breath, and the whites of his eyes were actually clear, giving good definition to the light blue of the irises. His blond hair was short and neat. He wore jeans and a gray plaid flannel shirt—not his usual style. People who met Theo Zimmerman for the first time had commented—occasionally within Mercy's disgusted hearing—that he was the handsomest man in Knolls. At six feet tall he didn't exactly tower over other men, but he stood out, and he knew how to do it to his best advantage. He'd used his physical attractiveness like a tool when he worked as a real estate agent—before he was fired for embezzlement.

His eyes held hers steadily. "I did everything they told me to do." He leaned forward, elbows on knees. "The day I hit Tedi I wanted to die. I wanted the police to stick me back in the darkest and farthest cell and throw away the key."

Mercy still did, yet she was aware of the fact that Theo had been the one to call the police on himself.

"I can never make it up to you or to Tedi," he continued. "Or to anybody else who's suffered because of me." He frowned, still watching her. "They appointed an attorney to my case, and he convinced me I could make amends a lot better outside of prison than inside. But he told me something surprising, Mercy. Somebody paid my debts. The embezzlement charges were all dropped because the money was returned."

She replaced the receiver on its base. "I've got patients who need me."

"Why did you do it? You didn't have to. You could've sold the house and car and kept the money."

"Don't flatter yourself that I did it for you, Theo," she snapped.

He frowned, and his eyes narrowed slightly. "Oh, don't worry. I wouldn't be that stupid. You never—" he began, then caught his words, closed his mouth, shook his head.

"And don't expect me to do it again," she said. "I was your meal ticket for too many years, and I've run out of meals."

"I'm not after a free meal, either. Can't you just listen to me for once?" That old blue blaze flickered in his eyes, then was forcibly doused. "No, Mercy, that's not what I'm here for."

"Good. Tedi didn't deserve to have an alcoholic father who not only tried to kill her, but was being dragged through the courts on embezzlement charges. She's had a hard enough time because of you."

He exhaled sharply, then inhaled again, as if to curb a quickly rising temper. "Look, I know that, okay? I've been locked up for it, the courts know it, everybody knows it! Why do you have to rub my nose in it, too? Can't you see I'm trying to change?"

Mercy held his glare until the fire in his eyes once more died, then she turned her back on him. "Get out."

# CHAPTER 5

Tedi Zimmerman always felt the darkness before she saw it. It wasn't really a feeling, though. It was more just a sudden discovery that something was watching her, waiting for her to close her eyes, to fall asleep, to forget for just one night. That was when it pounced like a monster.

And so she lay awake with her light on, staring at the lumps and bumps of texture on the white ceiling and fighting the sleep that weighed down her eyelids when she wasn't paying attention. She'd finished her homework hours ago. She'd come to bed hours ago, too, but she mustn't sleep, because tonight was one of those nights when she knew what was out there. Sometimes it caught her before she could brace herself.

Should she go climb into bed with Mom? The monster could never get her there, and she always slept so well then. Mom didn't, but she'd told Tedi to wake her up when the shadows got too close. Tonight they were lurking everywhere.

She reached up to pull the blankets back when she saw it, actually saw it! Darkness puddled in the closet corner, seeping across the wall in slow motion, trying to creep up on her. She pulled the covers back up over her chest and tried to breathe quietly. It wasn't supposed to come this close, not in the light!

Surely it couldn't come any closer than the corner. It was kind of dark in that spot—the darkest place in the room. It would have to wait there until she turned the light off, and she wasn't going to do that.

She lay frozen for a long time, watching the blackness as her eyelids grew heavier and heavier. Then the blackness moved. It crept a few inches from the corner, then slowly inched across toward the door along the white glow of the wall. A small tendril poked out from the rest of it like a huge bony finger. It nearly reached the light switch before she realized what it was doing.

"No! You can't do that! Stop it!" Her voice wouldn't reach across the room. The tendril snatched off the light, then grew to fill the room with its evil. It tried to suffocate her.

"No! Mom, stop the monster! Mom!" She couldn't make any sound. She couldn't breathe, couldn't even move her hands from her sides. The monster filled her mouth and nose and ears and slid over her face.

And then something changed. A warmth spread down her legs, wet and heavy, and the scream she had been trying to make finally broke through, loud and—

She woke up to find the light still on in the bedroom. The light snatched the monster away before she could see it. The door swung open, and Mom rushed in, her long hair tumbling across her face as she tied the belt of her robe around her waist.

"Honey? Tedi, what is it?" Mom's voice sounded strong. It sounded wonderful. She sat down on the edge of the bed and reached forward.

Tedi's face contorted in tears, and she scooted forward into her mother's embrace, hating the sharp, cloying smell that rose from the covers. She was too embarrassed to admit what she'd done, but still too scared to let go.

"It came again, Mom. He tried to get me again."

"It's okay. I'm here and he can't get you now." Mom's grip was firm. She held Tedi and let her cry for a moment. "Come back to bed with me. I'll keep that ol' monster away from you." She released Tedi and leaned back to look at her. "Okay with you?"

Tedi wiped her eyes and nose with the back of her hand and tried to keep the tears from falling, but her chin still trembled. "I can't." This was the third time since she'd been living with Mom that this . . . kind of accident had happened. She was sitting in a puddle of pee, and it was seeping everywhere. It felt awful, but how could she admit—

"Of course you can." Mom straightened and stood from the bed, then reached down and pulled the comforter back. "Get your pajamas off and go clean up while I throw this bedding in the washer."

The relief came strong and fast. Tedi looked down and grimaced. "How'd you know?"

"You never cry this hard over a bad dream."

Tedi thought about that for a few seconds and realized that was right. Usually the dreams went away soon after she woke up.

"Besides," Mom continued, "I know what urine smells like." She sighed and shook her head, her dark eyes resting on Tedi's face with sympathy and love. "It hurts worse when your whole body lets you down, doesn't it?"

Tedi nodded.

"I know. It happened to me when I was eleven, too."

"Does it still happen?"

Mom grinned. "Well, I don't wet the bed anymore, but our bodies will always let us down. That's why I decided to be a doctor. It's a part of life."

Tedi climbed out of the soggy sheets, taking care not to drip on the floor. "Does it have to be so embarrassing?"

"I always wondered that myself." Mercy bent down and kissed Tedi's forehead. "Come on. If we hurry we can catch a couple more hours of sleep before we have to get up and get you to school."

Tedi grimaced as she peeled off her stinky pajamas. Today was Thursday, and Mr. Walters always gave tests on Thursday. She had to go to school. Mr. Walters constantly told her what a good job she did, not just on test days, but lots of times. He liked her, she could tell.

She ran into the bathroom and turned on the shower. Mom liked her, too. Parents were supposed to love their kids, but they didn't always seem to like them or want to spend time with them. Tedi knew some kids at school whose parents didn't seem to like them very much, and she felt sorry for them. That was what she felt like when she lived with Dad.

By the time Tedi was clean and dry and in fresh pajamas, she wasn't scared anymore.

———

Mercy shoved the sheets into the washer with a little extra force, glad she'd decided to buy the protective mattress pad this summer. Tedi's brilliant, wonderful, little-girl mind was working out some nightmare issues that nobody should ever have to face—issues Theodore Zimmerman had caused. And how would he have reacted to tonight's mishap? With ridicule.

She slammed the lid on the washer. And now he thought he could just dance back into Tedi's life and turn it upside down again. He was the most selfish, thoughtless—

"Mom?"

Mercy turned to find Tedi watching her from the laundry room door. "What, honey?"

"Are you mad at me for wetting the bed again?"

Mercy realized her jaws were set and she was gritting her teeth. "You've got to be kidding." She made an attempt to relax her facial features into a smile and went over to put her arm around her daughter. "When have I ever been mad at you? You're the most important person in my life." She buried her face in Tedi's hair and squeezed her close for a long moment. If only she could make the nightmares go away. "I hate to see you going through this. Come on. Let's get to bed." She walked with her arm around Tedi to the master bedroom.

Tedi was silent for a moment, then said, "You're mad at Dad again, aren't you?"

Oh boy. There was no hiding anything from this child. Mercy motioned for Tedi to crawl into the queen-sized bed—a newly purchased luxury. "You're far too discerning for an eleven-year-old." She switched off the bedside lamp and reached over instinctively to tuck the covers around Tedi's shoulders.

"Will you always be mad at him?" Tedi asked into the darkness.

Mercy was tempted to tell Tedi to just go to sleep and stop worrying so much. But Tedi would keep worrying, and Mercy knew how that felt. Her own mom had done the same thing to her. Of course, Ivy had not only been a mother but a shield for Mercy when Dad got drunk, and sometimes a punching bag.

And after all that, Mercy had married a guy just like him.

"So will you, Mom? Always be mad at Dad?"

She had to be honest. "I don't know."

There was a long silence, and Mercy had just decided Tedi had fallen asleep, when the small voice came again.

"Will I?"

Mercy winced at the plaintive sound of her daughter's voice. "I don't know, honey. For your sake, I hope not."

"Me too. Grandma says we should always be able to forgive people who hurt us, or we'll just be hurt worse. I don't know what she means by that."

"Well, medically speaking, when we harbor anger within ourselves it hurts us physically. It makes us sick, gives us ulcers, and scientists are discovering a lot of other things it can do." And why was she lying here filling Tedi's head with more things to worry about? She glanced at the lighted numbers of her clock. It was four-thirty in the morning. She didn't feel up to a deep philosophical discussion.

"I asked Grandma how you're supposed to forgive someone." Apparently Tedi was in a philosophical mood.

"What did she say?" Mercy asked.

"She said it's a hard thing to do without God's help. Grandma uses God's help a lot."

Three months ago Mercy would have been irritated by her mother's attempts to indoctrinate Tedi into her spiritual thought processes. Funny how things could change in such a short time. Mom had been a Christian for the past five years, and there seemed to be a peace about her that wasn't there when Mercy was growing up. The peace seemed to increase with time, and Mom seemed to grow stronger, even through Grandma's horrible cancer and death this spring, and Mom's own heart problems, and the horror and helplessness of seeing Theodore mistreat Tedi.

Mom's God was also Lukas's God. After many talks with Lukas about it, Mercy had recently begun to consider the possibility that she might be interested in getting to know more about Him. But why would He want to get to know her? Her skepticism still ran deep.

Still, there was something about Christianity—not with every person who claimed the belief, but with enough people that she couldn't help noticing the difference. And lately she felt surrounded by those people. Even Arthur Collins, in the midst of all his pain the other day, had prayed for her. She'd thought about it often. . . .

"Mom?"

Mercy's eyes flew open in the darkness, and she realized she'd dozed off. "Mm-hmm?"

"Has Dad talked to you yet?"

Okay, that was a powerful wake-up. "Yes, Tedi." And how did Tedi know about that? What was going on here? Remain calm. "Did he talk to you?"

"Yes. He came to the school the other day to spy on me. Abby saw him standing in the trees, and she made me go talk to him."

"She *made* you?"

"Well, you know, she talked me into it."

Mercy kept her breathing even, rehearsing the speech she would give Tedi and Abby on peer pressure later. What was Theodore up to?

"He asked if he could see me."

Tedi didn't say anything else for a moment, probably trying to determine how much more she could safely share. Mercy knew she had been far too indiscreet in the past about her bitterness toward Theo.

Mercy waited until she felt she could control her voice sufficiently, then asked, "How do you feel about that, honey?"

"I don't know. He apologized." Tedi paused for a moment. "He's done that a lot of times before, hasn't he, Mom?"

"Yes."

"But Grandma's always talking about how we should be willing to forgive over and over again. I forget how many times, but it's a lot." She hesitated. "Do you want me to see him?"

No! Never again! Why couldn't he just cease to exist? If he truly realized the damage he had done to Tedi, why didn't he leave the state and never come back? The truth as Mercy saw it was that he still didn't care who else he hurt. He just wanted to charm his way back into their lives.

"Do you, Mom?"

Mercy sighed. It was far too early in the morning for this discussion. "I want to do what's right for you. Unfortunately, I don't know what that is right now. I think I'll hold off on a decision until you and I can make it together and be more sure about how we feel."

Tedi let out a little sigh, and Mercy could tell she'd given the right answer for the moment. Minutes later, the deep, even breathing of a somnolent child whispered through the room. Mercy relaxed.

But she did not sleep. Fear and anger filled her mind. If not for Tedi, this hatred wouldn't have such a stranglehold. Mom kept talking to Tedi about the concept of forgiveness, but that was such a foreign concept when it came to her embittered relationship with Theo. Would it ever be possible? Was it even advisable?

---

At six o'clock Thursday morning Lukas finally awoke to an intermittent alarm and reached out toward the bedside to slap the Off button. The shutoff didn't work. He hit it again, but it kept ringing. He opened nearsighted eyes, put on his glasses, and realized he'd been abusing the call room telephone. He picked up the receiver.

Claudia, the RN on duty, didn't wait for him to say anything. "Good morning, Dr. Bower." Her mellow alto voice was pleasant and soothing, as it always was with patients. She knew how to tread lightly with a deadhead in the morning. "You've had at least four good hours of uninterrupted sleep, and it's time for you to get to work."

He slowly pushed the blankets back with his free hand. "Yes, Mother."

"Don't get smart with me, young man." Lukas could hear the matronly nurse smiling through her words. "We've got an eleven-year-old girl in exam room three who is covered in blood and needs your attention. Looks like she's been playing jump rope with barbed wire. Her parents are in worse emotional shape than she is."

"I'll be right there." Lukas replaced the receiver and climbed out of bed, combing his hair with his fingers as he stumbled out of the room. Maybe Claudia had gotten really smart and brewed some of that typical ER coffee that took fifteen cubes of sugar to kill the taste.

After reading Claudia's initial assessment, he entered the exam room to discover that, as usual, the nurse had not exaggerated her description. The eleven-year-old girl, Abby Cuendet, lay on the exam bed in pink pajamas with bloody rips in both legs. Lots of blood. Lukas frowned.

Abby tensed when she saw Lukas come in, and her dark eyes, behind thick-framed glasses, did not leave his face. Her parents, a young couple looking tear-streaked and shaky, hovered at her left side, and they, too, had blood on their clothes. Claudia worked on the other side of the bed, taking vitals and gently removing the pajama bottoms.

"Hello, I'm Dr. Bower." Lukas stepped over to the parents and held out his hand.

They introduced themselves, separately, as Jason and Lindy Cuendet. Not Mr. and Mrs. Cuendet.

"I'll be checking Abby out this morning," he said, noting as they shook his hand that they avoided getting close to each other. "Can you tell me what happened?"

Lindy shot her husband a sharp glance before she answered. "Abby got up earlier than usual this morning, and we didn't know she was awake. She went out to feed the dog, and she got caught in a broken roll of barbed wire we had out back." Her eyes narrowed at her husband. "Jason just had to bring it home because it was such a good bargain."

Her husband didn't reply, but his chin jutted out and his face flushed with barely restrained anger.

Lukas smiled at Abby. "You're Tedi's best friend from school."

Abby's face brightened and she nodded. "You recognized me."

"Of course. Tedi talks about you all the time, and I remember you from the school picnic a couple of weeks ago."

"Tedi's supposed to spend the night with me tonight," Abby informed him.

"Well, we'll just have to get you all fixed up so you can do that." He watched Claudia set up the suture tray, and he saw Abby's eyes widen with fear.

He bent over the wounds. "Now, don't worry, Abby. I'm just going to see what these look like right now." She had three gashes on her left leg below her knee and one on her right ankle. They didn't look as bad as Lukas had expected from all the blood. They weren't deep puncture wounds, which was good, but they were fairly gapped, and a couple of them would need two-layer closures.

He bent to examine one of the gashes more closely, and Abby winced.

Her mother inhaled sharply, then let out a low moan. "I can't do this," she muttered and rushed out of the room with her hand over her mouth.

Lukas let her go. It was easier on the child for the parent to leave the room than to pass out or become sick right there by the bed. He returned to the wounds, noting with concern that there was still some active bleeding, but since there was no involvement of the muscle, he didn't worry too much about it.

"Jason, when was Abby's last tetanus shot?" he asked. "Does she have any drug allergies that you know of?"

The man glanced at the wounds, then at Lukas, looking helpless. "I'll have to go ask Lindy." He left to find his wife.

Lukas gave Claudia instructions for skin prep and topical anesthetic, then left to get more information from the parents. He had just reached the central desk when he heard low, angry voices in the entrance to the first trauma room.

"You have to blame me for everything, don't you?" Jason Cuendet spat. "But you can't even be there for your own daughter when she needs you most."

"You know how I hate the sight of blood. I just can't stand to see her like this."

"It's always about you, isn't it? Why don't you think of somebody besides yourself for once?"

"That's precious, coming from you. When do you ever think of—"

Lukas cleared his throat. "Um, excuse me, I'm sorry to interrupt. Is Abby's tetanus up to date?"

In a voice still filled with anger, Lindy replied that it was.

"Good," Lukas said. "And how about drug or antibiotic allergies?"

Lindy shook her head, glaring at her husband.

Lukas took a couple of cautious steps closer to the couple. He hated interfering in what appeared to be a deep-rooted family dispute, but he often saw parents blame each other when a child was injured, and it always made the situation worse.

"Your daughter is going to be fine. We'll stitch her up and have her out of here in good time. Has Abby had other accidents like this?"

Jason switched his brooding gaze from his wife to Lukas. "What's that supposed to mean?"

"Oh, stop it, Jason," Lindy snapped. "You're always trying to start something with somebody." She turned to Lukas. "She fell and cut her knee at school last year. That's when she had the tetanus shot."

"When was the last time her eyes were checked?" Lukas asked. "I had to have my glasses changed frequently when I was her age, and I was always tripping over things." He saw Jason relax. The suspicion of child abuse never seemed to be far from anyone's mind lately.

As they talked about that, he slowly led them back toward Abby's room, where Claudia had everything ready to go.

"It'll be okay," he assured Abby and her parents as he washed his hands and gloved.

But when he turned back to Abby, Lindy walked out into the hallway again.

Her husband's loud, disgusted sigh filled the exam room. "I don't believe this," he muttered.

Abby tensed, and Lukas repressed a strong urge to ask him to leave, as well. At times like this he had to remind himself that he needed to learn more patience. Looked like Jason Cuendet could use some, too.

He picked up the anesthesia syringe. "Claudia says I'm not too bad with stitches, and she wouldn't say anything nice about me if she didn't have to." He shot the nurse a teasing glance, then redirected his focus to Abby. "If the sight of blood bothers you, why don't you just look the other way?"

Abby shook her head. "I'm used to it. I've had some nosebleeds."

"Why don't we play my favorite Popsicle game?" Ordinarily Lukas didn't use this tactic with a child as old as Abby, but she could be a little less secure than others her age. Her parents were behaving quite immaturely, and he found himself wondering if they acted like this all the time. "If these shots hurt after the first little sting, you let me know and you get a Popsicle. What flavor do you like?"

Abby looked from him to the nurse, her lips pressed together, eyes narrowed, as if making a monumental decision. "Grape."

"I think we have that, don't we, Claudia?"

Claudia grinned at the girl. "Sure do."

"Good." He raised the syringe once more. "Now, we'll numb you up, and everything will go smoothly. Abby, you can't watch me when I do it, because that would be cheating."

She turned her head and looked away, but her father hovered in an almost threatening stance, watching every move Lukas made.

Lukas slid the point of the needle just underneath the edge of the skin cut.

"What're you doing it like that for?" Cuendet snapped. "Trying to kill the kid?"

Abby whimpered and drew back.

Lukas shot an irritated glance at the father, fighting the urge to plunge the needle into the wrong person. "Due to the nerve endings on the noninjured skin," he snapped, then took a breath and tried to slow his words and his annoyance, "it's actually more painful to inject through the skin surface. As long as the wound is not grossly contaminated, I prefer to do this so it won't hurt the child." He looked more closely at the man's pale, moist skin. "We have a water cooler and some paper towels out in the waiting room. Would you want to step outside for a moment?"

The man shook his head, but he didn't hover so close to his daughter. Lukas had barely stitched the first cut when Jason took a deep breath, released it, and walked out of the room.

With both parents gone, Claudia managed to divert Abby's attention from the procedure. She asked about Abby's brother and sister and encouraged her to talk about her favorite sport, baseball. Then Abby's attention caught and held on something past the open threshold of the exam room. Her eyes widened, and she stared for a long moment.

"I don't need that grape Popsicle now," she said at last, her voice soft, almost reverent.

Lukas finished tying off a stitch. "I'm that good, huh?" He winked at Claudia.

"That's not it."

Claudia laughed.

Abby looked back at the sutures Lukas had placed, then looked up at him. "I'm too old for stuff like that. You won't tell Tedi how scared I was, will you?"

"Of course not. You don't act scared now."

"Nope. Mom and Dad are more scared than I am."

"I noticed."

"At least I didn't get in trouble for making them miss work. I guess all that blood got to them. Wait'll I show Tedi my stitches. Are you going to marry Dr. Mercy?"

Lukas nearly dropped the needle driver he was using. "What?"

"She likes you. She always talks about you, and so does Tedi. You'd sure be a better father than Tedi's real father was."

He glanced at Claudia, who was at least keeping her laughter to herself.

"Are you sure you don't want a Popsicle?" he urged. Children were growing up too fast these days. "Aren't sixth graders supposed to still like Popsicles?"

Abby shrugged. "Nah, I'm not hungry." She glanced again out the exam room entrance.

Lukas looked up to see what she was watching and caught sight of Abby's parents standing side by side, and Jason had his arm around Lindy's shoulders.

"I should get stitches more often," Abby murmured.

# CHAPTER 6

At a quarter to seven Lukas finished his chart on Abby and decided to try to catch some more sleep. He had two meetings this morning before he could go home, but his shift would be over in fifteen minutes. Dr. Landon could handle it after that. Yawning, he walked into the call room and sat down on the side of the bed.

The day he unloaded the directorship would be a day for celebration. He would have so much time on his hands he might get a chance to check out more of the hiking trails in the Mark Twain National Forest, which surrounded Knolls. In the past few months he'd had very few opportunities to explore the countryside. Even though Estelle picked up a lot of the slack for him, there were still too many things going on at—

Someone knocked at the door he had just closed. "Dr. Bower, you got a minute?"

He opened the door to find Bobbie Jo White standing there, hands on hips, heavy brows drawn down farther than usual over a plump face. Bobbie Jo, an x-ray technologist, was the director of the radiology department, and although she rarely smiled, she seldom glowered this morosely.

"Bobbie Jo? What's wrong?"

She sighed, crossed her arms over her ample chest, and slumped, uninvited, into the room. "It's this BO thing. You've got to do something about it, Dr. Bower. I don't have that much authority, and everybody's griping about—"

"Uh, wait a minute, Bobbie Jo. What 'BO thing'? I don't know what you're talking about."

"Oh, sure you know. That new ER tech they hired last month, Amanda? Everybody's talking about it, and even some of the patients complained. She works nights. In fact, she worked last night." Her glower eased a little as she looked at Lukas hopefully.

"And you're telling me this because. . . ?"

"We all want you to talk to her about it. Tell her to clean up."

He definitely needed more sleep. Or maybe he already *was* sleeping, and this was just some weird dream. "Who is 'we all,' and why me?"

"You know several of the staff. You're the director. It's your job."

"It's the *nurse* director's job."

"She's not touching this one. It's up to you. The girl flat out stinks."

Lukas stared at her, dumbfounded. He hadn't noticed any unusually significant aromas emanating from the tech last night, or any other night—not that he'd been paying attention. Sometimes the patients got pretty rank, but an emergency department was not expected to smell like a field of spring clover. And he had come to Knolls to treat patients, not teach hygiene.

Before he could think of a kind but firm way to explain to Bobbie Jo how far off the mark she was, Claudia stepped up to the open doorway. "Oh, good, Dr. Bower, you're awake. I wasn't going to disturb you if you were sleeping, but we just got a call from Dr. Landon, and he's not going to be able to come in today."

Lukas groaned. This was the second time this week he'd been stood up for a shift. It was getting ridiculous. "What happened?"

"His brother was in a wreck last night up in Jefferson City. I tried to find a replacement, but so far nobody wants the shift." She took a step inside. "Are you up for a twenty-four?"

"No," he snapped and was immediately contrite. It wasn't Claudia's fault he was getting dumped on this week. "I'm never up for a twenty-four."

"Sorry. I'll keep trying to find someone if you want me to."

Did she even have to ask? "Please, Claudia."

She glanced hesitantly at Bobbie Jo, then back at Lukas. "Dr. Bower, we also got a call from your early appointment this morning." She came farther into the room.

"Dr. Garcias? Don't tell me she canceled."

"No, but she's coming earlier if you don't mind. She had something come up at home, and she has to be back in Little Rock, Arkansas, this afternoon."

"Dr. *Garcias*?" Bobbie Jo exclaimed. She put her hands on her hips, and her frown deepened again. "You're kidding. Our new ER doctor's a *Mexican*? Don't we have enough already?"

Claudia shot the woman a surprised glance, shook her head in irritation, and walked out of the room.

Lukas turned a sleepy glare to Bobbie Jo. "Was there something else you wanted to discuss with me?"

The technologist continued to rest her fists on her wide hips. "Hiring a Mexican is going to go over like a lead balloon. In this town people are already worried about all those people coming in. They're taking over the courthouse square with their grocery store and bakery and—"

"So? They're legitimate businesses, just like every other business in town." Funny how quickly a good attitude could dissipate. "I don't see how they're taking over if everyone in town reaps the benefits. Have you tasted the sopapillas at the bakery?" He and Mercy had eaten at the restaurant just last week, and their chiles rellenos, according to Mercy, were perfect. His church held Spanish-speaking services, and the attendance was increasing.

"What are you going to do about Amanda?" Bobbie Jo demanded.

Lukas wanted to tell her to take care of it herself, but she wasn't exactly a people person. Besides, she was right. It wasn't any of her business. "I'll talk to her." He specifically did not say what he would talk to her about, or when he would do so. "Now, if you'll excuse me, I'd like to get some rest." He walked over and held the door and waited for her to huff out, then closed it a little too loudly behind her. On a whim, he locked it. They would soon learn that he could get firm when necessary.

He had the blankets lifted and was ready to climb back into bed when the phone rang. He jerked up the receiver. "Yes?"

"Dr. Bower, I have to tell you something you're not going to like." It was Claudia.

He groaned. "More? Haven't we had enough bad news this morning?"

"I'm sorry. This is the worst."

Lukas immediately thought of his family. Were his father and stepmom okay? Was one of his brothers or their families—

Claudia sighed heavily over the phone. "Alma Collins lost her leg. They said there was too much damage for them to repair. Her husband, Arthur, called us this morning to thank us for all we did for them Monday, and he especially wanted us to tell you and Dr. Mercy how much he appreciated your kindness."

Lukas slumped onto the side of the bed and exhaled. He felt as if he'd been slapped. He closed his eyes and saw the faces of Arthur and Alma, remembered the pain they'd experienced, remembered the love and concern they had displayed so openly toward each other.

"I'm sorry, Dr. Bower," Claudia said softly.

"Me too. Thank you for letting me know. Why don't we send some flowers from the department?" That seemed like such a frivolous gesture under the circumstances, but he couldn't think of anything else to do right now except pray.

"Good idea," Claudia said. "I'll start collecting, and I'll call the florist when they open."

When she hung up, Lukas sank back against his pillow, too depressed, suddenly, to think about sleep. "Why, Lord?" he muttered. "They're your servants. They've dedicated their lives to serving you and helping others. Why did this have to happen to them?"

He knew the answer, of course. None of God's people were immune to the suffering brought to earth by sin, and it wasn't God's fault, but it sure was easy to blame Him.

A moment later, another knock sounded at the call room door. "Dr. Bower?" came a slightly familiar voice. "Bobbie Jo told me you wanted to see me."

Amanda.

Lukas gritted his teeth. As of now, he would start locking the call room door any time he was in here. Then people like Bobbie Jo White would not have the freedom to barge in and start adding to his already overtaxing duties. She had no right. Why couldn't he have just told her that in the first place?

He went to the door and opened it to find a young tech with curly brown hair and sea-green eyes waiting expectantly. She looked clean.

No dirt under her fingernails. In the month she'd been here, Lukas had heard no complaints about her work. In fact, she almost seemed to go at a run most of the time. Maybe she just worked too hard.

And maybe there was . . . yes, there was a slight hint . . . okay, make that a certain odor . . . yes, okay, she smelled.

"Dr. Bower, did you want me for something?"

Lukas hesitated. How was he supposed to tell this young girl that she needed a bath? Estelle would not appreciate it if he dumped this on her, and it would be more painful coming from the hospital administrator than it would from a doctor who worked with her.

"Yes, Amanda." He cleared his throat and willed his face not to flush. This was strictly a professional problem to be dealt with. "Uh, did you have an employment physical when you came to work here?"

Her light brown eyebrows raised in curiosity. "Yes. It was a requirement."

"Good." But those physicals were certainly not comprehensive. "Have you been having any health problems lately?"

She frowned at him. "No, I've been better than ever." She tugged at the waistband of her scrubs, which showed some slack. "I've been on a diet, and I'm almost down to my target weight. I've got all kinds of energy."

Target weight? She didn't look like she needed to lose any weight. "Are you under a doctor's care?"

"Nope, I did it on my own. I've been taking ma huang since I came to work here—one of the nurses up on the floor told me about it. It sure helps curb the appetite."

Ma huang? He didn't like the sound of this. He looked her up and down. "Why are you still trying to lose?"

She tugged at her scrub pants again. "Don't worry, there's still some flab. These baggy things cover a lot of cellulite. I've always had trouble with my weight, but when I moved to Knolls six months ago, the pounds just started to slip off. I don't know why. I guess I just got too busy moving, and I got a little homesick, too . . . anyway, I wasn't hungry. It felt so good to lose the weight, I decided to keep going. It worked! I've lost forty pounds since I came here, and it wasn't hard at all." She grinned at him. She had a sweet face, with dimples, rosy cheeks, the whole bit.

Lukas frowned. Forty pounds in six months? That was a little extreme. "Amanda, did you know that ma huang contains mostly ephedrine? That's an amphetamine-related compound. I don't like the idea of one of the hospital nurses recommending it for you." He knew he probably sounded like her father trying to lecture her.

"But I feel so good." Amanda looked around, then lowered her voice. "Except for maybe one thing. Lately I've been sweating a lot, and when I work twelve-hour shifts, I don't have a chance to shower." Her face turned even pinker. "Sometimes I'm afraid a patient might notice when I get too close."

Suddenly the odor was the least of Lukas's concerns. "Are you taking caffeine with the ma huang?"

"Well, I do drink a lot of soda, but I don't touch coffee, especially the ER brew. That stuff could kill a horse."

"Soda can have a lot of caffeine. Are you having trouble sleeping at night?" He resisted the urge to take out his penlight and check her eyes.

She shrugged. "Yeah, sometimes."

"You're overdosing yourself. That can be very dangerous, and it needs to stop." Why did young girls do this to themselves?

She frowned at him, shook her head, and spread her hands out. "But I don't want to gain all that weight back."

"Didn't you do well on your diet for five months before you began taking the herb?"

"Well, yeah, but—"

"Just try to cut down, Amanda. The drug could be hurting you."

She grudgingly agreed and left, and Lukas sighed with relief. He was congratulating himself on a situation well handled when Claudia came to the open threshold again.

"You know, Dr. Bower, you could use a revolving door if this keeps up. Sorry, but I can't find anyone to take the shift today. I've exhausted the list of prospects, and I can't even get Dr. Evans to come in early for you. His kid has a game. Hope you didn't have anything going on today."

By now *everybody* was getting on his nerves. "Just *sleep*."

"Oh, well, I hear that's overrated." She hadn't caught the friction in his voice. "Are you ready to talk to Dr. Garcias? She's here."

Lukas looked at his watch. "Now?" It wasn't even eight o'clock. "Sorry."

Lukas yawned and stretched. "I'll meet with her in the private waiting room in a moment." If he didn't fall asleep first.

He watched Claudia leave, then realized there was one person who wasn't getting on his nerves—possibly because she wasn't here right now, but there was a way to check out his theory.

He called Mercy at home, and she answered. Good, she hadn't left to take Tedi to school yet.

"Hi." His voice held weariness.

"Lukas? What's wrong? Are you okay?"

He closed his eyes and let the warmth of her voice and the essence of her concern float through him like healing balm. As was happening more and more often lately, she picked up on every nuance of tone. She could almost read his mind, and sometimes she answered his questions before he even asked them. He found himself turning to her whenever things went wrong. Occasionally, the realization concerned him. Shouldn't he be turning to God before he turned to anyone else, especially someone who did not claim a belief in God?

But right now he didn't want to think about that. "Sorry about the late notice, but I'm going to be a little late for our date tonight. I'm still working, and I have to cover today's shift."

Mercy groaned. "Oh, Lukas, not again. If you don't hire more doctors, you're going to work yourself to death. Can't you get a replacement?"

"Nobody wanted to come in."

"You coddle them, Lukas. Why don't I come in and relieve you for a few hours, at least, so you can get some sleep."

Lukas smiled to himself. Mercy to the rescue on her day off. No wonder he cared so much about her. She was so giving, but he refused to exploit their deepening friendship. "I got a few hours last night, and I have two meetings this morning, so I might as well stick around. Why don't you go check on Clarence and Darlene this afternoon?"

"I was planning to do that, anyway. Darlene's breathing didn't sound good last week, and I suspect she's hoarding her medication again, afraid to use it unless she thinks she's dying."

Clarence and Darlene were pro-bono cases Mercy had picked up a few months ago when Clarence's extreme obesity threatened his life. His sister, Darlene, suffered from bad asthma, and her worry over Clarence exacerbated the situation. Since then, Lukas and Mercy checked them regularly and administered medication—sometimes paid for from their own pockets—during frequent home visits. Lukas admired the brother and sister, who had fought their way out of a family of welfare abuse. It was a painful day when Clarence was forced to ask for state aid so that he wouldn't be such a dangerous burden on his sister. His goal was to be self-supporting again. Literally.

"How's Clarence's weight?" Lukas asked.

"He hasn't lost any more, but he's still about two pounds below five hundred. I know he's discouraged, but with his heart condition, I don't want him to start exercising any more strenuously without closer supervision. I'd promised he could start walking more when his weight dropped to four seventy-five. I'll fill you in on all the details when I see you tonight." She paused. "I *will* see you tonight, won't I?"

"Yes." But Lukas wanted to see just Mercy, not a large crowd of small-talking people. "I don't suppose we could just relax and have a casual meal at your house or something. I'd even spring for pizza."

"We'll have casual food at Jarvis's party, Lukas." Her voice had that familiar "this is for your own good" tone. "I'm sure they'll have some punch somewhere, and those little barbequed weenies you love so much. How could it get any better than that?"

"We could be lost in the Grand Canyon without water." He knew he should appreciate her attempts to heal the breach between him and Jarvis George. "We could be canoeing down Elk River in a hurricane." Maybe Jarvis really wasn't a vicious man when he didn't have tuberculosis teeming through his brain. "We could be dining on king crab in a den of rattlesna—"

"Lukas."

"Sorry. I can't get over this inner conviction that Jarvis will find a way to turn *me* into little barbequed weenies when he sees me tonight."

"Don't worry. I'll stop him before he takes his first bite."

"I may be late. You know how busy it always seems to get at shift change."

"Especially for you. I'll see you when you get here, and wear something besides your scrubs."

"I'll see if I have any clean clothes in the dryer." He hesitated, then said gently, "Mercy, I just got some bad news. Alma Collins lost her leg."

There was a quick intake of breath, and then a sigh. "Oh no. Oh, Lukas."

"Arthur called this morning to tell us he appreciated our help."

"But his wife lost her leg!"

"He especially mentioned you and me."

Another sigh. "Sometimes I wonder if it's worth it."

"It is, Mercy." He just wished he could find the perfect way to convince her that God was the One who made it all worthwhile. "I'll see you tonight."

---

Mercy glanced at the clock and thought again about Arthur Collins and his willingness to stay and interpret for the very man who had caused Alma to lose her leg. Mercy had no doubt that he would have done the same even if he'd already known the worst. It was the kind of man he was . . . like Lukas.

Did the spiritual belief of these men have something to do with their soul-deep kindness, or were they believers because of the kind of people they were to begin with? Lukas must have been as earnest and forthright at five years of age as he was now at thirty-five.

Chronologically, Lukas was almost five years younger than Mercy. Experientially, the gap was probably more like ten years. Here she was, divorced with an eleven-year-old child, and Lukas had never even had a serious relationship with a woman. It showed. Even though they had gone hiking together several times over the summer, and had gone on picnics with Tedi, and out to dinner, even though he'd been to her house several times, and had even helped her move, he did not engage in open displays of affection. He'd hugged her and patted her on the back a couple of times when she bowled a good game at the lanes. It seemed as if he was always physically drawn to her, always touching her on the arm to emphasize a point.

He'd taken her hand and held it once when they were walking in the park, almost without thinking, and then when he realized what he was doing he let go. ER staff teased her about the time she and Lukas spent together, and some of them had already jumped to entirely erroneous conclusions.

What was the future of their friendship? He displayed how much he seemed to care for her in every glance, in the inflections of his voice when he talked with her, and the amount of time he wanted to spend with her. But he'd never even kissed her, and never acted as if he intended to.

At first that was a refreshing relief. She hated men who thought a first date granted permission to paw her—not that she'd had many dates in her life besides Theo. But there were times, now, when she found herself wondering if Lukas found her physically unappealing. Were they really just good buddies, after all?

The brief thought about Theo reminded her of Monday. She picked up the phone again and speed-dialed her mother's number. She couldn't waste her day sitting here dreaming about a man, even one as special as Lukas.

Ivy answered on the fifth ring, her breath coming in hard puffs that sounded like wind across the telephone line.

"Hi, Mom, did I catch you exercising?"

"How did you guess?" Ivy asked dryly. "Did I tell you about my new treadmill?" She huffed a couple of times. "It measures everything, including calories expended, heart rate, practically my metabolic rate. The guys from the sports equipment shop delivered it last Saturday, and I've already put twenty miles on it." Her words were clipped and quick, as they always were, especially when she was excited.

Mercy smiled. At sixty-six years of age, Ivy Richmond was in excellent shape and worked hard at it, especially after developing some cardiac problems in the past few months.

She continued to breathe heavily, and the soft whine of a motor filled the background. "What's up? You don't usually call this early in the morning."

Mercy didn't hesitate. "Theo's out of detox and he wants to see Tedi." She waited for the motor to shut off and Mom to scream, but nothing changed. She continued. "He came to see me Monday." She paused again. Still no discernable reaction. "Mom, are you listening to me?"

"Of course. What're you going to do about it?"

"Good question. What if he tries to get Tedi back? He's already gone to the school to seduce Tedi into seeing him again."

"That's not the way I heard it."

Mercy bit her lip and suppressed a sharp retort. She should have known. "When did Tedi tell you?"

"She didn't."

"Then who—"

"Have you considered the possibility that Theodore might have had a change of heart while he was sitting in that cell with nothing to fill his time but memories about what he'd done to his daughter?"

Mercy couldn't believe it. "Mom, you talked to Theo!"

"He came to me Tuesday. He told me everything, including his trip to the school and to your office." There was a slight pause. "I heard you weren't too friendly."

"And you were?"

"No, I wasn't, but I didn't kick him out. I listened to what he had to say, and I believe he is truly sorry."

"I believe he is, too." Mercy couldn't keep the exasperation from her voice. "He's been sorry before, Mom, but that didn't precipitate any character changes. Are you actually saying you think I should let him see Tedi?"

"No, but I think you should talk to him again. He was encouraged by the fact that you used equity in the house and car to settle his accounts."

"And I explained to him very clearly that I did that for Tedi's sake, not for his."

"He told me that impressed him."

"Careful, Mom, he's playing you just right. You know how he operates."

Ivy was silent for a moment, and the whine of the machine diminished. "Talk to him, Mercy. The bitterness is building up in you like a volcano, and if you don't find a way to forgive him, it will hurt you and Tedi and everyone else who loves you. Don't let the past do this to you. Besides," she said, breathing deeply as she stopped her exercise, "sooner or later he can get legal visitation rights reestablished. If you can control the situation instead of the court, it'll only be better for Tedi. Like it or not, he's her father."

———————

Lukas liked Dr. Cherra Garcias, a slender woman with shoulder-length, curly black hair and laughing eyes. She, too, was a Doctor of Osteopathy about the same age as Lukas, and she had been in family practice in Arkansas for six years. She had moonlighted in a small ER near Little Rock. As Lukas had earlier ascertained, she possessed excellent references and a license to practice in Missouri, and her husband and three children were ready to move as soon as possible.

Unfortunately, she laughed when Lukas hinted about the possibility of her taking the ER directorship. "I have three active children and a husband who works at home so one of us can always be with the kids. I can barely manage them."

*Oh well, one can always dream,* Lukas thought.

Her laughter died and she grew serious, her dark, almost black eyes sober. "When I first went to work where I am now, I had a lot of trouble with prejudice because I'm Hispanic. This is a small town a lot like ours, and there's no reason for me to expect anything different here." She held Lukas's gaze. "I can deal with it if I know what to expect."

He appreciated her openness and wondered if she might have run into Bobbie Jo White out in the hallway somewhere. "Knolls has a growing population of Hispanics, drawn to the area by quickly advancing industry. Some of the native locals are paranoid, but we haven't really had any serious racial difficulties."

She watched him closely. "Yet?"

"Hopefully never, although it's hard for any outsider to penetrate the small-town social shell. I haven't managed to do so. In this region of the country, a person usually has to be around for twenty years before they're considered a citizen. I'm surprised I'm allowed to vote."

"How much impact will my Mexican heritage have on your decision to hire me?"

Lukas thought about the question for a moment. He probably wasn't even supposed to be addressing this subject with her. "The fact that you're bilingual will be a great help." There, that sidestepped the issue nicely. It was also the truth. "I need another doctor—in fact, more than one—and you come with good qualifications." He knew if he hired this doctor, Mrs. Pinkley would back him up. "Do you want the job?"

Cherra smiled and stood from the overstuffed chair where she sat. She reached out and shook his hand with a firm grip. "I'm ready when you are."

Some of the tension of the morning eased for Lukas. "How does Monday sound?"

She cocked her head sideways, eyebrows raised. "You must really be desperate."

"I'm on my second twenty-four-hour shift this week."

"Monday is fine."

He returned to the ER to find Claudia waiting. "Dr. Bower, I had a phone call for you while you were in your meeting. He insisted you call him back. I told him not to hold his breath."

"Oh?"

"He wanted an abortion pill. He said you'd know what he was talking about. I told him I was a registered nurse who worked closely with you, and that if I didn't know about an abortion pill for men, neither did you. Turns out he wants it for his sister, who's pregnant." She shrugged and bent her slightly chubby body over to pick up her purse from beneath the desk. "I assured him he had the wrong number. I'm out of here, Dr. Bower. My shift's over. You don't have any patients, so why don't you try for a nap." She glanced around and lowered her voice. "Brace yourself. Beverly's your nurse for the day." She waved and walked out the door.

He turned around and nearly collided with Beverly, the tall, slender RN who had scrambled for the whole summer, sometimes unsuccessfully, to keep her schedule from coinciding with his.

"Good morning, Beverly."

She blinked at him in surprise. "Hi, Dr. Bower. I thought Dr. Landon was on duty today."

"So did I until about an hour ago. Sorry, you're stuck with me." He heard the sharpness in his own voice, and he didn't care.

Beverly's freckled face suffused with color, and she looked away.

"How's Cowboy doing?" he asked as he reached over to check a chart on the desk.

"Better." She glanced at her own work area, as if to keep from making any unnecessary eye contact with Lukas. "He's still upset about Leonardo, of course. He's glad they locked up Berring, but now we've heard that Berring is trying to get out on bail. He may do it, too."

"I hope not."

Beverly placed her purse under the desk, glanced around the empty ER, then back at Lukas awkwardly. "I guess Lauren's our double-coverage nurse today, isn't she?"

"I think so."

"She should be here about noon, then."

"Yes." Lukas got tired of the tension and turned to go to his call room, when he heard Beverly clear her throat behind him.

"Um, Dr. Bower?"

He turned back. "Yes?"

She took a deep breath. "You got a raw deal with the Dwayne Little case this spring."

Lukas couldn't prevent his surprise from showing. "Yes, I did." And she hadn't helped the situation. It was her refusal to back him up—

"I hear we're being investigated by COBRA."

"Yes, we are." He waited for her to say something more, to admit she was wrong, that she'd behaved like a coward and allowed Bailey Little to coerce her, and that she would rectify the situation immediately.

"You want some coffee?" she asked, turning toward the break room in the back. "I'm going to make a new pot."

"No, thanks, I think I'll take a nap while the place is quiet." He kept his disappointment to himself.

# CHAPTER 7

After three and a half months of weekly visits, Mercy Richmond knew she could enter the Knight household without waiting for them to answer her knock. Like many citizens of Knolls, Clarence and Darlene left their doors unlocked and their fifteen-year-old car sitting out in the drive with keys in the ignition. She shook her head as she gave a quick rap at the threshold and opened the door. Her own mother was the same way.

"Hello, anybody here?" she called out, knowing there would be. Even after losing a great deal of weight, Clarence had a lot more to lose, and he remained in his bed most of the time. His sister, Darlene, was afraid to leave him in case he needed her, and so she earned an unsteady income by indexing nonfiction books for publishers on her home computer. In spite of her poor physical condition, she continued to refuse state aid. Clarence had only been forced to accept help when he realized the burden of his extensive medical problems could worsen his sister's condition. Both were in their forties.

"Hello? It's Mercy." She stepped farther into the small, dilapidated ranch-style house. "Darlene? Clarence?"

"In here," came a voice deep enough to vibrate the walls. It echoed from Clarence's bedroom at the end of a short hallway.

Clarence Knight had been a hardworking mechanic, in good physical health and only slightly above average weight just a few years ago. Then several unexpected blows had hit him in succession: he had lost his job, developed pneumonia, and gone into the hospital for a couple of weeks. Then he lost his insurance, and he couldn't find a job. He had to sell his house to pay the hospital bills, and he moved in with his younger sister, Darlene, who suffered from asthma. With Clarence's depression had come the weight, and it had snowballed into a near tragedy before Lukas Bower had discovered the problem last spring and invited Mercy to donate weekly time and money to help him and his sister.

Mercy lugged her medical paraphernalia to the open door of the room, then stopped and greeted them. Clarence looked no different from usual, dwarfing his old standard-sized bed with rolls of thick flesh, huge arms and legs, and a heavy growth of dark beard and mustache that matched his hair. His dark brown eyes welcomed her, but they held worry. He wore very little clothing because he was always hot, and just like anybody on a diet, he refused to buy more clothes until he had reached his target weight—not that he could have afforded clothing had he needed it. Since he never left the house, why bother?

Clarence gestured toward his sister, Darlene, who occupied the only chair in the room. She was as slender as Clarence was huge, and she kept her prematurely graying hair cut short—and she cut it herself. She never wore makeup, never dated, always kept busy. And she treated Clarence to the same adoration with which she had treated him since they were children.

Today she sat bent forward, shoulders stiff, back straight in what was known in the ER as the respiratory position, with obvious inspiratory and expiratory wheezing. The expiratory was much worse. Classic signs of an asthma attack.

"I tried calling your office this morning, Mercy," Clarence said in his growling voice. "All I got was your machine."

Mercy stepped to Darlene's side and put her things down. "You have my home number, Darlene. Why didn't you use it when you started having trouble?"

"She wanted to try to treat herself before she called you," Clarence answered for his sister, heaving himself up to a sitting position, quaking the bed in the process.

"And did it work?" Mercy pulled out her stethoscope and listened to Darlene's chest. "No need to answer that."

"I tried to get her to call," Clarence said. "The weather changed last night, and she was out in it, cleaning out the rain gutters. That's what made her worse."

Mercy grimaced at her patient and took her blood pressure. "Darlene, you know better." She kept her voice gentle but could not hide all the frustration she felt. "Independence is a wonderful thing, but risking your health like that could make you more dependent in the end."

Darlene's blood pressure and heart rate were a little elevated. She was agitated, but not crashing. Her skin wasn't cool or clammy, and though her capillary refill was a little sluggish, it wasn't bad. Yet. The peak flow meter didn't register great numbers when Darlene exhaled into it.

"She ran out of her inhaler," Clarence said.

Mercy reached into her bag and pulled out two different types of inhalers. "Time for a breathing treatment. And, Darlene, I want you to start taking your steroid again. I want to see you first thing in the morning in my office."

Darlene shook her head. "Not tomorrow."

"Please don't argue with me. This is your life we're talking about." Mercy began the treatment, giving Darlene no further chance to reply. Between treatments, she did a bedside glucose test on Clarence and was glad to see that his blood sugar was 260, much lower than it had been, even though it was still high. His blood pressure was lower, as well, at 160 over 98.

"How's that strain doing?" Mercy asked him as she reached down and kneaded the huge calf of his left leg. At his size and in his eagerness to recover, he had a bad habit of moving too quickly or overdoing his walks through the house. Strained muscles were common. He seldom got outside because of the steps.

"A little better," he said. "I'm trying to stay in bed, but I'm doing arm exercises."

"Do you still get short of breath when you get up?"

"Not as much."

"Still getting depressed?" She warmed the stethoscope in her hand and placed it on his chest.

"I hate being on welfare."

"I know. Just keep losing that weight and we'll get you healthy again. Are you still taking your Lasix?"

He grunted. "Don't you see that path to the bathroom?"

She heaved him forward and listened to his back, then nodded and straightened.

Clarence lay back after the exam, his bulk causing the bed to groan. He watched his sister with worry. "Wish you'd drag her to the hospital with you, Doc. I know I'm okay, but she just seems set on staying here with me. I can't talk sense into her."

Mercy sighed and bent over with another breathing treatment for Darlene. "She's your sister, Clarence. What do you expect?" His brow lowered in what appeared to be an angry glare, but Mercy had learned over the months that was his worried look.

"You've kept her breathing this long." He shrugged his burdensome shoulders. "I guess she thinks you can do miracles right here in the house, so why leave me alone to go to your office?"

"Stop talking about me like I'm not here," Darlene wheezed.

Mercy knelt beside her. "Darlene, I know what you're thinking—that you've been this bad before and our treatments kept you going. But you're not using your medication as often as you should be, and I've warned you about the danger of hoarding it for an emergency. If you wait to take it until you can't breathe, you're just guaranteeing that there *will* be an emergency."

Darlene nodded, still concentrating hard on each inhalation.

"You've pushed your body to the limit, sis," Clarence growled. "What's gonna happen to me if you . . . don't take care of yourself?" He glanced quickly at Mercy, then away. Mercy had used that very same argument on him this spring when his refusal to accept medical care endangered not only his life but Darlene's.

Darlene's jaw set in a firm line. "What happens to you if I leave now and end up in the hospital?"

Brother and sister held each other's stare for a long moment. Unfortunately, during that moment Mercy felt her skin tingle with the precursor to another bout of weakness and hot sweats. She nearly groaned aloud. Not now!

Clarence sighed heavily. "I can get my own food, sis. You need medical help." He had come a long way from the angry, belligerent man who hated all doctors and partially blamed them for the shape he was in.

"So are you going to come see me tomorrow, Darlene?" Mercy started to stand to her feet, but her legs quivered from the sudden weakness that had overtaken her. She stayed where she was.

"Not tomorrow," Darlene said. "I feel better. I'm breathing better."

"Not much," Mercy said, breathing deeply herself to try to fend off the wave of heat she knew would attack her soon.

"Just until Monday," Darlene said. "I've got a deadline."

Clarence bent his huge upper body forward. "Is it worth your life?"

Once again, Mercy pulled out her peak flow meter and tested Darlene's air flow. This was so frustrating! But she knew from experience that it wouldn't help to argue with either of the Knights. She also knew that it had taken just this streak of stubborn independence on both their parts to fight their way out of a second-generation welfare family. Clarence intended to fight his way back to health and discontinue state aid.

The wave washed through Mercy in spite of her silent, desperate attempts to stop it. Beads of perspiration attacked her from every pore, but she resisted the urge to grab a handy piece of paper or magazine and fan herself.

Stress. That was all this was. That, and lack of sleep last night because of Tedi, and worry about what Theo might do now that he was out of the detox center.

"You need to be resting, Darlene," she said at last, wondering if they could see the sweat dripping from her face and neck and darkening her clothes.

"I need to make a living. This house isn't paid for." Once again, Darlene's jaw jutted out stubbornly. "Monday. I said I'll come in Monday if I'm still having trouble."

Clarence explained. "Darlene got her check late last month, and we had trouble making the house payment." A hint of old bitterness entered his voice. "We had trouble like this before, and they threatened to call in the loan, even though we got the payment to them."

Mercy finally pushed herself to her feet. "I thought you had your house paid off."

"Second mortgage," Darlene said. "Had to get a new computer and have some work done on the car."

The heat continued to spread across Mercy's body. She took a slow, deep breath.

"Doc, you okay?" Clarence asked, his voice softening. "Something wrong?"

"I'll be fine, just a little flushed." Probably nothing that couldn't be cured by a disappearing ex-husband. "Darlene, I want to see you in my office as soon as you can get there. Don't worry about waiting for an appointment." She turned to Clarence. "If she refuses to come in, I want you to sit on her. We need to keep ahead of this thing, or she's going to be in serious trouble. I want both of you to drink plenty of water, no sodas, not even diet sodas. Try not to stress out too much, and get plenty of sleep." In other words, she wanted them to do a better job of taking care of themselves.

---

Estelle Pinkley was well acquainted with the hot seat, and she knew she could hold ground against Bailey Little. She refused to be intimidated by his steely glare at her across the conference table—the crafty attorney had seldom won a case against her in the courtroom when she practiced law. That this morning's combined meeting of twenty people held not only medical staff but also influential business owners and elected city officials did not frighten her, either. They knew and respected her for her ability to lead, especially the doctors. Besides, one did not show fear when facing down the enemy, and Bailey Little was a ravenous wolf in attorney's clothing.

As hospital board president, Bailey called the meeting to order and dispensed quickly with preliminaries. Several had complained about the suddenness of this meeting.

"I'd like to know why three active members of our medical staff are not present," Estelle interjected before Bailey could continue.

Bailey raised a silver brow that matched the steel of his hair. "It isn't my responsibility to take roll call, Mrs. Pinkley."

"But it *is* your responsibility to contact all members when you call a special meeting." Tension that had already permeated the room now crackled with energy. "Dr. Mercy Richmond, Dr. Robert Simeon, and Dr. Lukas Bower are all absent, and I would like you to state for the record if you called them." All three doctors had, from time to time in the recent past, resisted Bailey Little's requests and suggestions. "I'm sure we are all aware of the reason for Dr. George's absence."

Bailey waved his hand dismissively. "A secretary was issued a list of people to contact. If they weren't available it's no longer my responsibility."

Estelle did not pursue the issue further. Her point was made. The medical staff could usually be counted on to support one another, except in cases of negligence.

"In fact," Bailey continued, leaning forward and making eye contact with as many as possible, "of the three points we're gathered here to discuss, two of them involve two of our absent physicians."

Estelle glanced around the room. No one was surprised. Bailey was suing both Dr. Bower and Dr. George for medical malpractice. He had also attempted to use his influence to sway opinion within the hospital board to have Dr. George permanently removed from the medical staff. The best he could do was relieve Jarvis of hospital privileges until the doctor was completely recovered from the TB encephalitis. Ironic that tonight was Jarvis's get-well party.

"However," Bailey continued as his sharp, glinting gaze returned to Estelle, "first I need to share some news with you." He held up a one-page letter, and then a stack of pages that looked like a contract. "We have here a possible answer to all our problems, ladies and gentlemen. I'm sure you've all heard of RealCare Medical Group, one of the largest and most profitable health-care organizations in the Midwest." He indicated Estelle with a nod of the head and a practiced smile. "Our esteemed administrator has done such an outstanding job with this hospital that RealCare wants to buy us out."

The room grew silent. No one squeaked in their chair, no one moved. Estelle had trouble breathing, but she thought she managed to keep all expression from her face. While Bailey's eyes shot her a triumphant glare, it seemed as if everyone at the huge conference table began to talk at once.

"That's crazy! We'll be sucked dry!" . . . "How much are they offering?" . . . "I won't practice medicine for that company. They're sharks!" . . . "What'll happen to our county taxes? Knolls County may go for that, especially if it'll give the fire department more funds."

Estelle continued to hold Bailey's stare. A buyout could destroy everything the people of Knolls prized in their county hospital, and Bailey knew that better than anybody. The small-town warmth, the sense of community, the pro-bono cases they took for those truly in need, would all be gone. It was what Bailey wanted. Estelle knew what was going through his mind, knew he was remembering his visit to her house soon after his son died.

He had brought a sheaf of papers with him then, too—reports from the hospital and from the autopsy. Not only did Dr. Jarvis George give Dwayne an injection of morphine and a script for more, but he let the young man drive away high on the drug. And when Dwayne was brought back to him, battered from the wreck, Jarvis didn't even check for the internal bleeding that had killed Dwayne. Jarvis, in his own stupor from undiagnosed tuberculin encephalitis, concentrated on Dwayne's head injury.

"Your doctor killed my son," Bailey had snarled. "My only child is dead, and Jarvis George and Knolls Community Hospital are going to pay for that death!"

As Bailey called for order in the meeting, Estelle fervently hoped these people remembered that Bailey Little was not only taking Jarvis George to court for malpractice, but Knolls Community Hospital, as well. Further, he had not removed himself as hospital board president, which Estelle had protested fervently and often as a serious conflict of interest.

"In light of the circumstances," Bailey said, raising his voice to be heard over the din in the room, "I once again advise that we permanently drop Dr. Jarvis George from the medical staff before he can return to work and damage our reputation any further than it has already been damaged." As two of the doctors began to protest, he held up his hand. "Whether or not you agree with the idea of a buyout, I'm sure you agree that the reputation of our medical staff must remain immaculate. To that end, I also must disclose that this hospital and Dr. Lukas Bower are scheduled for investigation by the government watchdog COBRA."

A collective groan stopped his words for a moment, then he continued. "If Dr. Bower is found guilty, both he and our hospital could be fined. We could be denied all federal support, which means we would not receive a penny for Medicare and Medicaid. If COBRA so desires, however, they can limit the hospital's involvement if we dismiss the offending physician."

This time Estelle did not hide her amazement and outrage. "So in essence you're requesting termination of two staff physicians who are at this time being named in medical malpractice suits by the estate of Dwayne Little?"

"Perhaps everyone but you can see the logic." Bailey's voice dripped with condescension. He glanced at the rest of the group. "Do I have a motion?"

They stared at him in silence, and Estelle held her breath.

Bailey's brow lowered in sudden, amazed annoyance. "Don't everyone speak at once."

No one made a motion.

Dr. Wong stood up. "You're wasting our time here today, Mr. Little. I have patients, as I believe most members of the medical staff do." He turned toward the door. Chairs moved back on the thick carpet as others followed.

Bailey's eyes narrowed, and his face flushed with color as he sprang to his feet, pointing at Estelle. "What have you done?" He slammed the flat of his hand onto the table, and the sound of it froze the others for a moment. He studied the face of each member present, then turned to glare again at Estelle, who remained seated, her hands folded calmly on her lap.

"What did you do, call every member and poison their minds against me before the meeting? What did you tell them?" He glared around at the rest of them again. "What did she say?"

"She didn't have to say anything." Greg Frost, the bank president, stepped over behind Estelle's chair. "I think we are all intelligent enough to see the issue here for ourselves. Why don't you save the histrionics for the courtroom, Bailey?"

Dr. Wong shook his head and left the room. One by one, the rest followed, except for Greg, who continued to stand where he was.

Estelle finally pushed her chair back and stood to her feet, facing her old nemesis across the table. "What they know, they've learned from you, Bailey. I think it's long past time you resigned."

Bailey's lips whitened. His steel gray eyes burned with growing fury. "You're the paid employee here, Mrs. Hospital Administrator. I can have you fired."

His whole body quivered visibly with suppressed emotion, and Estelle only hoped he could retain enough self-control to leave without making a further scene.

"I don't think so, Bailey." Greg put his hand on Estelle's arm. "Mrs. Pinkley, may I walk you back to your office?"

———

"Dr. Bower, you got a minute?"

Lukas turned from his charting to find Buck Oppenheimer leaning against the counter of the circular central ER desk, his broad, thick shoulders drooping, his eyes bloodshot. He wore an old pair of gray sweats, which meant he was off duty—a rare condition for him lately.

"Sure, Buck." Lukas shoved aside his charts and waited for Buck to talk.

Buck glanced at Carol, the secretary, who clicked at her computer keyboard a few feet away, then he looked back at Lukas. "Alone?"

"Hmm, must be serious." Lukas got up and led the way across the pale green tile floor toward the private waiting room. "Come on in here." He opened the heavy oak door and stepped into the carpeted silence of the small, comfortably furnished room. He indicated an overstuffed chair for Buck.

"Kendra didn't take me back." Buck sank down on the edge of the chair with his head bent and his hands clasped between his knees.

Lukas sighed. "I'm sorry." What was he supposed to say? Admit that he thought Kendra was behaving like a spoiled brat? "Maybe she just needs more time, like Lauren said." He knew Buck didn't have any kids, so at least no one else was being dragged through this ordeal. He'd heard a rumor that they couldn't have children, but he tended to ignore hospital gossip.

Buck rubbed his face with his hands. "She wants me to quit my job. She doesn't want me to be a fire fighter anymore."

Lukas watched his big-eared, big-muscled friend and wondered how he himself might react if someone important to him asked him to give up medicine. But Mercy wouldn't do that.

With a start, he realized the direction of his thoughts and refocused on Buck. "Have you talked to her about it much?"

"I begged her to at least let me stay at the house and give me a chance. She threw a bunch of clothes at me and told me to stay down at the firehouse, said I loved my job more than I loved her. Now I'm bunking with our young Explorers." He scowled. "So now I'm baby-sitting even when I'm not on duty."

"You mean Kyle and Alex?"

Buck nodded. "Yeah, and Kyle's sulking because I had to shut him down after our competition on Tuesday. We did a training exercise where they had to raise a twenty-four-foot extension ladder, and Kyle tried to jump in and take over the show and forgot to tie off the halyard. That's a good way for a fireman to lose a foot if the dog doesn't click in."

Lukas stared at him. "Dog?"

"You know, the ladder lock. Anyway, I lost my temper and let him have it right there in front of everybody. I shouldn't've been so rough on him, but he needed to learn. The kid's smart, but he jumps into things before he thinks. A fireman's got to think things out. He's got to watch what's going on around him and make good decisions. Some people think we're just a bunch of fire junkies, but that's not true. We—"

"Uh, Buck, we were talking about Kendra."

Buck drooped again, and Lukas was sorry he'd said anything.

"Yeah. After five years, she thinks she can just throw me out like the trash."

"Well, not exactly, Buck. Does she cry when she takes out the trash?"

Buck slumped farther down in his chair. "No. I hate to see her cry, but, Dr. Bower, I've always treated her right. She knows I love her. I can't help it that sometimes I have to take risks."

"Would she take you back if you were . . . say . . . a paramedic instead of a fire fighter?" As soon as he said it, he knew it was a stupid question. *What if somebody asked me to be a nurse instead of a doctor?*

Buck sat watching Lukas for a moment in silence. "But that's not what I am. I'm a fire fighter." He scowled and shook his head. "And I'm not a teacher, either. Why can't I just be a fireman? Kendra wanted me to find out about paramedic school, but you know how much I hate riding the ambulance. I always seem to attract the drunks. Besides, they need me down at the station, especially since they're cutting back on the money. There've been two more fires since that one Monday."

"When? Anybody hurt?"

"Nobody was hurt, but there was one Tuesday night and one yesterday." Buck grimaced. "I wasn't on duty, but since I was just hanging around the firehouse anyway, I rode along."

"Buck, I told you—"

"I know, I know, I need to take time to heal." Buck held his hands up. "I didn't have to fight any fires. They were both small. I'm surprised you didn't read about them in the paper."

"The only papers I've had time to look at lately have been patient charts. Any idea what caused the fires?"

"The chief's not giving out any information yet. He's being awfully careful."

"Why? Could he be thinking arson?"

Buck looked away. "Maybe."

"What else could it be?" Lukas asked. "Three fires in three days? Where were the other two?"

Buck still didn't look at him. "One in a warehouse and one in another convenience store." He suddenly didn't seem as interested in talking.

Lukas felt a rush of sympathy for him. He was a fire fighter. His first toy had probably been a fireman's hat, and he'd probably wanted to do just that one thing from the time he could talk. And now he was faced with a heartbreaking choice.

"Buck, are you going to be okay?"

The big guy blinked at him, sighed, and his features drooped. "I've got to, Doc. I've got a job to do. I'll think about what you said. Thanks for talking to me." He pushed the door open with his shoulder and stepped out ahead of Lukas and nearly collided with Lauren, who was walking past.

She took one look at him, then glanced at Lukas. She placed a hand on Buck's arm. "I'm so sorry to hear about Kendra."

He looked at her in surprise, and his jaw stiffened. "Thanks, Lauren."

She shook his arm gently. "Hey, don't give up on her. She'll still come around when she realizes how much she misses you. You two have a good marriage, and you can't just give up and let it drop because one of you is struggling with demons from the past. She'll call you and ask you to come home."

Buck hung his head. "I don't know. Maybe not."

"Well, whatever happens, if you want to talk about it, I'll be glad to listen."

Lukas shook his head and turned away. Sometimes he gave stupid advice. If Lauren could learn to just listen, anybody could.

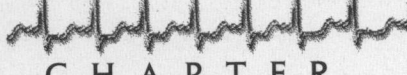

# CHAPTER

Thursday night at nine o'clock Lukas was attempting to tuck his T-shirt into his jeans when Mercy opened her front door and turned on the porch light, catching him in a glow that blinded him for a second. She stepped out wearing a gauzy bright green dress that draped around her calves and highlighted the darkness of her hair. Her coffee brown eyes reflected an inner warmth that seemed to glow more as Lukas and Mercy spent more time together.

In fact, right now the glow had ignited to a slow burn.

She placed her hands on her hips. "Lukas Bower, what are you doing?"

He stood staring back at her. "I told you I'd be late."

She rolled her eyes. "Jeans? Come on. I said casual, not bowling night with the boys."

That hurt. He'd gone to all the trouble to change out of his scrubs so he wouldn't embarrass her. "Where I come from, jeans are casual. If you want me to change—"

"No time for that now." She glanced at her watch. "We'll be an hour late as it is." She stepped back inside and retrieved her coat and purse from the hall tree. "If you didn't want to come with me, you could have just told me."

"I tried—"

She held her hand up. "Too late now. I don't even . . ." Her steps faltered. She took a deep, sharp breath through her nose. She closed her eyes and exhaled through her mouth.

Lukas reached over and touched her shoulder. "Mercy?"

Her face flushed, and she reached out to grab the doorjamb.

"Mercy? Are you okay?"

She took another deep breath and nodded, eyes still closed. "I'll be fine."

"You don't look fine."

She opened her eyes and shot him a scowl. "Thanks. Trust me, it'll pass."

"You know, we've had a lot of people in with the flu this week. Maybe you shouldn't be going tonight. Come to think of it, you didn't look that great Monday, either."

Her scowl deepened as she straightened from the doorjamb. "Lukas Bower, you should be ashamed of yourself, using my temporary weakness to get your way. Give it up. You're going through with this if it kills me." She handed him her coat. "Mom says Jarvis still resents you for taking over the directorship when he got sick. I want you to smooth things out with him tonight."

He shoved the coat over his arm. "I don't even want to be director, and everybody knows it. I'll be glad to let him come back and take over."

"That's not going to happen for a long time." Mercy checked her dim reflection in the storm door and adjusted her hair, which she had allowed to hang long and loose for once. "Maybe never." She looked back at Lukas. "Especially if Bailey Little gets his way."

"If Bailey gets his way the whole hospital could go under, but that won't stop Jarvis from being mad at you if you go to this party tonight and give him the flu. Tuberculosis isn't something to mess with."

"I don't have the flu. And besides, he's on so many antibiotics he's not going to catch anything."

"So if it's not the flu, what's wrong with you? You're awfully gripey tonight." Lukas reached up and raised her right eyelid before she could stop him. "Your eyes don't look too bad." He felt her forehead. "Do you have a fever? You feel hot and sweaty. Don't you think—"

Mercy pushed him away. "Would you stop! Lukas, you're the least romantic person in Knolls County."

"I'm not trying to be romantic. If you're sick—"

"I'm not . . . probably not . . . sick." She sighed and looked at him in silence for a moment, and just a hint of a smile glowed from the depths of her dark eyes. "Okay, maybe you are a romantic," she said at last, her voice suddenly deeper and warmer. "Sorry if I've been gripey." She reached up and touched his cheek. "Let's go."

Lukas stood and watched her walk to the car, her movements graceful, entirely feminine. For some reason, his heart rate and breathing increased. He felt like a nervous adolescent on his first date, which was ridiculous, because he and Mercy had been friends all summer. They'd spent a lot of time together when neither of them had to work. They'd gone on hikes, swam in the lake, and actually had a few real dinner dates. And they talked all the time. They found so much to talk about, and to laugh about, and to care about.

His heart rate slowed to normal by the time they reached the car. "Hope these jeans don't embarrass you. We could stop by my house and I could at least—"

"Your house is in the other direction." Without waiting for him to remember his manners, she opened the passenger door of his denim blue Sable and slid inside. "I don't embarrass easily, Lukas." She paused and fixed him with a stern glance. "That's not a dare."

He was pulling onto the street when she said, "I can tell you one reason I'm grumpy tonight. Theo's out of detox and he came to see me Monday."

Lukas's foot slipped from the accelerator for a second. "He's out already? How?"

She shrugged. "Good behavior, I guess. He even went and talked to Tedi and Mom, already trying to undermine me. That's how he's always operated. I told him to get lost. Mom thinks I should talk to him. I think he's charmed himself beneath that turtle-tough exterior of hers."

Lukas hated the thought of Mercy and Tedi having to deal with Theo again. Not only had Theo left a lifetime scar on Tedi's body, he'd left scars in her heart. One night when Lukas was helping Tedi with homework—she was a smart kid—she told him that her father used to try to convince her that her mother didn't love her. How could a parent—

"Maybe I'm just being paranoid," Mercy said, "but I know Theo. He manipulates people. He lies about people, especially me."

Lukas nodded. "How does Tedi feel about seeing him?" He couldn't help the tiny flicker of jealousy he felt, and he couldn't pinpoint its source, exactly.

"Her nightmares are back, if that tells you anything."

"Sounds like something to pray about."

She looked sideways at him as they headed toward Jarvis George's house, where the party was being held. "I'd appreciate it if you would," she said quietly.

He hid his sudden, hopeful surprise. "Of course."

"I saw Clarence and Darlene today," she said. "I did everything I could to convince Darlene she needs to start taking better care of herself. She promised to come to my office Monday, but you may see her sooner in the ER."

"She's that bad?"

"That bad."

"If she comes in I'll give you a call. Maybe you can slap some handcuffs on her and fasten her to a hospital bed."

They arrived at Jarvis George's home far too quickly, and Lukas had to park a block away because of all the cars. Oh great, a big party. Just what he always loved. His only hope was that Jarvis wouldn't see him in the crowd.

Even under the best of conditions Lukas had always hated parties. Though he graduated from high school as valedictorian of his class, his social ineptitude had always embarrassed his two older, more popular brothers, who were jocks and proud of it. The resulting shyness, which had not disappeared with continuing education, kept him from making many friends—especially of the female persuasion. The fact that he and Mercy had become good friends was something he still considered with amazement and gratitude. Deep gratitude.

He couldn't help watching her as they walked to the front door and rang the bell. Her features might be too strong for others to consider her beautiful—her black brows were thick and straight, her mouth was a little too generous in proportion to the rest of her face, and she had a strong personality, outspoken to the point of occasional brashness—but as he got to know her over the past months, he thought she was the most attractive woman in Knolls. Her tendency to bully patients and family and friends into submission was offset by her willingness to listen and change and nurture everyone from children to the elderly. Her only rough spot was her distrust of men because of her bad experience with Theodore Zimmerman.

Lukas could identify, because a few years back an unethical woman had cost him his job and his internal medicine residency in Kansas City. The shared pain had drawn Lukas and Mercy close from the very beginning.

And the increasing depth of their friendship continued to disturb him. His parents had always warned him never to become romantically involved with someone he could not marry. He and Mercy had never even kissed, but he couldn't deny that they shared more than a simple, platonic friendship. At least he thought so. He'd never discussed it with Mercy.

The door opened and the hostess greeted them. Jean had been Jarvis George's private nurse during his long illness and was now his fiancée. Talk around Knolls was that she was twenty-five years younger than Jarvis. She looked even younger, and friendlier. She dressed friendlier, too, with a boldness that spoke volumes more than it should have.

Lukas hesitated inside the doorway. Mercy took his arm, squeezed it, and guided him forward through the vestibule behind their chattering hostess into the large formal parlor beyond.

Lukas resisted dwelling on the obvious question—what on earth did Jean see in an old grouch like Jarvis? She even had the grace not to react to the sad "bowling night" outfit Lukas had chosen to wear. She had, however, chosen to wear a dress designed to continue holding the host's attention throughout the party—and that of several other guests, no doubt.

Jarvis—with his gruff voice, erect, broad-shouldered posture, and his gray hair still cut military length—held center stage with a fistful of his many guests in the center of the formal dining room. Mercy had too much compassion to drag Lukas through the crowd and lay his neck on the chopping block in front of the host. Instead, they wandered around the periphery of the mingling group in the general direction of the buffet table. They could talk with Jarvis later.

Lukas rounded a corner and nearly stumbled into Lauren McCaffrey, who stood talking to one of the floor nurses from the hospital. She had changed from her daytime scrubs to a silky-looking blue dress. Her long, naturally blond hair hung loose, and her green eyes widened with a smile when she caught sight of Lukas. Then Mercy stepped around the corner.

Some of Lauren's enthusiasm dissipated. "Hey, Dr. Bower, Dr. Mercy."

Mercy's sudden tension reached out and touched Lukas with an almost physical force. "Hello, Lauren, hi, Megan."

"Dr. Bower, I didn't know you were coming tonight," Lauren said.

"You mean I had a choice?" Lukas muttered. Mercy nudged him with her elbow. He glanced sideways at her. She was not smiling, but he saw a glint of humor in her eyes.

"Dr. Bower, I was just telling Megan what a workaholic you are," Lauren said. "We heard the new doc's starting a week from Monday. Good job. Now, if we had a couple more, maybe you'd get a break. Did you know they're trying to hire more nurses for the floor? Mrs. Pinkley had the jobs posted yesterday, and somebody already asked if I knew anybody who might be interested. I told them about that new lady in our church who's a nurse—you know the one I mean? She and her husband joined a couple of weeks ago. I've only spoken with her a couple of times, but she seems—"

"Yes, I think hiring more nurses was a good decision," Lukas interrupted, trying to staunch the freight train flow of Lauren's chatter. He could smell barbeque in the air, rich and pungent and smoky, and his stomach growled at him. It wanted food.

"Mrs. Pinkley is making a lot of good decisions," Mercy said.

"She sure is," Lauren said. "I don't think the hospital would still be in operation if it weren't for her. Her husband was a good judge, too. Dr. Bower, I don't think you've ever met Judge Pinkley. He retired a couple of years ago because of a bad heart." She glanced around the crowded room. "I don't think he came with Mrs. Pinkley tonight, but he sure is a character. He knows everybody he's ever met by their first name, and he remembers every case he ever had. I've never heard any complaints about his decisions, either, although I never—"

"Lauren," Mercy interrupted gently, "does Jarvis have his buffet table in the usual place?"

"Oh, I'm sorry," Lauren said. "Here I am talking away, and you must be starved." She smiled at Lukas again. "I know Dr. Bower is, since he worked so late tonight."

"I'm sure we'll be talking to you later," Mercy said as she turned and made her way through the crowd.

Megan stepped over to speak with someone else.

Lukas turned to follow Mercy, but Lauren reached out and touched his arm before he could walk away.

She took a step closer to him, glancing in the direction Mercy had gone. "Dr. Bower, I guess I should warn you. Dr. Mercy's ex-husband was here earlier."

"Theodore?" *What was he doing here?* "How much earlier?"

"I saw him about thirty minutes ago. I didn't even know he'd gotten out of detox, and I can't believe Dr. George would have invited him after . . . you know. But Dr. Mercy's bound to be upset if she sees him. I haven't seen him since, but you might want to warn her just in case he hasn't left yet."

"Thanks, Lauren."

"Hey, a bunch of us from church are going fishing Sunday afternoon. Want to come?"

"No, thanks, I'm taking a trip to see my dad and stepmom." Lukas caught sight of Mercy across the large room, already caught in another conversation before she could reach the buffet. She glanced in his direction, looked at Lauren, then dropped her gaze. He excused himself and turned to blaze a trail through the crowd across the elegant ivory carpet.

He had smelled the heavenly food before he saw the elaborate crystal punch bowl surrounded by what little food was left: finger sandwiches and salads and—sure enough—barbequed smoked sausage. He felt his mouth water even before he caught sight of the spring rolls and crab dip and caviar. He hadn't eaten since noon, and there were three spring rolls remaining on the gold-trimmed plate.

"Hello, Lukas!" Ivy Richmond, Mercy's mother, called out from the far corner of the room, where she sat on a sofa beside Estelle Pinkley. Ivy looked a lot like Mercy, with her high cheekbones and firm chin. She wore her long, liberally white-streaked hair up tonight. She smiled and held out a hand for him to join them.

Instinctively, Lukas glanced toward Jarvis to satisfy himself that the crusty doctor had not picked up on Ivy's hail. He hadn't. He was too busy watching his hostess circle the room in her low-cut dress.

"Don't worry," Ivy said, reading Lukas's mind. "He probably won't even recognize you."

"I'll have to trust your judgment." Lukas noticed that Ivy wore jeans more faded than his own. "I like your outfit," he said. "It's what I call comfortably casual."

"Thanks, Lukas." She glanced toward her daughter, who stood talking with an older couple by the buffet table. "Mercy got her fashion sense from her father, obviously. I'm glad to see it hasn't worn off on you, but by this time next year she'll have your wardrobe overhauled."

Lukas saw Mrs. Pinkley stifle a grin at Ivy's offhand presumption that Lukas and Mercy would still be together next year. Lukas glanced toward the buffet table again and saw, to his joy, that Mercy was approaching the buffet table with two plates. She was either very hungry, or she was going to take pity on him. He turned to go join her.

"Have a seat, Lukas" came Estelle's deep voice of authority. She indicated an empty folding chair beside the sofa where she and Ivy sat. "Mercy told us she was going to feed you. Shouldn't you be home in bed? You had to pull double duty today, didn't you?"

The lady looked more relaxed than Lukas had ever seen her, and for once her hair wasn't in perfect position, and her collar wasn't perfectly straight. Lukas sank down slowly on the chair in obedience to an administrative order. "I got a little sleep last night." He hoped his stomach wouldn't growl loudly enough to harmonize with the jazz music that floated across the room from Jarvis's big stereo system.

Robert Simeon, the local internal medicine physician, wandered by and spoke to Lukas and the two ladies, then ambled in Mercy's direction. He and Mercy had been friends before Lukas came to Knolls, and out of curiosity—and perhaps a little more—Lukas tried to keep a casual gaze on him, but Ivy's voice caught his attention.

"Oh, look," she said, putting her hand on Estelle's arm. "There's Jake Casey. Did you know his neighbor got out on bail today? What was that judge thinking? Now poor Cowboy has to worry if that crazy man's going to shoot him again or go after another one of his animals. Estelle, this county lost a great judge when your husband retired."

Lukas turned again to catch sight of Mercy laughing at something Simeon said. Then she turned away from him, and the plates were filled with food this time. Yes! She had probably heard his stomach growling from all the way across the room.

Lukas stood up and took her burden, then had to give it back while he scrounged for another chair. When he was finally seated with his plate balanced in an unsteady perch on his lap, he saw Mercy watching to see if he would bow his head and say grace before he ate, as he always did. This time he didn't. Why embarrass her at this function, which seemed to mean so much to her, when he could just as easily talk to God from his heart, as he did throughout the day?

So he picked up his first spring roll and devoured it while thanking God for it and for Mercy's generosity. She'd given him the rest of the spring rolls and crab dip, and an extra serving of barbequed smoked sausage. He tried not to gulp his food, though he doubted anyone was paying attention. Mercy chatted with Ivy and Estelle and greeted several others who came by to say hello. How she managed to have her mouth empty and free every time someone asked her a question, Lukas couldn't figure. He was usually chewing when someone greeted him, and once he almost choked when Dr. Wong slapped him on the back halfway through a finger sandwich.

He saved the best for last and had bitten into his first piece of barbequed sausage when he heard a familiar, sharp voice behind him. "Enjoy the power while you have it, Bower. I plan to take my job back in a few weeks."

Lukas turned to see Jarvis George standing over him. He picked up the plate from his lap and stood up while taking a breath for reply.

That was when the sausage lodged in his throat.

While Mercy and the other two ladies spoke with their host about his struggle with TB, Lukas tried with increasing desperation to breathe, but he could not cough, could not get any air. He couldn't even gasp.

Jarvis turned back to Lukas. "How's your lawsuit with Bailey Little progressing?" His voice was actually conversational instead of confrontational.

Lukas stared at the other doctor's face, which blurred through tearing eyes. He had to do something, or he would pass out and cause a scene, and Mercy would die of embarrassment. And he would just die.

He dropped his plate, placed a double fist in his mid-gut, and shoved hard. The obstruction cleared, but not without a price. He gasped for breath and looked down in horror at the barbeque sauce that had spilled from his overturned plate, staining Jarvis George's pristine ivory carpet.

Lukas groaned. He hated parties.

―――――

"See, look." Abby Cuendet sat gingerly down on the blue-and-white-plaid quilt on her bed and held up her legs for Tedi Zimmerman to admire. "I got twenty-two stitches altogether, and some of them had two layers!"

"So? Your skin has seven layers. That's no big deal." After all, it was just her legs, not her throat, like Tedi's had been.

"It's not the same thing," Abby said.

"Do they hurt?"

"They're okay. Dr. Bower gave Mom and Dad some medicine for me if it gets too bad. I bet I don't have to take it, though."

"Did you cry?"

Abby scrunched her face and pushed her oversized glasses back up to the bridge of her nose. "Wouldn't you cry if your legs had been sliced open by barbed wire?"

Tedi sighed. Abby could sometimes be a real pain.

Abby leaned closer. "I asked Dr. Bower if he was going to marry your mom."

Tedi gasped. "What! Are you crazy?"

Abby giggled.

"What'd he say?"

"I don't think he wanted to talk about it." She shrugged. "He's nice." She glanced toward her open bedroom door and motioned for Tedi to close it. Tedi almost refused, until Abby gestured toward her bandaged injuries.

"I thought it didn't hurt much," Tedi muttered as she went to the door, looked up and down the hallway, stepped back in, and closed them off from Mr. and Mrs. Cuendet's sharp hearing.

"You want to know the best thing about getting hurt today?" Abby whispered as Tedi jumped back onto the bed.

"There was something good about it?"

Abby leaned closer. "Mom and Dad were so worried about me, they forgot to fight. I even saw Dad put his arm around Mom at the hospital."

Tedi wanted to ask what was the big deal about that, but then she remembered how much Abby's parents fought, and how Abby had come to school a few times crying. Tedi's own mother and father had fought for as long as she could remember. At least Abby's parents still lived together. Tedi could barely remember the time when her mother and father split up, except she remembered how bad it hurt, and how much she cried, and how much Mom cried when Dad got custody.

"I heard Dad tell Mom last week that he was tired of fighting," Abby said. "He said he'd almost rather get a divorce. I don't want them to get a divorce." She looked down and traced the edge of one of the bandages with her finger, then looked up at Tedi. "How did it feel when it happened to you?"

"Awful. Everything went wrong after that."

"I bet you'd've done almost anything to stop it."

"Yeah."

Abby held her gaze, her eyes narrowing. "So would I."

"Yeah, but what can you do? You're just a kid."

Abby ignored the question. "Are you going to see your dad?"

Tedi frowned and shrugged. "I know Mom doesn't want me to, but she won't say it. She'll talk to Grandma, then she'll talk to Lukas, then she'll think about it awhile, and in the end she'll do what she thinks is best for me." Abby didn't seem to be listening, but Tedi kept talking anyway. "She'll ask me what I think, then she'll try really hard not to act hurt if I say I want to see him." She thought about it a moment. "I guess I want to see him, but in a way I want him to suffer longer. I don't want to go back to the way it was. And I guess if I told Mom I wanted to see him, she'd let me." Abby still wasn't listening, but Tedi didn't really care. She'd made her decision.

"I bet I could keep them from getting a divorce," Abby said softly, still fingering the gauze on her legs.

"How?"

Abby looked at Tedi. "I can make them forget to fight again."

"No, you can't. I think parents want to hate each other more than they want to love their kids."

"You're wrong, and I'll prove it. My parents love me enough to stop hating each other."

Tedi shrugged and shook her head. Abby had a lot to learn about managing parents.

# CHAPTER 9

Thirty minutes after the Heimlich debacle, Lukas continued to smart with humiliation. After Mercy had made sure he was okay, she had laughingly accused him of doing it on purpose to spite Jarvis. Then she had helped clean up the barbeque sauce and mingled deeper and deeper into the noisily chattering crowd, attempting, every few moments, to draw Lukas with her. He had refused. Now she was out of sight altogether. Why had he agreed to come? He wanted to go to his quiet home and crawl into bed and close his eyes. He was so tired. . . .

But he was a gentleman in spite of his poor table manners, and a gentleman did not leave a date at a party. He didn't want to leave Mercy, anyway. He wanted to take her with him, but she looked as if she was having so much fun. Perhaps he could find a nice soft recliner in a corner somewhere—

"Dr. Bower?" came another familiar male voice behind him.

Lukas turned in surprise to find himself facing Theodore Zimmerman. For a moment, all Lukas could do was stare.

Theodore looked different from the way Lukas remembered him. The prominent bone structure of his face was sharper due to apparent weight loss, and dark shadows hovered beneath his eyes.

"Yes?" Lukas glanced past the man's right shoulder in search of Mercy, but she was lost in the throng. "If you're looking for—"

"I need to talk to you." Theo turned and studied the crowd, his gaze darting quickly back and forth. He turned back to Lukas. "Sorry to bother you here. I wasn't invited. I overheard someone downtown talking about the party."

His voice was clearer and softer than Lukas remembered. But this was the first time Lukas had ever met him when he was sober.

"At the time it seemed like a good idea to come here and try to see Mercy, away from the office or the hospital, and also away from her house, where she'd feel threatened."

Lukas waited for a moment, but Theo didn't explain further. "So what do you want with me?" He couldn't keep suspicious resentment from his voice, couldn't push from his mind Mercy's warning about Theo's ability to manipulate people. And he couldn't forget Tedi.

"Just to talk." Theo's light blue gaze searched Lukas's face. "Please. Would you mind talking with me for a minute?"

"What about?"

Apparently taking this as agreement, Theo turned with a gesture for Lukas to accompany him and led the way out toward an adjacent sunroom, surprisingly empty at the moment. Lukas shrugged and followed. One false word about Mercy, just one attempt . . .

Theo turned back around, his gaze wandering around the small, windowed, garden-like room. "I know this house well. Mercy and I used to come here to parties and dinners when Mrs. George was still alive. That was when Mercy's father was still partners with Dr. George." He sat down on a cushioned wicker chair and gestured toward its twin.

Lukas sat on the edge, watching Theo. The man was the same age as Mercy, which would make him thirty-nine or forty, but he looked older. His blond hair was neatly cut and combed back, and his skin had a faded tan that made him appear slightly jaundiced. He had broad shoulders, and his gray silk shirt revealed lines of a muscular build. He was a couple of inches taller than Lukas, but he had an uncustomary slump to his shoulders that Lukas didn't remember seeing before. It gave him the appearance of a man defeated. The only two times Lukas had met him were in the emergency room, when Lukas and the ER staff were trying to save Tedi's life. There was no reason for this man to want to talk to him.

"First of all, Dr. Bower, I want to thank you for saving my daughter's life, not just once, but twice."

After a long hesitation, Lukas nodded. What was he supposed to say, "You're welcome"? He couldn't take credit for saving lives.

"Second," Theo continued, "I'm sorry for the way I acted this spring."

Lukas recalled the man's belligerence in the ER when Tedi had almost died from an allergic reaction to a beesting. The second time, when Theo realized he'd almost killed her himself, he was panic-stricken.

Theodore took a deep breath. "I've learned in the past three months to say, 'I'm an alcoholic, and that's no excuse for the way I behaved.' "

Lukas nodded. Okay, that was a step forward. But according to Mercy and Tedi, Theodore had been contrite about his actions before. They didn't trust him now. Neither did Lukas, and the issue wasn't just about the drinking. It was about the way he treated people, specifically Mercy. Lukas felt very protective of Mercy and Tedi right now, almost as if he had a right to feel that way.

Theo readjusted himself in the chair. "I know you've been friends with Mercy for a while. Word gets around in a small town like Knolls, and all I can say is I hope she's found someone who'll treat her right. I never did."

Lukas sighed. This was exactly why he hated parties. He never knew what to say at awkward moments like this. This subject had sure never come up at a party before.

Theo continued. "I learned a lot this summer. I had to face things about myself that were hard to face, and some things I haven't been able to accept yet. No wonder Mercy hates me so—"

"Uh, Theodore, shouldn't you be talking to Mercy about this? She might want to hear it."

A muscle jerked in the side of Theo's face. "Don't you think I've tried? I'm sure she told you all about—" He grimaced, glanced through the doorway toward the partiers, as if she might come out and catch him talking about her. "She won't listen. She's never listened to me, but she's always reminding me about what a jerk I am." He bent forward, gaze intent on Lukas. "If she'll listen to anyone, she'll listen to you."

Just as Mercy said, this was Theo's method—draw people into his confidence, then convince them to help him twist the knife in Mercy's back. "But you've also talked to Tedi and Ivy," Lukas said, feeling the resentment building. Ordinarily he didn't treat people like this. He did not like this man. "Now you're talking to me. How can you expect Mercy's family and friends to gang up on her and force her to allow you to have visitation rights with Tedi?"

Theo's eyes flashed briefly with irritation, then he sighed and slumped deeper in his chair. "That's not what I'm trying to do. Of course I want to see Tedi. What father wouldn't want to see his own little girl? But when I told Mercy I wanted to prove I had changed, she wouldn't even give me a chance to explain. How can I prove to her I've changed when she won't even give me a chance?"

"How've you changed?" That was funny, Lukas suddenly didn't seem to be having trouble with the conversation. He was having more trouble controlling several different emotions—like anger . . . indignation . . . and maybe a little guilt at his own sudden, obvious lack of compassion—but no trouble finding words.

"I haven't had a drink all summer, and I've gotten a job down at Jack's Print Shop on the square. I apologized to my former boss, Mr. Johnson, for using his money to buy that property to make a profit. He dropped the embezzlement charges."

Lukas watched him without replying.

The even features of Theo's face shot through with a grimace. He bent his head. "I know Mercy was the one who paid Mr. Johnson off. I thanked her for it, and she reminded me that she didn't do it for me. She did it for Tedi. She hates me, Lukas."

That wasn't exactly late-breaking news. "I still feel you should be talking to her about this, and if she won't talk tonight, try later, after she's had some time to grow accustomed to the fact that you're out of detox."

Theo glanced out the window to the darkness beyond. "I know I shouldn't blame her. In the past few weeks I've started hating myself. The other day, when I talked to Tedi, I could see in her eyes that she's still afraid of me."

"What did Ivy say when you talked to her?" Lukas asked.

Theo shook his head. "She said time will tell. She said I would have to pay my dues."

Lukas nodded. "I agree with Ivy. You can't expect anybody to believe you're suddenly a new person after years of abusive behavior."

Lukas caught the caustic tone of his own voice, took a deep breath, let it out slowly. "We all have to prove ourselves," he said more gently. "It sounds to me like you need to prove yourself to yourself."

"I know. I've got a temper. And the embezzlement . . . well, I told myself at the time that I was doing the right thing. I didn't mean to steal the money. I meant to use it for a profit, then return it before Mr. Johnson knew it was missing. I lost some of my own money in the investment, too. But I know now that I was wrong." He looked up at Lukas and gave a self-deprecating grimace. "Ivy asked me if I had anything to replace my old habits. Then she said if I was to read the Bible, like she's been telling me to do for years, I'd know what she was talking about. She said Jesus lays it all out when He teaches about evil spirits. I wouldn't even know where to start looking."

Lukas silently gave Ivy a nod of approval. It was an apt illustration. "I can't quote the chapter and verse," he said, "but I think she's talking about an incident in the book of Matthew, where Jesus warns the people about the impossibility of self-reformation. It tells about the evil spirit that left a man and wandered for a while and found no rest. When it returned to find the man still empty, the spirit called seven other spirits even more wicked, and they all entered the man, and he was worse than before."

Laughter reached them from the other rooms, and the chatter increased. Theo opened his mouth to speak, then his eyes widened, and he looked beyond Lukas toward the entrance to the sunroom. Lukas turned his head to find Mercy stepping up to the threshold, her face white, eyes filled with competing emotions of fear and anger as she watched him and Theo together.

———

Mercy felt the pain of betrayal even as she struggled to remind herself that Lukas would never betray her. But he knew how she felt about Theo. She'd warned him about what Theo was trying to do, and he knew she was afraid for Tedi. In this mixed-up world of crazy court decisions, what would keep some judge from making the same kind of mistake they had made before? How could Lukas sit out here so calmly and—

"Hello, Mercy." Theodore stood to his feet. "I was hoping for a chance to talk to you."

She kept her voice steady. "Were you? I've been here as long as Lukas has. You managed to find *him*, didn't you?" Her eyes flicked briefly toward Lukas but then shot back to Theo. "Who else have you cornered here tonight?"

Lukas stood and stepped toward her. "Mercy, it's okay."

"No, it's not!" The words came sharp and loud, betraying her fear, so loud that she heard people shushing each other in the room behind her. This irritated her. Oh no, they mustn't miss a single juicy detail. Why had no one told her Theo was here? Maybe they'd all been waiting for this show tonight, rubbing shoulders with good ol' Theo and waiting with anticipation for the fireworks.

She wouldn't give them fireworks, badly as she wanted to. She'd struggled too hard to rebuild her reputation with these people; she wasn't going to throw it all away by hurling the accusations she wanted to at Theo right now.

She kept her voice low. "Are you finished feeding your line to Lukas?"

Lukas stepped to her side and laid a hand gently on her shoulder. "Mercy, let's go outside and get some air and—"

Mercy jerked from his touch and turned to glare at him, but the calm, compassionate look in his eyes quieted something inside her. She heard whispers in the other room.

"This isn't what it looks like," Lukas said softly. "Jarvis did not invite him. He just came here to talk to you."

"Well, doesn't it seem strange to you that he never did? He found you instead. That's how he does things, Lukas. He weaves this net around me without actually touching me, and then he closes in for the kill. You and Mom and Tedi are just a part of his net." Her voice broke. *Stay in control.* She'd had too little sleep the past few days. "I don't want to talk to him."

"You don't have to, Mercy." Lukas had such a soothing voice, so full of kindness. "You don't have to do anything." He reached out and touched her shoulder again, and this time it seemed as if something of his own spirit came to her through that touch. "Why don't we go on a walk? It's going to be okay. Theodore is leaving." He turned toward Theo, and his voice became suddenly firm. "Aren't you, Theo?"

After a long silence, Mercy forced herself to look at her ex-husband again. His face was pale, his eyes bright, as if he were in shock.

He stared at Lukas, then at Mercy. "Yes, I'm leaving," he said hoarsely. He cleared his throat and took a step forward, as if to step past Mercy. He hesitated, stopped, shook his head. "You're right, Mercy. I'm still doing it. I didn't realize . . . I'm sorry." He took another step.

Mercy dropped her gaze from those pleading eyes. She waited for him to walk away. She concentrated on breathing evenly and deeply as a voice from the other room snapped out.

"What's going on in here?" It was Jarvis. "Zimmerman! What're you doing here?"

Mercy leaned against Lukas as she listened to her ex-husband apologize once more. She heard the front door open and shut, heard Jarvis grumble something about trespassers, then command the guests to remember they were supposed to be having fun.

Lukas put a protective arm around her shoulders and drew her close. "I'm sorry, too, Mercy. Lauren warned me that she thought she'd seen him, but—"

"And she couldn't have warned *me*?" Mercy snapped.

"Nice to see your temper's still healthy and strong," he said softly.

She would not cry. The chatter in the other room picked up again, and a little of the pressure in her chest dissipated. Someone stepped out and touched Mercy on the back.

"Honey, you okay?" It was Mom.

Mercy nodded, still relishing the feel of Lukas holding her so close.

Ivy patted her. "Theo's not going to get Tedi away from you."

Mercy felt a prickle of heat at the back of her neck. "How can you be sure? He's done it before."

Others came out to check on her, and Lukas stepped away to give her some room. Her nurse, Josie, hugged her, followed by Estelle. Suddenly it seemed as if the party had relocated to the small sunroom, and the din increased. Jarvis came out, and he, too, caught her up in a bear hug.

"That won't happen again, Mercy," he growled. "If you want me to call the police, I will. I swear I didn't see him come in, or I would have grabbed one of my hunting rifles from the den and loaded it for you and let you have a field day."

At another time, Mercy would have smiled. Jarvis was getting to be more like his old self. But somehow the noise became oppressive. The room grew hot. That old tingling sensation began at the core of her body, and she knew she had to get out or she would burst into tears or shout again in anger or scream with frustration. She felt as if she were swimming through people as she headed for the doorway. She heard Lukas call out, but when she turned toward the sound of his voice, she couldn't see him. People were talking to her, laughing around her, pressing against her from all sides, and she knew how Tedi felt when her body betrayed her this morning when she wet the bed. If she didn't escape this suffocating heat . . . She had to get out.

---

Lukas watched helplessly as Mercy stepped out a sliding glass door onto an open patio and disappeared into the darkness. He pushed through the crush of well-meaning people, ignoring their questions and their attempts to draw him into their conversations. He reached the door through which Mercy had exited, managing not to step on too many toes or knock over more than one glass figurine— which fell into thick carpet and did not break.

As soon as he stepped outside he heard her weeping. He barely saw the pale reflection of her skin in the darkest shadows in the farthest corner of the yard, and he walked carefully across the well-tended grass to her side. He put a hand on her shoulder and felt the quiet sobs that shook her body.

"Mercy, it's okay. He's gone, and it's just like your mother said. He doesn't have anybody fooled anymore."

Lukas slid his arm around her, and with a suddenness that startled him, she turned and buried her face against his chest, folding herself into his embrace like a child yielding to the care of someone bigger and stronger.

He put his other arm around her and let her cry. Occasionally he patted her shoulder and prayed for the right words . . . and the right reactions. The reactions he was having right now to her nearness, her tender trust, were more powerful than he'd expected.

After a few more moments the major storm passed enough for her to speak through the sniffles. "I'm sorry," she whispered. "I hope I didn't embarrass you too badly in there." She raised her head and looked up at him.

He could see the pale outline of her face from the minimal gleam of light that reached them from the house as she wiped at her eyes and nose with the back of her hand. Lukas forced himself to release her and move back just a few inches. "I'm not embarrassed. I'm sorry I don't have a handkerchief or Kleenex or anything." He pulled out his hastily tucked T-shirt and offered her the hem.

She looked at it, then back up at him, and she shrugged and took it. "Might as well. I can't be any more humiliated than I already am." She tugged the material up and patted at her face, concentrating on the makeup around her eyes.

"You don't have to feel humiliated, Mercy. Everyone understands, and nobody's laughing at you. They're all worried about you. They didn't want Theodore here any more than you did, and you heard what Jarvis said. As far as he's concerned—"

Mercy released his shirt and shook her head, swinging away to walk a couple of steps into the darkness. "That's not it, Lukas, not all of it." Her voice once more grew husky with tears. "It's just that everything's a mess right now. Tedi's having nightmares, and I can't stop worrying about her, and I don't know how good I am for her. I want her to get over all of this, but people keep telling me that in order to do that, she's going to have to face her father and come to terms with what happened. How can she come to terms when I can't? How am I supposed to know how to do the right thing for a child who puts her whole trust in me?" Mercy once again dabbed at her face with the back of her hand. "It was so much easier to deal with when Theo was tucked safely away from us. I know that's the coward's way, but I'm a coward."

"You're not a coward, Mercy." He stepped up behind her and placed his hands on her shoulders. He wanted to hold her even closer. "What you're being asked to do . . . the forgiveness . . . I don't think it's humanly possible. I think that's a God-sized job."

She stood in silence for a moment, then sighed and shook her head. "Guess I'll never get it right, then."

"Let God do it for you."

She shook her head again and stepped away from him, and all the warmth went with her. "You know, Lukas, in a way you've made my life worse since I met you."

Lukas blinked in sudden hurt bewilderment. "Worse?"

She turned and looked at him through the darkness. "Since you came," she said softly, "I've had to address the fact that God truly exists. It was so much easier before I met you to avoid the subject, and avoid God, even with Mom's constant harping. I could always blame the changes in her attitude on the changes in her life since Dad's death. But now, with you, I get so confused sometimes. There really is something different about you, and you make me believe in His existence. I get so frustrated because I don't have what you have, and yet I want to so badly. But it's like there's something inside me that won't let me."

"Fear," Lukas said, feeling a powerful surge of hope.

"More like anger because He's rejected me."

"He hasn't rejected you. What makes you think that? Because you've suffered a lot of pain? So do Christians. I watched my mother die of breast cancer, and I was kicked out of my residency program in Kansas City because of the power of one angry nurse. Throughout my childhood I was ridiculed because I was smaller than the other boys, and I was shy and I wore glasses. Mercy, we can all look at our lives and see the pain. We have to look past the pain to see God. He didn't put the pain there, but He's there to take it away."

"But He didn't take mine."

"You won't *give* it to Him." Lukas couldn't keep the frustration from his voice, and he was ashamed to realize that the frustration wasn't all for the sake of her soul, or for the sake of God's kingdom, but for the sake of his own desire to be more to her than just a friend.

She raised her hands as if to ward him off. "Enough! I've heard this all before." With a sigh she turned and strolled a few feet across the uneven shadows of the yard. "Lukas, before I met you I thought I was beginning to get my life back together after years of struggle. Suddenly, everything's turned upside down for me. I've been so miserable lately."

Lukas stared at her darkened form in surprise. "Really? You've seemed . . . I don't know . . . so much happier lately."

"Oh sure, that's when I'm with you." She gave a half laugh. "I'm always happier when we're together. You make me forget everything else. It isn't until you're gone that the depression starts to sift its way back in." She turned and paced back toward him. "I realize I've never worked through some of the unresolved consequences of a bad marriage and a nasty divorce. I had to fight so hard to see Tedi and to rebuild my practice that there wasn't any time to deal with the rejection of my husband leaving me for another woman and taking my daughter with him. Somehow, seeing that woman leave him soon afterward didn't ease any of the pain." She returned to stand in front of Lukas, and her voice dropped to a near whisper. "I closed my heart off for a while, Lukas, to keep it from shattering to pieces. Because of you it's opening again." She stared at him in silence for a moment.

Lukas couldn't control the sudden pounding in his chest. "I may not have anything to do with it." Although, in spite of an inner warning, he hoped he did. He wanted to have that kind of effect on her. "Look at everything that's happened since I came." He held up his hand and started counting things off on his fingers. "Your grandmother died, you got your daughter back, and—"

"And I discovered that I can fall in love again."

Lukas froze with the fear and longing and hope and pain her words brought. Was this love? The desire to spend more and more time with her, to protect her, share everything with her? But the most important aspect in his life, she wouldn't share with him.

"Mercy, I—"

"Please don't say anything." To stress her words, she placed two fingers against his lips, gently, like a butterfly landing. "I've got to be honest with you. I've wondered about a possible future for us. I've allowed myself to hope that you might feel the same way."

Lukas couldn't answer. He could barely breathe. Somehow they had jumped from the subject of God to the subject of their own future together, and he wasn't sure how they'd gotten there.

"Oh, Lukas, I'm sorry." She turned away. "I know I shouldn't be doing this to you." The long, heavy silence was so deep that the sounds of laughter and talk that reached them through the closed windows of the house seemed miles away. "Maybe . . ." She bent her head. "Maybe we shouldn't be spending so much time together."

Another shock. "What?"

"This is getting so hard. The more time we spend with each other, the harder it'll get." She turned back to face him, the tears in her eyes sparkling in the light from the house.

"But I don't want to stop seeing you."

She stood watching him for a long moment. "Why not?"

How was he supposed to put it all into words? "Because I care for you." He thought about it for a moment. "I love spending time with you and telling you about all the things that happen to me during the day that nobody else would understand. I've come to depend on your friendship . . . and your patience with my total lack of social skills, and I love to hear you laugh, and I love your compassion for people."

"But do you love *me*?"

Lukas hesitated. How was he supposed to determine the depth of their relationship after only a summer of friendship? Didn't it take a lifetime to know about love?

She sighed and bent her head.

He reached forward and tipped her chin back up. Touching her skin and looking into the shadowed planes of her face brought all the warmth back—more than before. More than even a few seconds ago. He wanted to forget everything else and just hold her, draw her closer, close his eyes, and feel her next to him. He wanted to protect her and never let her go.

For a moment she held his gaze, then smiled through the tears. She stepped up to him and put her arms around him, and he thought the sudden energy between them might ignite. She placed a hand on the back of his head and drew him forward. Her lips touched his with gentle caring for a brief moment, and they tasted sweeter and felt softer than he'd dreamed possible. Then she tilted her head back and looked at him quizzically. The look burned all the way to his heart. He wanted more.

He couldn't help himself. He grasped her shoulders tenderly and then wrapped his arms around her. His lips sought hers again, as if that was where they belonged. Her warm, exquisite arms came across his back. He thought he would drown. The whole night disappeared for him except for this one moment, her touch, her beauty. There was a spiritual bond between them, he could feel it. He immersed himself into it. He felt lost in the power of her presence, and he didn't mind at all. Lost . . .

Lost.

He stiffened. His eyes flew open, and he caught his breath. What was he doing?

She drew back. "Lukas? What's wrong?"

Even the sound of her voice transfixed him. He reached up and touched her face again, then drew back again quickly, as if she might burn him.

And she might. And she didn't even realize the sudden power she had over him.

"Maybe we should go back inside."

# CHAPTER 10

Monday morning at three minutes to seven Lukas pulled into the hospital parking lot and turned off the Jeep's windshield wipers. A fine mist floated between the trees and branches of the hospital grounds, and the delicate washing of water brought out the beginning golds and reds of the leaves that would soon deepen into true autumn beauty.

Lukas wrapped his stethoscope around his neck as he climbed out of the Jeep and pocketed his keys. He caught sight of his reflection in the window, and even with the blurring of moisture, he could see the dumb grin on his face as he thought again about Thursday evening with Mercy. He shook his head and walked toward the emergency entrance. It had only been a kiss. And a hug. And a hint of a future.

But what future? His grin flattened. With things as they were, there could be no future. He'd thought about it all weekend, all along the two-and-a-half-hour trip to his dad and stepmom's home in Mt. Vernon, Missouri, and all day Saturday, at Dad's seventieth birthday celebration, complete with at least forty relatives and friends. He'd endured the good-natured teasing from his brothers and their families about his lack of a love life and didn't once mention the fact that he thought he might be falling in love. About a month ago he'd talked with Dad about his friendship with Mercy, and he'd heard the concern in Dad's voice when he discovered that Mercy was not a believer. So what was there to talk about?

But Mercy's heart was changing. She'd admitted it herself. She was on the verge of belief. Lukas could almost hear it in her voice. Any day she might—

The sudden appearance of barrel-chested, big-eared Buck Oppenheimer standing at the glass entrance doors of the ER waiting room dragged Lukas from his daydreams.

Buck pushed the door open for Lukas, his muscle-bound arm flexing like well-crafted stainless steel. "Hi, Doc. I've been waiting for you." He glanced at his watch. "You're almost late, you know."

"No, I'm not. I'm sixty seconds early." Lukas slowed his steps, studying the look of eager anticipation in Buck's gray eyes. "What's up?"

"I've been thinking about what you said the other day." Buck turned to walk with Lukas through the quiet ER proper toward the call rooms in back. "How about I come to work here for you for a while? I can take a leave from the fire department, move back in with Kendra, and when we have to cut our finances and stop going out to eat every weekend and she can't buy all the clothes she wants, she'll realize how much better off I am with the fire department."

Lukas shot Buck a skeptical glance as he pushed his way through the door of his customary call room. "I thought you said the fire department was cutting back on expenses." Sometimes the guy didn't use common sense.

"They're not cutting my salary, just asking for more hours at the same pay because they're not rehiring when someone quits."

"Doesn't sound like they'd be willing to let you take leave."

"They've been relying more and more on the new recruits. You know those two eighteen-year-olds I've been working with? The chief wants to hire Alex as a trainee at minimum wage. He didn't even ask Kyle."

"Why not?"

"The chief actually listened to me when I told him Kyle didn't have the aptitude. That kid's a show-off. He's always trying to upstage everyone and be a hero. He's an accident waiting to happen. He trips over hoses, he slammed the door on Alex's finger yesterday, and he fell into one of my airplane models and broke it before the glue was even dry."

Lukas checked the tiny fridge, grabbed a can of Instant Breakfast, and popped the top. He walked back to the main desk. "Have you spoken with Kendra this weekend?"

Buck walked beside him, a new frown drawing down his features. "I tried Friday. When she found out I was still an employee of the Knolls Fire Department, she hung up on me."

"Sounds like she means business. Have you tried again since Friday?"

"We've been too busy. I had to help a guy with another group of Explorers doing community service on Saturday, and that night we had another fire, this time down at the pool hall. It wasn't very big, but they had some smoke damage. I just happened to be there when it started, so we got it out in time to save most of the pool tables and other furniture."

"But didn't you even try to call her Sunday?" Lukas asked.

"Well, I would have, but my cousin Reese asked me to go out to his farm and help him vaccinate some cattle. We didn't get finished till late."

Lukas shook his head. "Buck, I know I'm just an inexperienced single guy, but I get the feeling you're avoiding the issue with your wife, and if *I* get that feeling, then *she* does."

Buck shrugged. "Why should I keep trying to call her when all she does is hang up on me? She's not even trying. Why should *I*? Do you have any jobs for me here?"

Carol looked up from her work at the central desk as the two men approached. "Are you looking for some work, Buck? Our tech for today just called in sick."

"Oh, really?" Lukas asked. "Who's scheduled?"

"Amanda. She's got the flu. I can't find any of the other techs to fill in."

"I can do it," Buck said eagerly. "Can't I, Dr. Bower?"

Lukas shook his head at the puppy-eager quality of Buck's expression. "Fine with me, since you're already part-time with our ambulance service. Monday is traditionally a busy day, and Dr. Garcias is supposed to come in for her first shift. I want to break her in gently, and a full crew would be nice. Find some scrubs, Buck, if you can get any to fit over those football pads you call shoulders."

A huge gap-toothed grin spread across Buck's face. "All right!"

"That doesn't mean we can hire you full-time," Lukas warned. "And I don't think you're going to fool Kendra by just taking a leave from the station."

"You're not suggesting I actually *quit* the fire department?" Buck exclaimed.

Lukas shook his head. "Go get your scrubs on."

As the young man turned and rushed toward the back, Carol looked at Lukas and leaned toward him, lowering her voice. "Dr. Bower, you know they're looking for an arsonist, don't you?"

"Yes, I heard that."

"It makes sense. I wonder if they've got Buck on the arson team again."

"Again?"

"Oh sure. He teaches fire safety, you know. He's helped them catch three in the past. No wonder they've got him teaching those kids."

The glass entrance door flew open, and Lauren McCaffrey raced through it, tying her long blond hair back with both hands while trying to carry her purse and a lunch bag under her right arm. "Sorry I'm late. My freezer went out on me last night, and I had to find a way to store all those fish I've been catching this summer. I've got packages stored at the kitchen at church, but they're going to need the space tomorrow for the side of beef they're having—ouch!" Her hands got tangled in her hair, and her lunch bag and purse dropped to the floor.

Lukas went over and picked them up for her while she untangled her hair. "I've got a brand-new refrigerator," he said. "You can use the freezer in it if you want to. Catch any fish yesterday?"

"Seven white bass. Thanks for the offer, Dr. Bower, but I've decided to have a fish fry tomorrow night. I've got the day off. You like fish, don't you? I'd love to have you—"

"Excuse me, Dr. Bower!" Carol interrupted, swinging around in a frantic motion toward him. "We have a frightened caller on line one. He and his buddies just pulled a woman out of Norfork Lake, and they're bringing her in by private car. They're calling from a cell phone."

Lukas stepped over to the desk and took the phone, from which a man's shaking voice shouted from the receiver. "Hello? Is anybody there? I think the line's—"

"This is Dr. Bower. Tell me what's going on."

"Oh, thank goodness! We've got this girl in the backseat of our car. We found her lying at the shore of the lake, and she was barely breathing, so we just loaded her in and took off instead of calling for help and waiting for it to get here. Now she's stopped breathing, and we don't know what—"

"She isn't breathing? Is anyone doing rescue breathing?"

"We don't know how! She looks bad, and her skin's turning blue. She's cold, like death!"

"Is anyone in the seat with her?"

"Yeah, Chuck's back there. There's three of us. We just came down to fish for a—"

"Listen very carefully," Lukas said. "I want Chuck to lay her flat and gently tip her head back, then lift her chin up, then tell me if you hear her breathing. Put your ear next to her mouth so you can hear, and have someone watch to see if her chest is rising and falling."

He waited while the confused men chattered, held silent, then came back to the phone.

"We don't hear anything, Doctor. Is she dead? What can we do? We don't want a girl dying right here in the car!"

"About how old is she?" Lukas tried to keep his own tension from his voice.

"She's probably about eighteen or twenty."

"I want someone to pinch her nose closed, then take a deep breath, cover her mouth with his mouth, and exhale into her mouth deeply and slowly. Do it two times."

The caller repeated the instructions to his buddy while Lukas waited. He looked up to find Dr. Cherra Garcias walking through the entrance and saw Lauren greet her. Good, Lauren would take care of the preliminaries. Claudia should be here by noon for double coverage when it got busy. He caught sight of three cars pulling into the ER patient parking area at about the same time. Maybe Claudia could come in early.

"Hello?" he said over the phone. "Is she breathing?"

The caller came back on the line. "Not yet." His voice rose with increasing panic.

"Check for a pulse at the neck. How far out are you?"

"Probably about thirty miles, and it's foggy, so we can't drive very fast." There was a pause, then, "Hey! Chuck says he thinks he felt a pulse, but he just felt it once. He doesn't feel it now." There was a fumble, and then, more distant, "Chuck, don't let her die! Hang on!"

"Listen to me!" Lukas called. "Hello, are you there?"

More fumbling. "Yeah, help us, Doc!"

"Try to stay calm. Tell Chuck to keep breathing once every five seconds for her. You're going to have to do complete CPR. Is there someone else in the backseat?"

"I'll climb over. Just tell me what to do, Doc. I don't want to let this girl die!"

"Tell me where you are and which route you're taking. I'll dispatch an ambulance crew in your direction. I think we have one in the area out there. Turn on your flashers and lights and tell me what kind of car you're in."

The man breathlessly gave that info as he climbed over the seat. Lukas then turned to Carol, who hovered anxiously beside him. "Call an ambulance." He gave the details he had just received. "Do a weather check and get a chopper on standby if the fog doesn't have them grounded. Then call Claudia and see if she can come in early."

"Gotcha." Carol picked up the ambulance phone and punched a speed-dial number.

Lukas returned to his own phone and gave brief, concise instructions for CPR. He could hear them breathing for her, then pumping her chest five times, then breathing again, begging her to wake up.

Carol turned to him and nodded. "The ambulance is on its way out. I'll call for Air Care."

Lukas nodded and informed the rescuers, "An ambulance will intercept you shortly. Stay on the line until they arrive so I can answer any questions you might have. I also want to ask you some questions so I'll know how to prepare."

"Okay, but I'm handing the phone to the driver so I can have my hands free."

The rest of the phones at the desk rang one after another, and Carol was kept busy for the next few minutes answering them. "Sorry, Dr. Bower, but nobody's flying because of the fog," she said at one point before answering another call.

"Hello, are you there?" Lukas asked into his receiver, hoping the rescuers had made the switch.

"Yes, Doctor, they're doing the CPR back there," said a new man with a lower, calmer voice, apparently the driver. "Don't worry, we've got this thing floored."

Lukas could hear the roar of a motor in the background, and then the sound of rubber tires squealing on blacktop. "Getting yourselves killed won't help anyone. Watch those curves and slow down, especially since they can't wear seat belts in the back. Tell me exactly how you found this girl. Was she lying in the water? Was her head out?"

"We just went down early to fish, and Chuck saw something down by the rocks. She was lying with the lower half of her body in the water, and her face looked pretty beat up, like maybe she'd fallen on the rocks. But her hair was wet, like she'd been in the lake and had crawled out. We couldn't get her to wake up, so we just lugged her to the car real quick. Calvin called you right afterward."

"Is she breathing yet? Can they feel a pulse?"

The driver conferred, then came back on the line. "No, we can't! What do we do now?"

"Keep going. I'll hold." Lukas saw someone step up to the desk and recognized the curly haired ER tech Amanda. He pivoted the mouthpiece of the phone and put a hand across it. "What are you doing here, Amanda?" he asked softly. "I thought you called in sick."

She nodded and leaned against the desk. Her narrow face was flushed, and beads of perspiration coated her brow, moistening the soft brown bangs. "Guess I got the flu everybody had last week. I'm really weak and shaky, and I have diarrhea. Can you check me out, Dr. Bower? I feel bad." Her breaths came in rapid succession.

Lukas cradled the receiver against his shoulder and stepped over to take her pulse. Her skin felt hot, and her heart rate felt rapid and weak. "You're not still taking the ma huang for your diet, are you?"

She shot him a quick, guilty glance and nodded.

"Still drinking caffeine?"

"Not as much. But, Dr. Bower, I'm sick to my stomach. It's the flu. I know it is."

"How long did you say you've been taking the ma huang?"

"Since I started working here. A month."

Lukas shook his head. "You'd better go lie down in exam room seven. I'll have Carol check you in as soon as she gets off the phone, and we'll see if we can get you feeling better." He glanced in Carol's direction and found her still juggling two separate calls.

A deep phone voice shouted out at him from the receiver on his shoulder. "I see lights up in the fog! It's the ambulance. I think they've found us!"

Lukas sat back with relief. "Keep your flashers going. Pull well over to the side of the road and get out and wave them down, but let your buddies keep doing CPR until the crew can take over."

Lukas held the line open until the ambulance crew rendezvoused with the three amateur rescuers, and then he thanked the men and disconnected. A cordless headset would be nice for situations like this when he had other patients to treat and other calls coming in.

To his relief, he saw Buck come back into the ER, along with Lauren and Cherra Garcias. He also glanced through the window that overlooked the parking lot and saw another car pull into an Emergency Patient Only spot.

Carol turned around. "Dr. Bower, Claudia says she'll be here as soon as she can get here."

"Thank you, Carol." He stepped forward and greeted the new doctor with an outstretched hand. "Hello, Cherra." Her grip was as firm as he remembered. "Thanks for coming on such short notice." Her smile was as bright as he remembered, too.

"You're welcome. I'm sorry I'll only be able to do a few shifts these next few weeks, but my contract in Arkansas ends in October. Then I can come full time."

Carol finally disengaged from the phone and began checking in the three new patients that had come in. It wasn't even eight in the morning.

"Is it always this busy here?" Cherra asked Lukas.

"The numbers fluctuate. Mondays can be pretty hectic, and overall volume has been increasing steadily since I came in April."

Cherra smiled again. "So you're a popular doctor."

"No, that's not—"

"He's a great doctor," Lauren said as she stepped up beside them at the desk. "Some of our frequent flyers call to make sure he's on duty before they come in. Some of them recognize his Jeep in the parking lot, and word gets around the neighborhood."

Lukas felt his face flush. "My presence here is not the reason volume has increased."

Lauren shrugged. "You have your theories, I have mine."

Cherra's dark-eyed gaze went from Lauren to Lukas and back again, and she grinned. Lukas felt his flush deepen. He picked up a clipboard, went to the case template stand, with all its different pockets that held forms covering only a small gamut of human suffering, and pulled out the proper form for the flu, even though he didn't think that was Amanda's problem. The rest could be added later.

He placed the T-sheet on the clipboard and handed it to Lauren. "Would you please assess Amanda? She's in room seven." He jotted down orders for blood tests and a urine drug screen. He also gave orders for a tilt test on the tech to see how dehydrated she was. "She might need IV fluids. Be on the lookout for reaction to ephedrine."

"You think it's that ma huang she's been taking, don't you?" Lauren asked.

"Yes, I do."

Lauren shook her head. "I told her that stuff was bad news. Nice to meet you, Dr. Garcias. I'm looking forward to working with you." She left them and went to tend her patient.

Another patient came in the door to be seen, and Lukas and Cherra overheard him telling Carol he'd had a rash for a month and finally decided to get it checked out. Lukas met Cherra's wry expression and saw her shrug. It was going to be one of those days.

The ER entrance door opened again, and Lukas looked over to find Theodore Zimmerman walk through, wearing jeans and a chambray work shirt. He was apparently on his way to work at Jack's Print Shop downtown on the square. His steps were hesitant, and his tense gaze darted around the room until he caught sight of Lukas at the central station.

"Dr. Bower," he said, walking over to the station. "Can I talk to you for a minute? I won't take much of your time."

His voice cracked, and Lukas noticed that his eyes were bloodshot, his face puffy. "I'm sorry, Theodore, but I can't talk now." Lukas gestured toward the patients coming in. "I'm just beginning what looks like a busy shift. Perhaps—"

"Why don't you let me take them for you, Dr. Bower?" Cherra interrupted. "I need to break in sometime, and I might as well make my trip up here worthwhile for you, too."

Lukas shrugged, trying not to allow frustration to show on his face. "Thank you, Dr. Garcias. I would appreciate it if you would take exam room seven first." He took her arm and walked with her a few steps away from any listening ears. "She's one of our techs, and she's been taking ma huang and caffeine to lose weight for the past month or so. I suspect she's overdosed. I warned her to slow it down, but apparently she hasn't. Maybe she'll listen to you."

Cherra nodded and headed toward the exam room, and Lukas turned back toward Theo.

"I'm sorry, Dr. Bower," Theo said. "I was on my way to work, and I thought I'd better stop by and apologize for last Thursday night. I probably got you into trouble with Mercy."

With anyone else, this wouldn't irritate Lukas. "You didn't 'get me into trouble' with anybody."

Theo paused. "I also need to talk with you about something else."

Lukas watched the man's face for a moment. What was he up to now?

"What do you want to talk about, Theodore? And please, call me Lukas."

Theo took a deep breath and let it out and reached up to push his short blond hair back from his forehead. "Thanks, Lukas. Could you come outside with me?" He glanced around at the filling ER waiting room, and at Carol, who was looking their way. "What I've got to say is kind of . . . personal."

"If it's about Mercy again, I don't—"

"It isn't. Honest. Please." Theo held his gaze.

Lukas relented and turned to the secretary. "Carol, we'll be in the private waiting room. Call me immediately when the ambulance contacts us about the drowning victim." He turned to lead the way without waiting to see if Theodore followed.

The thick carpet and comfortably overstuffed chairs and sofa were decorated in peaceful shades of green and blue, and the windows overlooked a small rose garden. Soft classical music drifted through speakers in the ceiling. Lukas stepped in and took a chair across from the sofa.

Theodore paused at the threshold and peered around. "I'll never forget this room. It's where I waited the night I hit Tedi. It's where

Estelle sat with me and bullied me into telling you what I'd done."
He shook his head and walked across to the sofa. His step was steady
as he sat down with slow, deliberate movements, as if wary of disturbing too many painful memories, or maybe a headache.

"I wasn't always this way, Lukas," Theodore said. "I didn't drink
much when Mercy and I first started dating." He gestured around the
room. "I spent a lot of time here at the hospital then, when she was
first in practice with her father in his office. She had a lot of spare
time back then, and when she wasn't busy we would sit in the cafeteria between her appointments and talk for hours." He sounded so
wistful and sad. "I was working as a real estate agent then, and when
I didn't have to be in the office I was here. There was something
about Mercy that . . ." He glanced swiftly at Lukas. "Well, anyway, I
know this hospital well. I was here when they did the remodeling in
this wing, and I even helped nail Sheetrock. But what I really wanted
to do was x-ray. I loved it. It got to where I thought I knew those
machines as well as anybody, just because I spent so much time
watching and learning. I thought I might make a good x-ray technologist."

"So why didn't you?"

Theo shrugged. "I was already a real estate agent, even though I
didn't like it. I thought if I sold a lot of property Mercy might consider marrying me. I mean, how much can an x-ray tech make compared to a family practice physician?"

Lukas watched him and felt a tug of pity.

"Mercy was right Thursday night," Theo said softly. He rested
his elbows on his knees and leaned forward, his light blue eyes filled
with self-reproach. "I haven't changed. I still treat her the same way,
building my case against her with the people closest to her. I've always done that. I even used Tedi against her when I could." He
looked down and rubbed his face with his hands. "She hates it."

"Wouldn't you?"

Theo looked back up at him. "Yeah. I do it even when I don't
know I'm doing it, just like with the booze. My apartment's about
three blocks from a liquor store, and about ten times this weekend I
had myself convinced that one little drink would actually be a good
thing, just to prove to myself that I was cured of it." Theo slumped

back into the soft cushions and laid his head back with a sigh. "I was lying to myself."

Lukas waited. *I don't know what it's like to be addicted, and I can't identify with him. Why can't he get what he needs with all the AA meetings they have around Knolls?* Lukas cleared his throat and started to mention that very thing, when Theo sat back up.

"You said something the other night about this guy in the Bible who couldn't straighten out his own life and just got worse. Whatever happened to him?"

*So that's it.* "The Bible doesn't say, but I gather from the words that he died still lying to himself."

Theodore stared at him. "That's all?"

"It was a warning. Jesus was telling the people that they couldn't just keep evil out of their lives by the force of their own will. Evil is stronger than we are, and it will control us. Even if we manage to extricate ourselves from bad situations, like alcohol or drug abuse or child abuse or manipulative behavior, we can't keep ourselves from doing it again, or from doing something worse. We are susceptible to the control of Satan and his evil spirits unless we allow a stronger Spirit to control us, and that can only be the Spirit of Christ, God's Son."

Theo did not break eye contact, but his gaze intensified, grew pleading. "That's what I want."

Lukas stared at him. *Just like that?*

Theo spread his hands. "Can't you see? That's my only hope."

Lukas took a moment to digest what Theo was saying. As though Christ were just some tool for Theodore to use, to manipulate the way he manipulated everyone else? Once, when Lukas was in his third year at UMC, another student had pretended to seek out his friendship. He'd attended worship services with Lukas, listened to him tell about Christ, and feigned interest in learning more. Then he had hit Lukas up for money, saying he needed help to buy textbooks. And Lukas had loaned him the money. Later he discovered the money had been used to buy pornographic magazines.

Was Theo setting him up the same way?

Theo dropped his hands to his lap and bent his head. "I can't live like this anymore."

Lukas took a deep breath and let it out slowly. He thought of Mercy and her continuing struggle to accept God's offer of salvation because of her own feelings of unworthiness—much of which came from the way this man had treated her for the past ten years. Why should Theo's sins drive him to Christ before his victim could bring herself to come?

"Please, Lukas," Theo said. "Tell me what I need to do. My own daughter tried to tell me about Christ, but I wouldn't listen. I want to listen now." He leaned forward, and his reddened eyes filled with tears. "I'm drinking again." His face contorted, and a sob shook his broad shoulders. He looked down and covered his face, and for a moment he cried. His nose ran. His neck reddened. He wasn't manipulating anyone.

And then Lukas felt the compassion. This was real. He reached over and pulled a couple of tissues from the container beside his chair, then got up, stepped silently across the deep carpet, and sat down beside Theodore. He placed the tissues in Theo's hands and waited.

Lukas had no idea what it would be like to be caught in such a deadly habit. How would it feel not to have known about Christ from your earliest memories of childhood? Lukas knew from Mercy that Theodore's parents divorced when Theo was ten years old, and he was still in high school when his father died. Lukas could only imagine all Theo had gone through.

*Lord, forgive me. Now I know how Jonah felt when he tried to escape his mission to Nineveh. Don't send the giant fish just yet. I really do want to do your will. All these years I've asked you to use me, and now that it looks like you are, so quickly and with so little effort, I'm resentful. Help me to forgive.*

Theodore used the tissues to wipe his face and nose, and he rested his elbows on his knees and continued to cover his face with his hands. "Thursday night after Jarvis kicked me out of his house, I walked home." He shrugged. "I don't have a car now, so I walk everywhere I go. Anyway, I passed the liquor store three blocks from my apartment, and then I turned around and went in. I bought a pint of whiskey, promising myself I wouldn't drink the whole thing, just a couple of swallows to kill the pain."

Lukas leaned forward. "Pain from what?"

Theo wiped his face again and sat back. "From seeing myself more clearly than I ever have. Mercy was right—I hadn't changed, and I knew it. I couldn't stop thinking about it." He looked at Lukas. "I drank half the bottle Thursday before midnight, then I was so sick for the next three days, I barely got out of bed. I finished the bottle last night, and I couldn't get any more because the liquor store was closed. This morning when I woke up I decided that if I buy any more booze, I'll just buy a couple of gallons and keep on drinking until it kills me." He continued to hold Lukas in his gaze. "I can't . . . I won't live like this anymore." Tears once more spilled from his eyes. He still looked sick.

Before Lukas could think of any comforting words, the door flew open and Buck rushed in. "Dr. Bower, Dr. Garcias sent me to tell you that Amanda's crashing. Also, Carol caught me on the way in here, and the paramedic with the drowning victim is calling for you from the ambulance. We need you—now!"

# CHAPTER 11

I want birth control pills." Fifteen-year-old Shannon Becker did not make eye contact with Mercy but sat slumped on the table after her female exam, shoulders curved forward in a position that demonstrated a discomfort with her rapidly burgeoning female contours.

Mercy tried not to allow her sudden shock to show on her face. "I see." Oh boy, did she see. What was she supposed to do about this? She refused to allow this sweet child to join the meat market parade. "You mentioned a concern about your complexion." That was lame and she knew it, but she had to stall for time. That could be Tedi sitting on that exam table in a few years. She turned toward the small desk along the wall of the exam room. "I can prescribe a cream for acne that will be safer than—"

"No, I don't want the pills for zits." Shannon reached up and wrapped a strand of her shoulder-length light brown hair around her right forefinger. She blinked, looked at the floor, then back at the delicate cloud pattern of the wallpaper, anywhere but at Mercy. "My friends told me that a doctor can't report to a girl's parents if she gets birth control pills."

With a silent sigh, Mercy stood and assisted her young patient down from the exam bed and gestured toward a chair. "That's right. Legally I can't tell your parents about your request for contraceptives." And right now Mercy hated the legalities of her profession.

She'd watched Shannon grow up for ten years, ever since her parents, Zach and Lee Becker, sought out Mercy to be their family physician. Even during the divorce and the rumors about Mercy's mental problems, the Beckers had been faithful to her, had trusted her judgment and medical expertise. And now she felt like a traitor.

"Our discussion will be confidential."

Shannon's expressive gray eyes flicked toward Mercy for the first time during the visit. "Discussion?" Her face flushed.

"Of course."

"But you gave me the exam. Can't you just write me a prescription for the pill now? Why do we have to talk about anything?"

Mercy made a notation on Shannon's chart and checked the noticeable weight gain since her last visit a year ago. Adolescence had attacked this child with a vengeance. "I talk to all of my patients, or their parents, about the treatment they will be receiving."

"And you really won't tell Mom?" There was a faint quiver in Shannon's voice, the scared little girl hiding behind the crumbly veneer of a teenager.

Mercy patted the girl's slightly plump shoulder. This was the Shannon she had always known and loved. "Get your clothes on, honey, then come down the hallway to the second door on the right. It's my office. We can talk there." She grinned. "Don't worry, I'm not going to eat you."

———

Lukas rushed back into the ER from the private waiting room. "Buck, tell Dr. Garcias I'll be there as soon as I can." He glanced at Theodore, who came out behind him. "Can you wait for me?" He suddenly wanted to continue the conversation he'd been so anxious to avoid earlier.

"I've got to go to work."

"If you're serious about what you said in there, can you find a Bible somewhere today?"

"My boss sells them at the print shop."

"Then find time on your break to read the first chapter of Isaiah and start on the book of John." Lukas stepped to the radio and pressed a button. "This is medical control."

It was the ambulance with the young drowning victim. "We are currently inbound to your facility with a class-one medical full code. Repeat, patient is a full code. She is in v-fib, and we have attempted defibrillation three times without success. Patient is intubated and IV established times one. C-collar in place, patient on backboard. ETA of ten minutes. Further orders at this time?"

"Does patient have obvious injuries?" Lukas looked up to see Claudia coming through the ER entrance. The cavalry had arrived.

The voice came back over the radio. "Patient has numerous abrasions, no active bleeding. Full assessment not done due to patient severity."

"Understood. What was the initial rhythm?"

"Pulseless electrical activity."

Lukas frowned. You couldn't shock someone with pulseless electrical activity. It did no good. Then he realized what had happened—they'd had to intubate her, and that had thrown her into v-fib. He'd seen it happen before.

In the background Lukas heard Lauren greeting Claudia with a patient assessment when Lauren's words registered.

"Claudia, would you withdraw an ampule of Inderal from the drug dispenser? We need it in exam room seven. Amanda's in there, and she's crashing."

Lukas jerked around. "Hold it! Lauren, what's going on?"

She glanced over at him in surprise.

"Dr. Garcias is requesting Inderal for Amanda?" he said. That drug would not work for an ephedrine overdose. In fact, it could be lethal. "What's happening in there?"

Lauren stepped toward Lukas. "Her heart rate and blood pressure went up, and she's much less responsive. Her fever shot up, and she didn't improve with fluids."

"Lauren, I need you in here," came Cherra's voice from the exam room, and Lauren turned to obey.

The radio sparked to life again. "Medical control, be advised patient is extremely cold. Recommend you initiate hypothermia protocol upon arrival. Over."

Lukas ignored the radio. "Lauren, wait! Tell her to wait!"

The voice from the radio came back. "Medical control, are you there? Did you copy our last transmission? Over."

Lukas reached back quickly and punched the button. "Yes, we copied your last transmission. Keep us advised. This is medical control out." He jumped up and ran into exam room seven.

Amanda lay on the bed with a clear oxygen mask on her face and a large IV tube attached to her left arm. Monitor leads were attached to her chest beneath her hospital gown. Tears streamed from her sea-green eyes and dripped into fine tendrils of curly brown hair around her face.

Claudia entered the room with the Inderal and handed it to Lauren.

Dr. Garcias bent over Amanda with her stethoscope. "You're going to be okay, hon." She looked up and saw Lukas. "Dr. Bower, I just happened to notice this a few minutes ago." She reached over and gestured toward the center of Amanda's throat. "Feel that?"

He stepped forward and gently palpated her neck. There was an unmistakable midline mass. He looked up at Cherra in surprise. "Goiter." Immediately he remembered what Amanda had told him about her easy weight loss over the past few months, long before she'd begun taking the natural herb. He nodded at Cherra. "Thyroid storm, possibly precipitated by the ma huang." He'd overlooked the obvious. Why hadn't he listened better to his patient?

"Exactly what I think," Cherra said. "I just ordered a thyroid profile plus TSH level, but we won't get that back for a while, so I decided to do this clinically. The curly hair confused me, because fine, straight hair is typical of hyperthyroid, but Amanda told me she has a perm." Cherra indicated her own curly black hair. "That shouldn't surprise me, since I have one myself."

Lukas exhaled heavily and nodded. "Nice pickup. You obviously know how to treat this. I'll leave you to it. I've got to get ready for a code."

------

"Dr. Mercy, we have a little more time this morning than we expected." Josie, Mercy's nurse, placed a chart on Mercy's desk. "Those Knights are a stubborn family." Her short black hair reflected the rays of sunshine streaming through the window.

Mercy looked at the chart and felt a thrust of familiar frustration, something she often experienced when dealing with the Knights. "Did Darlene cancel another appointment?"

"Yes. That makes three times in two months."

Mercy sighed and picked up the phone, but Josie shook her head.

"I just did that. Clarence told me he tried to get his sis to come in, but that she's stopped wheezing, and she says she's too busy. She's promised him she's doing her inhalers and drugs."

"Just great." Mercy slumped back in her chair. "I'm not going to have a chance to visit them for a few days, and I doubt if Lukas will. We're both teaching classes at the health seminar this week, and there's a weekend conference in Springfield that we're scheduled to attend."

Josie sat down in the straight-backed chair across the desk from Mercy. "Then maybe you should just stop playing superdoc and let Darlene take care of herself for once."

Mercy blinked and straightened. "Is this *my* nurse talking? The one who gives free blood pressure checks to every person over the age of fifty in her church? The woman who has been known to pay patient bills when she knows they can't pay?"

Josie didn't smile. "You and Dr. Bower have been treating Clarence and Darlene free of charge for the past summer. Clarence is losing weight as a direct result of your bullying, but what about Darlene? She is totally noncompliant. Maybe pushing her just makes her more stubborn."

Mercy thought about that for a moment, then shook her head. "I don't think so. I think she is afraid to let up on the work she's doing at home because they're struggling financially."

"But she should realize for herself that she's sick. She needs help."

"She's like a lot of patients who think they can push themselves past the limits, and then the doctor will make everything okay."

"So what are you going to do about her?" Josie asked.

Mercy picked up the chart, thumbed through it, and placed it back on her desk. "I guess I'll just try to be there for her when she needs me. Call them back, Josie, and try hard to set up an appointment for Darlene as soon as possible."

A timid knock sounded at Mercy's open office door, and both women looked up to see Shannon Becker slumped there in her jeans and T-shirt, her straight, light brown hair combed as much over her face as possible to hide the slight decorations of acne scattered across pale skin. She still would not make eye contact with Mercy.

Josie jumped up. "Come on in, Shannon, I was just leaving. I've got temperatures to take, shots to give, and patients to placate."

The ambulance was running hot, and Lukas heard the echo of its siren long before it pulled into the bay and stopped. He looked around at his assembled team to get their attention.

"As you already know, this patient is coming in as a full code, and you know how to handle a code. Remember, however, that this case is complicated by hypothermia, so to give her any chance at all we've got to get her warmed up."

He turned to Lauren. "I want a rectal temp as soon as possible, and then you can assist me in placing a central line. Claudia, heat the IV fluids and switch them out from the fluids she's getting in the ambulance."

He turned to the respiratory therapist. "Mary, we need a heated aerosol generator hooked up to the ET tube. I also want a blood gas."

He turned to the ER tech. "Buck, get me a central line kit, and then you can take over on the compressions. Carol, I want basic blood work and alcohol level. I'll also want a chest x-ray and c-spine series, but we won't break CPR to get it, so that'll have to wait."

The door opened with an ambulance team guiding a cot with a young woman on board. One EMT walked alongside the cot pushing against the patient's chest, one pulled the cot and squeezed the ambu bag to breathe for the patient, and another pushed from behind. They wheeled her into the cardiac-trauma room and transferred her to the bed.

"Okay," Lukas said, "let's get to work."

---

"So, Shannon, tell me what's been going on in your life." Mercy sat back in her chair and tried not to see this young innocent girl as just an older version of Tedi. *Don't condescend. Don't lecture.*

Shannon tangled her fingers together in her lap, a flush creeping up her neck.

"I gather there's a special person in your life now?" Mercy prompted, trying to sound matter-of-fact and ignore the sound of Josie ushering a patient into an exam room.

Shannon shook her head jerkily, then hesitated and nodded. "I guess."

"It's a wonderful feeling to be falling in love. I'm not surprised someone noticed a beautiful young woman like you. What's he like? Are you going steady?" She would not ask "parent" questions—Zach and Lee could do that.

The flush deepened. "No, we're not going steady or anything."

Mercy stifled a sigh and waited for this suddenly silent girl—who used to be such a talker—to give her some hint about what was going on in her life. The burden of professional responsibility weighed heavily. Mercy couldn't helping noticing, once again, that Shannon's young body had developed dramatically in the past year—and that her body language screamed out her feelings of awkwardness at this development.

"I met him while we were cruising the square this summer," Shannon said softly. "One of my girlfriends is sixteen and can drive."

"So you met him a month or so ago?" Finally she was talking.

"A couple of months ago. He's from another town, and he's seventeen, so Mom and Dad wouldn't let me go out with him even if I asked." She shot Mercy another glance, and this time held it longer. "You said you wouldn't tell Mom and Dad."

"That's right." Much as she wanted to warn them to protect their daughter, Mercy was prevented from doing so by the laws heaped more and more often on physicians.

"Well, I keep running into him on Friday and Saturday nights, and lately he's been taking me out driving." Shannon continued to tangle her fingers around each other. She glanced again at Mercy, this time more bravely.

Mercy kept her expression composed, serene. "You really like him, do you?"

Shannon nodded. "A couple of weeks ago he drove me out onto this logging road in the forest, and we parked and kissed for a while. Then he asked me if I wanted to . . . you know . . . go further."

Mercy did not allow herself to react like a parent but like a logical family doc. "Did you discuss birth control and VD histories?"

Shannon shook her head. "I just said no. It would be too embarrassing to . . . you know. Anyway, he kept looking at me . . . that way . . . like he liked what he saw."

Mercy bit her tongue for a moment. She wanted to ask if this kid even knew what Shannon's face looked like, or appreciated her sense of humor, or knew how many brothers and sisters she had. "Why don't you tell me what you like about this guy."

Shannon grinned and rolled her eyes, then shrugged. "He's cute, and he's older. He's got a great car. The guys at school don't even know I exist, but he's started looking for me in town on Fridays."

"Has he taken you out to dinner? Met your parents?"

Shannon looked down at her hands. "It's not like that. We just kind of hang out."

And for this she was thinking about sacrificing her body?

Shannon shrugged. "My girlfriend says it's just sex. No big deal."

The phrase irritated Mercy. She knew she hadn't intended to lecture, but she couldn't help herself. "Shannon Becker, I've watched you grow from a sweet little five-year-old to a beautiful young woman, and I must tell you that you are very special to me."

Shannon looked up at her. "I am?"

"Yes, and because of that I hate to see you give something precious away to somebody who probably doesn't even see the beautiful flecks of gold in your gray eyes, or hear the lilt in your laugh when you're not too self-conscious to let loose."

"But he's always telling me I'm pretty."

"Do you laugh with this boy? Do you share your thoughts and dreams with him? Does he share his with you? Shannon, the physical intimacies between a man and a woman are life changing and beautiful—or they can be with the right person. It's never 'just sex.' It's always a 'big deal,' something to be anticipated and cherished."

Shannon looked down at her hands, her face reddening again. "He thought I was weird because I'm still a virgin. Some of my friends do, too."

"A lot of people will say or do anything to convince you that you're weird if you don't live the way they do. Don't listen to them. Your virginity makes you special."

Shannon stared down at her hands as she thought about that for a moment. "Mom said something like that a long time ago, when she told me all the stuff about the facts of life. But kids at school say—"

"Not everybody at school has discarded their virginity. Those who have will try to convince you to join them because they know they've lost something valuable, and they don't want to feel they're the only ones."

Shannon hesitated. She sighed deeply, slowly. "I really think this guy likes me. He says he does."

"Lots of people *like* you, Shannon. It takes a lot more than that to share the most intimate part of yourself." This girl was already beautiful, with a look of joyful anticipation that often came into her eyes when she talked. And in spite of her awkward adolescence, she had a graceful way of moving. Zach and Lee would have their hands full with her the next few years, starting now.

"Shannon, sex is more than just physical, but it affects you physically. You can get pregnant even if you do use birth control. There are diseases out there now that can dramatically change your life or even end it. They're right here in Knolls, and teenagers are one of the highest risk groups."

Shannon's eyes widened. Okay, so fear was the best tactic with her.

"Your friends won't tell you about that even if they've got it," Mercy continued. "Nobody talks about it, but it happens all the time. I know because I see it all the time, even with first-timers. And even if you talk to this boy about it and he tells you he's clean, he doesn't know for sure, not if he's been with anybody else."

Shannon sighed and leaned back in her chair. "You're not going to give me birth control pills, are you, Dr. Mercy?"

Wasn't the kid listening? But then, what if she didn't get the pills, and then she got pregnant? "Okay, let me give you some information about oral contraceptives. You have to take them faithfully, every day, or they aren't reliable. They do not protect from venereal disease of any kind. Also, there have been studies lately linking breast cancer later in life to an extra surge of estrogen now. Remember the lump your mother had last year? Breast disorders run in your family." Mercy reached toward her prescription pad. "However, if you still feel you must have this medication in order to prevent pregnancy, I'll write this out for you and—"

"Um, well, Dr. Mercy, wait."

Mercy paused and looked at Shannon across the desk.

Shannon bit her lip, thinking. "Maybe I *could* have another talk with Mom about this. You know, before I decide for sure. Maybe I can get Mom to herself for a few minutes, away from my brothers and sister, and when she's not working, or not cooking. Maybe." She made a face. "Or maybe I could even corner Dad."

Mercy nodded, relieved. "That's good, Shannon. If you want me to talk to them, I'll be happy—"

Shannon gasped. "No! I don't want them to know it's *me* I'm talking to them about. I mean, I've got great parents, but get real. They'd spaz."

Mercy thought again of her own daughter. Was it possible Tedi could have a future relationship with her *own* father?

And then as she said good-bye to Shannon and watched her walk out the door, thoughts of Lukas came bursting through. She thought about last Thursday night and the sudden, powerful awareness that had caught them both. She smiled and allowed the warmth to seep back through her, allowed the hope to lift her. They were more than just buddies—a lot more. She even appreciated Lukas moving cautiously, because it meant their relationship was something very important to him, too.

She would give him more time.

———

"Temperature is going back down from 93 to 92.4," Lauren said sadly.

"Stop CPR." Lukas placed his stethoscope once more on the young woman's chest. He heard nothing. No heartbeat, no breath sounds. He looked at the monitor. The rhythm was asystole, flatline, as it had been for the past fifteen minutes. He checked the pupils. Fixed and dilated. He felt that old specter of grief catch him. "Claudia, what time is it?"

Claudia, the official recorder for the code, looked at her watch. "Nine-thirty A.M."

"Time of death nine-thirty A.M. Sorry, everyone. This one wasn't meant to be."

A collective aura of disappointment echoed through the room. Slowly, as if in shock, code team members removed gloves and other gear and gathered up scattered plastic and paper containers that had held the equipment they'd used.

Lukas stood looking at the wreckage of the body that had belonged to a young girl with a future just a few hours ago. He knew that technically she was dead long before she reached the ER, but he couldn't help wondering, as he always did in cases like this, if there was something he could have done to change the outcome. Her temperature had been only 86 when she came in. It looked as if she'd fallen into the lake and probably hit her head against some rocks and inhaled water.

The three fishermen who had found her were now back at the lake with the police, scouring the shoreline for some kind of ID so they could locate and inform the girl's family.

A gasping sigh registered behind Lukas, and he turned to find Buck standing by the doorway, his hands clasped in front of him, his face drenched with tears as he stared at the dead girl's white face.

"Buck?" Lukas took a step toward him. "Are you okay?"

He nodded, but the tears continued, his face reddening with the effort to control his emotions.

Lukas looked again at the face of the dead patient. Of course. Why hadn't he noticed? She looked like Buck's wife.

"Kendra's father was a fireman," Buck said at last, sniffing and wiping his face with the back of his hand. "Year before last he was killed in the line of duty down in Mountain Home, Arkansas. He was pulling a little kid out of a burning house, and a wall fell in on him."

Lukas watched Buck continue to struggle with his emotions. "I didn't know about that, Buck. I kind of picked up on some of the things you said, but I didn't realize—"

"He got the kid out, though. Fred's death kind of sent Kendra off the deep end for a while. She was upset one night after I came in from a big fire, and she said she might as well just kill herself now, because she didn't want to live if the same thing happened to me." Buck shook his head. "She almost succeeded, too, before I caught her with an empty bottle of sleeping pills her doctor had prescribed for her after Fred's death. She looked as dead as this gal." He reached over and grabbed some tissues, blew his nose with a loud honk, and then wiped his face. He jerked his head in the direction of the patient. "What happened here, Doc?"

"I don't know." Lukas patted his friend on his broad, muscular shoulder. "But I know this isn't Kendra. You still have a chance to try to convince her how good life can be. You obviously love her. Make sure she knows it."

The evening sun still peered over the rolling Ozark hills in the western horizon when Lukas stepped out of the hospital for the first time in thirteen hours. The clouds that had begun on the ground this morning were now far to the east, just visible enough to reflect a brilliance of peach and mauve from one of the Missouri sunsets that were famous for their beauty and variety. Lukas wished he'd been out in the forest today, taking a long, much-needed hike on one of his favorite trails. Instead, he'd been busy here misdiagnosing a young ER employee. He had also filled out a death certificate on the drowning victim, young Julie Walters. The three rescuers had found ID at the scene of the accident at the lake. And that was before lunch.

On the upside, Lukas had discovered that the new full-time physician they had just hired would be worth the wait. Not only had Cherra Garcias caught Amanda's thyroid storm—which Lukas himself had missed—but she had covered most of the patients in ER for the rest of the day while Lukas plowed through hours of paper work and committee meetings. Amanda was going to be fine and would improve quickly with proper treatment.

Which reminded him that even though tomorrow was covered and no one had canceled yet, he still had to come in for another meeting and a stack of—

"Lukas?"

The sound of Theodore's voice came from behind him. He turned to find the man walking across the empty ambulance bay toward him.

"I just got off work, and I thought I'd walk over and try to catch you before you left the hospital." Theo fell into step with Lukas. "Whew! That's quite a walk."

"Working late?"

"We had an extra order that needed to get out tonight, and since I'm the newest employee, I got to stay and help." Theo reached into the right back pocket of his jeans and pulled out a small book. It was a New Testament. "Jack gave me this today."

Lukas couldn't miss the sound of excitement in Theo's voice. They reached the Jeep, and he unlocked the passenger side. "Sounds like you've got a generous boss. Hop in, Theodore, and I'll drive you home."

Theo stood at the open door, the glow from a nearby security light pole illuminating a smile on his face. "I found a Bible at work and read all the verses you told me to read, and everything fell into place. No wonder I've never been able to do anything right my whole life. I've always tried to do it myself. I don't want to do that anymore." He took a deep breath and let it out slowly. "I'm giving it all to Christ." Emotion broke his voice, and the whiteness of his teeth showed in the glow of the light. "I believe."

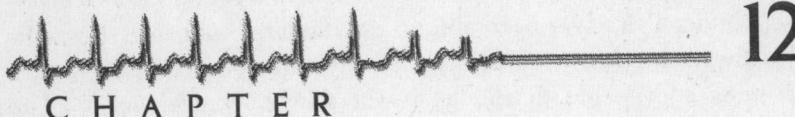

# CHAPTER 12

A week later, on Monday morning, Lukas heard a squeal of car tires outside in the parking lot just as he prepared for his first meeting with Mrs. Pinkley and the COBRA investigator. He glanced out the double glass doors of the waiting room and saw a man jump out of a late model Chevrolet with a small camcorder hanging from a strap around his neck. The man raced around the front of the car and opened the passenger door, then reached down to help a very pregnant woman out of the seat. An older woman emerged from the back, and the three of them walked toward the ER entrance.

Halfway across the parking lot, the pregnant woman stopped and grabbed the man's long, lanky arm with both hands. She bent over with a grimace of pain.

"Judy," he called to the secretary, "better get a wheelchair. Looks like we've got a patient for Labor and Delivery." Even as he spoke, the older woman also doubled over, hands to stomach. "Judy, make that two wheelchairs. Where's Lauren?"

The slender secretary with short salt-and-pepper hair jumped up from the desk and rushed toward the wall where the wheelchairs and gurneys were parked when not in use. "I think she's in the supply room helping Amanda restock."

Lukas took the wheelchairs from Judy and aimed them toward the door. "Would you get them both, please? Have them meet me out in the parking lot."

He pushed the automatic button for the doors and managed to get both chairs out at the same time without breaking glass. Reaching the struggling man and two moaning women, he caught the pregnant woman just before she fell and eased her into the first wheelchair.

"Is Labor and Delivery expecting you?" he asked, then looked up to find, to his amazement, that the man was backing away from the scene and focusing his camcorder.

"Not yet." The older woman grabbed the other wheelchair and sat down with a groan. She shot a wounding glance at the man. "Useless," she muttered. "To him this is just one big movie scene." She reached over and patted the younger woman's arm. "Told you not to marry the nut. But I'm here for you, Melinda. Just hang on."

Melinda nodded, her face red and perspiring. She took a couple of deep breaths, then once more grabbed her abdomen and bent forward with another loud moan.

Lauren and Amanda came running out, and Lukas straightened to meet them. He gestured toward Melinda. "We need to take this one to Labor and Deliv—"

The older woman cried out and nearly fell out of the wheelchair. After a long, deep moan, she gasped. "Jeremy, get over here and help your wife before I choke you with the strap on that thing!"

The man nodded. "Just one more second, Mom. I want a shot of them wheeling her in."

"Now!" Mom screamed loudly enough to awaken every patient in the hospital. She bent over again, eyes squeezed shut from the pain.

Lukas helped Amanda push Melinda's wheelchair onto the sidewalk, then turned back to Lauren. "Would you please take the mother to the ER. She's apparently in pa—"

"Oh no you don't!" the woman shouted. "I'm part of this package. This is my first grandbaby, and I'm not going to miss it. Ever heard of *couvade*? Jeremy, get over here!"

Lukas nodded in understanding. Of course. Melinda's mother-in-law was having sympathetic labor pains. It was a little unusual—usually if anyone suffered with *couvade* it was the husband, but other family members had been documented.

Reluctantly, the son powered down his precious cargo, and Lukas walked toward him, relieved. "We'll need you to provide some information for us over in the ER, since our admitting office isn't open yet. Who's your obstetrician?"

The man grinned. "Dr. Mercy. Can you call her for me?"

---

"Hello, Mercy."

At the sound of Theo's voice over the telephone, Mercy nearly spit out a mouthful of coffee. She swallowed instead, and it burned all the way down. Setting her cup on the counter, she looked over to see Tedi wandering into the kitchen in her pajamas, her tangled dark brown hair falling across her shoulders, her brown eyes muzzy with sleep.

"I hope I didn't wake you," came Theo's voice as Mercy pushed a bowl of hot cereal across to Tedi's place at the breakfast bar.

*Be nice. Don't alarm Tedi. Keep it polite.* "No, I've been up awhile." Mercy poured some orange juice with extra pulp and placed it beside the bowl of cereal, then motioned for Tedi to sit down and start eating.

"I was just getting ready to leave for work, and you probably are, too," Theo said. "I wanted to apologize for barging in on Jarvis's party a week and a half ago. It took me this long to work up the guts to talk to you again."

Mercy frowned. There was no hint of sarcasm in his voice. He sounded sincere—but then, how many times had he fooled her and everyone else?

Still . . . she'd been thinking about things, and Mom was right. If she kept putting him off, he could get mad and go back to court and demand visitation rights. She did not want that.

"It's okay," she said.

There was a shocked silence from the other end of the line.

She reached down and pushed Tedi's hair back from her face so it wouldn't fall into the cereal. "Actually, I know there are some things we will need to discuss." She heard a swift intake of breath over the line, and she felt her own heart beating faster. Was this a good idea? She still despised the man, but her own personal feelings were not as important as Tedi. "I'm still off on Thursdays. Do you suppose we could have a telephone discussion? Or we could meet—"

"Yes. Anything. Name the time and I'll be there. I've been putting in some overtime, and if I explain to my boss—"

"That's not necessary, Theodo—" Too late, she caught the slip. She saw Tedi drop her spoon at the sound of his name, saw her eyes widen. She sighed inwardly. "When is your lunch hour?"

"I get off at eleven-thirty. I have thirty minutes, but I could take long—"

"No, that's okay. Little Mary's Barbeque is next door. I'll be there at eleven-thirty."

"Would you make it eleven, please? I told my boss everything, and he understands how important this is to me."

Mercy rolled her eyes. Everyone in town knew about their situation. She felt a rise of anger but quelled it for Tedi's sake. "Okay. Eleven."

"I'll buy lunch."

"No."

There was a pause, then, "Thank you, Mercy." She thought she heard a catch in his voice. "This means . . . so much. Thank you." There was another pause. "You probably won't believe me, but I've been praying about this for the past week."

*Oh sure, and Billy Graham is a Hindu.* "I'll see you then." She hung up and looked down at her wide-eyed, openmouthed daughter.

"Mom, you're going to see Dad?"

"I need to talk with him."

"Can I go with you?"

Mercy sank down onto a stool at the breakfast bar. Had she lost her mind? What was she putting into motion with this meeting? Why was she even agreeing to talk to him? The fear of losing custody of Tedi still stalked her thoughts like a nightmare that wouldn't go away.

Tedi stepped over and took Mercy's hand. "Mom?"

Mercy sighed and drew Tedi forward. "Do you want to see him, honey?"

Tedi stared at her with big solemn brown eyes for a moment, then nodded. "I think so."

The telephone rang again, and for an instant Mercy entertained the wild hope that it was Theo calling back to tell her it was all a mistake, that he was leaving the country, never to be heard from again.

When she answered, it was the feminine voice of a stranger. "Hello? Is there somebody there by the name of Dr. Mercy?"

"Yes, that's me. May I help you?"

"Well, I live over here on Monroe Street, and this huge half-naked man just came and knocked on my door and asked to use my telephone."

Mercy caught her breath. Clarence.

The woman continued. "Said his phone's disconnected, and he needed to talk to you real bad. Well, this guy was so big I wasn't about to let him in my house. I mean to say, this man is—"

"What did he say?" Mercy snapped. Did this woman think Clarence was contaminated or something? "Is he okay?"

He wanted me to call an ambulance, but I thought they might bill me for the call, and I don't have extra money lying around for other people's emergencies and—"

"For goodness sake, this is an emergency and they're in danger. Just make the call!" She slammed down the phone and turned to Tedi. "Honey, get your clothes on now. We've got an emergency, and I've got to take you to Grandma's."

In five minutes, Mercy and Tedi were out the door. The last thing Mercy grabbed as they left was her beeper.

———

The ER secretary hung up her phone in distress. "Dr. Bower, Dr. Mercy doesn't answer at home. At first when I called, it was busy, and now I'm getting her answering machine."

"Try her work number. She'll be around somewhere."

Lukas's phone rang, and he picked it up. "Emergency room."

"Dr. Bower, could you please come down to Labor and Delivery?" It was Lauren, who had accompanied the soon-to-be mother. "This baby's coming fast, and we need a doctor."

"How far apart are the contractions?"

"Every one to two minutes."

"I'll be right there." He put down the phone and looked up to see Mrs. Pinkley walking into the ER with a grim-faced silent woman with a briefcase. It didn't look like he was going to make his first meeting. Great first impression with the terminator. *Mercy, where are you?*

He turned to Judy. "Do you have Dr. Mercy's beeper number?"

"Yes. I'll try it if she's not at the office."

"Good, and meanwhile I'll go down to see if I'm needed to catch a baby or run interference." With a helpless shrug at Mrs. Pinkley and guest, he rushed out the door, leaving Judy to explain his departure.

---

Using well-known shortcuts, Mercy delivered Tedi to Ivy's house and drove across downtown Knolls in ten minutes. She reached the Knights' dilapidated home, screeched the car to a halt in the driveway, and grabbed her bag. Just as she reached the front door, her beeper sounded in her pocket. She pulled it out and checked the calling number as she barged through the front door. A quick glance told her the number belonged to the ER desk. She could only hope that the neighbor who had called her must have also broken down and called the hospital. There was no way Mercy could leave Clarence and Darlene right now in search of a telephone.

"Clarence? Darlene? Where are you?" she shouted, trying to keep the alarm she felt from her voice.

"Doc!" came Clarence's deep, frantic voice from Darlene's bedroom. "In here. Hurry!"

Mercy raced down the short hallway to Darlene's tiny room, which was crammed with a twin-sized bed and a chest of drawers on one wall, with a computer, desk, and filing cabinets completing the cramped space. Clarence crouched in the tiny floor space between the bed and the closet door.

He was battling valiantly to continue holding his massive arm up and balance his weight to keep from falling as he helped his grayfaced sister with her inhaler. He was losing the battle, and fear and pain covered his face like an open wound.

Darlene was barely sitting up in bed, leaning back against the headboard, eyes closed. What Mercy noticed first was the silence. No wheezing, no breath sounds at all in the room except for Clarence's loud, frantic panting. Darlene looked as if she hadn't slept in two days.

"Take it in, sis!" Clarence turned pleading dark brown eyes to Mercy. "I can't help her. She won't do it for me. Can you do it, Doc?" His arm gave out, and the heavy load it had balanced now slumped back against the closet door with a groan of wood. His gaze reverted back to his sister's sagging form.

Mercy stepped in and squeezed past the computer to the other side of Darlene's narrow bed. She pulled the stethoscope from around her neck, but she knew what she would hear before she even placed it on Darlene's chest and back. She pulled out her breathing equipment and set it up, then placed the pulse oximetry unit onto Darlene's finger and waited for the $O_2$ sat and heart rate readings to kick in.

Nothing happened.

She took Darlene's pulse, and it was 125 BPM. To be expected. She removed the attachment from Darlene's finger to her ear and watched for a tiny *blip, blip* of reading to jump on the screen. It was disappointingly low. Darlene had maybe a reading of 75, and normal was 95 or better for a nonsmoker.

"What's it say, Mercy?" Clarence asked, still huffing, beads of sweat dripping from his face.

"Not good." Mercy glanced over at him. "You okay?"

He nodded. "Just take care of her, Doc. Please save her. Are they coming? Is the ambulance coming? I told the neighbor to call them."

"So did I. Just listen for the siren."

———

Scrubbed, gowned, and gloved, Lukas entered the delivery room to find the mother-to-be and her attendants the unwilling stars of an amateur movie production. While the husband, Jeremy, focused his camcorder from a few feet away, the OB nurse and Lauren placed the patient on a fetal monitor. She was already draped with cloths on a delivery table and had an IV in her left arm. Lukas knew Mercy's standing orders for blood work would have already been completed. An OB pack lay open on a metal tray beside the bed—cord clamps, forceps, scissors, baby towels, 4x4's, bulb syringes, tubes for drawing a cord blood and a cord gas. There was also an anesthetic for a midline episiotomy.

"I can't do this!" the patient said with a gasp, grabbing Lauren's arm. "Please, you've got to give me something. Why isn't Dr. Mercy here? She'd give me something for the pain."

Lauren glanced at Lukas. "Dr. Bower, she's fully dilated."

Lukas stepped forward and quickly checked beneath the draping. She hadn't crowned yet, but she would anytime. "I'm sorry, Melinda, but it's too late to give you anything now. We can't risk respiratory depression with the baby."

The mother-in-law snorted from the reclining chair at the other side of the delivery table. "Melinda, you should've listened to me. I told you not to take the time to change your clothes after your water broke."

"Rats!" Jeremy cried. "I forgot to change the battery before we left the house. I'll be just a second. Hold on."

"Are you crazy?" his mother shouted. "I can't believe I raised such a . . . Get over here and help your wife before I take that camcorder and hit you over the—"

Melinda cried out with another contraction. Lukas checked her again and instructed the OB nurse to prepare the anesthetic for the episiotomy. He checked the monitor and was relieved to find the heart rate holding well.

The perineum stretched, and Lukas injected and cut.

"Got it!" Jeremy shouted eight inches from Lukas's right ear.

Lukas gritted his teeth, held steady, and completed the procedure.

Just in time. The baby crowned. The nurses coached. The mother-in-law cried out in sympathetic agony, and Melinda screamed.

"All right!" Jeremy said. "Keep it coming! Yeah! Come on, honey, you can do it!"

Lukas watched the crowning head and gently coaxed it farther. "Okay, Melinda, good, the head's out. Now stop pushing and breathe deeply for a moment." He cleaned the baby's pale face of the heavy coating of natural lubricant that resembled cottage cheese while the father jockeyed noisily for a better viewing position.

"Doc, can you just move to the left a little? I want to see his face."

Lukas ignored him. "Okay, Melinda, now you can push again, but gently. We don't want—"

A low moan, followed by a loud crash of metal came from directly behind him, where Jeremy had been avidly taping the whole scene.

Melinda groaned again in pain. Her mother-in-law cried out and jumped up from the recliner and ran behind Lukas.

"Okay, the movie producer's out of the way for a moment," the OB nurse announced. "Too bad we didn't catch that moment on tape, Melinda. You'd have loved it. Dr. Bower, don't back up. You've got a crowd behind you. Lauren, I can take it from here if you want to check on the proud father."

As Lukas and the other nurse helped the new mother complete the birth, Lauren called for reinforcements with c-collar and backboard for Jeremy.

Lukas reached out and caught the emerging slippery baby boy—like a football, just as he'd been taught. The tight little face scrunched and his mouth opened. No sound came out. Lukas flicked the feet with his fingers, grabbed a towel and rubbed the baby's back, and felt a flood of relief when the cry came, strong and clear. He clamped and cut the cord and turned around with the baby—just in time to catch Lauren in the new little boy's urine stream.

———

Mercy's beeper went off again as she continued to work on Darlene. Once more, it was the hospital, but she couldn't do anything about it. She glanced at Clarence, whose puffy, bearded face betrayed his own physical pain. He had probably pulled one or two major leg muscles in his hurried trip to the neighbor to call for help.

And now that neighbor, who had even refused to allow Clarence into her house, might not have called an ambulance. Mercy vowed that once this whole thing was over, she would personally go to that woman's house and sock her in the mouth.

But this whole thing wasn't over, and as Clarence lay watching her with fear-filled eyes, Mercy realized that he and his sister were both getting worse. Darlene now had an irregular heart rate of 140. Her breath sounds, fast and shallow, were barely perceptible. She was failing.

Mercy reached into her bag and pulled out an ampule of Brethine, a bronchodilator that should open Darlene's bronchial tubes. Unfortunately, it could also increase the heart rate and drop the blood pressure even lower. But this was Mercy's last play. She injected the drug and hovered over the woman, waiting.

"I thought she was better until I saw her blue lips this morning," Clarence said, his deep voice seeming to rattle the closet door against which he leaned. "She stopped wheezing yesterday. I thought that meant she was getting better, but she wasn't, was she?"

"We don't know that for sure, Clarence." Mercy placed her stethoscope over Darlene's chest. Was that a slight wheeze she heard?

"Don't try to fool me, Doc. I should've caught it, and I didn't. I was so busy feeling sorry for myself, letting her wait on me and carry food and give me my medicine that I didn't even know she was getting worse."

"You're not a doctor," Mercy snapped. "Hush for a moment and let me listen."

At the sharp sound of Mercy's voice, Darlene opened her eyes.

"Feeling pretty rough?" Mercy asked her.

Darlene nodded. She opened her mouth to try to speak, but Mercy placed a finger over her lips. "I've given you a drug that I hope will help, and we're waiting for an ambulance."

*But what if no ambulance is coming? Shouldn't they be here by now?* Another reading of blood pressure showed no change. The heart rate did not increase past 140, but Mercy heard no sounds of wheezing, which would have indicated an improvement. The drug wasn't working yet.

"Just hold on, Darlene. Keep breathing for us."

"She's been quiet the past few days," Clarence said, "but I knew she was worried because she was behind with her work, so I didn't think about her being sick. They cut our phone off last Friday because we couldn't pay the bill, and Darlene was afraid she might not be able to make the house payment."

Mercy adjusted the mask over Darlene's gray face. "Clarence, the oxygen is helping some, but not enough. The breathing treatment isn't helping because she's not moving enough air, and we don't even know for sure if that neighbor of yours called for an ambulance. I've got to go find a telephone and—"

"No."

"I can't do anything else for her right now. We have to get help soon."

Clarence shook his head and rolled forward to heave himself up. "I've gotta do it, Mercy. You've gotta stay here in case . . ." He reached up for the threshold casing of the closet and pulled himself to his knees with a deep groan of pain. His face turned purple with the exertion of lifting five hundred pounds.

"Clarence, please."

"Get my cane." He gestured toward the far corner of the tiny room by the computer, where an old aluminum cane leaned against the wall. "I can make it. I've gotta make it for Darlene."

As he pulled himself to his feet, Mercy grabbed the cane and placed it in his hand. Sweat popped out on his face and bare torso. "Take care of Darlene." He heaved himself out of the room, leaning heavily on the thick cane. Mercy could hear his deep, gasping breaths and the groaning strain of the floorboards in the hallway until the front door closed behind him.

"Take care of him," came a breathy, whispered croak.

Mercy jerked back around to find Darlene watching her with tears in her eyes. "Hold on, Darlene."

"I'm not going to get through this, am I?" She was struggling for breath, fighting to stay awake, and Mercy could barely hear the words.

"Yes, you are. Clarence is going for help." Mercy returned to Darlene's side and once more inflated the blood pressure cuff. "We'll get you to a hospital and get you on a ventilator. Just keep going a little longer, Darlene."

Darlene reached up and touched Mercy's arm, her eyes closing once more. "Take care of my brother."

Ten minutes later, while Mercy did another check on Darlene's unchanging breath sounds with her stethoscope, she heard the faint, welcome call of a siren. Clarence had reached help.

# CHAPTER 13

Lukas winced at the disharmony of strong baby lungs and strident grandma lungs as he pulled off his gloves. He bent down and gently moved Jeremy's mother aside so he could examine the new father. Her labor pains had ended when her own baby dropped the camcorder.

The woman scrambled as close as she could to her son's other side. "He's bleeding, Doctor. Oh, my . . . what if he's got a concussion? Jeremy? Jeremy! Wake up, honey. I didn't mean those things I said."

"What happened?" Melinda demanded from the birthing cot. "Did something happen to Jeremy? What's going on?"

A two-inch-long streak of bright blood angled across Jeremy's forehead where he had connected with the corner of a metal utensil tray that had interrupted his sideways fall. Lukas checked Jeremy's airway, breathing, circulation, looked in his eyes, and nodded to himself. The man would be coming around any moment.

"We need to check him out," Lukas told the others. "He'll need some stitches, but he fell because he fainted at the sight of his son."

An exhausted chuckle reached him from the birthing cot. "Oh, is that all?" Melinda said weakly. "He'll be okay, then. He gets sick at the sight of blood. I told him he couldn't take it."

The mother's eyes widened behind her wire-framed glasses. "You're kidding! The big baby fainted?" She stared back down at her son, her expression metamorphosing from concern to disbelief to disgust. "How typical!" She shook her head and climbed to her feet with a grunt, then walked back over to the bedside. "Oh, Melinda, honey, I'm so sorry," she said, patting her daughter-in-law's hand. "This is so humiliating."

Jeremy opened his eyes and blinked up at Lukas, then groaned and tried to rise, but Lukas put a hand on the young man's bony left shoulder and eased him back down. "Just stay put and we'll all be safer. Someone is on the way down to take you to the emergency room so we can check you out."

"Are they okay?" Jeremy asked.

"Your wife and baby are fine, but I'm not an electronics expert, so you'll have to get a diagnosis on your camcorder from somebody else."

Amanda rushed through the wide delivery room door with a gurney, on which lay a c-collar and spine board. "All right! A new baby! Way to go!" She instantly saw Jeremy splayed out on the floor and lowered the adjustable gurney to make it easier to transport the patient. "Lauren, will you give me a hand? Dr. Bower, as I was on my way in here, we got a call about a bad asthma coming in by ambulance. They're about six minutes out."

"Okay, thanks. Keep me posted." Lukas took the c-collar from Amanda and placed it around Jeremy's neck. Together, he and Amanda logrolled the patient onto his side, strapped him onto the backboard, then transferred him onto the gurney. As Lauren and Amanda wheeled Jeremy out, Lukas grabbed another pair of gloves and turned back to his other two patients. The efficient, seasoned OB nurse had already shown the baby to the mother and taken him over to place him beneath a radiant warmer. Melinda, the new mother, needed attention.

"Oh, and, Dr. Bower?" Amanda continued as they started to push Jeremy out of the room. "The ambulance attendant told us that Dr. Mercy is with them. She was at the scene with the patient when they arrived."

Lukas frowned. "She's in the ambulance?"

"That's what they said."

Immediately, Lukas knew. Darlene. . . . Hadn't he discussed this very thing with Mercy a few days ago?

"After all that trouble, I hope he didn't break that stupid camcorder." Jeremy's mother once more leaned over her daughter-in-law and dabbed the younger woman's forehead with a wet towel. "My boy means well, even if he is a wimp. He's just always loved his gadgets." She glanced in the direction of her new grandson. "How's that baby doing?"

"Looking good," the nurse assured her without looking up from her work. "Great Apgar test scores. He's got a good strong heart rate, and he's pink from head to toe."

"Now we just have to deliver the placenta," Lukas said as he positioned himself to complete the job.

Melinda grimaced. "Jeremy's going to be okay? Ouch, I'm cramping! Did he even get the baby on film?"

"Now, now." The new grandmother continued to pat Melinda's face with the towel. "He's going to be fine, just like the baby. Maybe a scar on the forehead will make my son think about *you* next time you're in labor, instead of his little gadgets."

Melinda's eyes widened at her mother-in-law. "*Next* time?"

———

Tedi found Abby sitting out by the trees on the playground, watching a last-minute game of baseball before school began for the day. Mr. Walters had been encouraging them to practice for the past two weeks so they would be ready to play the other sixth-grade team Thursday. Tedi dreaded it. She could beat everybody in sixth or seventh grade in a spelling bee but couldn't control a baseball with a bat or a glove, and she didn't want to learn.

She walked over and sank down onto the grass beside her best friend. "Why aren't you playing, Abby? You're their star hitter."

Abby pointed to her bandages. "I don't have my stitches out."

"So? That didn't stop you last week."

Abby shrugged and looked down, ignoring the game. That wasn't like her, either.

"What's wrong?" Tedi asked.

"Nothing."

Tedi knew what it was. "They're fighting again, aren't they?"

Abby pushed her glasses up her nose and nodded.

"Sorry."

"Yeah, I know."

The bell rang. Tedi groaned and started to get up, when the bell rang again, and then again, in short bursts.

"All right!" the pitcher on the mound shouted. "Fire drill! We're gonna get out of class."

Tedi groaned. "That's silly. Why are we having a fire drill before we're supposed to be in—"

Abby gasped and pointed toward the cafeteria at the east end of the long elementary school building. Gray smoke billowed from one of the open windows. "It's a real fire!"

The fire alarm continued its blast, echoing across the large grassy playground behind the building. Wide-eyed with excitement and fear, Tedi and Abby got up and joined the ballplayers at the spot by the flagpole where their class was supposed to stand. They watched kids and teachers and the principal and secretaries file out of the doors of the building and walk toward them, just like they'd done during the drill they had three weeks ago.

Mr. Walters came rushing out from the west exit, herding two other kids in front of him. His slightly chubby belly jiggled over his belt, and his right hand grasped his attendance book. He directed the two kids to join Tedi and Abby and the ballplayers, and as soon as he reached them, he started roll call, just like the other teachers.

The bell continued its sharp report. Before Mr. Walters finished calling out the list of kids' names, a siren joined the jangle of the bell. Another siren soon joined it. The flashing red lights of two blaring red trucks raced toward them down the street from the direction of the fire station.

The smell of the smoke reached Tedi as the trucks pulled into the school drive. More trucks arrived, and men jumped out and unwound huge hoses from their trucks. They connected the hoses to the fire hydrant at the back of the school, and with two men per hose, they shot their forceful streams of water at the fire.

The smoke turned to sizzling steam as the men shouted to one another and fought the hoses. One skinny man kept running around, tripping over the hoses, until another fireman walked over to him and jerked on his arm. Together they entered the school building.

"Do you think the cooks are okay?" Abby asked.

Tedi nodded and pointed toward the school staff. The cooks all mingled with the secretaries at the far end of the group.

About the time the final wisp of smoke disappeared, Tedi saw Grandma pull her car into the front drive and wave at them. They'd been dismissed from school for the day.

That was it? That was all the excitement they were going to have today? No screams, no explosions, no collapsing buildings? Just wisps of smoke and a few fire hoses, and it was finished?

Tedi sighed and walked toward Grandma's car. Oh well, at least nobody was hurt. Time to go home.

---

In the ambulance, Mercy's physical tension rose and fell with the sound of the siren above her and the constant *beep-beep* of Darlene's monitor. Sitting in the jump seat at the head of the cot, she squeezed the ambu bag with increasing frequency. Darlene had to struggle to take in a breath. This left Connie, the paramedic, free to keep track of the blood pressure and monitor and establish a second IV en route to the hospital. She was just as efficient inserting the second IV as she had been with the first, but Mercy noticed with concern that this time, when the needle pricked Darlene's flesh, there was no reaction, not even a flinch. And Mercy was having to use more and more force to move air through the ambu bag because of Darlene's decreased responsiveness and muscle tone. Darlene was too worn out to breathe.

Less than four minutes from the hospital, Connie rechecked the monitor and inflated the blood pressure cuff. "Dr. Mercy, I can barely hear a pressure." She checked for a pulse, then looked up at Mercy in alarm. "She's in shock. We've got to intubate."

"Give her fifty milligrams of lidocaine first."

"I've got it ready."

Mercy watched Connie administer the drug through the IV, then she removed the bag mask and changed places to allow the paramedic to do the intubation. "You do it, Connie. It's what you're good at, and you do it often." Mercy was too emotionally involved at this point.

Connie was smooth, very experienced, and the tube slid in quickly, but too late they saw that in spite of the medication, the tube triggered a sudden bad reaction. The monitor alarm shot through the van.

"She's in v-tach," Connie said, checking the pulse again. "I'm not getting anything."

Mercy pressed Darlene's throat in search of the carotid artery. Nothing. She turned toward the driver. "Bernie, call the hospital. Tell them to call Air Care. Tell them we're coming in with a code."

———

Lukas stood in the ambulance bay as the code team continued to assemble in the ER. He had already told the secretary to call the chopper, on Mercy's instructions. He saw Mercy and Connie bent over someone in the back of the van. He knew for sure it was Darlene Knight before they opened the double back doors and wheeled her out.

He felt sick.

He stepped forward to help them. Connie recited the patient summary to him, continuing chest compressions as she spoke.

Lukas caught sight of tears shining from Mercy's face, but he had no time to dwell on that. Darlene had crashed hard, and they would have their hands full bringing her back. And they had to bring her back. They *had* to. *Please, God.*

———

Mercy continued to squeeze the bag as the code team worked over Darlene and Lukas ordered drugs. She only released her position when Lukas placed the paddles on Darlene's chest for defibrillation. All stood back.

"Clear."

The body arched, the monitor sang, and then a steady rhythm beeped across the room from the monitor. Mercy felt fresh hot tears— this time of relief. She ducked her head and blinked, scattering the tears over her flexing arms. This was no good! She couldn't fall apart like this. She felt a hand on her arm and looked up as Lukas gently took over the bagging for her and nudged her aside.

"We've got extra help now, and the chopper's almost here," he said under cover of the monitor beep. "Go blow your nose."

She went, feeling helpless, inept. After working with patients for more than ten years, she had learned to protect her emotions, to distance herself from the suffering so that she could most effectively help those who depended on her calm judgment. This one had cut deep, had shaken her more completely than her first code blue as an intern, and she hadn't even run this resuscitation effort herself.

And what about Clarence? She'd left him slumped on the front porch of his house, frantic about his sister, and grimacing in pain from pulled muscles. There was no way to call him.

She did as she was told and blew her nose and wiped her face, but she would not leave the ER. After rechecking the progress on Darlene, she turned to watch through the plate glass windows for a helicopter to appear in the sky. She listened for the pulsing thrusts of echoing blades that would be her first assurance that help was arriving.

Instead, she saw Buck Oppenheimer wheel into the ambulance bay in his big red pickup truck. He wasn't supposed to be doing that. What was going on?

Then she saw Clarence Knight riding shotgun, his massive bulk taking up half the cab.

Mercy ran into the ER proper, grabbed their sturdiest wheelchair and pressed the automatic sliding doors of the ambulance entrance. When she stepped out with the chair, she saw two more cars pulling up behind Buck's pickup. Altogether, five men climbed out.

Buck jumped from his truck and came around the front. "Hi, Dr. Mercy. I heard about what was happening over the radio. I drove over to check things out, but you had already left with Darlene. I saw Clarence sitting on the front step of their porch." He shrugged. "I was off duty, so I rounded up a few friends. I think he's pulled some muscles in his right leg, and his lower back is hurting pretty badly, but as far as I can tell, he's okay otherwise."

"Thank you, Buck. Is he complaining of pain anywhere else? Is his breathing—"

Clarence shoved the door open and leaned out, his big body nearly toppling from the truck as the men rushed forward to catch him. His hair and beard were wet from perspiration. He wore his usual short pants, covered by a huge ragged T-shirt that barely covered his torso, and the worn pair of black house shoes Mercy had seen many times before—the only ones he owned.

"Where is she, Mercy? Is she okay?" He allowed the men to help him squeeze into the big wheelchair, but his deep brown eyes held

Mercy's, and he reached toward her. "Tell me she's still alive!"

"We had to resuscitate her, Clarence, and we're airlifting her to Cox South in Springfield." She spread her hands helplessly. "Lukas is working on her now. I'm sorry, but she hasn't regained consciousness."

"But she's alive?"

"She's alive." Who knew how long that would last?

"I've got to see her. Please let me see her." He let his arms fall over the sides of the wheelchair and looked down at himself, at the men struggling to push him into the ER, and his face contorted. Tears filled his already reddened eyes. "What have I done? I let this happen. What have I done?"

Mercy put a hand on his shoulder.

He leaned back and moaned as the men wheeled him through the doors.

Mercy bent over him. "Clarence, are you having pain in your chest?" His numbers had been good the past few weeks, but—

"It's not my heart. It's just pulled muscles." He laid his head back. "Please let me see Darlene."

They pushed him to the broad door of the first trauma room. Lukas and Lauren worked with two nurses from upstairs as they continued to watch Darlene and take her vitals and help her breathe.

Clarence's gaze shot immediately to the monitor. "Is she awake, Doc?"

Lukas shook his head. "No, Clarence, not yet, but we just got word that the chopper's getting ready to land. You could probably hear it if you were outside." He gestured toward the group of men who encircled Clarence's wheelchair. "We'll have to clear out for them to come in and get her."

Mercy stepped forward. "Let's put Clarence in room three, guys. There's a sturdy Stryker bed in there, and I want to do an assessment on him and take care of some of that pain."

"I'll take him, Mercy," Lukas said as the rotor echo of the helicopter reached them and the shadow of a huge bird darkened the landing pad outside. "I'll be with him as soon as they take Darlene. You've got patients in Labor and Delivery."

Connie came rushing over to them from the central desk, where she'd been working on her ambulance-run sheet. "We just got word that there's been another fire." She glanced at Mercy and grimaced. "Sorry, Dr. Mercy, but it was at your daughter's school, in the kitchen."

The breath left Mercy's lungs as if she'd been kicked. As the flight team trooped through the automatic doors to collect their patient, and Buck and his buddies unloaded Clarence into room three, Mercy rushed to the nearest desk phone to call the school.

The line was busy. She disconnected and started to punch her mother's number, when Judy turned around from a phone call.

"Dr. Mercy, that was your office. Your mother called to let you know that Tedi's safe. Nobody was hurt except for one fireman. They're bringing him in."

———

"If I tell you something, will you promise not to tell anyone?" Abby asked Tedi as they waited for Grandma to end another long conversation with another friend in the supermarket.

Tedi studied Abby's serious expression. "Okay. What?"

"I'm not going to call Mom or Dad."

"But you have to! They'll hear about the fire, and they'll call the school and find out you're not there."

Abby pushed her glasses up, scrunched her face, and nodded. "They'll come looking for me, and they won't find me. That'll scare 'em to death."

"That's stupid." Tedi forgot to keep her voice down. "Why would you do that? You want them to worry about you?" She would never do that to her parents. Never on purpose, anyway.

"Shh! Shut up! You promised not to tell!"

Tedi lowered her voice. "But Grandma told you to call right after she called Mom's office. Why would you not tell your parents?"

"I told you Friday night, remember?" Abby pointed to her bandaged leg. "Every time something happens to me, they forget to fight. Mom will cry, and Dad will put his arm around her, and then they'll remember they are part of one family, and they belong together."

Grandma said good-bye to her friend and turned back to them with sandwiches from the deli section. "Ready to go, girls?" She strode toward the checkout counter. "Let's get out of here before we run into somebody else we know."

Abby nudged Tedi. "Remember, you promised."

# CHAPTER 14

Mercy checked on Melinda and baby and did the episiotomy repair. Lukas had done an excellent job. He had cut just right, and Melinda needed few stitches. In fact, Mercy made such good time that Lukas was still working on Jeremy in the ER when she returned downstairs.

She walked into exam room three to find Clarence holding on to both sides of the Stryker bed as if he thought he might tumble off. His eyes held the glazed look of a drugged patient hovering just above the grip of pain. Mercy checked the chart and discovered that Lukas had already assessed him and administered a muscle relaxer and pain medication.

"You don't have to hold on so tight, Clarence," she said as she entered and patted him on the arm. "The rails are up. You won't fall."

His eyes shifted to her, and he blinked in slow motion. He didn't reply, but his fingers loosened their grip slightly.

"You're going to be okay, pal. Are you feeling a little woozy from the muscle relaxer Lukas gave you?"

"Kinda . . . some . . . little," came Clarence's weakened, out-of-focus voice.

"Good, that'll keep you out of my hair for a while," she teased. "Looks like Lukas also gave you a shot for pain."

"Hate drugs."

"Nonsense, they're good for you. They saved your hide this summer, didn't they?"

He grunted. "Maybe that's not all that saved me." His eyes closed again. "Lukas said he was praying for me."

Yep, Clarence was drugged. He resisted help from everybody. Why should God be any different?

"Clarence, you've got some badly pulled muscles, and we're going to admit you and keep you on IV muscle relaxants and pain medication for a while so you can heal. In the meantime, I'll keep in touch with Cox South about Darlene."

" 'Zat the best place for her?" The big man's words slurred, and his eyes remained closed.

"I think so. They'll take good care of her there."

"C'n I go up?"

"Sorry, Clarence, I'm admitting you here. You're in no condition to travel."

His eyes opened with a great deal of effort, and his expression, with those dark, fathomless eyes, was one of helplessness, like a trusting child's. "But—"

"You're not in any condition to argue, either, so don't start with me." Ordinarily, Mercy couldn't get away with this, so she was going to use her opportunity while she had it. "We'll monitor Darlene's progress, and they'll call us when anything changes. You'll know as soon as we hear anything." She adjusted the sheet that covered him and watched his lids drift back down slowly with great effort, as if he fought their closure with every ounce of wakefulness he could muster.

Five minutes later, as his deep, rumbling snores echoed out of the room and across the ER, Mercy adjusted Clarence's heavy arms into a more comfortable position and patted him gently on the shoulder.

---

Lukas smiled to himself as he finished Jeremy's stitches to the bass accompaniment of Clarence's sleeping serenade. Mercy and Clarence had struck sparks off each other from their very first meeting last spring. Clarence the bullheaded giant had met his match in Mercy. Lukas wondered if he had, too. She was all he thought about lately.

Another ambulance pulled into the bay soon after Lukas stepped out of the laceration room. He watched as the EMS crew wheeled young Explorer fireman Kyle Alder from the back of the van and turned to push him through the automatic doors. Unlike Buck's blackened and singed appearance after the fire two weeks ago, Kyle's face was clear and unburned. Only a faint whiff of smoke accompanied him and two of the seasoned firemen into the ER.

". . . don't think it was a grease fire," one of the firemen was explaining to the EMT who pushed the patient in. "They found an empty baby jar that was still wet inside. Smelled like some kind of solvent. The fire was going good when the cooks came in, but it didn't take much to put it out."

The EMT looked up at Lukas. "Where do you want him, Dr. Bower?"

Lukas gestured toward exam room five and noted with approval that the BLS, basic life support, ambulance team had properly placed the oxygen mask over Kyle's face and immobilized him on a backboard with a c-collar.

The EMT gave Lukas the vitals. "He's complaining of pain in his right shoulder, Dr. Bower."

As Lukas bent over Kyle with his stethoscope, he caught sight of the two older firemen standing in the open doorway to the room.

Kyle moaned, and Lukas turned his attention back to the curly haired eighteen-year-old, whose smooth face sported only a few sparse hairs along his chin line. "Hello, Kyle, I'm Dr. Bower. Remember me? I was here when you brought Buck in a couple of weeks ago."

"Yeah, I remember," Kyle said hoarsely. "You're the guy who found that metal in his—" he broke off and moaned again.

"Are you having any trouble breathing?" Lukas asked.

"No, but my shoulder sure hurts. I hit it rolling, and I guess I didn't fall just right."

One of the firemen in the doorway cleared his throat. "Instead of assisting the real firemen who were putting out the fire, this fancy pants kept tripping over hoses and getting in the way. When I took him inside to get him out from underfoot, he decided he had to check the storeroom for people, so he went jumping over the fire, hit the floor with his shoulder, and rolled against the wall."

Kyle grimaced. "I thought I heard somebody back there."

The fireman shook his head in disgust. "If you'd've listened to me, you'd've known the cooks were already out. I wanted you to follow orders. You should be glad your time's about up with us, or you'd get yourself or somebody else killed."

The man's partner muttered, "He should thank Buck. We'll be waiting out in the hallway, Dr. Bower. We've had orders to baby-sit."

At the hurt expression that crossed Kyle's face, Lukas felt irritated by the older firemen. They didn't have to be so cruel.

Lukas gestured for Lauren to begin her assessment while he checked Kyle's shoulder for pain and point tenderness.

"Guess I really blew it," Kyle murmured as Lukas pressed his fingers against the boy's collarbone.

"Your shoulder doesn't look broken or dislocated," Lukas assured him.

"I mean with the fire," Kyle muttered. "Everybody's mad at me. Nobody thinks I can do anything right. Buck won't even show me how to handle a hose, and when I tried to do it when he wasn't on shift, I lost control."

"Maybe they'll give you another chance," Lukas said. "Nobody gets everything right the first time."

Kyle looked up at him with grateful eyes. "Thanks, Dr. Bower. I needed that. Buck just doesn't like me for some reason, but I know my stuff. I've read everything I can get my hands on ever since I was in eleventh grade. I'll get it down. I know I will. I just need more time." He reached up and tugged at the c-collar. "This thing feels like it's choking me."

"I think we can remove it and the backboard in a moment."

"Did you hear what they said about the solvent in the baby jar? At least they got that part right. We found it as soon as we got into the kitchen." He glanced around the room and lowered his voice. "I saw that same jar at the firehouse. I think it's an inside job. Everybody knows Buck uses that stuff for his model airplanes. He's got them spread out all over the place."

"You mean you think somebody's trying to set Buck up?"

"Looks like it to me." Kyle winced again. "Man, that hurts. Are you sure it isn't broken?"

"I can't be sure of that until I've checked the x-rays. Don't worry, Kyle, we'll take care of you." Lukas walked out the door to the desk.

The firemen who had brought Kyle in sat talking in straight-backed chairs ten feet away from the central desk, and it was difficult for Lukas not to hear their words as the conversation floated over him.

"Did they check the jar for fingerprints?"

"They're doing it now. Don't guess anybody saw anything around the school this morning."

"Some old woman across the street claimed she caught sight of a man running out the back way about fifteen minutes before the cooks got there."

"Any description?"

"Just that it was a big man with broad shoulders. He was wearing a ball cap. Shoot, she could've been describing me."

"Only if he looked like he had a watermelon under his shirt."

There was a grumble of protest, then a moment of silence.

"No sign of forced entry."

"Nope. That don't mean anything. Half the town has keys. Speaking of security, the police hadn't been by there in a couple of hours." There was another moment of silence, and they glanced at Lukas and lowered their voices. "We'd have money for more manpower for police *and* fire department if we didn't have to spend it all on—"

"Watch it, Joe."

They fell silent and looked at Lukas again, then changed the subject.

"Guess Buck's leavin' town for a few days. He needs the break from his training duties."

"I'll say. He's been acting awfully weird lately. Did you see the fit he pitched down at Little Mary's Saturday? You could've seen steam coming out of his ears. Could've heard him shouting out on the street. Never seen him do that before. He's about to lose it."

"I wasn't too happy with that waitress, either. She's blaming us for the fires. Told Buck we were probably starting the fires just so he could play hero again."

"She was just teasing."

"Buck didn't take it that way. He's scheduled to work again Saturday. I just hope he comes back."

"You'd better, 'cause until he gets back, we're stuck with that kid in there."

The partner groaned. "Maybe this injury will keep him out of commission for a week or so, at least until we can dump him back in Buck's lap."

————

When Mercy finally walked into her office Monday morning, her small waiting room was filled with gossiping patients and groaning complaints and laughing, mixed with squealing children as they played with the new toys and books in the playroom. Josie had done some rescheduling, but they would still have to hustle to get a lunch break today.

Mercy was reading a chart on her first patient when she caught the faint whiff of White Shoulders perfume, Mom's signature fragrance. She turned to find her mother and daughter standing at the entrance to her office. Several strands of Ivy's long white-streaked hair had fallen from a knot at the back of her head, and her shirttail was untucked. They had all been rushed by the excitement this morning.

Tedi, in a long-sleeved T-shirt and worn jeans, rushed from her grandmother's side to Mercy's open arms. "Is your patient okay, Mom? Did you get to her in time?"

Mercy kissed her daughter's forehead. "I don't know yet, honey. She's in a coma, and we flew her to Cox South. Did you have an interesting time at school this morning?"

"Yeah, it was fun to watch the firemen. They put the fire out fast, though, so it wasn't as exciting as in the movies. They let school out for the day. I wanted Grandma Ivy to bring me here to see if everything was okay with you, and then she's taking Abby and me to a picnic on the river, since Abby's parents are both at work, and she doesn't have anyplace else to stay. Abby's out in the car."

The sound of Tedi's chatter calmed something in Mercy, and she leaned back to look down into her daughter's concerned eyes, then hugged her again, relishing the feel of her sturdy five-foot-tall body.

"Were you worried about me, Mom?" Tedi asked.

"Yes. I'm glad you came by." She kissed Tedi again, then looked past her to Ivy. "Does this upset your plans for today, Mom?"

"Are you kidding? I've been going stir crazy this past month with Tedi back in school. We'll have a great time, and we'll see you tonight." Ivy held out her hand toward her granddaughter. "Come on, kiddo. We've got to get back to that car before Abby drives off and leaves us."

Tedi paused and looked once more into Mercy's eyes. "Mom, are you going to be okay?"

"Yeah, thanks, honey. I'm much better now."

---

Estelle Pinkley's large upstairs corner office had tinted windows that took up a third of the wall space and overlooked a quiet residential neighborhood interspersed with mature oak and maple trees. The maples were showing the change of season with a golden warmth that Lukas took time to admire while he waited for Mrs. Pinkley to bring the COBRA investigator into the room. He sat down in a straight-backed chair facing the windows, then wondered if the light coming in would put him at a disadvantage in the interview. He stood up and crossed to the chair at the far right of Estelle's huge desk. There, that was better. It was probably silly for an interim ER director to play musical chairs, but since he was two hours late for his meeting, he'd better take any advantage he could get.

Voices alerted him to Estelle's arrival with the investigator, and he silently began to quote one of his favorite verses. *"Do not be anxious about anything, but in everything, by prayer and petition, with thanksgiving, present your requests to God."* Now, if he could just keep that going in his mind as a constant litany for the next hour or so. *Thank you, Lord, for Mrs. Pinkley's indomitable will. Protect us both from COBRA.*

Mrs. Pinkley stepped into the thick-carpeted room wearing her usual attire of suit jacket and skirt, this time in gunmetal gray with a white blouse. She had every hair in place, and her face held no expression. She stood aside as a woman followed her into the room.

Lukas remembered his manners and stood while Estelle introduced him to Ms. Francis Fellows, a young woman who couldn't have been more than twenty-five, with short straight blond hair and wire-framed glasses. Her complexion looked as if she'd made up this morning with pale pink Liquid Paper. She shook Lukas's hand weakly and did not smile. Lukas felt as if he could inhale the tension in the room. He waited for the two women to be seated, then managed to sit down without turning the chair over.

"I'm sorry I wasn't able to meet with you earlier," Lukas began. "We had several emergencies at one time, and I couldn't leave."

"That's fine." Ms. Fellows pulled a pad of forms from the wide pocket of her tailored suit jacket. "This is a preliminary meeting and shouldn't take long." Her voice lacked inflection, as if she had memorized the lines. "Dr. Bower, I need to ask you some questions about the Dwayne Little case and your refusal to prescribe pain medication for a patient obviously in pain."

"Dwayne Little was not obviously in pain." Lukas kept his voice as monotone as hers. "I did not refuse to give pain medication. I offered two different medications for his alleged migraine, and he became angry and left against medical advice."

Ms. Fellows wrote something on her pad. "We show no AMA report from anyone other than you, Dr. Bower, so you had no witnesses?"

"I had one witness, my nurse, who did not fill out a form."

The woman looked up at him. "We will want to interview her, if possible. Would you have given Mr. Little a suitable narcotic if he had not left?"

"Objection," Mrs. Pinkley said suddenly from her place of observation behind her desk. "That question calls for conjecture, not facts." She smiled to temper her words, but the smile did nothing to cover the keen intelligence and insight behind Estelle's calm gaze. "You'll have to excuse me. I was an active attorney in this county for thirty-five years before I retired and took this position as hospital administrator. Sometimes I have trouble keeping my opinions to myself."

Lukas watched as some of the already sparse color drained from young Ms. Fellows' face. He could tell she did not appreciate the intrusion, but she was going to have to get used to it. For fifteen years Estelle Pinkley had been known as the most formidable prosecuting attorney in Knolls County, and her reputation had spread all the way to the state capital in Jefferson City. Several times she had been urged to run for the office of state senator, and as many times she had declined nomination. Estelle's roots were always solidly in Knolls, and now they were just as solidly rooted in this hospital.

Ms. Fellows turned back to Lukas, her gaze cold, her tone colder. "What I will be striving to discover during this investigation is whether or not this case falls under COBRA jurisdiction, which I believe it does. Next I will be determining whether or not Mr. Little received ethical treatment for pain. If I find—"

"Excuse me, Ms. Fellows," Lukas interrupted, suddenly angry. "I can tell you what ethical treatment entails. First of all, it does *not* entail handing out morphine every time someone comes in off the street and demands it. I'm not a pusher. I'm a doctor. I took a solemn oath to that effect, a part of which is to employ only those recognized methods of treatment consistent with good judgment. I could not in good conscience give morphine to Dwayne Little that day." He glanced at Estelle and caught the barest shake of her head, and he fell silent.

"If I may continue," Ms. Fellows snapped. "If I find this case to have been inappropriately managed, we can fine you and the hospital twenty-five thousand dollars for each violation we uncover, and we can recommend that the hospital dismiss you. If this hospital does not dismiss you, we can give them six months to correct the problem, or they will lose Medicare and Medicaid funding." Her voice went from cold to antagonistic.

"I'm sure you are aware that emergency departments are not allowed to refuse Medicare or Medicaid patients," she continued, "and that without government funding this hospital would go out of business. Some hospitals receive up to eighty percent of their funding from government entitlements."

"How long will this investigation last?" Lukas asked, this time with an attempt to keep his voice well modulated.

She held his gaze with a hard stare. "As long as I see fit to continue discovery. And my discovery does not have to be limited to this one particular case. If I even sense a lack of cooperation from you or Mrs. Pinkley or anyone else in this hospital, I can, and will open other files at my discretion, including confidential peer reviews. Your malpractice insurance will not cover our fines." She stuffed her pad back into her pocket and stood up. "I'll be in touch." Without waiting for him to play gentleman and stand, she saw herself out the door.

Lukas felt cold tingles of anger and worry make tracks up his spine. After she disappeared out the door, he slumped in his seat and stifled a groan. "Oh boy, I blew it that time. Why can't I learn to keep my mouth shut at the right time?"

"Don't get all worked up, Lukas," Estelle warned him. "I like the old commercial that says 'never let 'em see you sweat.' If they sense any weakness, they think they have something on you, and they'll go for the jugular."

Lukas scowled. "She's after more than my jugular. She's already got it in a death grip."

"Don't let her fool you. Most COBRA investigators try to be fair-minded." The older woman's eyes narrowed thoughtfully. "This one's got another agenda. I picked up on that when she first got here. Let's just wait and see what she's up to."

"And use me as bait? In this gal's eyes I'm guilty until proven innocent. That's not the way the justice system's supposed to work. How can they get away with this?"

"She hasn't—yet."

"That's encouraging."

"Oh, come on, Lukas." She sat back in her chair and folded her hands together. "You know doctors are always in the hot seat. You're not allowed to be human and make mistakes like the rest of the human race. Lives are at stake."

"I don't think it's lives people are worried about as much as money," Lukas complained, surprising himself with his own bitterness. And he realized after he said it that he meant it. "Even when we do everything right, some money seeker is going to look for a way to cry foul, and there's greed at every level. They can always find plenty of 'expert' physicians willing to help them turn the screws on a colleague for a cut."

Estelle nodded, unfazed by his cynicism. "Hey, this is America. We're nothing if not litigious, but keep in mind this isn't a lawsuit. If it were, your malpractice insurance would cover you, no matter what the decision about your actions."

"Thanks for the reminder," Lukas grumbled. "I didn't make a mistake with Dwayne Little. He was a drug seeker." And Lukas was at the mercy of Francis Fellows, who had obviously already made her judgment.

He thought about the whopping school loans he had yet to pay off, and the house mortgage, and the bills he had willingly incurred for Clarence and Darlene. There was very little in his pockets except for lint. He had a generous income, which was good, but his bank account worked like a financial sieve. If the hospital didn't pick up his malpractice insurance, he'd be living in a tent in the Mark Twain National Forest. Come to think of it, that might not be so—

"The present legislation is a reaction to fraudulent medical personnel," Estelle said, breaking into his thoughts. "Many hospital emergency departments used to have the unethical practice of checking on a patient's ability to pay before they accepted the patient for emergency treatment. Hospitals would play 'hot potato' with unwanted patients. COBRA is the result of government reaction to that practice. Unfortunately, human beings also operate the government, and so the corruption continues."

"And the honest people suffer for it on both sides of the medical fence." Lukas had to remind himself that the only perfect society would be heaven, and his expertise would not be needed there.

Estelle nodded and stood. "Sorry, Lukas, it's a part of your education as a director."

Lukas stood and took her outstretched hand. The meeting was over, but he didn't feel any better. He never did want to be the ER director. Now was not a good time to address that, but after this was all over, if he still had a job, and if the hospital was still a hospital and not just another money-maker for some power-drunk HMO, he would resign from his red-tape duties and concentrate on treating patients.

# CHAPTER 15

A t ten o'clock on Wednesday morning, Mercy walked down the street from her office to the hospital. She had lab reports to collect and patient rounds to do, and this short walk was the only exercise she would have for the day, except for her hops between exam rooms in the clinic. If she wasn't careful, Mom would buy her a treadmill and attach a pedometer to her waist.

To prevent this from happening, Mercy climbed the stairs to the second floor instead of taking the elevator.

She knocked at the threshold of room 232, then stepped into the room. All rooms in this sixty-bed hospital were private. It was one of the first things Estelle Pinkley did when she became the administrator.

Clarence lay in drugged listlessness in his bed with the raised cold metal rails pressing into the flesh of his right side. The hospital gown he wore looked like a bib on his huge shoulders, and a sheet was pulled up to his waist for modesty—probably by a kindhearted nurse, since it would have been difficult for him to reach down for the sheet, even without his injuries. His eyes were closed, but at the sound of Mercy's quiet footsteps he opened them.

"Good morning, Clarence. Did you get my message earlier about Darlene?"

"Yeah." His voice was heavy with worry. His sister was still in a coma.

"As I told you yesterday, Darlene is in the best place possible, and my secretary will be checking on her again today. They promised they would call if there was a change. How's the pain?" She retrieved the clipboard with his chart from the end rail of the bed and stepped over to his side.

"Still there."

His voice, usually loud and rumbling, barely reached her, and she watched him worriedly as she checked the chart for vitals, medication, and urine output. "You know, Clarence, your weight has gone down extensively with fluid loss since you've been in here. Are you sure you were taking the Lasix at home every day?"

He looked away and didn't answer.

She pulled a pen from her pocket and jotted a memo on the chart. "I thought Darlene was the only one I had to lecture about hoarding drugs."

A muscle twitched at the side of his mouth. He stared out the window. "Just trying to stretch it out. I got tired of going to the bathroom every ten minutes. I figured if I just cut it down a little, that would make it easier on me and the floor. And my back."

"Your back?" Mercy crossed her arms and leaned against the windowsill. "You mean you were having trouble with your back and you didn't tell me about it?"

He shrugged and looked at her. "And what could you do about it? You've already said it's just pulled muscles."

"I didn't say *just* pulled muscles. Pain is a real thing, a signal that your body is not functioning properly, or that there is a threat to your health. It is not something you can ignore until it goes away." She had to stop and remind herself not to lecture too severely. He was worried about his sister, so she softened her voice. "You don't need me to tell you what happens when you ignore your body's signals, do you?" Clarence had been fighting all summer against the effects of type II diabetes and chronic heart failure—both due to his obesity.

"If you damage the muscles further, you'll be out of commission longer. And if you don't take the medication the way I've prescribed, you're going to have trouble, not just with your body, but with *me*." She leaned forward and tapped his arm to emphasize her point.

He watched her for a moment. "How much weight did I lose?"

"Would you believe twenty-five pounds?"

He stared at her in disbelief. "In water weight?"

"Exactly. If you'd taken your medication the way I asked in the first place—" She broke off, once more biting back irritable words.

She took a slow, deep breath, reminding herself of the pain and worry Clarence had suffered in the past two days. "I just wish you'd trust me a little more. Now, tell me about the pain. And this time, tell me the *truth*."

He took a deep breath and looked once more out the window. "My back's killing me."

"The muscle relaxers aren't helping?"

"Yeah, they help for a while, and then the pain comes back."

"Then why didn't you tell me?"

"Because you'd just give me more drugs."

When it came to macho stubbornness, Clarence held a master's degree. That was one reason for his condition right now. He refused to ask for help. Mercy and Lukas had been making house calls to the Knights all summer, and the only way either of them ever found out if Clarence was hurting was when Darlene whispered it to them.

"I don't want to be doped up all the time, Mercy," he growled.

"I understand that, and I know how you hate drugs, but you're not in here for the fun of it. We need to keep those muscles relaxed so they have time to heal. You don't want to keep reinjuring them, do you?"

"That stuff constipates me."

"Then we'll unconstipate you. What about your leg?"

He grimaced. "It doesn't hurt unless I move it."

"Then don't move it. Later, when you do start getting up and around, we'll set you up with some ace bandages."

He shifted in the bed, and the side rails rattled. "They won't let me get out of this bed to go to the john, so I don't move it much. If I'm good, how long before I can get out of here?"

"It's a moot question, Clarence, because you don't know how to be good. Remember that IV we had in your arm when we admitted you?"

His mouth opened slightly, and his eyes widened in surprise. "You wouldn't."

"This time I'll stick the needle in myself. I'm not as gentle as Lauren."

He looked away again, and his glower returned. "Fine. I could check out of here."

She watched him in silence for a moment. Someone had washed his hair and bathed him, and the dark hair set off the pallor of his skin in spite of his usually florid complexion. "Clarence," she said, then hesitated.

He turned his head back to look at her, and the bleak expression in his eyes and the knowledge of his situation saddened her. Beneath all of that, Clarence was a handsome, intelligent man who had always reminded Mercy of Tom Selleck.

"Have you called your family about Darlene?" she asked.

His eyes darkened, and his lips set in a straight line between his beard and mustache. "Don't even think about it."

"I wouldn't do it without your consent."

"You'll never get my consent, and if you knew my parents you'd know why. They never did anything but take, take, take. They lived off the government all their lives and didn't even try to get jobs. They took advantage of so many people in our hometown that everybody avoided them. That's why Darlene and I left home and never went back. Why do you think I hate being on Medicaid and Welfare so much?"

"I understand that, Clarence, but they don't even know—"

"They don't care! They won't care if she dies!" A sudden expression of shock on his face showed his inner reaction to his own words. Slowly, tears filled his eyes, and he looked at Mercy helplessly. "I can't believe she might die."

"I can't, either."

He covered his face with his right hand, and a silent sob shook the bed. Mercy pulled some facial tissues from the small box on the bedside stand and placed them in his left hand, then waited in silence. What were she and Lukas going to do about him? Clarence and Darlene had been recluses for the past two years. As far as Mercy knew, they had no friends. Their neighbors didn't even know them, and therefore distrusted them. That was evident when Clarence had gone to a neighbor to call for an ambulance.

It had taken some blunt conversation from Lukas to convince Clarence last spring that if he didn't start taking care of himself, he could die a slow and painful death and could also ruin his sister's health. Unfortunately, Darlene had turned out to be even more stubborn and independent than her big brother. And now Clarence was blaming himself. Even if Darlene did come out of her coma, who was going to take care of her and Clarence? Darlene couldn't even afford insurance for herself.

Clarence wiped his face and blew his nose, then laid his head back against the raised pillows and took a deep breath. "Sorry."

"It's okay."

"What'm I gonna do, Mercy? I was four when Darlene was born, but as long as I can remember, I took care of her. Up until two years ago, I always watched out for her, made sure she was okay. Then when I lost my job and my insurance, I couldn't take care of her anymore. She had to take care of me. How did I let it get this far?"

Mercy laid a hand across the broad expanse of his forearm. What was she supposed to say? "You're not alone, Clarence."

———

A timid knock sounded at Lukas's call room door, and he looked around from his small work desk to find Beverly standing there—Beverly, the redheaded, hot-tempered nurse who had avoided him all summer.

Lukas turned in his swivel chair, unable to keep the surprise from his face.

She entered the small room without waiting for an invitation. "Dr. Bower, I've been thinking about the COBRA investigation."

"Yes?"

She left the door open and stepped over to perch on the corner of the bed—the only other place in the room to sit. "I hope the investigator didn't give you too bad a time in that interview."

Lukas shrugged. "It's her job."

Beverly's thick red brows drew together in a frown. "Half the hospital staff is mad at me. Claudia flat out told me it's my fault you're being investigated, and I know Lauren thinks so, too, although she didn't say it."

Lukas tried not to let himself hope.

"Lauren did say that she thinks the reason I've been avoiding you is because I feel guilty." She looked at him, then looked away again. "Maybe she's right." She took a deep breath and let it out. "There, I've said it."

But she hadn't actually said anything. "Beverly, what are you—"

"The thing is, Dr. Bower, that you scared me last spring. When you refused to give Dwayne Little the narcotics he wanted, I was upset."

"I am aware of that."

"But I've known, deep down, that it wasn't because I disapproved of your treatment plan. It was because I knew the Littles could hurt my future."

"So Bailey did threaten you."

Beverly nodded. "I'm sorry, Dr. Bower. I guess I hoped all summer that since Dwayne was killed in that car wreck, Bailey would drop everything. Didn't he realize it was morphine that caused the wreck?"

"I don't think he's able to accept the truth right now."

"Bailey and truth have never gotten acquainted. I've never liked that man. He—" Beverly caught herself, shook her head, and spread her hands. "And who am I to talk? I've tried to convince myself all summer that I was mad at you because your actions threatened the security of my kids. I was really just mad at myself because I didn't have the guts to stand up to Bailey the way you stood up to Dwayne."

"As you told me, Beverly, I didn't have a family to support."

A smile chased the heaviness from her face. "And I won't have to worry about that so much, either, in a couple of months." A blush touched her cheeks.

"Oh? Did your ex-husband suddenly decide he could pay child support?" It was common knowledge that Beverly struggled to support herself and her two kids. She openly complained about it and didn't take offense at his question.

"Ha! That deadbeat?" The smile didn't quite leave her eyes. "Jacob Casey asked me to marry him."

All right! "Cowboy? The confirmed bachelor, the Lone Ranger, Jake of the Jungle?"

The tenor of her rich laughter filled the small room. "In fact, he heard about the situation with Bailey"—she held her hands up—"don't blame me, I didn't give away patient confidentiality. Somebody else told him, but Jacob talked with me about it and told me I needed to do the right thing. Then he told me he would help me. He proposed."

Lukas returned her enormous grin. "Congratulations. Somehow I get the impression that you accepted."

"You'd better believe it! You know how I feel about his '66 Mustang."

"You obviously care a great deal about him." Lukas couldn't resist thoughts of Mercy. Would it ever be possible. . . ?

Beverly nodded. "I think he kind of likes me, too, although we're going to have to work on communication. The next time he gets shot, or when he gets kicked or bitten or trampled by one of those exotic animals on his ranch, he'd better tell me before he tells anybody else."

"Have you heard anything more about the guy who shot him?" Lukas asked. The last he'd heard, some idiot had released the guy on bail.

"He disappeared. Hasn't shown up at his house, and I hear it's going to be repossessed because he didn't make his payments. They think he skipped out of the state." The laughter in her eyes died. "Jacob is having trouble coming to terms with what happened. He's so softhearted and trusting, he expects everyone to be the same way. Violence doesn't fit in his vocabulary." She slapped her hands on her knees. "Anyway, Dr. Bower, what I came here to tell you is that Mrs. Pinkley now has a filled-out AMA form on her desk. All it needs is your signature. It's already got mine."

"She does?"

"Yes. I just came from there. She was happy to see me. Surely this will call off the investigator." She stood up. "I wish I'd done it sooner. I would have had a much better summer, and I wouldn't have been stuck on that long guilt trip . . . and a good, honest doctor like you wouldn't be going through this investigation now." She paused and sighed. "There, have I groveled enough?"

Lukas chuckled, stood up, and took her hand. "Thank you, Beverly. Maybe we won't have to worry about an investigation at all now."

"There's just one thing I don't understand about all this, Dr. Bower," she said just before she walked out the door. "Why did Bailey Little turn your name in to COBRA? Dr. George was the one who gave Dwayne the drug that caused him to have that wreck. Why are they making such a big deal out of your *not* giving a narcotic?"

"Because that's the only way Bailey can manipulate COBRA to do a witch-hunt on me and the hospital." Lukas shrugged. "COBRA can't fine the hospital for killing a patient with drugs. They can only get them for not giving the drug in the first place. Now maybe the hospital and I will both be off the hook, at least with the government. There's still a lawsuit pending." And there was still a hospital buyout looming over them.

———

Tedi Zimmerman looked up at the clock on the wall, then looked up at Mr. Walters and tried to concentrate on the things he wanted them to include in their partner interviews. For an English assignment, he had everyone in the class choose a partner, and then they were going to interview each other and write a biography. It was going to be a homework assignment for tonight, but he was going to let them use class time to get started in case they had any questions. Mr. Walters didn't give a lot of homework assignments. Tedi glanced to her right across the aisle at her partner, Abby, then picked up her pencil and started to write.

She caught her breath and stared back at her friend.

Something red and shiny seeped through the long sleeve over Abby's left forearm, forming a stain about three inches long and an inch wide.

Tedi peered more closely at it, leaning across the aisle to see it better. Sure looked like blood. She tried to catch Abby's attention by waving, but Abby was listening intently to Mr. Walters' instructions.

"Psst!" Tedi waved again.

"Yes, Tedi," Mr. Walters said. "Did you have a question?"

Tedi froze midwave. Finally Abby looked at her. Tedi turned to look at her teacher. "Um, yes. Do we get extra credit if our reports have more pages?"

"Not this time, Tedi. This is a journalism assignment. I want exactly two handwritten pages, no more, no less. And I will deduct from your grade," he said, pulling his glasses off for a moment to make a point, "if you manipulate space on your papers by writing extra large or extra small. We have a word count, and I want you to stick to it. Okay, class, break into teams and get to work." He turned and looked at the clock. "It's ten-forty, so you have twenty minutes to work together and ask me any questions. After that you're on your own." He clapped his hands. "Push your desks together and get started."

There was a general scraping and clatter while the kids moved around to meet with their partners.

Tedi checked the clock again. Mom should be here to pick her up in ten or fifteen minutes for lunch with Dad, and Tedi wanted to be ready to go. Thank goodness she and Abby knew each other so well.

She scooted over two feet and pointed at Abby's arm. "What happened to you?"

Abby looked up at her, then looked down at her left forearm. She quickly placed her hand over the stain. "Scratched it."

Tedi watched her eyes behind the glasses. Abby wouldn't look at her. Something was up. "How'd you scratch it?"

Abby shrugged. "I guess on one of the bushes out on the playground."

"I didn't see you do it, and your sleeve isn't ripped. I was with you all the time on the playground." She reached over suddenly and slid up the sleeve before Abby could stop her. Blood had seeped through three bandages placed there. "You've got to go to the nurse. You didn't do this during recess." She narrowed her eyes at her best friend. "What's going on?"

Abby's thin lips tightened. "Shh!" She glanced toward Mr. Walters, who was grading papers up at his desk. All the other kids were making so much noise doing their interviews that the teacher didn't notice Abby and Tedi arguing.

"But it's still bleeding," Tedi said. "Don't you know you can get an infection if you don't take care of this? Why don't we ask Mr. Walters if I can go with you to the nurse's office, and—" She turned and raised her hand to get the teacher's attention.

Abby jerked it down. "Shut up!" Her fingers pressed hard into the flesh of Tedi's arm. "I don't want to go to the nurse."

"That's stupid, unless it's fake blood or something." She pulled away from Abby's tight grip and examined the bandages closer. "It's not fake, is it?"

"No! Just leave me alone. I'll show my parents tonight, and they'll take care of it."

Tedi kept watching her. Abby kept her gaze focused downward on her notes.

"You *want* your parents to see this," Tedi whispered.

Abby's face flushed. She jerked the sleeve of her blouse back down over the blood and turned away from Tedi.

Tedi leaned forward and hissed into Abby's ear, "You did this on purpose!" Her voice got louder. "You did it to yourself!"

With a sudden movement, Abby swung back around and shoved Tedi away. "I said shut up! You promised you wouldn't tell, remember? You promised."

"Girls," came Mr. Walters' voice from the front of the room. He moved his glasses down on his nose. "Is there a problem back there?"

Tedi started to speak, but Abby kicked her in the ankle. "Ow!"

"No, Mr. Walters," Abby said, smiling up at him as if everything were fine. "We're just really getting into this interview."

He watched them a moment longer. He didn't looked convinced. Finally he said, "Tedi, it's time for your mother to come and pick you up. You can wait in the office."

Tedi closed her notebook and scooted her desk back into place. She didn't look at Abby again. What was she supposed to do? She'd promised not to tell.

---

"Are you ready to take your baby home?" Mercy wrote her orders onto a sheet attached to Melinda Mason's clipboard, then smiled at the new mother, who sat up in bed holding her sleepy newborn, Christopher.

The pretty young woman, with freshly scrubbed face and shampooed soft brown hair, smiled into the camcorder held by her eager husband across the room. "I'd love it, Dr. Mercy. I can't wait to take my turn with that camcorder. Jeremy has promised to change baby diapers for a week, haven't you, Jeremy?"

The tall bony young man with a bandage over his right eyebrow lowered his toy for a moment. "Did I promise, exactly?"

"Yes, and your mother heard you, too. That's better than any recorded tape. I want to catch your expression on film when you get your first big dirty one. Dr. Mercy, he's really a good husband. He just likes his gadgets."

"That's okay, as long as I get to see a tape of him changing Christopher." Mercy shook hands with the happy couple, wished them well, and walked out of the room.

Her smile died as she walked down the hallway and stepped into the stairwell to the first floor. Jeremy and Melinda were so young, so eager, so inexperienced. And in contrast Mercy felt so old. Thirtynine wasn't old. Intellectually, she knew that. But lately when she looked in the mirror she saw the lines around her eyes, the fine streaks of white hair mingled with the dark, and she wondered where her youth and eagerness had gone.

Just before lunch, Mercy stopped at the lab to check on test reports for her patients. She had six today. One was for an FSH—follicle stimulating hormone—test for a fifty-one-year-old patient, Sharon Hawkins. It confirmed that Sharon was in menopause.

Mercy made the call from a private phone in the lab to break it to Sharon.

"All right!" Sharon exclaimed when she heard the news. "I've been hoping for this for months!"

Mercy shook her head as she thumbed through the other printouts. "Congratulations," she said dryly. "I'm glad this makes you happy. I'm not in my office right now, but if you'll call over there and schedule an appointment, you and I can discuss hormone replacement therapy to help you with those hot flashes."

"But they're not that bad, Dr. Mercy. I don't want to take the chance of getting breast cancer from the estrogen."

"That's one of the things we'll discuss. We'll look at your family medical history and see what your health risks are. Tests have shown that estrogen is protective against heart disease, osteoporosis, and possibly Alzheimer's, among other things. You're in great health, Sharon, and I want you to stay that way."

"But I took birth control pills in my thirties, and I had trouble with blood clots."

"We'll take that into consideration, too, but the estrogen I prescribe is only a tiny percentage of what you would have taken in your thirties. Please make the appointment, Sharon. And even if you decide not to take the therapy, we can keep a very close eye on your overall health. Are you getting enough calcium in your diet?"

"I drink a glass of milk every day."

"That's all? Not good enough. Do you want a broken hip in a few years? You're a small-boned woman, which would put you at high risk for osteoporosis. Start drinking a can of evaporated skim milk every day, at least. I also want to check your cholesterol, which could skyrocket as you lose your natural estrogen."

Sharon sighed. "You make menopause sound like some kind of disaster."

Mercy glanced at her watch and grimaced. It was past time to leave. "It can be, but it doesn't have to. Why don't you make that appointment, and I'll explain everything to you then. There are a lot of things to consider, and I won't be able to discuss it all on the telephone."

"Okay," Sharon said grudgingly. "Are you going to poke me with more needles?"

"Afraid so, but Josie's the best. She'll be gentle with you. See you soon."

As Mercy hung up she studied another sheet with FSH test results. She sighed and closed her eyes, leaning back in the chair. "I guess it's time I got started on hormone replacement therapy, too."

She couldn't help thinking about Lukas. How would this affect their relationship? Granted, life had been so hectic for the past couple of weeks that they'd had no chance to talk about that night at Jarvis's, and about the hope that had flared within her at Lukas's reactions, his tenderness . . . and the depth of emotion he had displayed. Just thinking about it warmed her all over again.

But was she being fair to him now? Shouldn't she . . . somehow . . . tell him about this before things went further? Lukas had never been married, never had the opportunity to have children, and now she knew she couldn't offer him that.

And yet, could she bear it if he turned away from her now?

Little Mary's Barbeque, on the square in Knolls next to Jack's Print Shop, always had smoke rising from its chimney, even on the hottest days. The smoke advertised the tender, spicy pork, chicken, and beef better than any billboard or newspaper ad. The locals flocked there for noon and evening meals, and sometimes a stray visitor wandered in. Fame had spread fast, and now the rustic café was open on weekends.

Tedi loved Little Mary's Barbeque, but she hardly ever got to eat there anymore. Dad used to take her there when she lived with him, but Mom cooked at home a lot, and so did Grandma. Grandma said Little Mary's didn't trim their meat, so Tedi was doomed to a healthy diet.

The little downtown café already had a dozen customers when Tedi stepped inside ahead of her mom at exactly eleven o'clock. The wooden floors and plain wooden tables and chairs made it look like the dining room at the Cartwrights' on *Bonanza* reruns. The sound of their footsteps echoed against the walls, the way Little Joe's boots would echo. The smell of the special barbeque Little Mary made was sharp and smoky and wonderful, probably as good as Hop Sing's, and Tedi stopped to get a whiff.

Mom stumbled into her from behind. "Tedi, keep moving!"

"Sorry." Tedi turned to look up at her mom, who'd been grumpy ever since she picked Tedi up at school. "Don't worry, Mom. He can't do anything to us here in front of people."

Mom took a deep breath and let it out slowly. "Sorry. Let's go sit at a booth in the back, since he isn't here yet. Maybe we can have some privacy that way."

They had just scooted together into the booth at the far back of the room when the front door squeaked open again and Dad walked through, looking as worried as Mom was. Tedi sucked in her breath.

He saw them right away, and the worry seemed to disappear. He smiled and raised his hand in an eager wave, then walked toward them, the clomp of his work shoes making the wood floor sound hollow. Dad didn't dress like he used to. Before, he always wore suits and silk shirts and ties and shiny shoes to work. Now he had on worn jeans with a gray plaid shirt. His shirt sleeves were rolled up to his elbows, and he had a stain of purple ink on his arm. He wore no jewelry now except for a watch. When he looked at Mom and bent to sit down across from them, he was still smiling.

"Thanks for coming, Mercy. I was afraid you might not be able to get away." His smile widened when he looked at Tedi.

Tedi didn't smile back. Just because she wanted to come to lunch and see him today didn't mean everything was back to normal.

"We haven't ordered yet." Mom's voice was sharper, higher than her usual warm, comforting tones. Even as she spoke, a waitress came to take their order.

Tedi felt her stomach clench, and she couldn't tell if it was hunger or worry . . . maybe fear. This whole thing felt weird, and Tedi wondered if it was just because this was the first time since she was five that she'd ever seen her parents actually sit down and eat together. Would they get into a fight? She'd never seen them when they got along, even before the divorce.

After the waitress left, Dad looked at Tedi and smiled again. "I'm glad you came, Tedi. I'm sorry if I scared you at school the other day." He looked at Mom. "I wasn't really trying to talk to her without permission. I just wanted to see her again. It's been so long, and I really missed her."

Mom took a deep breath, let it out, and shook her head. "Theodore, you've apologized a lot lately." Her voice wasn't sharp or angry, but it sounded nervous. "I appreciate the thought, but we came here today to discuss setting up some kind of a schedule for Tedi to see you. Why don't we talk about the work you're doing now, the hours you might have off when you can visit with Tedi under supervision, and maybe what kind of visitation time you have in mind, what kinds of activities you might want. I think Tedi has a few questions for you, too." She reached over and patted Tedi's shoulder reassuringly.

Dad held up his arm with the purple ink stain. "Well, as far as work goes, I have a lot more fun now than I used to, and I get a lot dirtier. Jack's teaching me how to run all the presses." He looked at Mom. "You know how much I used to love working on the machines."

She nodded. "I remember." She looked across at Tedi and explained. "Ten years ago your father spent so much time at the hospital watching the maintenance men work, I thought he would get a job there. He knew every x-ray machine in Radiology."

"So now I'm learning printing," Theo continued. "This morning we printed out a special handout sheet advertising a school dance coming up in a couple of weeks. Jack's got some old-fashioned printers, and since I did typesetting in journalism class in high school, I remembered a little bit about the machines."

The waitress brought their drinks, and Tedi's attention went from Dad's face to Mom's face and back again. Mom grabbed her lemonade and gulped down half of it before she put it down. According to Grandma, that always meant Mom was nervous.

"You took journalism?" Tedi asked Dad. "That's what we're doing in class right now. I'm supposed to write a two-page interview on Abby tonight, but I don't think I can keep it down to two pages. I know too much about her."

Dad shrugged. "I didn't do any more writing than I had to in school. I just liked the machines. All I remember about the writing was that you're supposed to put the important stuff first, because if the editor cuts it, he starts from the end and works his way to the beginning. Why don't you just write as much as you want to write, putting the big stuff first, then turn in the first two pages?"

Tedi sat back in her seat. "Maybe I will."

"Knowing how much you love to do homework," Dad said dryly, "you'll get to the bottom of the second page and decide the teacher doesn't need to know as much about Abby as you thought he did. By the way, Abby who? I thought you hated the Abby in your class last year. Is it the same one?"

"Yeah, but I didn't really hate her. We just fought a lot. She was jealous of me because I was smarter than she was, and the teacher liked me better. She wasn't so bad after my grades dropped last spring." Tedi was vaguely aware of Mom and Dad exchanging a quick glance, and she remembered that Mom had always blamed Dad for that. "Then when we started school again this fall, after everything that happened to me when you were drinking, and when you went to jail, most of the other kids wouldn't have anything to do with me at first. But Abby did. She told me she knew how it felt to have your mom and dad fight, because her parents fight a lot. Only they still live together. They're not divorced."

Mom picked up her glass of lemonade and gulped several more large swallows, then set the glass down and looked at Dad. "I guess you might call them best friends by default."

Dad picked up his own glass of ice water and held it against the side of his face for a moment. He looked like he was having a "hot flash" like Mom's.

The waitress brought the food—three mixed grill barbeque sandwiches on kaiser rolls made from scratch. They used to call them "homemade," but for some reason Little Mary changed the menus and the sign out front last week. The coleslaw was Tedi's favorite. They made it with lots of carrots and raisins, green onions and purple cabbage, and the dressing was sweet.

Tedi was wondering if she should say a silent blessing on her food, the way Grandma Ivy had taught her, when she glanced at Dad. He sat hunched over his sandwich, head bent, eyes closed.

Tedi turned to her mom in alarm. "Is Dad sick?" she whispered.

Mom shook her head slightly, her mouth set in a firm line as she picked up her lemonade glass one more time and gestured toward the waitress across the room for a refill.

Dad raised his head. "No, Tedi, I'm not sick. I've been . . . praying before I eat."

Mom shot him a startled look. "Afraid you'll choke?"

He leaned back in his seat, watching her cautiously. "No. My boss, Jack, has taken me to lunch a couple of times, and he prays before we eat, so I've started doing it the past few days."

Tedi sat up farther in her seat, afraid to hope for too much. "Why do you do that, Dad?"

Dad looked at Mom for a moment, then turned his attention to Tedi. "Because I gave my life to Christ last week."

Mercy snorted. "And He took it?"

He ignored her and kept his gaze on his daughter. "I know I don't deserve it after all I've done, Tedi. I was trying so hard to change my life—to stop drinking and stop hurting people the way I have in the past—and I discovered I couldn't do it on my own." He looked down at his food as if it had suddenly sprouted bugs. "About two weeks ago, after a whole summer of being sober, I bought a pint of whiskey and drank it over the weekend."

Mom caught her breath. "Two weeks?" She paused, as if calculating the time in her head. "You were drunk at Jarvis's party?"

"No, I bought the bottle afterwards on my way home."

"You're drinking again!" Mom exclaimed.

He spread his hands. "I told you, Mercy, I can't stop on my own. I'm an alcoholic, and I guess I always will be if I keep feeling the need to take that first drink. The morning after I finished the bottle I went and talked to Lukas."

Mom stiffened and caught her breath. "Why him? Why didn't you just call your counselor?"

"Because Lukas was the one who made the difference. He's the one who explained to me for the first time why Christ's Spirit has to control mine, why I'm helpless against the alcoholism without His strength."

Tedi felt a great rush of hope. "Does that mean you're saved now, Dad? You're a Christian?"

Dad's eyes reflected her joy. He nodded. "That's right. I've got my own New Testament, and my boss prays with me every morning. He says I'll still have to fight against that old Zimmerman temper, and I'll still be tempted to drink. But I can tell the difference in my life. Now all I have to do is pray about it, and think about you, and how much I want to be with you again."

"Supervised," Mom said quickly. "Don't forget that, Theo."

He looked at her and held her gaze and nodded. "You're right. So I've joined a new AA group that meets on Wednesday nights at Covenant Baptist."

Mom picked up her glass again. "Lukas and Mom go to that church." Her voice was still as sharp, her face even more worried-looking than it had been. Her movements were jerky, and she squeezed the lemonade glass—so hard her fingers turned white.

Dad sighed, and his shoulders slumped just a little. "It isn't what you think this time, Mercy. Honest. I haven't been trying to turn your mother against you. In fact, I haven't even talked to her at church. I doubt if she wants to have anything to do with me. But did you know her pastor is a recovered alcoholic?"

"*Recovering*," Mom reminded him. "They're never totally recovered."

Tedi looked up at Mom impatiently. She could let up on Dad just a little bit now. He said he was a Christian. He was really trying to change . . . of course, Mom didn't believe in Christ. So maybe she just didn't understand the change that was taking place in Dad's heart. Maybe Grandma and Lukas could explain it to her again.

"I'll never forget that, Mercy," Dad said. "I've attended one of their worship services, but I sat in the back, and Ivy didn't see me. The church has two morning services, and if you don't want me going to your mom's service, I'll go to the other one."

"Why should it make me uncomfortable?" Mom took another big swallow of her drink. "I don't even attend."

"You could, Mom," Tedi said. "You could take me, and that could be a way I could see Dad while I was being supervised."

"You already go with your grandmother."

"So don't you want to make sure for yourself that Dad's not going to kidnap me or something?"

"Kidnap?" Mom shook her head and rolled her eyes. "Honey, I don't think—"

Dad's sudden laughter interrupted her. "Watch it, Tedi. You're trying to manipulate your mom. You sound like me."

Mom picked up her sandwich, then put it down again, folded her hands at the edge of the table, and looked straight at Dad. "Why don't we start slowly?" Her voice was soft and calm, not angry. "We could do like we did today, meet for lunch, only do it on Saturday when we don't have work or school. We could plan to meet a week from this Saturday and see how things progress from there."

"All right!" Tedi picked up her sandwich and took a big bite. It tasted great. Maybe they could come to Little Mary's again. Or maybe they could go to the Cantina across the street from the hospital. Lukas had taken them there a couple of times, and even though Mom complained about the fat content of the Mexican food, she always agreed that it sure tasted good.

Tedi could tell by the look on Dad's face that Mom's idea made him happy. He took a big, hungry bite of his drippy sandwich. Tedi took another bite of hers. Mom kept drinking her lemonade, and she finally asked the waitress for a bag for her food, explaining that she wasn't hungry.

"Mom," Tedi said while the waitress was still at the table. "Can I have a piece of chocolate pecan pie?"

"Me, too," Dad said. "I feel like celebrating. My boss told me to take all the time I wanted for lunch." He leaned back and stretched, looking happier than Tedi had ever seen him.

Tedi took a long swallow of her root beer. "So, Dad, what's it like in the slammer?"

# CHAPTER 17

At one o'clock Thursday afternoon, the first day of October, Mercy pulled into the farthest slot of the Knolls Community Hospital employee lot and parked beside the old red Jeep Lukas had driven to work this morning. He wasn't even supposed to be working today. In fact, he'd invited her to have lunch with him at Antonio's. That was before Dr. Cobb called in with strep throat yesterday. Lukas had declined Mercy's offer to split the shift with him.

She sighed and got out of the car, then bent to retrieve her picnic basket from the passenger side of the front seat. If Lukas couldn't go to Antonio's, then Antonio's would come here, complete with salad, low-fat seafood pasta, and hot Italian bread. No horseradish. On their first date last spring, Lukas had accidentally grabbed a bottle of horse-radish and sprinkled it liberally over his bowl of plain noodles, mis-taking it for Alfredo sauce. The resultant fire flying through his sinus cavities had sent him rushing blindly into a lavatory—the ladies' room, complete with outraged lady. To complicate things further, Lukas had forgotten his billfold, and Mercy found him afterward hanging upside down from the rear seat of his car searching beneath and between the front seats for enough loose change to pay their bill. Who wouldn't be charmed?

Mercy breezed into an empty waiting room and through the dou-ble doors of the emergency department. A new, very young secretary, Tonya, sat at the large U-shaped central desk, the top of her curly auburn hair just visible above the waist-high counter that surrounded the multistationed work center. She was bent over a computer keyboard, and she spoke softly into a telephone headset, then giggled and snapped her gum.

Mercy resisted the urge to say something to her. Several people had complained that the girl made too many personal calls, and therefore made too many mistakes. The one time Mercy had worked with Tonya, she'd had to check and recheck to make sure the orders for patient tests were right. A lackadaisical attitude had no place in an emergency department, where lives were at stake.

More laughter reached Mercy from behind and to the right, and she turned to find Lukas and Lauren in the laceration room, restocking supplies from a cart, their heads close together for a moment as Lauren murmured something to him. They laughed again.

A prickling of jealousy swept over Mercy before she could control her thoughts. She squeezed on the handle of the picnic basket. It seemed to her as if Lauren was always working when Lukas worked, even when it was due to a last-minute schedule change. Coincidence? Mercy didn't think so. Who could miss the way Lauren tagged around after Lukas like a puppy dog, or the way her gaze followed him all around a room?

Mercy took a deep breath and loosened her death grip on the picnic handle. And what did it matter if Lauren was romantically interested in Lukas? It wasn't like she was out to nab some woman's husband.

Lauren's teasing laughter rang out again, and she reached up to straighten Lukas's glasses for him while his arms were full of sterile 4x4's and cotton balls. Did she have to be quite so obvious? Didn't Lukas see what she was doing?

Mercy's hand went slack, and she dropped the picnic basket with a loud clatter. Tonya, at the desk, choked on her gum. Lukas dropped his burden and turned around, then lit up with a smile. Without a backward glance he left the exam room. Lauren's laughter died.

"Hey, what's this?" He stopped when he reached the central station and sniffed the air, then he reached down and picked up the basket. "Do I smell garlic?"

Still stinging from the remnants of jealousy—an emotion she loathed—Mercy forced a smile. "Thought I'd save you from cafeteria cholesterol surprise." She glanced over to find that Lauren had turned back to the chore of restocking.

"I'm free," Lukas said, leaning close and smiling even more brilliantly into her eyes. "And I'm hungry. Lauren was just telling me to eat because my stomach was growling loudly enough for them to hear it in Radiology. We've been busy all morning, so I'm glad you didn't come earlier." He gestured toward the back part of the ER, where the staff break room was located. "Want to eat at a table? For some reason, that COBRA investigator is still hanging around. If she finds us with food in here, she'll call one of her buddies at OSHA and have a fine slapped on us so fast we won't have time to eat." He led the way toward the back of the department.

Mercy followed him, keeping up with his swift stride without difficulty, and feeling, as always, the lifting of her spirits at his very nearness. They matched each other well. Those times they had gone hiking together in the shady depths of the Mark Twain National Forest Lukas kept the pace strong while she pointed out sparkling rocks and discovered hidden waterfalls and found natural gardens of concealed wildflowers, which were abundant in the area surrounding Knolls. They hadn't been hiking in a few weeks—there hadn't been time—but she would make a point of suggesting it soon. He loved a good hike, and she loved spending time with him.

While Lukas prayed over the food, Mercy inhaled the warm scent of the garlic and felt her mouth water. As they ate, he gave her a blow-by-blow account of a patient who had come in this morning with a viral gastrointestinal upset. She was glad there weren't any nonmedical personnel within earshot. A doc's dinner conversation could sometimes be an effective appetite suppressant . . . maybe they could try that with Clarence. Lukas loved to talk about his cases, although he was always careful to respect patient confidentiality.

Against her will, Mercy's mind flashed to lunch yesterday and to Theo. She'd done the same thing to him when they were married. She would arrive home every night, usually late, and talk about work, sometimes ruining his appetite. Her work had consumed her. It still did.

". . . and so I prescribed a bottle of aspirin and a jug of cyanide, and she went home happy."

Mercy frowned and looked up at Lukas. "What?"

He put another forkful of pasta in his mouth, not quite able to conceal a grin.

"Sorry, Lukas, I wasn't listening."

He finished his bite of food and took a drink of the iced tea she had brought him. "You do seem a little preoccupied. Does it have anything to do with your lunch date yesterday?"

She shrugged. Why did he have to be so insightful? How had he gotten so good at reading her mind? That was one particular subject she wished she could forget right now. She just wanted to enjoy Lukas's company.

Lukas grew serious. He put his fork down and leaned forward. "Really, Mercy, how'd it go?"

"Well, I didn't throw anything at him, and I didn't poison his food."

"Wow. You've come a long way. Did Theodore behave himself? Did he treat you well? Did you come to some kind of understanding about Tedi's visitation?"

Mercy picked up her drink, suddenly not wanting to meet Lukas's gaze. She didn't want him to pick up on the little chord of resentment that shot through her.

"Mercy? How did it go?"

"He behaved himself. He didn't yell at me, and yes, we made plans to meet again." She looked at him at last. "You could have warned me about his so-called 'conversion.' Tedi was so excited about his little announcement that she didn't even eat all her coleslaw. And now she's trying to get me to take her to church on Sundays." Mercy shook her head. She hadn't intended to spout, but she couldn't help herself. "Especially since Theo told us he's attending worship services at Covenant. I refuse to drag her down there so we can all sit together like some happy family."

Lukas remained silent, and for once Mercy couldn't read what he was thinking. She picked up her fork and put it down again. "It's still the same, Lukas. Theo has manipulated it so that once more I'm on the outside looking in. And now he's dragged God into it, as well as you, and Tedi, and before long he'll have Mom singing his praises."

Lukas bit into a breadstick and chewed it thoughtfully for a moment. "Do you really think he's manipulating you this time?"

"See what I mean?" Mercy took a long swallow of her drink and set it down. "You're defending him." She felt betrayed. She picked up her fork to attack the food in front of her. It tasted as much like sawdust as the Little Mary's lunch she'd ended up taking back to work with her in a doggy bag yesterday.

"Did he tell you about the struggle he's going through?" Lukas asked.

She chewed, swallowed, washed it down. "Yes, he told us all about the booze. It's what I expected. Have you forgotten that my father was an alcoholic? I know how it works."

"But has Theodore ever been honest with you about it before?"

Mercy put a couple of strands of pasta in her mouth and stared out the small window that overlooked a small lawn dotted with cultivated rosebushes. This lunch date had lost its appeal in a hurry. Why shouldn't she still resent Theo? What made everybody suddenly think he could change the habits of a lifetime in just a few months? Or just because he blurted a few words to God in a desperate moment of need?

Lukas leaned toward her and placed a hand gently on her arm. "Mercy, he doesn't have a chance of turning me against you. If he's trying, he'll lose. If he's sincere, everybody wins, including you. Will you give him one more chance?"

She swallowed again and allowed herself to be soothed by the compassion she read in Lukas's eyes. "Do you know how many chances I've given him?"

"I can't even imagine, but judging by your generous spirit when you're putting up with me, I would expect a lot. Just one more?"

His hand stayed on her arm. On a whim, she reached out and took the hand and squeezed, then released it. "We've set up a visitation schedule for him to spend time with Tedi. Sorry, that's all I can bring myself to do for now."

His eyes held hers for a moment, then he turned his head to gaze pensively out the window. "I know it's hard for you. It isn't easy for me, either. I'm dealing with a lot of resentment on your behalf, and on Tedi's. I think all we can do is wait and see what happens." He sat staring out for a moment longer, then turned back to her, as if shrugging off his thoughts. "Feel like risking your life tomorrow night?"

"What?"

"I owe you a meal, and if you're game I'll do the cooking."

Mercy struggled with the sudden subject change. "You know how to cook?"

"If all else fails, I can heat up a frozen pizza, and I can buy a bag of salad and some dressing. Feel brave?"

Mercy couldn't help returning his smile—a smile that started the blood pounding through her veins. It was a smile filled with affection . . . maybe more. She thought again about the kisses they had shared the night of Jarvis's party and the sudden life and joy that had sung through her heart when Lukas held her in his arms, pressing away the pain and humiliation that had attacked her only moments before.

Yes, she was feeling brave. She reached out once more and took his hand, and this time she didn't let go but relished the power of that connection to him. His very touch was a healing balm.

Lukas looked down at their hands clasped together, and his smile died as he raised his gaze to meet hers. The affection warmed to something deeper, bolder, more serious. He leaned forward and brought his other hand across to cup the side of her face in a feather-light touch. With a sense of wonder, he also seemed to acknowledge the strength of attraction that started to spin out of control.

*I love you, Lukas.* She couldn't speak her thoughts aloud, but they reverberated inside her in a continuing echo. And she acted on them. She leaned forward and found his lips in a moment of unthinking ardor, and pleasure spiraled. She heard him catch his breath and felt his hand tighten on hers.

That was when the door swished open behind them. They broke apart to find Lauren standing there, a blush creeping up her neck and face.

Mercy glared at her. Did she know what the word "private" meant?

"Sorry to interrupt you, Dr. Bower, but a patient was brought in by ambulance a few moments ago. His wife called 9-1-1 when he fell and was knocked out in the garage of their house. He presented drunk but alert, but while I was doing my assessment his condition deteriorated. Dr. Mercy, you're listed as his family physician. It's Abner Bell."

Mercy groaned, and Lukas looked at her as he pushed back from the table. "Alcoholic," she muttered. "What's new? Sometimes I think half the world is alcoholic."

Together they followed Lauren out the door and down the short corridor in quick-step. Lauren continued her report. "His wife told us he fell and hit his forehead on a concrete step going into the garage. His blood pressure started rising just before I left him, and his heart rate started to drop, although it was hard to tell because he was so belligerent." She led the way into the second trauma room.

Abner Bell lay strapped to a backboard and c-collar on the exam bed, wearing a worn, stained white T-shirt and dirty jeans. His feet were bare, and he had a couple of days' growth of bristly beard on his face. From what Mercy could see of it beneath the nonrebreather mask, it was matted with blood from a contusion on the right side of his jaw and a bloody nose. His dark blond hair fell across his brow. He also had an IV in his left arm, and the monitor to which he was attached beeped in perfect rhythm.

Mercy recognized his wife, Delphi Bell, standing in the far corner of the trauma room, her eyes swollen and red from crying, her arms crossed over her chest. She was a short, plump woman in her late twenties with light brown hair and a glassy expression in her hazel eyes. She always had that glassy expression, along with the occasional black eye, broken finger, or cut lip. Mercy knew there was spousal abuse, but she could never get Delphi to admit anything. It was a good thing the couple had no children. No telling what kind of a mess that would be.

While Lukas tried to rouse Abner with a sternal rub, Mercy stepped over to his wife and laid a hand on the woman's shoulder. Delphi winced, as if in pain.

"Delphi, why don't you come out to the other room with me," Mercy said.

Delphi gave a curt shake of her head, her gaze trained on her husband, arms held tight to her body. "I wonder if he'll die." It was not a question, and it held no emotion.

Mercy turned to watch as Lukas poked at Abner's foot with a neurological pinwheel and got no results.

Lukas turned to Delphi. "Mrs. Bell, you did say your husband hit his forehead on a concrete step going into the garage just before he lost consciousness?"

Delphi blinked at Lukas, then turned to Mercy. "He fell on his face. I told them that." Her arms crossed even more tightly in a self-protective gesture.

"Did Abner display any evidence of nausea or vomiting after he woke up?" Mercy asked. "Any headache?"

"Yeah." Delphi glanced at Lauren. "I told you that, too, didn't I? He was sick to his stomach, and his head hurt just before the ambulance got there, but he wouldn't tell anybody but me. I told the nurse about that when she asked him."

Lauren picked up her chart and checked it. "No, I don't remember that."

Mercy gave Lauren an irritated glance.

Lauren shook her head. "I'm sorry. He was yelling so much when he came in I must have missed what was said."

Delphi snorted. "Figures. He does that to me all the time."

Mercy made eye contact with Lukas. "Unconsciousness, then a lucid interval, then deterioration," she said. "We need to get him to a Class I trauma center."

Lukas nodded in agreement.

"What?" Delphi asked. "What's that?"

As Lukas issued orders for an Air Care lift, and lidocaine and vitamin K through Abner's IV, Mercy turned her attention back to the patient's wife. "Delphi, we think he could be suffering from an epidural hematoma, which is bleeding and swelling between the protective sheath of the brain and the skull. The swelling could be dangerous to him. We need to do a head CT on him to see if he needs surgery to relieve the pressure."

Lukas turned to Lauren. "Call Respiratory Therapy. We need to intubate him and get him on a ventilator stat, and we need a noncontrast CT. Mrs. Bell, if we find an epidural hematoma, we'll call a neurosurgeon."

"How long will that take?" Delphi asked.

"Depends on how soon we find something," Mercy said. "And we need to find it as quickly as possible."

While other staff members filed into the room to work on Abner, Mercy urged Delphi out of the room at last. As they stepped into the suddenly busy ER proper, Mercy noticed a telltale sign of dried blood on Delphi's right hand. Then she noticed fresh bruising on the side of the woman's face. She brushed the hair back from her neck to get a better look, and Delphi winced.

"Okay, what aren't you telling me?" Mercy asked.

Delphi's wary gaze flitted to Mercy's face, then away again. "What do you mean?"

Mercy guided her into exam room four. "Get on that bed. I want to take a look at you. He's been hitting you again, hasn't he? Did you have a fight?" She turned to call for a tech.

"No, don't!" Delphi cried. "I'm okay. I've got to see what happens in there."

"They'll keep us posted." Mercy reached for a stethoscope in the side drawer of a metal cabinet, wiped the bell with an alcohol swab, and turned back to Delphi. "Just let me check you out, okay?" She used her motherly, forceful tone and gently helped her patient onto the exam bed. "He hit you again, didn't he?"

Delphi's jaw clenched. She jerked when Mercy touched the stethoscope to her chest, and Mercy pulled the collar of the button-down shirt aside to reveal another bad bruise on her shoulder.

"Delphi, why do you keep covering for him like this?" Mercy demanded. "Breathe deeply." She checked breath sounds and was satisfied. Stepping back, Mercy looked down at Delphi. "Don't you know this is dangerous? I want you in a gown, and I want to check you over thoroughly. Are you going to tell me what happened this time?"

Delphi crossed her arms back over her chest and bent her head. "No gown. No check. He hit me a couple of times when I mouthed him. It's all he did this time."

"He broke your finger once."

"I'm no better than him. I've hit him, too. Just like today I—" She broke off and looked away. She pursed her lips together.

"Today you what?" Mercy prompted.

Delphi shook her head.

Mercy curbed her own frustration. She could understand how it felt to want to hit your husband. She could understand the need to protect herself. A big man like Abner could do a lot more damage . . .

She bent down and looked Delphi in the eyes and finally got so close she forced eye contact. Why wouldn't this young woman trust her? "Honey, tell me what happened."

The eyes welled with tears. Delphi closed them. "I told myself I was trying to protect myself."

"How were you trying?"

For a long moment, Delphi didn't respond. Then she took a deep breath. "He fell on his face, just like I said."

"Okay. What else?"

"There's a goose egg on the back of his head."

"On the *back* of his head? But—"

"When the drunken skunk turned over onto his side and tried to get up, I was afraid he'd hit me again. I grabbed him and shoved him over onto his back." She looked at Mercy, then away. "I shoved hard. It felt so good I shoved him again. I heard his head hit the concrete, but instead of backing off and calling for help, I grabbed him by his stupid ears and shoved him back down again." Her eyes narrowed, and the words came faster, more forcefully. "That's when he passed out. I did it to him this time, Dr. Mercy. I put that goose egg on him. I got him back for all the times he hit me and shoved me around. I don't need to call the cops on him because I took care of him myself!"

Mercy couldn't afford to give in to the shock that tried to freeze her. She pivoted and ran out to find Lukas. He was watching the CT tech wheel his ventilated patient out.

"Better check the back of his head," Mercy said when she reached Lukas. "Delphi forcibly slammed him into the concrete, cerebellum first. I don't think it's an epidural hematoma. It sounds like a—"

"Cerebellar hemorrhage." Lukas's eyes mirrored her own shock. "Wow. Good thing you caught that, or we wouldn't have known to look."

Lukas notified CT. They found the bleed immediately, and Lukas contacted the neurosurgeon on call. They had just started the patient on mannitol and fresh frozen plasma when Air Care arrived.

Mercy was in the exam room with Delphi when she heard the chopper's blades as it carried Abner away.

"I really did it this time, didn't I?" Delphi said with a sigh. The bruise on her shoulder had deepened in color to purple-magenta.

"I want to x-ray your shoulder, Delphi."

The woman shook her head, strings of light brown hair falling across her forehead.

In frustration, Mercy stepped out of the room, saw Lukas standing at the central desk, and walked toward him. "Lukas, I could use a consult on—"

Two uniformed police officers came through the front entrance doors and walked to the desk. "Hello, Dr. Bower, we got your call. Where is Delphi Bell?"

Mercy stopped as if she'd rammed face first into a wall of ice. "What? Lukas, you called the police?"

Lukas looked around at her in confusion. "Of course, I had no choice. It's an assault case."

"But the woman was defending herself!"

"I'm not making any judgments. As ER physician, I'm required to report any act of violence that comes into this department. You know that, Mercy."

Mercy planted her fists on her hips. "Then you'd better examine Delphi, too, because she's the real victim here, and she has been for a long time!"

He glanced at the police, then back at Mercy and lowered his voice. "They're the police, Mercy, not the bad guys. It's not like they're going to—"

"I should never have told you about Delphi," she snapped. "I should have kept my mouth shut and let you keep looking for the hematoma in his forehead."

"And Abner might have died," Lukas said quietly. "You know how difficult a cerebellar hemorrhage can be to pick up on a CT. Would you want that on your conscience?"

"Do you want *Delphi* on *your* conscience?" She heard the outrage in her own voice, felt it on her face, and she sensed the sudden, waiting silence that surrounded them.

Lukas stared back at her, prolonging the silence another few seconds. "I'll go check Delphi."

A moment later he returned. "She's gone."

———

"Dr. Bower, Mrs. Pinkley is calling for you," Tonya's voice came through the call room speaker thirty minutes after the helicopter lifted off with Abner Bell.

Lukas glanced over at the blinking button on his phone and sighed. Mercy's anger and her words still hurt more than he would have ever imagined. He had learned something else about himself and their relationship—if her tenderness, her tears, and her kisses had power over him, her anger felt as if it would break him in two.

He punched the button and picked up the receiver. "Don't tell me the police already called you, Estelle."

There was a short silence, and then came Mrs. Pinkley's voice, the deepest nonsmoker voice in a woman that Lukas had ever heard. "And good afternoon to you, Lukas. I gather you're having a good day?"

"I'm not even supposed to be here. It's the same old story—Dr. Cobb called in sick, and I couldn't get a replacement." He grimaced at the whiny sound of his own voice. Something about Estelle's motherly ways brought out the little boy in him.

"You'll learn how to be a department director in time. Hang in there."

"But I don't want—"

"The police did not call me, Dr. Bower. I called them. I don't think you need to worry about Delphi Bell. They're not going to much trouble to find her, and if they do, they will treat her like a battered wife who fought back."

Her words soothed something inside him. "How did you read my mind?"

"I spoke with Mercy a few moments ago. She wanted to make sure Delphi was treated well."

"Mercy called you?"

"Relax, Lukas. She wasn't calling to complain about you. She didn't even mention your name. She was just concerned about her patient. You did what you had to do. You followed hospital protocol and reported an obvious act of violence. Anyway, that's not what I called about. We have other problems."

Lukas stifled a groan. There were always *other* problems.

"Have you read today's *Knolls Review*?"

"I haven't had time to—"

"I didn't think so." There was a long silence and a huff of air over the receiver. "Brace yourself, Lukas. We've got another rough ride ahead of us." Her voice was nearly a growl now. "Bailey Little has issued a public letter of resignation as the hospital board president, and it came out in the 'Letters to the Editor' column of the paper. I could kill that editor, but the letter will probably increase ratings. Harvey is surely expecting a rebuttal from me, and he's certainly going to get one."

Lukas didn't doubt that. "I thought you wanted Bailey to resign."

"You'll see what I mean when you read the paper, but let me give you the highlights. Not only has Bailey broadcast the news about our COBRA investigation, but he states that he is resigning due to 'alleged' faulty conduct in our hospital, led by the administrator. That would be me."

Lukas could feel a headache coming. He rolled his head around on his shoulders and took a deep breath. "What kind of conduct?"

"Taking on pro-bono cases like Clarence and Darlene Knight, by paying their bills with public assets."

"That's a lie! You and Mercy and I paid those bills out of our own pockets. And there's a special fund designated for—"

"Bailey didn't bother to include that. He also complained about the hospital retaining the services of a physician with life-threatening tuberculin encephalitis who has a compromised mental capacity."

"But everyone in town knows Jarvis George hasn't been back to his office since his collapse."

"This letter was meant to place doubt in their minds." She paused a moment. "A further complaint, which he says he has tried to rectify, is about how the acting emergency department director—"

"That would be me."

"—was dismissed from his residency program due to questionable professional conduct and came here with his tail between his legs because he couldn't make it in the city."

Lukas got that old sick feeling in his stomach. "I told you I shouldn't be the director."

"Are you questioning my administrative expertise?"

"Not with anything else."

"Just trust me with this, Lukas. Consider it a growing experience."

"Haven't I grown enough?" Here came the whiny kid again.

In her years as attorney in this community, Estelle had probably won cases for or against half the citizens. People either loved her or hated her. Most loved her.

"There's more," she said.

"You're ruining my day."

"From what I hear, it was already ruined. Bailey also announced RealCare's interest in purchasing Knolls Community Hospital and suggested that the county might have more cash flow for other important community-oriented services, such as the police and fire department, if they didn't have to spend all their tax dollars on us."

"Is that how the county financial policy is set up?"

"No, and Bailey knows that. He's just stirring up trouble. I've seen him work too many times to be surprised by anything he does. He knows how powerful his little innuendos can be to a mob mentality, and this letter is going to stir things up. He also hints at the trouble they're having apprehending the arsonist." She fell silent, as if catching her breath.

Lukas waited a few seconds. "Anything else?"

"Just expect repercussions in the ER. You'll get the backlash from the patients, and you need to be warned. Everybody who has had any experience with Bailey will see through this ruse, and that could put us ahead of the game."

Lukas was still reeling from the shock of the news, but he thought he detected a familiar quality in her voice. He shook his head. "I think you're almost enjoying this."

She hesitated a moment, then chuckled. "You know, I think you're right. When I first took over this job, I thought I would be bored. That isn't proving to be the case. I'll be in touch."

As soon as she hung up, Lukas got another call.

"This is the emergency room, Dr. Bower speaking."

"Yes, Dr. Bower, you're the person I wanted to talk to," came a woman's voice over the line. "I'm calling from Cox South ICU, and we thought you might like to know that Darlene Knight just woke up."

Lukas thanked her and hung up, then sank down onto the nearest chair. Once, when he was about nine years old, his big brothers took him on a wild roller coaster ride at Six Flags in St. Louis. They thought he was enjoying it until he lost his lunch. He felt like that now.

"Lord, thank you," he whispered. "And, Lord, help!"

# CHAPTER 18

It was late Thursday afternoon, and Mercy was making a final check of Clarence's vitals before she left the hospital for the day. His blood pressure was better than she'd seen it in a while.

"I talked to Darlene on the phone today," Clarence said, his deep voice vibrating the bed.

Mercy placed her stethoscope against his chest, listened to the muffled *lub-dub* of his flesh-enfolded heart, and nodded, satisfied. "She sounds good, doesn't she? They're still checking her, but they don't think she's lost any mental function. She should come home in a few days, and so you need to concentrate on getting better. How's the pain?"

"Not as bad. But they're starving me in here."

"I don't want you to be starved. I just want you to lose weight and keep losing. Try drinking more water during the day, at least three quarts."

He gasped, then choked. "Three quarts! Are you crazy?"

"We're already having your intake and output measured." She jotted down some instructions on his sheet. He needed vitamins and minerals. "Trust me, you won't drown or overdose." She looked back at Clarence. "I heard you had visitors today."

"Yeah."

"Lukas?"

"Yeah, he came and talked with me awhile. He prayed with me for Darlene."

Mercy stepped back in mock amazement. *"You prayed?"*

Clarence's thick eyebrows drew together in a scowl. "I let him do all the talking." He hesitated. "Ever do that with patients?"

Mercy thought about Arthur Collins, the missionary whose wife had lost her leg. "Not willingly."

"It helps. Ever pray by yourself?"

"Only when I'm desperate." Mercy hung his clipboard back on the end rail of the bed. "I'll be back to check on you later, Clarence." She turned away.

"Everything okay between you and Lukas?" Clarence blurted before she could get out the door.

She stopped and turned back. "Why, did he say something about it?"

"Nope. Didn't have to. Everybody else in the hospital is. I heard a couple of nurses talking about a fight in the ER today between you two, and when he came in here I could tell he wasn't too happy."

Mercy stifled a groan. This place had too many ears and too many loose lips, and that new secretary, Tonya, was a gossip. Time for Lukas to have a talk with her if the hospital didn't want to get slapped with a charge of violation of patient confidentiality. "You'll hear rumors floating through here all the time, Clarence. I learned a long time ago not to listen." And she wished she'd learned long ago to keep her mouth shut when she was mad. She'd never been able to do that, and she couldn't forget the expression of hurt surprise on Lukas's face when she snapped at him for calling the police about Delphi. There had been no time since then to discuss it.

Clarence grunted. "When you've been cooped up in a room with a television as long as I have, you'll learn to listen to everything. Did they ever catch that gal that escaped from the police?"

"No." Estelle had assured Mercy that they probably wouldn't even try. Abner had come through surgery fine, and if he knew what was good for him, he would not press charges against his long-suffering wife. "Clarence, you should write soap operas."

"Maybe I will, if I don't go back into auto mechanics or start my own weight loss clinic. I had another visitor today, too. You know that guy that brought me in Monday? Buck? He came up to see how I was doing."

Mercy stepped forward and leaned against the side of the bed. This was the most she had ever heard him talk. She knew the depression he fought would probably come back to haunt him, but as long as this mood held, he could recover more quickly.

"He told me he just got back into town this afternoon from a fishing trip. The poor guy is all alone. He told me about his problems with his wife," Clarence explained. "Buck says to call him when I get my weight down some, and he'll start me exercising, maybe help me lift some weights." He reached forward and slapped his huge stomach with his right hand. "I told him I already lift nearly five hundred pounds every time I stand up. I bet even Buck can't do that."

"That's why you pull your muscles so easily," Mercy said.

"Think Buck and his wife'll get back together?"

"I hope so. He's a nice guy."

"He's lonely."

Mercy knew Clarence could identify with that. "Friends are important. When do you think you'll start breaking out of your shell and meeting new people?"

The big man gave a bitter laugh. "Who'd want to meet me? I'm a fatso. I live off the state. Other people are paying for this hospital room."

Mercy stifled a wave of irritation at this old story. "We both know how hard you fought that. Why don't you give yourself a break?" She hesitated for a moment. "Clarence, may I have your permission to discuss your case with an outsider?"

That old characteristic blanket of wary cynicism crept back down over his large, handsome features. "Are you going to sic another social worker on me?"

"You need more help than a social worker can give you. What are you going to do at home when I release you?"

"I'm not going home. I'm going to Darlene in Springfield. Now that she's awake she'll need me to help her get back on her feet."

Mercy hesitated. "Clarence, use common sense. Darlene will probably be out by the time you are, and she needs you to be as strong as possible when she gets here. I don't want you taking any chances with those pulled muscles. You both need someone to help you when you go home, and I know someone who takes causes like a bee takes pollen, and she loves it."

Clarence narrowed his eyes suspiciously. "Who?"

"My mother."

He watched her for a moment, as if waiting for a punch line. "You've gotta be kidding."

"Nope."

"You're talking Mrs. Ivy Richmond, one of the richest widows in town, who practically supports this hospital? You're talking about that lady?"

"I think you've got it all wrong, Clarence. My mother's no lady."

"Is she anything like you?"

Mercy scowled at him. "Do you have a problem with that?"

"She'll be bossing me all the time. I won't even be able to sneak in a candy bar, because she'll have eyes in the back of her head, just like you do. I don't need another prison warden."

"You know, it's a good thing you never got married," Mercy said, mimicking his grumpy drawl. "Your wife would've killed you by now, and I wouldn't have the pleasure of your company."

He curled his lip in a mock grin, then took a deep breath and let it out slowly. "I don't have a choice, do I?"

"Not if I can convince you to use your brain and lay off the self-pity."

He glowered at her. "Anybody ever tell you that you have a charismatic personality?"

"Nope."

"Didn't think so. I've been reading this book about the four personality types, and you're choleric. That means bossy."

"I'm a doctor. It's my way. You should be glad I have a tough enough hide to put up with you. Will you see my mother?"

"Fine. Call out the cavalry."

Mercy patted his arm. "Knew you'd see it my way. I'll be in touch."

The overhead page reached Mercy before she could get out of the hospital. She walked to the nurses' desk and dialed the operator, who connected her to the ER.

"Oh, thank goodness, Dr. Mercy!" It was Tonya's voice. "Dr. Bower hoped you'd be there. We have a rape victim down here in ER, and you're her family doctor. She came in by ambulance with a police escort, and her parents are going nuts. She doesn't want a man to touch her, and Dr. Bower was wondering if—"

"Who's the patient?"

"She's a teenager. Shannon Becker."

Mercy caught her breath and nearly dropped the phone. For a moment shock held her as if she'd been poured in concrete. "Oh no." With an ambulance in attendance, it couldn't possibly be statutory rape, could it?

"Can you come down, Dr. Mercy?"

"I'll be right there."

---

Lauren and a female police officer in an imposing full black uniform stood in the OB room with Shannon and her parents when Mercy entered. Ignoring the others for a moment, Mercy went straight to her bruised, sobbing patient sitting in her torn, bloodied clothes on the exam bed. It was not merely statutory.

The skin around Shannon's left eye had swollen nearly shut, and a streak of blood caked the right side of her chin. Tears and sweat had smeared mascara down her cheeks, and her limp light brown hair matted around her neck and shoulders.

Shannon reached for Mercy on a fresh sob, and Mercy drew her into a gentle embrace.

"I don't want to be here, Dr. Mercy," Shannon murmured in a voice that was hoarse from tears—and maybe from screaming. "I want to die. I can't do this. Why do all these people have to be here? Tell 'em to go away. Please! I can't go through with this!"

Mercy held her more tightly and gazed over the girl's head to Zach and Lee Becker, at their tear-worn faces and tortured eyes. How could something so horrible happen to their sweet, bubbly, life-loving daughter?

"Please, Dr. Mercy, can't we be alone?" Shannon asked, still gripping Mercy's hand with both of her own. "Can't everyone else go outside the room, like when you do my exam?"

Mercy nodded for the policewoman to step just outside the door.

Lee stepped over to Shannon and took her hand. "Honey, are you sure? I can stay here with you through the exam. I don't want you to be alone." Her voice wobbled.

Zach put his arm around his wife. "Come on, Lee. Shannon's a big girl, and she needs to do this on her own right now. She knows we'll be right here for her." He placed a callused hand on Shannon's leg. "We'll get the guy who did this. The police are looking for him now. You did good, getting that license number for us." His voice grew husky and shaky. "We'll get him."

Lee looked up from her daughter. "How could this happen, Dr. Mercy? Shannon's a good girl. She doesn't deserve it!"

Mercy patted Lee's shoulder and urged her out the door. Parental tears and questions would only make Shannon feel worse, and her ordeal was far from over.

Shannon pointed at Lauren, who was busy filling out her section of a questionnaire. "Does she have to be here?"

"Yes, honey. In this case we need a nurse present as a witness that I did my job correctly. Don't worry. Lauren's on your side. We'll be gentle, and we'll get those clothes off of you and check you over from head to toe and take care of any injuries." Mercy knew she was talking to Shannon as if she were a little girl.

Lauren stepped over to the other side of Shannon's exam bed and took the girl's trembling hand. "That's right, sweetie. We'll take good care of you. Dr. Mercy's going to ask you a lot of questions, and we want you to take your time and answer everything as completely as you can. Then we'll take our kit, here"—she held up the sealed white cardboard rape kit that was about the size of a John Grisham novel— "and we'll take specimens that can help us prove who did this to you and put them into the little envelopes and seal them. That way we'll stop this guy from hurting you again, or hurting somebody else." Lauren looked at Mercy. "Social Services is sending a victim advocate."

"No." Shannon shook her head. "I don't want anybody else in here."

"That's okay," Mercy said. "She can talk to you after we're finished. I think it'll help you and your parents get over this more quickly. Lauren, would you please get us a hospital gown?" She reached forward and gently touched the bruise on Shannon's face. "Does it hurt badly?"

"It did when he hit me. Now I feel kind of numb."

"We'll check it out. Now we'll help you get out of your clothes, and we'll seal them in a plastic bag. They'll be examined for evidence that can be used in court."

As Lauren and Mercy helped Shannon remove her clothes, Mercy used her stethoscope to listen to the girl's chest, back, and stomach, then checked more thoroughly for injuries on the rest of Shannon's body. She found other cuts and bruises and nodded. "Lauren, did you bring the Polaroid?" She took note of drying blood beneath Shannon's fingernails. The police would want a specimen of that.

"What do you mean?" Shannon asked, stiffening. "Why do you need a camera?"

"We need to take pictures of your injuries, honey. We've got to prove that this was rape."

"You mean everybody's going to see me like this?" Shannon's voice rose in a crescendo.

"No, not everybody," Mercy said quickly. "And not in any private areas." She took Shannon's hand. "But see the blood under these fingernails? I'd like a picture of your hands, and of your face, and the scratches on your arms and legs. Any jury that looks at these pictures will know you were not a willing participant."

Shannon relaxed a little and allowed Lauren to help her with the gown and chatter a nonstop monologue about what they were going to do and how they would do it. For once, Mercy was grateful for Lauren's gift of constant verbalization. It kept Shannon calm while Mercy took supplies out of the kit—fine-tooth comb, swabs, blood tubes, slides. It had been at least a couple of years since Mercy had done a rape case. Knolls was a peaceful, quiet community with very little violent crime.

Shannon allowed them to photograph her face and other injuries, then looked at Mercy again. "Do Mom and Dad have to know about our visit the other day?" She glanced at Lauren, then back at Mercy. "You know, when I came to your office? And what we talked about?"

Mercy shook her head. "I already told you that's doctor-patient confidentiality. It doesn't have anything to do—" She broke off, and stared with growing dismay at Shannon's bruised face and apprehensive gray eyes. "Oh, Shannon, is that who did this?"

The girl shook her head as tears spilled down her cheeks. "I told Lance no last Friday night, just like you said. He took me right back to town and dumped me off without even trying to find my girlfriends who were cruising somewhere on the square. I had to walk home." She looked over at her torn, bloodstained jeans as Lauren placed them carefully into the plastic bag. "Today after school this guy drove up and stopped on the road beside where I was walking. He told me his name was Cody, but I don't believe him. He was lying. He said Lance wanted to see me and he would drive me there." She stopped talking and glanced hesitantly at Lauren. "You can't tell anybody this, right?"

"That's right," Mercy said, "but you can. What happened?"

Lauren turned from her work and looked at Mercy, then at Shannon. Lauren put an arm around Shannon's shoulders. "It's okay, sweetie. You can go ahead and talk to us. You can tell us anything you want."

Shannon sighed. "I thought maybe Lance had changed his mind and he really did like me for myself." Her face scrunched up, and she wrapped her arms around her stomach and bent forward. "The guy who called himself Cody took me to the woods and told me Lance was spreading it around their school in Radium Springs that I was . . . you know . . . giving in. He said he could prove he was more of a man than Lance was." Her face puckered with more tears. "I tried to tell him the truth, but he wouldn't listen. He just started pulling at my clothes, and when I fought back, he hit me." She gestured to the swollen skin around her eye, and the sobs once again rose to a crescendo.

"It's okay, Shannon," Mercy said softly. "Take your time."

"I got out of the car, and he chased me through the trees, and that's how I got all scratched." For another moment she couldn't talk. She leaned into Lauren's shoulder and allowed the nurse to hold her and murmur reassurances to her until the sobbing hiccups subsided. She shook her head and looked up at Mercy. "None of the fighting did any good, Dr. Mercy. He kept telling me what a nice body I had, and that I should share it." Her face contorted again. "You warned me about a lot of stuff, but you never told me anything like this could happen."

# CHAPTER 19

L ukas drove down a dark, quiet street accompanied by the rough hum of his out-of-tune Jeep and the mutter of his growling stomach. The Antonio's breadsticks and pasta that Mercy had left scented the cab with garlic. The only thing that kept him from ripping open the little Styrofoam box and devouring the food was a stop he had to make first.

He parked in front of the apartment building where Theo lived, stared for a moment at the dimly lit window of apartment C, then got out of the Jeep and walked toward the front door. He didn't want to do this. Social visits rated right up there with parties on his pet peeve list. He didn't even know why he was doing it, except he needed to make sure Theo was okay. So this was kind of like a spiritual chore.

He was halfway up the uneven sidewalk when the front door opened. Theo stepped into the threshold, still wearing a blue chambray shirt and work jeans, his outline darkened by a glow from the room behind him. It took Lukas a moment to realize that Theo didn't see him in the darkness.

Theo raised his hand to his head and combed fingers restlessly through his hair, took a deep breath, and stepped out onto the concrete porch.

"Hello, Theodore," Lukas said.

Theo froze, caught his breath, squinting as he stared out into the darkness. "Who's there?" He took another step out. "Lukas? Is that you?"

Lukas stepped forward into the light. "Yes."

The breath came out of Theo in a rush. He bent his head.

This didn't seem like any social visit Lukas had ever been on. "Are you okay?"

Theo stood with his right hand gripping the doorframe for another moment. He nodded. "I think I will be now." He sighed the words. "God really does answer prayers. Come on in." He stepped back for Lukas to enter, then reached over and switched on a lamp as Lukas sat down on a chair inside the doorway.

From what Lukas could see of the apartment, it was the antithesis of his home. It was spotless. "What's wrong, Theodore?" he asked.

Theo shook his head and sank down on a second-hand sofa. "You caught me just in time. I shouldn't've rented a place so close to a liquor store, but this apartment came cheaper than anything else in town. I was just sitting here thinking about how good a few sips of bourbon would taste right now, and then I was praying, kind of half-heartedly, that God would keep me from doing something stupid. I was just stepping out to buy one of those little tiny travel bottles with a couple of swallows in it, but I know it wouldn't have stopped there." He heaved a sigh and looked at Lukas. His face was a deep well of dismay mixed with relief and wonder. "God brought you here, didn't He?"

Lukas nodded, unable to hide his own surprise. "Yeah, I guess He did."

"I was using all the arguments I could come up with to talk myself out of it. I was thinking about my date next week with Mercy and Tedi, and about how disappointed Tedi would be, and how mad Mercy would be. And then another part of me argued that it was just a couple of drinks, and that nobody would find out anyway."

"Oh yeah? Have you forgotten the town we live in? This is Knolls, Theo, not New York City."

"I know. I kept trying to remind myself how I'd be letting everyone down. I don't want to do that again. You don't know how much Mercy's suffered, and she didn't deserve it. I just want to be able to prove to her that I can do this."

"You can't," Lukas said.

Theo blinked at him. "What?"

"You can't do it. What do you think this whole salvation thing is all about, Theodore? You have to let God do it, because you've proved to yourself that you can't. Every single time you feel the temptation, you have to give it to Him." Lukas felt like a hypocrite. How did he know what it was like to be an alcoholic?

But he knew what it was like to be a sinner. And sin was sin. "Ask Him to take the temptation away," he continued. "Stay in His Word. Recite Scripture. One of my favorites is, 'I can do everything through Him who gives me strength.'"

Theo leaned forward, elbows on knees, hands clasped. "But that's the problem. I'm not doing everything. I belong to Him now, and I'm supposed to be a brand-new person, but I'm still struggling."

Lukas shot him a dry grin. "You thought you'd be Superman."

"I thought I'd be a holy Christian, not the same old drunk. I thought I wouldn't need the booze anymore."

"But you still have a human nature, a human body. Accepting Christ as your Savior isn't like waving a magic wand and making everything perfect. You still have to learn and grow and be fed. When you first took algebra in school, you didn't pick up the book and automatically know the material. You had to learn it step by step." Lukas glanced over at the side table and saw the New Testament Theo's boss had given him. He picked it up and turned to a passage he'd been trying to learn in his life ever since he starting treating patients. "You should mark this one, Theo, where God tells the apostle Paul in Second Corinthians, 'My grace is sufficient for you, for my power is made perfect in weakness.' You have to keep acknowledging your own weakness daily in order to allow God to control your spirit. You give up your own will, and—"

Suddenly, Lukas's own personal truth drove through his heart like a white-hot probe. He caught his breath at the discovery, and at the pain.

For him, the feelings that were growing inside his mind and heart for Mercy—and the powerful physical reactions that had helped drive them—were forbidden to him, just as forbidden as alcohol was to Theodore.

"Lukas?" Theo said, concerned. "Are you okay?" He leaned forward. "You were talking about giving up my own will."

Lukas tried to swallow back the pain. This talk wasn't about him, it was about Theo. "You've got to give it to God," he said softly.

"We all have to turn it over to God. We don't control our lives any longer. He does." The future Lukas had recently begun to dream about with Mercy seemed to disappear in the darkness. He was going to have to let her go. He couldn't think of marriage at this point, couldn't continue a budding romantic relationship with someone who did not share the Spirit that made up who he was. He knew it, had known it all along, but he'd conveniently grabbed at the fact that she seemed more and more open to discussions about spiritual things. It was almost as if he'd been trying to pressure her for his own selfish reasons.

And the thought of losing her now caused a pain reminiscent of the grief he felt when his mother died. He knew he would see Mom again. With Mercy, how could he know?

While Theo took the Book from him and read, Lukas felt his heart grow softer for this struggling man and his pain. And for the first time in his life he could identify.

And as he listened, he also argued with God. The answer remained the same. Let her go.

Was he going to be alone for the rest of his life? He should have listened to Mercy when she tried to break it off in the first place. She was right—it would have been less painful two weeks ago, when he hadn't even allowed himself to acknowledge the possibility that he was in love with her.

Theo put the New Testament down and sighed. "Lukas, I've started saving some money from my paycheck, and I'm going to try to pay Mercy back everything she spent to protect me from the embezzlement charges. I want to pay child support. I know she doesn't need it, but she paid me all those years. It's my turn."

Lukas struggled to answer past the ache inside him. "That's good, Theo."

"I sent the first money order today. She should get it in the mail at her office tomorrow. I just hope I can keep doing it."

"Talk to God about that, too," Lukas said. "Talk *to* Him, not just *about* Him. He'll be there when you ask."

He would be there for both of them. Lukas swallowed his pride and realized he needed God's constant presence as desperately as Theodore did.

————

Ivy Richmond still left her front porch light on and the door cracked open when she expected company, even if it was just her daughter, Mercy. It was her own brand of hospitality, her way of saying welcome.

Mercy needed that welcome tonight. She needed a warm comforter wrapped around her, a steaming cup of apple cider, and a good mystery novel. She needed something to get lost in, to help her forget about Shannon's pain-filled face. Every time she closed her eyes she saw the bruises. Every time it grew silent, she heard the shock-filled voices of Shannon's parents.

And then she thought about Delphi Bell's life of struggle and the bruises she suffered so often from a man she couldn't seem to get away from. There were too many battered people in this world.

Mercy stepped into her mother's house without knocking and found Ivy and Tedi together on the overstuffed blue love seat, Ivy reading the *Knolls Review* by lamplight, and Tedi watching Steve Urkel getting hit by a pie on *Family Matters*. They looked so much alike. Like Mercy, they had Cherokee blood from a not-too-distant ancestor.

Tedi laughed out loud, a free, unrestrained sound that always brought a smile to Mercy's face. A commercial blasted past the canned laughter at the same time Tedi saw Mercy.

"Hi, Mom!" Tedi jumped up and ran over to hug Mercy—a wonderful tendency she hadn't yet outgrown. "Can we stay long enough to see the end of the show?"

"You've seen that episode four times."

"Yeah, but I like it. Please? By the time we get home it'll be over."

Ivy stood up and added her voice to her granddaughter's plea. "If you stay awhile, I'll heat you up a serving of my baked cinnamon apples with some frozen yogurt on top."

Mercy shook her head and pulled at her already too-tight waistband. In spite of her lack of appetite lately, she was gaining weight. Blame menopause. Hormone therapy should help with that problem along with the irritability and hot flashes. "We can stay, but I'd better stick to water." She walked into the dining room and plopped down on a solid wooden chair while Tedi returned to the television for the final segment of slapstick comedy.

Ivy came into the dining room and turned on the overhead chandelier. Soft, warm light revealed a spotless kitchen, something that had been more in evidence since Ivy found herself with few daily activities besides watching Tedi after school four days a week. The kitchen and dining room took up only about a third of the great room, which held a computer area, exercise area, and skylights over an indoor garden. Leave it to Ivy Richmond to grow life anywhere she was.

Ivy stepped over behind Mercy and reached down to knead her shoulders. "Tense day?"

The press of her strong fingers against overtight muscles felt great. "In a lot of ways." Mercy sighed as Ivy continued to massage her stiff muscles.

"Did you hear about Bailey Little? He resigned his position as hospital board president. His nasty letter to the editor is in the *Review* today."

Mercy didn't reply. She'd heard, but she was on emotional overload and didn't even want to think about that.

"Today was supposed to be your day off," Ivy said, still massaging. "I thought you were just going to have lunch with Lukas and then go home."

"Lukas had to work today, and a couple of my patients ended up in the ER. Mmm . . . that feels great." She sat for a moment in silence, letting the massage ease away some of the stress that had been taking over her shoulder muscles since this morning. "Mom . . . are you bored?"

"What?"

"You know, do you find a lot of excess time on your hands?"

The massage stopped for a moment, then continued. "Why do you ask?"

"You mentioned the other day that you were suffering from the empty nest syndrome, and yet you're stuck taking care of Tedi after school, so you can't go to Springfield as a volunteer at the free clinic with your friends. Are you looking for something else to keep you busy?"

Ivy's hands stilled on Mercy's neck again. "I help take care of an active eleven-year-old, and I love it. Do I act bored?"

Mercy shrugged, hoping that would reinstate the massage. It didn't. "Well, you sent home three meals for Tedi and me last week, you cleaned my house Tuesday, and you volunteered to host a slumber party for Tedi and three friends Saturday night. I don't know, maybe it's a stretch, but you could be looking for a little more to keep you occupied."

The massage regained momentum at last, accompanied by Ivy's skeptical voice. "I get the feeling you have some input for me."

"He weighs about four hundred and seventy pounds, and right now he's totally bedridden. His sister—the only family he will claim—just came out of a coma at Cox South. That was the emergency I had Monday morning when I dropped Tedi off with you. Clarence and Darlene have no friends. Lukas and I have been making house calls on them this summer, and Clarence is finally on state aid, but it isn't enough."

"You need money for them?"

"It may come to that, but right now, while Darlene is recovering, they both need a friend who is as bullheaded and tough as they are." The massage got a little deeper. "Ow! I meant that in the nicest possible way."

Ivy stopped kneading and started chopping out the muscles with the sides of her hands. "You say this guy weighs four hundred seventy pounds? How'd he get that way? I don't think—"

"He isn't what you think, Mom." Mercy gave an abbreviated history on Clarence and Darlene.

"Sounds like a big project," Ivy said at last. Then she realized what she'd said. "You know what I mean." She pulled out a chair and sat down across from Mercy at the dining room table. "You have a giving spirit, Mercy. I'm proud of you. Let me pray about it and sleep on it." She leaned forward, wisps of gray-streaked hair falling, as usual, from the clasp that held them. She reached forward and laid a hand on Mercy's. "Now, why don't you tell me what's really bothering you."

Mercy held her mother's dark, insightful gaze for a moment, heard the sound of Tedi's laughter in the other room, and tears sprang to her eyes. "I'll never have another child, Mom."

# CHAPTER 20

At nine o'clock Friday morning Lukas fastened the top button of his worn Wrangler jeans, pulled on an old red-plaid shirt, and stuffed his double-stockinged feet into his Danner hiking boots. A good mud-eating hike in the Mark Twain National Forest would clear his head. He should probably call Mercy to make sure she was still coming over tonight, but he couldn't. He knew it was sheer cowardice that kept him from picking up that phone, but the thought of talking to her brought too much pain. He didn't want to think about his sudden revelation at Theodore's apartment last night.

If Mercy did come for dinner tonight, it could be the last time. He couldn't think about it right now.

He was stuffing a water bottle, an apple, and a package of Kellogg's Pop Tarts into his small backpack when the telephone in the living room rang. His immediate thought was that it was Mercy, and then his automatic reaction to that thought was to rush to the phone to pick up. In spite of everything, he wanted to hear her voice.

"Hello, Dr. Bower? This is Judy at the hospital. Dr. Garcias asked me to call and see if you could please come in for a little while. We're having a rush like you wouldn't believe, and we just got ambulance calls with more coming in, one class one and two class twos. They're supposed to be here in about six minutes."

Lukas sighed. "I thought Dr. Hill was on backup call today." He wished it were Mercy on the line.

"I just tried him. He told me he didn't have time to come over and coddle the new doctor. He said that's your job."

Lukas stifled his frustrated anger. Here went the squeeze play again. Members of the medical staff were required to take medical backup for ER, which meant that if the ER doc got into trouble or was overwhelmed with serious emergencies, the on-call doc would come in. It didn't always work that way when the backup doc had his own practice and a waiting room full of patients.

"Want me to call Mrs. Pinkley about it?" Judy asked. "Sounds like prejudice to me. One of Dr. Hill's office assistants overheard him complaining because you hired a Mexican. If you're busy, maybe I could call Dr. Mercy to—"

"No, Judy, don't call her. I'll talk to Mrs. Pinkley about it later." Lukas knew Dr. Hill disliked ER call, but in a small hospital setting like Knolls, with no interns or residents to take up the slack, medical backup was important.

"Tell Dr. Garcias I'll be there." He hung up, grabbed the package of Pop Tarts, and left his backpack on the overly cluttered kitchen counter. No time for a long hike today, but maybe he could take a shorter one if he escaped the hospital in time to clear out the congestion of clothing, dirty dishes, and old mail that had accumulated around the house in the past few months.

As he drove his Jeep to the hospital, he thought again about Dr. Hill. What if there had been no one else to back Dr. Garcias up? What if someone died?

Hospital politics was one of the most frustrating aspects of ER practice. The ER doc and patient often became the components of a hot potato tossed back and forth between the family practitioner and the specialist. The family practitioner—often called a "gatekeeper" in an HMO—was unwilling to admit an unstable patient. The neurologists, cardiologists, pulmonologists, and others didn't want to take cases they felt could easily be managed by the family practitioners. Too many times there was a margin between the two opinions, through which the patient fell while the ER doc begged and pleaded and did a lot of ego stroking. Sometimes it was the patient who called the shots, when the condition worsened.

Ten minutes later Lukas drove into an overflowing ER parking lot. Two fire trucks were double-parked along the street with their lights still flashing. Three police cars took up space in patient parking, and two ambulances sat in the bay.

Inside, the scent of smoky clothes stirred through the air, and the ER proper sounded like a loud party minus the laughter, crowded as it was with fire fighters, ambulance attendants, police, and concerned family members. Somewhere in the chaos there must be patients. Judy had said so.

Lukas searched through the din and caught sight of the secretary at the desk waving toward him frantically.

"Thank goodness, Dr. Bower!" she called. "Dr. Garcias is doing a needle decompression in trauma room two, but the woman in one has some bad burns and smoke inhalation, and they need you in there. Beverly's in with her now doing a saline soak. Then we have a fireman in three who also has some smoke inhalation and a possible concussion from a collapsed ceiling. We already had five others in exam rooms. We're full and running."

Lukas pulled out the trauma gear. "Where was the fire this time, Judy?"

"Little Mary's Barbeque burned to the ground."

"Oh no." Little Mary's was practically a historic institution in Knolls. It was where the ambulance attendants and police and fire fighters and courthouse employees all took their dinner breaks. According to Mercy, it was a community heart attack waiting to happen.

Lukas loved barbeque, but he'd had an unfortunate incident at Little Mary's soon after his arrival in town, and he was afraid to return for fear of arrest. He'd been mistaken for a pervert when he'd innocently carried a medical textbook in with him to study one evening— a textbook complete with illustrations that would have been considered graphic anywhere outside a medical classroom. The café employees did not seem to take it well.

Lukas walked into the first trauma room to the accompaniment of coughing and groans of pain. Beverly, soon-to-be-Mrs. Cowboy Casey, was bent over a woman with a blackened face and singed hair and a deep grimace beneath the transparent blue oxygen mask. Sterile cloths were draped over burned portions of the woman's chest and arms, and Beverly murmured soothing words as she applied cool saline. She had already established two IV's with lactated ringers and had placed the patient on a monitor—carefully, between patches of red, blistered skin.

Beverly looked up long enough to see who came in. "Oh, good, Dr. Bower, you're here," she said, then returned to her work. "We have a fifty-year-old burn victim here, Mrs. Rose Dotson. She's in a lot of pain, with at least ten percent of her body covered in second-degree burns. She was one of the cooks who was trapped in an enclosed space with the fire."

"Ouch."

"Yeah, but not as bad as she could have been. The other cook was hit when the ceiling collapsed. Dr. Garcias did a needle decompression on her just a couple of minutes ago. We've had basic blood work and an arterial blood gas done on Rose, and the results should be back anytime." Beverly glanced again at Lukas as he checked the monitor, then she looked down at his hiking boots. "You didn't waste any time getting here. Going on a field trip?"

"Not anymore. Get out the morphine. We'll give it to her IV." Through the clear blue oxygen mask, he could see soot around Mrs. Dotson's mouth and nose, and she continued to cough between groans of pain. Lukas raised the mask long enough to check the patient's throat. She had soot there, as well. He checked Beverly's chart. Mrs. Dotson's heart rate was fast, with her pressure a little high, but most of that came from pain. The respiratory rate was elevated into the 20s. The $O_2$ saturation on a nonrebreather was 94. Initial saturation was 88, so he would leave the oxygen mask on her, but there was no sign of imminent airway compromise. Lukas located the intubation kit just in case he might need it.

While Beverly went out to the computerized drug dispenser for the morphine, Lukas rechecked the patient's vitals. He couldn't help overhearing the buzz of conversation throughout the ER. He heard Cherra Garcias talking in a calm, slightly accented voice in the next room. The needle decompression had been a success, and the patient was now conscious. Dr. Garcias was doing well, working with staff and patient, using just the right combination of authority and compassion. Now, if Lukas could hire a couple more docs just like her, he'd be happy.

When Beverly walked back into the room with the morphine, Lukas stepped out past a jumble of people and equipment. "Judy," he called to the secretary, "make arrangements to transfer Mrs. Dotson to a burn center."

Judy nodded and signaled to him, then picked up the phone. By the time Lukas grabbed a T-sheet for patient records and stepped back into the room, Mrs. Dotson's groaning and coughing had already begun to subside. Morphine was wonderful stuff . . . unless you were driving.

"Beverly, I want to start her on high dose steroids IV." He glanced at the monitor again, then began his own assessment, checking off pre-worded comments on the T-sheet.

"Have you heard from Mrs. Pinkley this morning?" Beverly asked.

He looked up. "No. Was she supposed to call me for something?"

"Well, I am either going to be fired, or the COBRA investigation is going to be called off, or both."

Lukas waited.

"That woman interviewed me this morning when I first got here." Beverly leaned forward to check Mrs. Dotson's IV's. The groaning had stopped, and the woman's eyes were half closed.

Beverly stepped a couple of feet from the bed and lowered her voice. "You might say Ms. Fellows and I didn't hit it off. The woman's a witch. She even looks like one, with that pasty complexion and eyes like a shark. And did you see her fingernails?"

"No, I don't think I—"

"She demanded to know why I was just now turning in an AMA form about Dwayne Little. I tried to explain that I was afraid the president of the hospital board would fire me if I did, and that I had a family to support. She asked me if you or Mrs. Pinkley were trying to coerce me in any way. Then she accused me of trying to impede her investigation! Of all the vicious, unprofessional . . . I tried to keep my cool, but I asked her when this suddenly became 'her' investigation instead of a COBRA investigation. She told me I was out of line, and I told her I'd read the book on COBRA rules and that I wasn't even close to any line as far as I could see. I told her she needed to take a refresher course."

Lukas controlled his facial muscles with effort. Yep, this was the old Beverly, all right. He'd missed working with her.

"So Ms. Fellows implied that I could lose my job over this," Beverly continued with a shrug. "I suggested to her that Bailey Little was either blackmailing her or having an affair with her, and she turned pale and left. But then, she's always pale, because she's a witch. Did you get a load of that hooked nose?"

"I didn't notice."

Beverly shook her head. "If I lose my job, I lose my job. I wish I'd had the guts to do this months ago, and we wouldn't have this problem." She adjusted the IV and checked the blood pressure again. "It's coming down. Looking good, Dr. Bower. Mrs. Dotson doesn't look like she's feeling much pain." She poured some more saline onto the sterile cloths. "I got some Silvadene cream out. Want me to use it?"

"No, we'll leave that up to the burn center. They don't like anything sticky on the skin. Give her a gram of Kefzol. We need to get her started on an antibiotic."

Judy stepped into the open doorway. "Dr. Bower, the ambulance crew is getting ready to transfer Mrs. Dotson. They were still here from the run from Little Mary's, so they'll just take her now. The St. John's burn unit is waiting for her." She looked around behind her, then stepped into the room and lowered her voice. "One of the patients is refusing to see Dr. Garcias. He saw you come through, and he wants you to treat him before you leave."

"Why is he refusing to see Dr. Garcias?" Lukas asked.

Judy lowered her voice further. "He said he wants to see a 'male American' doctor."

"Tell him Dr. Garcias is the only American doctor on duty today. I'm not officially on duty. I'm just helping out with the emergency." Lukas stepped to the sink to wash his hands. He would take care of the fireman in three, then escape this place before any of the department directors discovered he was here. If he waited around he could get sucked into hospital politics for the rest of the day. Somebody always had a gripe or a bright idea that just happened to involve the ER in some way.

He glanced over his shoulder at Beverly, who had just walked back into the room with the steroids and antibiotic he had requested for Mrs. Dotson. "Beverly, how's Cowboy doing these days? Is he giving that gunshot wound time to heal?"

"His arm is healing well. His heart's a different matter." She placed the needle of the syringe into the injection port of the IV.

"He's still upset about Leonardo. For the past few days he's been talking about getting another lion cub, and I told him when we get married he'll have enough wild animals to handle without adding more. My kids are a little on the spunky side. Good news, though. Berring is up to his old tricks, apparently. He jumped bail, and they found him over in Barry County, robbing a convenience store. They caught him and he's behind bars. From what I hear, he's practically in a straightjacket. The guy's nuts. Crazy. I just hope they keep him locked up tight this time."

———

At ten o'clock Friday morning, Mercy's secretary-receptionist stepped into the office with the day's mail. "Got something besides bills today, Dr. Mercy." She placed the stack squarely in front of Mercy and pointed to the top envelope, which had been slit open. Loretta always opened all the mail. "I stuck it back in the envelope. Just let me get out of here and close the door before you look at it." She made an exaggerated dash for the hallway and pulled the door shut.

Mercy rolled her eyes and shook her head. Like Josie, Loretta had been a fixture in this office for five years. Both were loyal, trusted friends.

The envelope had no return address, but Theodore's precise cursive grabbed Mercy's attention. She eased the envelope open cautiously, as if a spider might be lurking inside. She pulled out a sheet of triple-folded notebook paper, and when she unfolded it, another piece of paper fell out onto the desk. It was a cashier's check for fifty dollars.

She stared at it for a moment, then looked at the note he had written on the paper.

> *Mercy,*
>     *Please don't burn this. I know you don't want my money, but this isn't my money. It's yours and Tedi's. If you don't want to use it, just put it into a fund for Tedi's education. I'm going to try to do this every two weeks. That's how often you paid child support for all those years. When I make more money, I'll send more.*
>                                         *Theodore*

Mercy's fingers tightened on the paper. Okay, she was touched. Part of her wondered if this was genuine. Another part of her wanted to mail it back to him. She didn't want this kind of a connection with him, even if he never drank another drop of liquor. But this effort wasn't something the old Theodore would do. Had he truly had a change of heart?

And if she were convinced that he had, would she be able to forgive him? Logically, it was something she knew she needed to do, whether or not he had changed. Emotionally, she still felt within her a solid barrier of powerfully woven links of pain, anger, fear. What would it take to dislodge this hardened mass?

She wanted to try to do the right thing for Tedi's sake.

Still, she wasn't about to go to the trouble of opening a separate account with this little check, because it would probably be the last one she'd see from Theo.

She would hold the check and see what happened next.

---

Lukas treated the fireman for smoke inhalation and a slight concussion and released him to his family's care. Time to escape. Maybe a hike would still be possible.

He stepped out of the exam room to find Estelle Pinkley looming over him, waiting to pounce, every silver hair on her head in place, every movement genteel.

"How bad were the injuries this time?" she asked, turning to glance at the fire fighters outside the front entrance, then at the ambulance attendants at the central desk.

Lukas pulled off his gloves and mask. "Not as bad as expected. We flew one cook and transported another by ambulance, both to the burn unit at St. John's. The fireman wants to go home. His family will watch him."

She nodded soberly, then gestured for Lukas to follow her down the hallway, away from the lingering crowd. She lowered her voice. "Do you see an increase in the severity of each successive fire?"

"Not really. The first one caused a dangerous explosion that could have killed two people."

"The first one wasn't arson. The barbeque grill ignited a box that was too close, and the investigator found a faulty valve on the grill.

That fire might have been a trigger for the arsonist, though. We could be in for more major injuries, worse than this. Do we have all the supplies we might need in ER for a disaster?"

"We're completely stocked, but—"

"Good. I want to hire more staff, perhaps a float nurse, another tech, as quickly as possible. I've already asked Personnel to contact part-timers and see if they're interested in full-time for a while. We need to be prepared." She paused and shook her head. "It's hard to catch an arsonist. To do so, one must think like him, and then get him to confess." She straightened the hem of her suit jacket and then her already perfect posture. "I have a good conviction rate."

"Who're you going to convict?" They walked past a wall mural of a forest trail, and Lukas wished he were there now.

"No one I'm ready to make public." Estelle moved closer to him and lowered her voice. "I don't like the direction the evidence is pointing, and I'm not sure I trust it. That's all I can say at this point. I know whom I would *like* to be able to accuse, but it's safe to say that Bailey Little is only out to destroy the hospital, not the rest of the town."

Lukas gave her a sympathetic nod, and she continued.

"Speaking of Bailey, I just found out that Beverly's AMA report didn't call off the investigation."

Lukas stopped walking and stared at Estelle. Disappointment overwhelmed him for a moment. "How is that possible? I was under the impression that was all we needed. I thought if we had a witness that I had offered the proper medication, and that I offered drug abuse rehab, they would drop the investigation."

"I asked Ms. Fellows the same question." Estelle pressed her lips together for a moment of thought. "She believes Beverly was coerced."

"That woman is malicious, vindictive—"

"And digging herself deeper into trouble every day she stays here." Estelle smiled at Lukas and patted his arm. "I'm not just sitting on my hands up in that office, Lukas. Trust me."

————

"I hate him. I hate him." Abby Cuendet sat down next to Tedi in class, hands gripping the sides of her desk, glasses fogged over from tears that flowed from her eyes. Nobody else in the class noticed, because all the students were doing one of the work projects where they were allowed to talk to one another.

"Who do you hate?" Tedi asked. Abby had just arrived three hours late, with no note for Mr. Walters or the principal. No excuse. Mr. Walters was looking in Abby's direction, but he just shook his head sadly and stayed at his desk.

Abby didn't act as if she'd even heard Tedi's question. She stopped saying the words out loud, but her mouth continued to move. She closed her eyes, and more tears spilled out.

"Abby?" Tedi leaned across the aisle and touched her friend's skinny arm. "What's wrong? What happened?"

Abby checked to see if anybody was looking at her, then she took her glasses off and wiped her eyes and nose with the cuff of her long-sleeved T-shirt. She wiped off her glasses, then sniffed and put them back on.

Tedi sighed and returned to her work.

Five minutes later, Abby said, "He blames Mom for losing me Monday."

Tedi looked back over at her. "Who does?"

"Dad. I heard them fighting this morning, and Mom followed Dad outside so April and Andy wouldn't hear them. I had to stay and keep an eye on them. Next thing I knew, Dad was peeling out of the driveway toward work, and Mom was running back into the house crying. Then she had to get ready for work, and she was afraid she'd get fired, because this is the third day she's been late in two weeks."

"Your *dad* blamed your *mom* when *you* didn't call Monday?" Tedi stressed the words and got a dirty look from Abby. "Your mom called all over trying to find you that day, Abby. How was she supposed to know where you were? Grandma had three messages on her recorder when we got back. Mom had two."

"I know. My mother finally called your mother's office, and they told her I was okay. But before that Mom called Dad at work when she couldn't find me."

"It doesn't sound to me like you're bringing your parents closer. It sounds to me like they're fighting because of you."

Abby shot Tedi a narrow-eyed look and didn't say another word.

Lukas walked back into the house at one o'clock in the afternoon. He'd been at the hospital for four hours. It seemed as if every department director in the hospital had discovered he was there and wanted to talk to him before he got away. He hadn't gotten away; there would be no hike today. He pulled off his boots and unloaded his backpack.

The telephone rang.

He groaned. That couldn't be the hospital again. Let the telephone ring. It was probably a telemarketer, and when the recorder kicked in, they wouldn't leave a message and he would be off the hook.

But after the recorder finished its spiel, he heard Mercy's voice on the other end of the line. "What's for dinner tonight?"

Lukas dropped his boots and backpack, raced to the phone, and picked up before she could say another word. "How about Wheaties? I've got a package of Rice Krispies Treats somewhere for dessert."

There was a pause, and for a moment he wondered if he'd cut her off. "Mercy?"

"Should I dress up?"

"It'll be pretty casual."

Another pause, then, "So I'm still invited?"

Oh yes, she was invited. "Of course."

"And you're not mad at me?"

Lukas couldn't stop the smile, and the sense of relief, and the sudden reaction of warmth he felt at the plaintive tone of her voice. "I thought you were mad at me."

"I'm mad at myself. I've been that way a lot lately. I've got to go. Patients are coming in."

"Does eight o'clock work for you?"

"Sure. Then maybe I'll have everybody cleared out of here in time. See you, Lukas."

He hung up, looked at the clock, panicked. He had to go to the store. He had to take a shower and do some laundry because he was out of clothes. And he had to find a cookbook somewhere in this town and learn how to cook in one afternoon. He was going to see

Mercy tonight. He could think no further than that.

The theme song of *Mission Impossible* pounded through his head, and he jumped up from the sofa and ran into the kitchen. It seemed like the best place to begin.

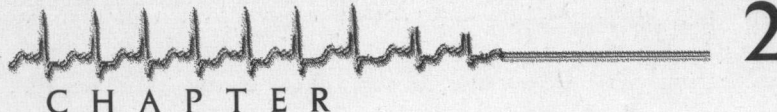

# CHAPTER 21

F riday night Lukas decided to barbeque hamburgers on his out-door gas grill. He'd never done it before, but he'd watched his brothers do it a couple of times, and it didn't look too hard. Besides, how complicated could it be to throw a couple of handfuls of ground beef over a fire and let them brown? He had more important things to think about. He had some more arguing to do with God.

For instance, why did he have to completely break it off with Mercy? Why couldn't they just take a backward step in their relationship? They'd been friends for six months without any dire conse-quences, and Mercy was more open to the subject of spiritual things now than she had ever been before. She had changed. Even Ivy had noticed, and she gave Lukas partial credit. Wouldn't it even hurt Mercy's growth toward God if Lukas broke off their friendship now? Wouldn't she feel ostracized? Abandoned?

Smoke from the dripping grease in the grill made his mouth water, until it thickened and blackened and aimed for his eyes. He coughed and tried to move out of the way, but a slight breeze picked up and seemed to swirl the smoke directly at him no matter which way he moved. He finally ducked and let the smoke rise over his head.

What a stupid way to cook food.

Before he could straighten and close the lid to the grill, a shrill, pulsing scream reached him from inside the kitchen. It took him about five seconds to realize it was the smoke alarm. By that time another scream joined it from the hallway. He leaped forward, slammed down the lid to the grill, and raced through the sliding patio door into the dining room.

By the time he reached the kitchen, another alarm joined the first two for an effect straight out of a sci-fi movie. He grabbed a dish towel to wave it at the alarm. It didn't help. Reaching up he opened the alarm casing, jerked out the battery, and ran toward the hallway to do the same. That was when he caught sight of the living room clock. Great, he only had ten minutes to turn off the alarms, clear out the smoke, and stuff away some of the clutter around the house that he hadn't taken the time to pick up and hide earlier before Mercy arrived.

He was pulling a stepladder through the hallway when he saw movement from the corner of his vision. He turned to find Mercy standing in the living room. She wore a simple red T-shirt and black jeans and sandals, and laughter mingled comically with a grimace on her face. She was shaking her head and covering her ears with her hands. He waved at her, pulled the battery, and carried the ladder into the bedroom to do the same.

Quiet came at last. Boy, these were sensitive alarms!

He went back to apologize to Mercy and found her in the backyard, sliding blackened discs from the grill onto a paper plate.

"I rang the doorbell," she explained, "but I heard the smoke alarm, so I thought you might need some help." She replaced the lid to the grill and picked up a hamburger. "Mmm, looks delicious," she murmured. "I can tell you've done this lots of times before."

She led the way back into the kitchen, where she set the plate of furnace-heated burgers. She pointed toward a large paper bag she had set on the counter. "Mom sent us a grilled green tomato salad to go along with . . . dinner."

"You can put the stuff in the refrigerator." Lukas glanced helplessly at his battered, hand-me-down dining room table, where he had plowed through enough stacks of unopened mail to clear two spaces. He had laid out two place mats decorated with scenes from the Jurassic era, and two dinosaur-decorated glasses filled with Mercy's favorite pink lemonade—the scenery on the glasses disappeared when filled with cold liquid, then reappeared as the liquid was consumed. Somehow, it didn't look as appealing as it had an hour ago. It looked childish. But it was all he had.

Mercy placed her bag in the refrigerator, coughed, and stepped over to close the kitchen window, where smoke from the grill continued to drift inside.

This evening was nothing like Lukas had hoped it would be when he'd first issued the invitation. The staff at the hospital teased him because he always ordered extra when he ate out, then took the left-overs home and lived on them for a couple of days. They called him the Doggy Bag King. So far, Mercy didn't seem too impressed with his domestic abilities, either.

But he wasn't trying to impress her.

He thought again about his discussion with Theo Thursday night, and his long, heartfelt arguments with God later.

Lukas watched as Mercy stood gazing around the kitchen and dining area. On a borrowed hutch in the corner sat a nice little array of old Star Trek paraphernalia collected from his nephews, who knew he was a Trekkie. Alongside them sat a box with a GPS navigational system for hiking, which he hadn't yet opened.

His stereo cabinet held a clock with stainless steel balls that rolled down a series of tracks every hour. The walls were still bare.

"Let me guess," Mercy said. "You didn't hire an interior decorator."

"Why would I want to? Most of these things are gifts from my family."

Mercy strolled over to a curio stand by the patio door. "Do you realize I've never even been past your living room before today? I'm discovering a whole new side of you, Lukas."

He thought of her expertly decorated home, her matched towels, her perfectly cooked and served dinners on fine china—which he happened to know were antiques given to her by her grandmother. She wasn't a snob, but compared to her home, his was a flea market wonderland. He thought of the Rolls Royce replica alarm clock in his bedroom and the bulletin board with pictures of his family stick-pinned to it.

He cleared his throat. "Ready to eat?"

"I can't wait." She continued gazing around the roomy, though cluttered, kitchen and reached up with typical feminine curiosity to open a cupboard door.

Lukas suddenly remembered what gadget he had hidden behind that particular door. "No, wait! Don't—"

A stuffed, coiled rattlesnake seemed to pounce from the cabinet with fangs bared. Mercy screamed and stumbled backward, and

Lukas rushed forward to grab her before she tripped over the step stool behind her. Every spot he touched seemed to tingle with awareness. He didn't want to let her go. Not in any sense of the word. Already, she felt like a part of him, and when she gently stepped from his embrace, he felt as if a piece of his heart went with her.

She stared at the snake, then looked at Lukas. "Don't even bother to explain."

"It's authentic." He swallowed and willed his breathing to return to normal. "My oldest brother's kids got it for me for my birthday when they took a trip out west this summer. I usually keep it on top of one of my stereo speakers."

She chuckled. "Why don't we just eat?"

To Mercy's voiced surprise, the hamburgers were good—once they got past the burnt and crunchy exteriors. They used part of the salad on the burgers, since Lukas had forgotten to get lettuce and tomatoes. Lukas didn't realize they didn't have napkins until they finished their meals.

He reached over and lifted a stack of mail and mistakenly uncovered a set of realistic-looking foam rubber replicas of a heart, a brain, and a kidney, which he had received from drug reps at various medical conferences over the years. Beneath the heart replica lay a roll of paper towels. He tore off a section and handed it to her.

Mercy wiped barbeque sauce from her lips, then formed a tent with her hands and placed her chin on it, still staring at the various body parts. "Did anybody ever tell you that you've still got a lot of little boy in you?" She smiled at the cluttered corners of his dining room and the stacks of mail he hadn't opened in two weeks. "Do you ever get behind on bills?"

"I lose them sometimes, or I accidentally throw them away. So far the electric company has been forgiving. I've got to stop some of the junk mail I get."

"I have never seen a bachelor more in need of a companion."

The living room bird clock suddenly sang out its cardinal call as Lukas considered Mercy's obviously leading comment. He said nothing. He wanted to tell her how wonderful a companion she would be.

Her smile slowly vanished, and she bent her head.

Lukas swallowed hard and changed the subject. "I think you're doing the right thing by agreeing to let Tedi see Theodore again . . .

and by going with her." He hadn't realized it would be so hard to say those words. He didn't want to think of Theodore and Mercy rebuilding a relationship, but he had no right to be jealous. Not now.

Mercy stood up to clear the table. "I didn't come over here to talk about Theodore. I came to sample your cooking and enjoy your company and forget about this past week. It's been a killer."

He hesitated, took a final swallow of his drink, and stood to help her. "I really think he's sincere about his new faith."

She found the dishwasher and jerked the door open with more force than necessary. "You don't know him as well as I do."

"It's been over five years since your divorce. How well do you really still know him?"

"And you've been in town less than six months and talked to him probably five or six times." She shoved the white Corelle plates into the dishwasher rack and straightened to look at Lukas. "You really think you can tell me anything about him I don't know?"

"I think I can look at the situation from a less biased standpoint. You're so filled with anger you can't see anything but bad memories. You must have some good ones somewhere."

She shook her head. "Why would I want to? *He* rejected *me*, remember? Do you know how traumatizing that is? And don't give me all that garbage about how it takes two to ruin a marriage." She shook her head and raised her arms in a silencing gesture. "I've heard it."

"I wasn't going to—"

"Enough about divorce, okay?"

Lukas sighed and walked back over to his chair. He sank down into it, watching Mercy. "Until you learn to forgive him you won't be able to get on with—"

"I've heard that, too."

Lukas tried to curb his growing irritation. "Well, you're not listening, so you need to hear it again," he snapped. He saw the surprise in her eyes and was surprised at himself. He had never spoken sharply to her. "Mercy, your bitterness is still showing. It's crippling you emotionally, and it's going to damage every relationship you have if you don't deal with it."

She leaned against the edge of the kitchen counter and crossed her arms over her chest. "Even ours?"

He heard the plaintive sound of her voice, the same tone he'd heard over the telephone this afternoon. It touched him deeply. And painfully. He knew there would be no backing off just one step. There was no going back to the friendship they had shared over the summer. Something had changed between them, and he knew he couldn't control the power of it. So far, the power had controlled him.

"Lukas?"

He looked up at her. She was so beautiful . . . so vulnerable. So open. And he needed to be open with her. She deserved that from him. He cleared his throat. "You can't have healthy future relationships until you can allow forgiveness to heal your past—all of your past. I'm not just talking about your forgiving Theo."

She watched him for a moment, her eyes holding his steadily.

He couldn't look away. "I'm also talking about your forgiving your father for his alcoholism. And while you're at it, you might try forgiving yourself." He swallowed, shifted in his seat, and breathed deeply. He could tell by her expression that this was going to become more and more uncomfortable. He couldn't even bear the thought of not seeing her again. He had reason to believe she wouldn't be too crazy about the idea, either.

"Lukas, if I was able to do all this forgiving, do you think all my relationships would improve?" There was a breathless, expectant quality to her voice.

"Yes." *Tell her. Say it! Say you can't see her again.*

She hesitated. "Yours and mine?"

The chair became very uncomfortable. "We already have a good . . . friendship." *You coward!* But this was so . . . impossible. *God, if you want me to back away from her now, you'll have to do it through me. I can't do it myself. I can't do this to her!*

"How good, Lukas?" She pushed away from the counter and walked back over to kneel next to him. He could almost touch the bond that connected them. "Is there some kind of future for us? Is there some possibility that this 'good friendship' will turn into more?"

He took another deep breath and willed his heart to stop. Period. This was too hard.

But he couldn't fantasize about a future with her, and he couldn't allow her to do it, either. "Mercy . . ." He hesitated, looked into her eyes, looked away.

"Because I think it already has," she said quickly, as if she was afraid of the answer she could already read in his expression. "I'm not trying to pressure you. It's just that I can't help believing you feel the same way I do."

She reached up and squeezed his arm, the touch of her hand sending warmth and pleasure all over his body. The power there could paralyze him. Her affection was such a new experience for him. And frightening.

And he had no resistance. He had to rely on God's power for this. He didn't understand it. He just knew the truth. The powerful need he felt between them right now was not something that would draw her to Christ. It might well be something that could draw Lukas away from his convictions and, eventually, destroy their relationship. He had no human hope of controlling the emotions between them. Only the Spirit of Christ could do that, and she did not belong to that Spirit.

He saw it now. It didn't make this less painful, but he understood.

"Isn't that important?" she asked. "The way we feel about each other? The way we communicate so well, even without words a lot of times? That we have so much in common?"

He had to be honest with her. He couldn't lead her on or lead himself on any longer. He knew what he had to do. He looked back down at her. "There is one major thing we don't have in common, and for me that's the most important thing," he said quietly.

At the widening pain of her eyes and the swift intake of her breath, he felt a shaft of resistance shoot through him. But only for a moment. *Yes, Lord.*

There was a long silence. Lukas felt the weight of her disappointment. Was this how it felt to have your heart break?

"Why are you doing this all of a sudden?" she asked at last. "I thought . . . there was such a connection. You've been so tender, so . . . honest. I'm not some silly little schoolgirl who thinks of a kiss as a promise, but you waited for so long, and everything was suddenly so right. I thought it meant something to you, too."

"It meant a lot." It meant . . . too much. "I'm sorry, Mercy. You can't imagine how much it has meant to me to have you in my life. I—"

"Is there somebody else?" Her voice held an unaccustomed tremble.

He shot her a startled look and saw tears shimmering in her dark eyes. "No!"

The tears spilled over. "It's the menopause, isn't it? Somebody told you about my test results. Why should I be surprised in Knolls, Missouri? Of course you'd want children. A man like you—"

"Menopause? You're in menopause?" The knife pierced a little deeper into his heart. What had he done to her? Now she was going to think—

She nodded. "The hot flashes . . . I had an FSH—"

"Oh, Mercy, no." He reached out and touched her then. He couldn't help himself. Couldn't help the tender compassion that flowed through him. She leaned against his chest, and his arms reached out to her in an irresistible embrace. He felt the softness of her hair against his face. This time it was she who drew away.

"You deserve children, Lukas."

"Of course I'd love to have children someday, but I'm not looking for a mother for future children. I want a mate to share my life with, the one whom God has chosen for me, and if He chooses not to give us children, then that would be something I could accept."

Sudden understanding dawned on her face. "Oh." His own pain reflected in her eyes, and then a flash of confusion. "It's a God thing."

He took a deep breath, held her gaze a moment longer, and nodded. That was one way to put it. It was the correct conclusion, but how could he explain something she would not be able to completely understand without that same Spirit in her?

"Mercy," he said gently. "I care so much about you. A great deal. I don't know what I'm going to do without you, and I'm going to miss you like crazy. It will be hard to get over you." His voice broke.

She slumped back in her chair and shuffled her fingers through her hair in frustration. "Lukas, you sound like a man in love to me." Her voice still had that plaintive quality in it that broke his heart.

He pushed away from the table and stood to his feet and reached down to draw her up with him. "I'm sorry. I know how you feel, because I think I feel the same way, but, Mercy, this is wrong for us now." What he didn't say was that it might always be wrong for them.

What about Theo? "You were right the night you suggested we stop seeing each other. I was wrong to argue."

"No, Lukas." A quiet urgency entered her voice now.

"I kept telling myself . . . but I know you haven't come to that place in your life where you can allow God to take control, and we shouldn't get any closer—"

She dropped her hands to her sides and stared at him. *"Control?"* Anger gradually replaced the tears in her eyes. "You're telling me I need to give my soul to a heartless God who leads me on with the hope of a future with you and then supposedly tells you to dump me?"

"He didn't tell me to dump—"

She backed away from him. "Where's all that compassion I see you sharing with your patients, Lukas?" The anger deepened and grew. "Where's that intelligence you displayed when you brought Darlene back from death Monday?" Her fists clenched together at her sides. "How can you stand there in your self-righteous judgment and tell me I haven't given enough to your demanding God?" She shook her head, looked around for her purse, found it, and jerked it from the counter. "I'm out of here. You're crazy."

"No! Please, Mercy, wait." He followed her through the house. "I know I'm saying this all wrong, but I need to explain—"

She shoved open the front door and rushed outside before he could reach her. The door slammed in his face with a heavy thud, and seconds later her car started.

He ran out onto his front porch in time to see her reversing from the driveway onto the street. Her tires squealed against blacktop as she drove away, and she did not look back.

———

Mercy drove down the last block to her house at ten miles per hour, tears still dripping down her face and onto her shirt. She managed to find a Kleenex in the seat of her car and dabbed away most of the obvious signs of her crying. But inside she was bleeding, and no amount of tears could wash that away.

She knew she was arriving home far too early, and Mom and Tedi would wonder why, but she wasn't in the mood to drive around and kill time just to keep up a pretense.

Had this whole summer been a pretense? Had she been fooling herself into believing that something good was actually going to happen to her?

Something inside her must be inherently ugly and unlovable, and she had been rejected once again. No matter what she did, how hard she had tried to be a good doctor, a good mother, a good daughter, a good wife, she had never measured up. She felt worthless.

She pulled into her driveway alongside Mom's car and turned off the motor. She slapped the dashboard with her hand, winced at the pain, and glared up into the nearly dark sky. "What do you want from me?" she asked through gritted teeth. "Why don't you just strike me dead if you hate me so much? Do you just enjoy torturing people?" She grabbed her purse and forced herself to get out of the car.

Though still raw, she stepped inside the quiet house and walked back to Tedi's bedroom to find Ivy sitting on the side of the bed while Tedi read to her. They both looked up in surprise.

"Hi, Mom," Tedi called.

Mercy frowned at them. "Bed already? It's Friday night."

"I coerced her," Ivy explained. "I told her if she'd go to bed early, I'd take her on that cancer walkathon with me in the morning, if that's okay with you."

Mercy nodded. The hospital had been advertising something about that this week, but she'd been too busy to take much notice.

Ivy leaned over and kissed her granddaughter, then stood up and crossed the room toward Mercy. "And since Tedi just finished reading me the end of the third chapter in her book, I think I'll make my escape." She frowned and sniffed at Mercy. "You smell like smoke."

"I had barbequed house for dinner," Mercy explained. *And barbequed heart.*

Ivy nodded. "Oh yeah, Lukas was supposed to be cooking tonight, wasn't he? Hope you had a good time."

Mercy avoided Ivy's questioning glance. "If you like rattlesnakes and dinosaurs and Star Trek." *And being dumped.*

"No kidding?" Tedi exclaimed from the bed.

"Yeah, you would've loved it."

"A real rattlesnake?" Tedi asked.

"It was dead, but it was real."

"I've got some good news for you," Ivy said. "Tedi and I visited Clarence Knight this afternoon. He's quite a character, isn't he?"

Mercy nodded, feeling her hopes rise in spite of her heartache. "What did you think?"

"I've never met anybody quite so . . . big, and not just physically. He really loves his sister, doesn't he? I'll keep an eye on him for a while, but I think he needs more help than that."

"Oh? What kind of help? They can't afford to have anyone move in with them."

"I know. I've got some ideas, but I want to think about them overnight. I'll talk to you about it tomorrow." Ivy paused, studying Mercy's face more closely. "Honey, is everything okay?"

Mercy didn't have the energy to lie. She shook her head. "I don't want to talk about it."

Ivy nodded in silence. "Okay. Maybe later." She pulled Mercy into a quick, unaccustomed embrace, then wrinkled her nose. "Phew, you stink. You'd better wash your hair before you go to bed." She turned to her granddaughter. "I'll be seeing you in the morning, Tedi. Can you be up by seven without waking your mom?"

"Yes, Grandma. I used to do that kind of thing all the time when I lived with Dad."

"Good for you." Ivy shot Mercy one more questioning glance, then left.

Tedi pushed back her blankets and scooted up in bed until she was sitting up against her pillows. "Mom, what's wrong? You look sick."

Mercy nodded. In a way she was. "I'll be okay." She strolled over and took her mother's place on the side of Tedi's bed. "What book are you reading?"

"It's called *Another Chance*. I got it at the school library. It's about this teenaged girl named Gordy who's always getting into trouble—a lot like me, except I'm not a teenager yet."

Mercy couldn't help smiling at her daughter. "So what happens to Gordy?"

"She goes out to this lake to keep a girl from killing herself, and she makes her boyfriend swear not to tell anybody she's going, and she won't let him go with her."

"And what happens then?"

"Her boyfriend tells on her anyway, and her father and a teacher come out just in time to rescue her from drowning. I've already read the book three times. I like it because Gordy's parents are divorced, like mine. It makes me feel like somebody else knows what I'm going through." Tedi hesitated. "You know what, Mom? There's even a place in the book where Gordy thinks her parents are going to get back together, and everything will be the way it used to be. It doesn't turn out that way. I guess I'm not the only one who thinks about stuff like that."

Mercy sighed heavily and closed her eyes. "No, you're not." Lukas was a dreamer, too. Far too idealistic. And sincere . . . He really had meant what he'd said about letting God take control. That thought eased some of her anger. It didn't help with the frustration, but she had to admit that he wouldn't have lied just to get rid of her. He really was going to miss her, probably as badly as she would miss him.

"Mom?"

Mercy opened her eyes again. "Yes?"

"What do you think about the boyfriend in this book who broke his promise and told on Gordy? Do you think he did the right thing? It saved Gordy's life."

Mercy thought about Abner and Delphi Bell. "I'm sure that's what the writer of the book wanted you to believe."

Tedi's eyes widened. "You mean he shouldn't have said anything?"

"I didn't say that. My concern is the principle involved. I don't believe in breaking a confidentiality." And she felt as if she had done just that yesterday, even though it might well have saved Abner's life. In retrospect, would she have done the same thing again?

"But what if it would be saving somebody's life?" Tedi asked.

Yes, Mercy knew she probably would have done the same thing again, because it was a human life, even though it was somebody like Abner Bell. But was she right? "I know there are exceptions to every rule, but when it comes down to breaking promises, then I feel that leads to a breakdown in ethics. When someone feels it's okay to break a trust, how far will they go?" And look what happened to Delphi.

Now she had a police record. Sort of.

Tedi heaved a sigh of obvious exasperation. "But, Mom, it was to save lives. She was doing something she shouldn't've been doing in the first place."

Mercy echoed the sigh and shook her head. Why did Tedi always choose the worst possible times to introduce a deep philosophical discussion? "Sorry, honey, I'm not up to the subject tonight. Why don't we sleep on it? Maybe you can read the book to me next week, and then we'll talk about it."

"It's a long book. It'll take a while." Tedi sounded disappointed.

"Fine, we'll do three chapters a night. Surely that won't be too difficult." Mercy leaned over and kissed Tedi good-night.

Tedi's nose wrinkled. "Grandma's right. You smell like smoke."

"Good night," Mercy said firmly.

As she made her way to bed, without washing her hair, she re-played the angry words she'd hurled at Lukas tonight. *"Where's all that compassion . . . where's that intelligence?"* And she knew the de-scriptions were appropriate. Lukas *was* compassionate and intelligent. He wasn't some Bible thumper who got carried away with religious emotionalism. He didn't hear voices in his head. He made good de-cisions about patient care, and he had always treated her with respect.

She had known him for nearly six months, and she'd never known him to be impulsive. And he was obviously sincere about why he was ending their relationship.

Should she pay more attention to his words?

# CHAPTER 22

"C larence, I don't know what to do with you." It was eight o'clock Saturday morning, and Mercy had been awake for over an hour. She leaned on the end rail of her favorite patient's extra-sturdy hospital bed and pushed the empty breakfast tray toward the door so an aide could collect it without disturbing them.

"I know one thing you could do," he growled. "Go away and let me finish my dream."

"You'll get your chance. Was it a good dream?"

"Real good. I could see my toes. And I could walk without having to use a cane to help carry the load, and my back didn't hurt."

Mercy stifled another yawn. She must have been crazy last night when she thought she could just burrow under the covers and forget everything. She'd fallen asleep sometime after two and had awakened long before Tedi's alarm clock went off at seven. So here she was on hospital rounds for the day, being glared at by Clarence's sleep-swollen eyes.

"It'll happen, Clarence. Give it time. You have to take care of yourself and lose more weight."

The big man grunted and shook his head. "Do you know how hard it's been to lose thirty-eight pounds?"

"Sixty-three pounds," she reminded him.

"Yeah, but you told me twenty-five of that was water, so all I really lost was thirty-eight pounds of fat and probably a bunch of muscle. I thought I was dying. I've got two hundred and fifty pounds to go, and I'm so hungry I can't see straight, even with the drugs I'm taking to keep me from being hungry. And you've been telling me that I've got to eat even less because my metabolism is slowing down because I'm not getting enough food. It's crazy! What if my metabolism stops altogether?"

"That will mean you're dead, and we're not going to let that happen."

"I can't even get out of bed."

"That will change." Mercy reached across the rail and picked up the chart that hung on a hook there. Except for complaints from one nurse who couldn't get a good blood pressure reading because of his size, his numbers looked good. "We don't want to exercise those parts of your body that are still injured," she said, "but you can go back to your arm exercises." She patted the biceps of his right arm. "Lots of weight to lift there. We just want to be careful not to pull any more muscles, or to reinjure the ones that are healing."

"I just hope I can still walk when I get out of here. And that reminds me, when *am* I getting out?"

She raised a warning hand. "One thing at a time, Clarence. I'm scared to even let you out of the bed to go to the bathroom yet, and I don't trust you to go home. My mother wants to help you, but I've got to be sure you're emotionally stable enough to work with her. She can be a tyrant."

"Oh yeah? I met her yesterday. She's not as bossy as you."

"You just saw her good side. Wait until she gets you alone."

"I've put up with you all summer. I can put up with her."

"How do you feel about surgery?" Mercy shot back. "We could have your stomach stapled. If you think your pathway to the bathroom is well worn now—"

"Okay, okay, I'll be good and eat my lettuce leaf and drink my water every day." His eyes betrayed a spark of humor, then grew serious again. "When's sis coming home?"

"Soon, we hope." And that was one reason Mercy hesitated to release Clarence too soon. "Dr. Weathers said he might be able to send her back here Monday or Tuesday, although he doesn't want her to be alone."

"Then let me out of—"

"Not so fast, pal. Just let me finish. My mother has promised to clear her schedule to help you and Darlene while you're both convalescing. Mom's rounded up some friends at church to help out, but . . ." Mercy hesitated.

Clarence narrowed his eyes in suspicion. "But what?"

"You're not going to like this part."

"What part?"

"I know how independent you are, and this would be hard on you, but I think it would be best for both you and Darlene while you recuperate."

"What're you talking about?"

"I don't want you to refuse immediately. Take some time to—"

"Mercy!" His voice echoed through the room in a low roar.

She grimaced. "Mom wants you and Darlene to stay with her."

He stared at her for a moment. "You mean, like spend a couple of days there?"

"More than a couple, Clarence. There's a little apartment at the far end of her house. My grandmother lived in it for a while." She paused, trying to read Clarence's expression.

His continued stare veiled his thoughts.

"Mom also has a lot of exercise equipment," Mercy said. "You can use it as you lose weight."

"What do you mean? It's gonna take me a long time to . . . oh no, you don't! I'm not anybody's permanent houseguest. We can't just pick everything up and leave our home and—"

"Aren't you forgetting something, Clarence?" Mercy asked quietly. She waited a moment, and she felt his pain when realization dawned in his face. Because of his situation, he had been a permanent houseguest for two years.

"She wants to coach you back into a trim, healthy body. She wants Darlene to join you. With the apartment you would have privacy, but my mother—who prides herself on her healthy cooking and lifestyle—wants to take you on as a challenge. My grandmother lived with her until last spring, and Mom has been taking care of my daughter this summer, but she's lonely." Mercy knew she was chattering to ease the awkwardness. It was unusual to have this much contact with a patient, but her heart went out to both Clarence and Darlene. "Would you at least think about it?"

He closed his eyes for a long time, then took a deep breath. "I'm not stupid, Mercy. The setup Darlene and I had wasn't working. I've gotta try something else for her sake." He opened his eyes and fixed Mercy with a glare. "But we'll pay our way."

Battling the shock she felt at this unexpected capitulation, Mercy smiled her first smile of the day. "I wouldn't expect anything else from you."

He took another deep breath and changed the subject. "So how's your love life?"

———

Tedi drank another cup of Gatorade that some people passed out to walkers from the pickup truck that drove along the country road and kept track of everyone. She had a blister on her right big toe and another one on her left heel, and she was tired. They'd walked four miles, and Grandma just kept walking faster, passing at least half of her fifty million friends, catching up on gossip—although Grandma didn't call it gossip. She called it concern for your neighbors. After a while, Tedi stopped listening. Grown-up stuff got boring after a couple of hours. And Tedi had other things to think about besides county taxes and hospital finances and suspected arsonists.

Last night, after Mom went to bed, Tedi had called Abby to invite her to the walk this morning. Abby said no. She didn't even bother to ask her parents. She just refused, which was not like Abby.

She'd been acting so weird lately, getting mad and shouting one minute, then laughing too loudly the next. She'd slapped three other kids in the past two weeks during recess, and Mr. Walters had seen it. He'd called Abby in and talked to her after class one day, but Abby never said anything about it, and Tedi was afraid she'd get slugged, too, if she asked.

Tedi was worried about her, but what was she supposed to do? She couldn't tell anybody that Abby might hurt herself to keep her parents from fighting. Nobody would believe her. And Mom had said it wasn't ethical to break a promise.

She should never have promised.

". . . saw Dr. Mercy peeling out from his house last night like she was a race-car driver. First time I ever saw somebody lay rubber with a front-wheel drive. Dr. Bower ran after her down the driveway, but she didn't even look back. She didn't see me across the street, either. . . ."

The words of Grandma's chatterbox friend suddenly registered. Tedi looked up and saw Grandma's suddenly grim expression.

"So you're saying my daughter seemed upset," Grandma said quietly.

"That's the understatement of the month!" her friend replied. "It sounds like Dr. Mercy and Dr. Bower broke up. Hope it doesn't put Dr. Mercy in a bad mood, 'cause I've got an appointment with her Monday."

Tedi stared up at the woman in shock. Mom and Lukas broke up? That's what Mom was so upset about last night?

How horrible! They couldn't break up! Mom was in love with Lukas.

"You know what this could mean, don't you?" the friend said. "A family reconciliation. It's biblical, and now that the ex has straightened out his life . . ."

Grandma walked faster, and Tedi had to hustle to keep up. They left the one gossipy friend behind and in a few minutes joined Dr. Hugh Heagerty, the retired doc that Grandma liked.

Tedi sighed. "Here we go again," she muttered under her breath. This was why she always hated going to town with Mom or Grandma. They knew everyone in Knolls, and every time they stepped out of their house, it seemed, they ran into one of their friends—no, make that fifteen of their friends, one at a time. And, of course, they had to "catch up" on news. Tedi was moving to another state when she grew up.

While Dr. Heagerty and Grandma talked, Tedi thought about last night. Mom had been really upset about something. *And all I could do was tell her about my stupid book and ask stupid questions about breaking promises.*

How could this happen? Mom and Lukas never fought. Even when they argued about something, they never got mad. Tedi would know, because she'd listened to Mom and Dad fight plenty of times. Mom was always in a good mood when Lukas was around. So was Tedi. Lukas had helped Tedi put up a rope swing this summer under Grandma's big tree in the backyard, and even though the rope came untied three times while Lukas tested it, he finally got it right.

And Lukas never got mad and shouted or threatened the way Dad used to.

Lukas was also the one who had introduced Dad to Jesus. Dad said so himself.

Grandma and Dr. Heagerty caught up with three more walkers. To Tedi's relief the pace slowed. These were more friends of Grandma's, and the same old routine began that Tedi had witnessed at least a dozen times already this morning, with at least two and sometimes three people talking at once.

". . . haven't seen you in weeks. Where are you hiding out?"

". . . read that Bailey Little's letter in the paper the other day . . ."

". . . ever catch that guy who shot Cowboy?"

The chattering voices continued to float over Tedi, and after they exclaimed over how pretty Tedi was, and how much she looked like Grandma and Mom, they ignored her. Thank goodness.

". . . hear they're narrowing down the suspects for the fires, but I think they're sniffing up the wrong tree . . ."

". . . think they'd have the arsonist already if they had money for a real investigation . . ."

". . . you have to think like an arsonist to catch an arsonist. That's what my cousin told me at the dinner last week . . ."

". . . hospital's taking up all the revenue . . ."

". . . RealCare could buy us out and shut us down or raise the fees so high we couldn't afford medical care . . ."

". . . Dr. Mercy and her fella breakin' up . . ."

Tedi was not going on any more of these cancer walks.

---

"You win," Mercy muttered as she turned into her driveway at home. She didn't designate the subject of her address. He knew who He was. "I get the message. I'm not good enough for Lukas. I'll leave him alone. Is that all you want from me?"

She heard the bitter challenge in her own voice, but she couldn't help it.

She got out of the car and went into the house. Tedi wouldn't be home yet, thank goodness. She was having lunch with Mom. It would be hard to put on a smiling face today.

The answering machine beeped that someone had called. Mercy looked over to find that she had one message. She hit the Play button and then caught her breath when she heard Lukas's voice.

"Hello, Mercy. I hope this doesn't wake you. I had a lot of trouble sleeping last night. I hope you slept like a log."

There was a pause, and Mercy realized he was trying to choose his words so that it wouldn't be too traumatizing in case Tedi got the message instead of her. He sounded wonderful to her, and she drank in the flow of his voice like a kid who had been given the last chocolate candy bar she would ever eat.

"You know how I have a bad habit of sticking both feet in my mouth?" he continued. "That's what I did last night. I didn't say anything right, and I'm sorry." There was another pause. "I just called to tell you the same thing I've been trying to tell you all summer. You count with God. You count . . . with me. Very much. We just don't know what the future is. I only know what I'm supposed to do right now, and it's one of the hardest things I've ever done in my life." He stopped and cleared his throat.

Mercy tried to resist a surge of hope at his use of the word *future*. Was Lukas suggesting that maybe, sometime in the future, he may rethink his position?

No. Lukas wanted her to rethink hers.

"I'm going on a long hike today," the gentle voice continued. "I've got a lot of praying to do. I'll be especially praying for you, Mercy." He paused once more. "Good-bye." It sounded as if he choked on the final word, and then he hung up.

Mercy sat down on the chair beside the telephone. He was praying for her. She buried her face in her hands and cried.

---

While Grandma cooked an early lunch at her house, Tedi excused herself and walked the four blocks to Abby's house, blistered feet and all.

When she reached the house, she rang the doorbell, then knocked and waited for a moment, then tested the door and pushed it open. The Cuendets were used to her coming in and out of their house without knocking when she stayed overnight with Abby. Maybe they wouldn't get mad if she walked in alone just this once.

"Hello?" she called out, standing in the threshold of the front door. The house was dark and quiet. She stepped down a few feet to the hallway, paused again, then headed toward Abby's room. "Anybody home?" They always locked their doors when they went some-where, so somebody had to be around. "Hello?"

A shadow came out at her through Abby's open doorway, and Tedi stepped back with a gasp, then recognized her friend's short straight brown hair and glasses.

"What're *you* doing here?" Abby crossed her skinny arms over her chest, and her chin jutted out.

"I came to see how you were doing. You didn't sound too good last night when I called, and so—"

"I thought you were going on that stupid walkathon with your grandma this morning."

"We just got back. You could've gone with us, you know. I invited you."

Abby stood in the doorway for another few seconds, glaring at Tedi, then she turned and walked back into her room. "Mom went to the store with April and Andy. I didn't want to go with them, so she let me stay home, but I'm not supposed to have company while she's gone."

Tedi could understand why Abby didn't want to go. Abby's mom knew everyone in town, too. It could take her two hours to run to the store and get a gallon of milk. But Mr. and Mrs. Cuendet usually didn't let Abby stay home by herself.

"Where's your dad?" Tedi asked, stepping into the room.

"None of your business." Abby plopped onto her bed, refolded her arms, and turned to glare at Tedi again.

Tedi returned the glare. "Abby, what's wrong with you? Are you mad at me about something? What did *I* do?"

Abby held her gaze in the dim bedroom for another moment, then looked down. Her expression lost some of its fierceness, and then her eyes filled with tears.

Tedi walked over to the bed and perched on the side. "What's wrong?" she asked quietly.

Abby shook her head. "Mom told me not to talk about it. No-body's supposed to say anything."

"About what?"

Abby's chin quivered, and her tears spilled over. Her glasses fogged up.

"Is somebody sick?" Tedi asked.

Abby shook her head.

Tedi lowered her voice even further. "Are your parents fighting again?"

"Yeah."

"What about this time?"

"Same thing. Me. I heard them in their bedroom."

Tedi sighed.

"Dad . . . moved out last night," Abby said.

Tedi caught her breath. "Oh no. Why? Where'd he move to?" That felt awful, she knew.

Abby cried harder, ignoring the questions, and for a moment neither of them spoke. Tedi wanted to cry with her.

"You can't tell anybody," Abby said at last.

"I won't." Tedi wondered if there was another woman, like when Dad left Mom. She remembered the shouting and the door-slamming and the threats. And always Dad's booze breath.

"He never even told us kids what he was doing," Abby said on a sob. "He just came out of the bedroom carrying two suitcases. I asked him if he was going on another trip for the company, and he said no. Then he told all of us good-bye except for Mom, and he left."

They sat there in silence. Tedi didn't know what to say, and Abby couldn't talk because she was crying too hard.

Things seemed to change so fast sometimes. Last night, Tedi's biggest worry was whether or not she could get up in time to be ready when Grandma picked her up this morning. And, of course, she'd been worried about Abby. She still was.

"Um, Abby, you're not going to do anything . . . you know . . . stupid, are you?"

Abby wouldn't look at her. "Like what?"

Tedi frowned. She didn't like the sound of her friend's voice. "You know what. Cutting yourself didn't help anything last time."

"It did when I had to get stitches from barbed-wire cuts."

"Not in the end. Your dad still left."

"If something happens to me, he'll have to come back. Look at your dad. He turned himself in to the police and went through detox because of you. And now he's off booze, and he's a lot nicer. You said so yourself. And I bet he wants to get back together with your mom, too."

"That's not the same thing at all. Mom doesn't—" Tedi suddenly realized something. With Mom and Lukas broken up, and Dad acting so nice lately . . . "Oh no!"

"What?"

What if Dad really did want to get back together with Mom? Was that what Grandma's friend was talking about this morning? Was that what reconciliation meant?

Abby sniffed and wiped the tears from her face with the back of her hand, and Tedi saw the faint line of the scar left from the last time Abby had cut herself.

And she might do it again.

# CHAPTER 23

The first Monday in October looked like frequent-flyer day in the ER, and Lukas felt his frustration mounting as he swabbed throats for strep, wrote orders for cough suppressant, explained over and over again to mothers why he would not write a script for antibiotic for a mild earache. He wanted to ask everyone if they knew what a family practice doc looked like—and how much less one would cost than a trip to the emergency room. Perhaps he could print out the description of EMERGENCY from the computer and post it on the wall in the waiting room.

Of course, most of these people were covered by Medicaid, so why would they care? Most private practice docs in the Knolls area had their quota of Medicaid patients. Sometimes it seemed as if half the town was on Medicaid.

Lukas knew there were struggling people who desperately needed Medicaid, but he had a hard time stifling his resentment toward the abusers. His attitude was getting worse by the minute, but he didn't feel like praying about it. He was in the mood to be in a bad mood.

One woman trooped five kids through the front door—all under the age of seven. She then stepped outside for a Coke and a smoke while the "poor, sick, weak" little children chased one another around the chairs of the waiting room, screaming at the tops of their voices. They sure didn't act sick to Lukas.

Later, the woman cussed every staff member in the place when told she could not have the whole neighborhood gang—only two of whom were her children—treated in the emergency department compliments of Missouri taxpayers.

Then halfway through a telephone call with an admitting physician, he heard a familiar voice at the reception window. He looked up to see the round, lined face of Odira Bagby standing beside her great-granddaughter, Crystal, holding her hand. She wore a threadbare size twenty dress. Some of the tension left his neck and shoulders.

It was easy to tell when Odira entered the department, because her familiar baritone voice seemed to reverberate from the rafters, and her heavy breathing was nearly as loud.

"Tell the doc I'm sorry to come in again so soon!" she told Lauren as she lumbered in behind the nurse. The quiet undersized six-year-old followed behind her. "Crystal cain't seem to get rid of this crud. Fever's worse today, 'bout 103 when I last checked, and I done everything, even a spongin'."

As Lukas finished his telephone call, he listened to Odira's voice continue to plunge past the fragile barriers of walls and curtains. The sixty-six-year-old woman had been taking care of Crystal for the past year, ever since the mother—Odira's granddaughter—had disappeared. With Odira's daughter dead, and no other living relatives, Odira got the child. She did the best she could in a one-bedroom apartment with nothing but income from her Social Security check.

Minutes later, when Lukas stepped into the exam room, Odira broke into a wrinkled, gap-toothed grin, and her voice boomed out once more. "There's our doc! Sorry to come in like this, Dr. Bower! We had an appointment with Dr. Mercy late this afternoon, but I was scared to wait that long. I'm always coddlin' this gal, don't you know!"

Lukas returned her smile, feeling more needed than he had all morning. Crystal had cystic fibrosis.

While Crystal watched him with silent water-blue eyes, he felt her throat and looked in her ears, checked for swollen lymph nodes, and ordered something to break the fever. Crystal didn't look too bad, but he didn't want to take any chances. He ordered tests to check for pneumonia while he assured Odira that she'd done the right thing, then stepped out to check on another patient.

Claudia, the double-coverage nurse today, caught him at the central desk. "We've got a good one in eight, Dr. Bower. She's a school bus driver, and this morning one of the kids on her route bit her leg."

Lukas turned to Claudia. "Did I hear that right?"

"Yep, you heard me. Just above the ankle. He was throwing a fit on the floor of the bus."

"Did it draw blood?" And it was still morning. What else would turn up?

"Yes. I'll clean it up, but it doesn't look like it needs stitches. She had a tetanus shot last year." Claudia leaned forward and lowered her voice. "She told me she didn't want to come in after that bad write-up in the paper about us the other day, but her boss told her she had to." She shoved a chart across the desk so hard it nearly toppled over the other side. "That Bailey Little sure has a lot to answer for. He's out to destroy this hospital. I hope I don't pass him on the street some day when I'm in a bad mood."

Lukas couldn't prevent a grin at his iron-jawed nurse. "I hope you don't, either, Claudia. We're the only emergency room within an hour's drive from here."

"You know," she said, "that makes the fourth person in three days who's mentioned that letter to me. Two people wanted to know if we were going to be closed down by the government, and one grouchy old man—who wasn't even a patient, mind you—wanted to know if you'd 'manhandled' any more nurses lately. I'd like to know who started *that* rumor. I'd like to show him 'manhandled.' "

As Lukas went to check the bus driver with the bite, he felt his resentment mounting again. Not only had Bailey Little written a misleading letter to the *Knolls Review*, but he was also apparently spreading rumors that made Lukas look like a masher.

The bus driver's bite had bled well, which would help cleanse the wound, and it didn't need stitches. It was best not to close bite wounds anyway. Lukas left Claudia to do further cleaning and went back out to the central desk, where Lauren sat talking quietly with Judy. They fell silent when he approached.

He frowned at Lauren and sat down in his chair at the end of the nine-foot-long counter. "Please don't tell me about all the patients who are complaining about our service or asking about the COBRA investigation or our sale to RealCare. I don't want to hear any more."

"You won't hear it from me." Lauren wheeled her chair over to him and scooted to a stop. "All I've heard the patients talking about this morning is the fires. It's making everyone nervous. You've got to admit, it tends to make you smell smoke everywhere you go." She leaned closer. "I did hear one other thing just now."

Oh boy, here it came. "Lauren, I told you I didn't—"

"Did you and Dr. Mercy break up?"

Lukas felt a fuse short out somewhere in his brain. That was the last thing he wanted to talk about. It was all he'd thought about this weekend. "Break *what* up?" he snapped.

Her voice grew even softer, and she laid a hand on his arm. "Are you doing okay?"

Lukas breathed an impatient sigh. How did that get out so quickly? A person couldn't even sneeze in this town without everybody talking about it. "I'm fine, Lauren." He moved his arm from her touch, rolled his chair backward, and stood, feeling a rush of unaccustomed anger that mingled perfectly with his already bad mood. "Maybe you should reread the passages in the Bible about gossip. Maybe you should read it out loud to the whole town. Do you think you could get back to work?" He picked up a clipboard. "Are the test results back for the patient in four? What was Crystal's temperature last time you checked?"

A pink flush crept up from Lauren's neck. "It's only a hundred degrees now. Sorry, Dr. Bower, I'll get busy."

He watched her get up and rush away, and for a full minute he refused to feel guilty for snapping at her. Hadn't she learned there were times a person did not want to be accosted with the pain in his life? Hadn't anyone in Knolls County ever heard of the word *privacy*?

He slammed a drawer shut and saw from the corner of his vision that Judy turned to cast him a worried glance. He immediately felt embarrassed. His temper had been spilling out all morning, and he needed to get it under control. He knew Lauren had a good heart. She cared about people. Still, her intrusiveness could be irritating at times. He would apologize later, when he had thirty minutes or so to listen to her nonstop monologue.

Finally, he paused to mentally repeat to himself a verse he had memorized for just such circumstances . . . *"Whatever is true, whatever is noble, whatever is right, whatever is pure, whatever is lovely, whatever is admirable—if anything is excellent or praiseworthy—think about such things*." He would try hard to push the rest out of his mind. But it was becoming a battle.

He missed Mercy.

"Good news, Odira," he said moments later as he pushed past the privacy curtain. Crystal's color already looked better, and her timid smile greeted him. "No pneumonia, and the temperature's going down." He listened once more to the little girl's breathing. It was better.

He bent down and looked her in the eyes and, as always, was struck by the aura of silent resignation in her expression. He'd never heard her laugh or seen her play. He handed her three scratch-and-sniff stickers, and her eyes widened.

She looked at him, then back at the stickers. "Thank you," she said softly.

"All right!" Odira shouted, struggling to get to her feet. "Knew you'd take care of her, Doc!" Once upright, she reached over and gave Crystal a bear hug. "Hear that, honey? My gal's gonna be fine." She turned back to Lukas. "You want me to keep that appointment with Dr. Mercy this afternoon?"

"No, but she'll want to recheck Crystal in a day or two. Be sure to reschedule her appointment," he said as he lifted the child down from the exam bed.

"I'll do it!" Odira straightened the thrift-shop dress over her rolls of flesh, beaming at Lukas. "Don't know what we'd do without you, Dr. Bower. When I read that letter in the paper the other day, I called ol' Harvey's office and told them if they did anything like that again, I'd cancel my subscription and tell all my friends at the senior center to do the same! Cain't stand Bailey Little anyway. Never could. Why, if that man's too stupid to recognize a quality doctor when he sees one, then he's just too stupid!" She jerked her head in Crystal's direction. "Why don't people pay more attention to the important stuff in life, like this little girl here? Why don't they stop tryin' to make life miserable for good folks like you?" She took Crystal's hand and waddled out of the room with her.

Lukas wanted to kiss her.

He was getting too emotional these days.

———

Zach and Lee Becker sat with their daughter, Shannon, in Mercy's office. So far Lee had managed not to cry, but Zach's eyes had dripped tears since they entered the office. He and Shannon had made a hefty dent in the box of Kleenex on the desk.

"The tests all came back negative," Mercy announced, feeling the relief in the room. "No pregnancy, no disease. Shannon, you'll have a black eye for a while, but it'll go away. What I'm concerned about right now is how you're dealing with this psychologically. Your counselor says you're doing well, but she wants to continue to meet with you every weekday after school for at least another week and then taper off from there. Is that okay with you?"

Shannon nodded as new tears formed in her eyes. "I told Mom and Dad everything, Dr. Mercy, about when I came to see you last week. They know you couldn't tell them that I asked you for birth control. They were upset I even thought about it. I can't go riding around with my friends anymore."

Good.

Zach grabbed another tissue and blew his nose. "I just wish I knew where we messed up, Dr. Mercy. I wish Shannon had felt she could talk to us."

"If you feel that way, I think you and Lee should see the counselor again, as well. This is going to take a long time to work through. I'll call today and have her schedule all of you for a meeting."

Lee clenched her hands tightly in her lap. "That monster who raped her is out on bail. We're going after him with everything we've got. He's not getting away with this."

"No, he isn't," Mercy said. "I called the prosecuting attorney's office and told them I'll be happy to testify or produce any evidence they need that I can give them."

After the grieving family left, Josie came to Mercy's open office door and knocked. "Dr. Mercy, we've had two cancellations and one walk-in who thinks she might be pregnant."

Mercy couldn't prevent the scowl that crossed her face. It seemed as if every other patient these days was pregnant, and right now it felt like a slap in the face from God, a reminder of what she'd lost. Maybe she should stop taking OB cases. After all, she was family practice, not ObGyn. Maybe she could start referring—

"Dr. Mercy?" Josie stepped into the room. "You okay?"

"I'm fine."

"I guess Shannon and her parents are taking things pretty hard." The nurse sank into the chair closest to the door. "I know I would if I had a teenaged daughter who'd just been raped." She sighed. "I guess I won't have to worry about teenagers for a while, though . . . if ever."

Josie's voice sounded so despondent, suddenly, that Mercy looked up at her. Josie had been married for five ecstatic years, and never in that time had she openly lamented the fact that she had, as yet, been unable to conceive. "I'm sorry. Don't give up, Josie."

"Oh, I'm not. There's time yet. I'm not even thirty. How about you? Think you'll ever get remarried and have more kids?"

The innocent question buried itself deep in Mercy's heart like the point of a blade. She forced herself not to react. All she could do was shake her head.

"Well, don't give up." Josie stood up and headed toward the door. "If grumpy old Dr. George can find somebody to marry him—"

Mercy looked up. "Jarvis is getting married?"

Josie turned back and shrugged. "Didn't you hear? It's all over town. I heard about it at church yesterday. Jarvis took off with his fiancée this weekend to get married."

Mercy shook her head and leaned back in her chair. Was she the only person in the world who would be alone for the rest of her life?

# CHAPTER 24

After the noon rush was stitched up, cleaned up, and written up, Lukas sank once again into his chair at the central desk. The secretary, tech, and double-shift nurse had all escaped for lunch in the break room, leaving Lauren to call them if more patients arrived.

Lukas glanced over at her, where she sat charting. "Uh, Lauren, do you have a minute?"

She looked up from her clipboard, her blond brows drawn together in concentration. "Sure, Dr. Bower. What d'you need?"

Something in him relaxed at the easy tone of her voice. Lauren never held a grudge. He liked her. She was a friend.

"Sorry I said what I did this morning. I'm just always amazed at the speed with which information travels in this town, and I was feeling—"

"You were right, and I'm the one who's sorry," she said. "I am a gossip. I guess I try to tell myself that if the words I'm saying are true, it isn't gossip. I always go to the source to see if it's true, and that way I don't feel so guilty. But it doesn't work that way. The truth gets changed, and somebody always gets hurt. Like, for instance, it's true that you're a doctor, and word spread all over Knolls when you moved in here. I bet you got charged double the price to have your lawn mowed or gutters cleaned, because everyone knew you were a doctor, and they think you're rich or something, and that they have a right to your money. So even though it's true you're a doctor, it's nobody's business outside the hospital. When I look at things like that, I know I've got to start trying to keep my mouth shut. I've always had trouble with that."

Lukas decided he'd better get a lawn mower next spring.

She continued. "Gossip or not, I did hear that you and Dr. Mercy broke up. That's hard. I know." She cleared her throat and looked away. "You and Dr. Mercy were getting really close. I was afraid this might happen."

He still didn't want to talk about it, but he didn't want to snap at her again. "You were?"

She shrugged. "I dated a guy once who wasn't a believer. I couldn't have married him. Two people can't be unequally yoked, so I had to break it off with him. It was really hard. My friends all thought I was crazy. Ever since then I don't date anyone who doesn't believe the way I do. If I meet a guy and he asks me out, I ask him right off if he believes in Christ, and then I ask him to give me his personal testimony. It's hard to do, and I've scared a few guys off like that, but it's probably the best for both of us. But with you and Mercy, you started off as friends and colleagues, and I guess you were caught off guard. How's she taking it?"

To his relief, before he could answer the question, the ER door opened, and a man walked through pushing a woman in a wheelchair.

Lukas thought he recognized the man, but it wasn't until he looked down and saw the woman in the wheelchair that he realized who these people were.

He jumped up and walked around the end of the central desk. "Arthur and Alma Collins!" He shook Arthur's hand, then bent down to take Alma's proffered one. "You've been released!"

"That's right," Alma drawled in her southern accent, pressing his hand between both of hers. Alma had short light brown hair and eyes the color of honey that smiled into his with warmth. "You got me to Springfield so fast, they were able to save more of my leg than they expected." She indicated the right leg, which revealed a below-the-knee amputation. "When I get my prosthesis, walkin' will be a lot easier because of you and your staff, Dr. Bower. If you hadn't been in such a rush to get me to help, I might've lost the knee, too. That's what they told me up there."

Alma Collins' positive attitude and heartfelt appreciation for what he'd done felt great.

"We wanted to come by and thank you in person," Arthur said. "For that, and for your prayers, and for the flowers you sent us."

Arthur stood about two inches taller than Lukas's five feet ten, and he had wavy red hair mixed with gray. His face expressed the same serenity as Alma's. "Are we keeping you from your work? We won't take long."

"I was hopin' to meet that lady doctor who prayed with Arthur," Alma said, glancing around the empty ER. "He told me all about how nice she was to him, and the way she helped Mr. Martínez when everybody else was so mad at the poor guy for causin' that wreck. Did you ever get a translator for him after Arthur left?"

"Yes, we called the man Arthur told us about." Lukas urged them to follow him into the private waiting room. "I'll let you go see Mercy, but I want you to myself first, if you have the time to talk." Lukas held the door open while Arthur pushed Alma through. "Amazingly, we aren't busy right now, and that's unusual for us at this time on a Monday." He gestured for Arthur to sit down on a chair beside Alma's wheelchair, and then he sat across from them. "You've been on our minds a lot around here."

Arthur smiled and looked sideways at his wife. "Hear that, Alma? They've been thinking about us, too. You're the intuitive one. Do you think that's a sign?"

"I should say it is. It's an answer straight from God." She looked back at Lukas. "We're up to somethin', Dr. Bower. We've done some checkin' with the Knolls Chamber of Commerce, and you folks don't have a Crosslines in this town."

Lukas stared at her blankly. "A Crosslines?"

"Yeah, you know, kind of like the Salvation Army, only it's supported by the local churches. We're thinkin' about startin' one here."

"You? But I thought your mission in—"

"We can't go back to Mexico now," Arthur said quietly. "Not for a long time, not with Alma's leg the way it is. It's going to take a lot of rehabilitation. Our mission board suggested that we might want to start a home mission in Missouri. They'll still support us, and we can choose a place where we can work with Hispanic people and put our experience to work. You have a lot of Mexican people around Knolls. We feel there's a definite need here, especially since you had so much trouble finding an interpreter the day we had the accident."

Lukas nodded. This was too good to be true. "How serious are you about moving here?"

"We have an appointment in an hour to look at some real estate," Alma said. "We've already received money from supporters throughout the state to help with our medical expenses, but the mission board had us insured. We'll use the money we received for a down payment, and then next Sunday we're beginning our rounds to the area churches to share our plan with them."

Lukas whistled through his teeth. "You people don't waste any time, do you?"

"Time wasted is souls lost," Arthur said. "We're not out of commission. God's just pointing us in a different direction."

"We thought we might also check and see if your hospital has a chaplain call list," Alma said. "We know how important it is to have somebody prayin' with you when you're hurt and scared. Do you think your board of directors might—"

"You'd better believe it," Lukas said. "I'll talk with Mrs. Pinkley, our administrator." He was sure she would approve. He was sure, also, that the Collinses were an answer to several prayers. *Lord, you know what we need before we even ask. Thank you.*

---

Mercy sank down at her desk between patients. She shouldn't be surprised that grumpy, cantankerous Jarvis George had actually convinced a woman young enough to be his daughter to marry him. He had a certain charm about him, sometimes. And he was worth a bundle.

Immediately, Mercy was sorry for her cynicism. She blamed it all on her inability to keep a relationship going with Lukas.

Was she that hard to get along with?

No, that wasn't it at all. She had to remember that. It was the fact that she wasn't a Christian. She was being rejected not only by Lukas, but by God.

Wasn't she?

She shook her head and picked up the chart she'd been working on as a knock sounded at the open threshold of her office. She looked up to find a man standing there behind a woman in a wheelchair.

"Hello, Dr. Mercy. I almost didn't recognize you without your trauma gear on," he said.

She frowned at him and then suddenly recalled that awful day last month, and she remembered the kind eyes. "Arthur Collins?" She stood up and circled her desk, automatically searching for a healing scar on his head. She found it. It was him. She took his hand, and then Alma's. They had actually gone to the trouble to come and see *her*?

"Come on in, have a seat." She couldn't help glancing at Alma's bandaged leg, which ended about four inches below the knee.

"After we explained to your nurse who we were," Arthur explained, "she told us you wouldn't mind if we came on back." He pushed Alma's wheelchair into the office and parked it beside the two chairs facing Mercy's desk.

"So you're the lady who helped God put my husband back together that day," Alma drawled. "Honey, I just wanted to tell you in person what a blessin' you were to him, and therefore to me. Thank you for prayin' with him, too. We'll never forget it."

Mercy stood staring at them for a moment while the words soaked in, then she sat down in a chair next to Alma. "Thank you," she said softly. "You can't possibly know how much it means to me to hear that." To her humiliation, she felt her eyes fill with tears. Her poor timing with her emotions had become a big problem lately.

Alma reached out and laid a hand over hers. "I guess you see a lot of sufferin' and sorrow over there at the hospital."

Mercy nodded, thinking about Shannon Becker, and Delphi Bell, and Clarence Knight. Compared to them, her life was wonderful. So why did she feel this way?

She dried her eyes and listened as Arthur and Alma described their plans, and she felt some of the depression lift. She couldn't help being affected by the eagerness with which they shared their dreams. And it sounded as if their dreams might easily become reality.

"That's perfect," she told them when they'd finished. "Maybe . . . maybe God sent you to us for more than one reason." It was hard to admit that God had such an active role in the lives of these people, but the truth was too obvious to ignore. "We need you here. There are so many people who have so many needs . . . sometimes it can be overwhelming."

"Don't be overwhelmed, honey." Alma reached out to touch Mercy's arm. "Just give it all to God, and He'll work out the tangles for you. Look what He's doin' for us. I figure if I have to lose a part of my leg so Arthur and I can find direction about where to lead people to God, then that's okay. Jesus Christ gave up His whole life on this earth for you an' me. He had the Roman soldiers beatin' and spittin' at Him, and I had a nice soft hospital bed and lovin' people all around me." A sudden grin spread across her face like sunshine. "We're in the lap of luxury."

Arthur looked at his watch and stood up. "Well, Dr. Mercy, we won't take up any more of your time. We've got an appointment to see a Realtor about a place for our Crosslines headquarters." He took Mercy's hand in another gentle grip as she stood. "Thank you again. We hope to be seeing a lot more of you."

"You bet, honey!" Alma said as Arthur wheeled her out of the office and down the hallway. "Remember what I said. Just give it all to God."

Mercy stood watching them until they rounded a corner out of sight, and then she walked slowly the other way to her patient in the OB exam room. Was it simply a coincidence that they had come at just this time, like a loving answer to her angry prayer? And what about Lukas calling her Saturday, just when she needed it most? Was that, too, a coincidence?

Did she have the courage to believe that something else might be going on here?

———

Lukas had just finished stitching an arm laceration on a local factory employee when he walked out and found Buck Oppenheimer leaning at the counter of the central desk. The man's ears looked more prominent than usual because he'd just had a haircut so close his scalp showed through. Maybe he wasn't happy with the haircut. His expression looked grim.

"Hi, Dr. Bower," Buck said morosely.

"Hi, Buck. What's wrong with you? Did your teenaged sidekicks desert you?"

Buck sighed and shook his head. "Guess *I'm* deserting *them*."

"Don't sound so depressed about it. I thought you didn't want to be a trainer."

"What I want never seems to matter." His words sounded tired, defeated. He sighed. "I just came from the Personnel office to apply for a job as a full-time tech."

"Really? Full time? But how can you work two—"

"I'm not with the fire department anymore."

Lukas knew he had to be missing something. Buck would never quit the job he loved. "Buck, is this some kind of riddle?"

"I wish." Buck slumped against the counter in an attitude of despair. "I've been suspended."

"What?" Lukas was still missing something. "Who suspended you?"

"The fire department," Buck said. "Pending further investigation. I can't believe they'd do this to me, not after all these years. Eight years I've been with them. Eight! They're on a witch-hunt. That's what this is, a witch-hunt."

Lukas had heard the rumors, though he hadn't listened to them. He knew Buck too well. The idea that he could be an arsonist was ludicrous. "Did your chief give you any good reasons?"

Buck gave a heavy sigh. "He said there were some leads they wanted to check out." He buried his face in his hands, rubbed his eyes, shook his head in frustration. "Eight long years down the drain." He pounded the counter with his fist. "It's crazy! And they don't want me here, either. I guess I'm just bad news wherever I go."

"What do you mean they don't want you here?"

"They just told me they didn't have any full-time openings for me." He scratched his head, then shrugged with growing restlessness. "I bet the chief talked to them, told them I was dangerous or something. Now nobody wants me."

Lukas would speak to Personnel. Hadn't Estelle told him just the other day that she wanted the staff beefed up? "Give it a couple of days, then come back in, Buck. I think they'll add some shifts to your schedule. Have you spoken with Kendra?"

"Oh no. No way. I'm not going to go crawling back to her. She didn't want me as a fireman, and she won't get me as a part-time EMT. I'm done begging. Besides, she'd probably believe everything they're saying." He straightened from the counter and swung toward the exit. "See you later, Doc."

"Wait a minute. Buck, where will you go? Why don't you come and stay with—" But Buck was out the door, striding away from the hospital as if he'd received a call about a fire.

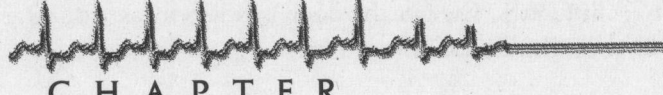

CHAPTER — 25

At eleven-thirty Wednesday morning Mercy and Tedi passed the burned, collapsed shell of Little Mary's Barbeque on their way to lunch. The half-bricked face of the old storefront café was all that remained intact. Cleanup had begun the day after the fire, and now all the shattered glass was cleared from the sidewalk and the debris pushed into a blackened pile in the center of the spot where the cooks had smoked their meat and shredded their county-wide-famous cole-slaw for so many years.

A charred and broken wooden floor pointed ragged, helpless fingers at the sky between the scorched walls of the neighboring buildings—and those buildings that surrounded the space served as a reminder that in a small town like Knolls, where walls and lives were intimately connected from the outset, nothing could happen in isolation. When one life was affected by tragedy or joy, others could not remain unaltered.

Mercy glanced sideways and caught sight of tears shimmering in Tedi's eyes. "Honey, you okay?"

"Yeah. It just looks so sad."

Mercy felt a loving pang at her daughter's tender heart . . . of course, she might also be thinking about the chocolate pecan pie and the best smoked chicken in the Ozarks, but her first thought would be for the—

"How are the ladies who got caught in the fire, Mom?"

Mercy suppressed a smile. Yes, Tedi would think of the people first. She could make a good doctor someday. "They're going to be fine. I saw one of Little Mary's waitresses yesterday, and she told me both the cooks will be okay. Little Mary is going to rebuild with the insurance money." Mercy drove a half circle around the courthouse and parked in front of the Mexican restaurant, then turned to look at Tedi, whose eyes continued to shimmer. "Everything's going to be as good as new."

Tedi shrugged and bent her head, letting the tears spill. She swiped at her eyes with the back of her hand, then reached up to finger the scar at her throat. "As good as new doesn't mean as good as old. I like it the way it used to be."

Mercy reached across and placed a gentle hand on Tedi's shoulder. "We can't look at it that way. We have to see how we can make things better for the future." Which was exactly what she was doing here today.

After making the lunch date with Theo for this Saturday, she had realized that she was already scheduled for a Pediatric Advanced Life Support recertification class. This gave her a wonderful excuse to cancel the date, and the temptation to use it had been powerful. But Tedi needed a more normal life, and that included a relationship with her dad.

"Are you hungry?" Mercy asked, punching the unlock pad for the doors with a *snap-click* and reaching for her purse.

"I guess."

"Good, because your father knew I wouldn't have much time today, and he already ordered for us. He should be waiting inside for us. He got soft tacos with guacamole and sopapillas for you. Your favorite. And you'd better enjoy it while you can, because next time we're going to eat healthier. I already told him that, and he agrees." He'd been very agreeable lately. It was not in his character to be this nice for this long. Was it possible that there truly was an inner change?

Tedi hesitated, her solemn gaze finding Mercy's. "I wish you and Lukas could keep seeing each other." The tears once more spilled over.

"Oh, honey." Mercy reached across the seat again, this time to feel her daughter's forehead for a temperature. Tedi wasn't usually this weepy. But she didn't feel hot. "I know, so do I." How could she have been so blind to Tedi's feelings of loss? Had Lukas even considered who else would be hurt by his rejection? How many times could a child's emotions spring back from losses like this?

She drew her daughter into her arms. "Honey, you must feel as if the whole world is falling out from under you." Mercy certainly did.

Tedi squeezed back and held on for another moment, burying her face against Mercy's shoulder. "Grandma had me memorize a verse from the Bible where Jesus says He will never leave us or forsake us." Her voice came out muffled by Mercy's sweater. "He took care of me when the bee stung me, because those people found me just in time. He took care of me when Dad hit me. I know Jesus is watching out for me." She drew back enough to look up at Mercy.

Mercy took a deep breath and let it out and forced a smile. "Then I guess we'll just wait a little longer and see what happens, okay?"

"Okay." Tedi glanced toward the front window of the café. "Dad's watching us from a front table."

"We'd better get in there."

They got out of the car and walked toward the glass-plated front door, but just as Mercy reached for the handle, Tedi tapped her on the arm. "Mom?"

Mercy hesitated and turned back, frowning at the continued serious tone of Tedi's voice. "What is it, honey?"

"Are you and Dad going to get back together again now that you and Lukas aren't going to be seeing each other anymore?"

Mercy caught her breath. The door opened and two people stepped out of the café, and Mercy and Tedi had to move out of their way. Mercy saw Theodore talking and laughing with a man at the table next to his, then glance their way. She raised a hand to signal to him that they would join him shortly. She had to make this explanation fast and firm.

"No, Tedi. That isn't something that will ever happen. Don't even think about it, don't worry about it, and please, please don't ever suggest it to your father. He will always be your father, but he will never be my husband again. If Lukas and I . . . well, I may never get remarried. I'm sorry if you have hopes that your dad and I—"

"I don't, Mom." Tedi glanced toward Theo's image through the glass, then lowered her voice. "I just wondered."

"Don't wonder any longer."

———

Lukas pulled as close to Ivy Richmond's front porch as he could without destroying the blooms on her rosebushes. Until Clarence healed completely from his injured muscles, he shouldn't walk any more than necessary. Lukas glanced across at Clarence. The big man's expression was lit with the excitement of a child on his birthday. He'd come a long way from the rude, cantankerous patient Lukas and Mercy had first visited last spring, and even though he still had an independent spirit that kept him from accepting help easily, he also had a logical mind. He knew staying here with Ivy Richmond was the best chance Darlene had for a healthy future, since she would never abandon him. He still struggled with depression, some days worse than others, but he had a desire to get better.

"You say Darlene's already settled in here, Doc?" Clarence reached up to open the passenger door.

Mercy had wrapped Ace bandages around his massive legs for better support while he healed and had given him crutches to assist with walking while he continued to lose weight. He had lost three more pounds while he was in the hospital, and when he heard the news, he'd whooped loudly enough for the nurses to hear him at the other end of the hallway.

"Not only settled, but ready to get back to work on her computer." Lukas grabbed the crutches that he had placed in the backseat, then got out of the car and rushed around to Clarence's door. The scent of the roses filled the air with sweetness. "Smell that, Clarence? Ivy Richmond has a green thumb. She just started growing flowers over the summer, and she keeps them all over the house. Plus she has an indoor garden. You'll love it here." He reached forward to help the big man out.

As expected, Clarence waved him away with a gesture of impatience, heaved himself to his feet with a firm grip on the doorframe, then took the crutches. He wore a pair of blue jeans and a T-shirt that actually covered his huge stomach. Ivy had enlisted the skills of a friend who did seamstress work, and she had presented the clothes to him three days ago.

An aide at the hospital knew how to cut hair and trim beards and had worked a miracle with Clarence's bushy mop. He was more completely groomed than Lukas had ever seen him. In fact, Lauren had remarked that as Clarence continued to lose weight, he might become one of Knolls' most eligible bachelors . . . of course, not counting Dr. Bower.

Lukas and Clarence made their ponderous way up the walk as the front door opened and Darlene stepped out. She greeted him with a broad grin, the lines around her eyes fanning out in a frame of excitement.

"Clarence, you look great!"

He stopped halfway up the walk and gazed at her, his breath already coming in deep, whooshing puffs from the exertion. "So do you, sis. How do you feel?"

She came down the walk and gave him a hard hug and a smack on the cheek, taking care not to overbalance him. "Better now that I'm out of the hospital." She turned to lead the way back toward the house. "I can't stop wondering about the bills, though."

Ivy stepped out of the house, her long graying hair floating over her shoulders. "Now, Darlene, none of that." She came over to join them. "I told you I'll take care of it, and you can settle with me later. Lots later. Concentrate on getting well, both of you." She held the door open and stood back, allowing the scent of pine cleaner to waft out at them. "I've been scrubbing corners that haven't been scrubbed in weeks."

Clarence huffed his way past the threshold and peered into the house, leaning hard on his crutches. An expression of awe spread across his face as he looked up at the knotty wood beams that arched across the cathedral ceiling of the foyer and front parlor.

"Knew you had a nice spread," he growled and moved back slightly, as if afraid to go farther and mess anything up.

"Step on in there, Clarence." Ivy poked him in the back with her fingers. "You're going to have to learn to make yourself at home."

Clarence continued to hesitate, then turned back to look at Ivy in deepening alarm. "I can't sit on those flimsy chairs. What if I break something?" He shook his head. "I don't think you know what you're getting into."

"Of course I know. Now, get on in there and I'll show you to your apartment."

Clarence hesitated a moment more, then looked down at the small hump of the threshold, pushed forward with his crutches, and eased himself inside.

"There you go," Ivy said with satisfaction. "Darlene, you go with him and show him around. Clarence, turn left at the hallway and go to the end. There's the door to your apartment."

As Darlene and Clarence explored further, Ivy turned to Lukas. "I had the doorway built extra wide to make room for Mother's wheelchair when she lived with me." Her eyes reflected the same dark beauty Lukas remembered from Mercy's last smile. "It sure did help when I had their furniture brought in yesterday. Darlene's going to have a bedroom next to mine here in the main house, but her computer's in an alcove of the apartment so she can be close to Clarence. That way neither of them will feel alone."

Lukas strolled down the hallway alongside her. "You sound like you're enjoying this."

"I am. Mercy told me all about Clarence, and I knew the moment I heard about his problem that this was something I could help with. I just didn't realize how involved I would get. Mercy knows how fanatical I've been about healthy cooking and exercise, and that's exactly what Clarence needs."

Her steps slowed, and her eyes narrowed at Lukas. "Mercy and Tedi miss you," she said in her usual forthright manner. "I guess you know Mercy's devastated by your breakup."

Mercy couldn't be any more devastated than he was. "I'm sorry. I should never have let it go on so long, but I guess I just didn't realize—"

"You don't have to tell me. I know. I just wish it could have been different. You would've been a great addition to the family. You'd be good for Mercy and Tedi . . . and for me. I could use a good son-in-law for a change."

Warmth spread up Lukas's neck, but before he could think of something to say, Clarence gave a shout from the apartment, then turned and limped his way back out to the hallway.

"Hey, you brought my bed!"

Ivy grinned and clasped her hands together. "Welcome home, Clarence."

———

Tedi leaned back from her empty plate, watching Dad finish his ice cream and sopapillas. He'd offered her some of his, but she had already eaten two desserts, and her jeans felt as though they might squeeze her in half.

Mom was crunching the ice from a third glass of lemonade, and she and Dad had just finished discussing the weather, Tedi's grades, and the most recent fire. It seemed as if they'd run out of topics to talk about. Tedi didn't feel like trying to keep the conversation going this time. She had more important things to think about. What was she supposed to do about Abby? Would Abby really do the strange things she talked about doing? She'd already cut her arm.

Tedi cleared her throat. What would Mom or Dad do about something like this? She watched Mom crunch the ice in her glass and glance around the crowded room. She watched Dad put the last forkful of sopapillas in his mouth and look everywhere but at Mom.

"Mom," Tedi said, trying to sound as if she had just suddenly thought of this subject, "if I was doing something that would hurt me, and I made a friend of mine promise not to tell anyone, do you think she should tell?" She picked up her fork and slowly, casually ran the tines over the sweet-smelling leftover honey on her dessert plate. She did not look up.

"Of course she should," Mom said. "I would want to know."

"Even if she promised not to?" Tedi still didn't look up.

The ice crunching stopped, and Tedi felt Mom's attention focus on her. "You already asked me this the other night."

Tedi looked up at her. "Yeah, and the other night you told me it wouldn't be ethically correct to break a promise."

"I was not discussing the subject of your safety the other night. I was discussing a story in a book."

"What's the difference?" Tedi asked. "Isn't right always right? If someone makes a promise, shouldn't they keep it no matter what? If they don't, doesn't that mean they're a liar?"

Mom put her glass down and leaned forward, eyes narrowing. "Tedi, why is the subject so important to you all of a sudden?"

Tedi bit her lip. Uh-oh.

Dad put his fork down and pushed his plate away. "What's going on?"

Tedi blinked up into his blue eyes, keeping her expression as innocent as possible. "Mom and I are reading a book called *Another Chance*, where this girl, Gordy, goes out to meet another girl, Chrissy, late at night, because she's afraid Chrissy is going to do something stupid and get hurt. Gordy makes her boyfriend, Smitty Joe, promise not to tell anyone, but he tells anyway. She almost drowns, but her father gets there in time to save her. I think it was wrong for Smitty to tell on her, and Mom did too, at first, but now she's changing her mind, and—"

"What kind of parents would name their kids Gordy or Smitty Joe?" Dad interrupted.

He wasn't getting the point. "Dad, *you* named *me* Theadra. What could be worse than that? Besides, I just think—"

"I don't think Tedi's talking about a book now," Mom said. There was a soft suspicion in her voice. Her gaze broke from Tedi, and she looked across the table at Dad. "Something's up."

They both turned their attention to Tedi.

Rats. This had never happened before.

Tedi tried one more time to bluff. "Mom," she said with a long-suffering sigh, "don't you think a promise should be a promise, whether it's in a book or in real life?"

Mom opened her mouth to speak, but Dad answered. "Tedi, what would you have thought about the book if Gordy had died?"

Tedi put her fork down and sat back in her chair. "It would've been awful."

"What would you have thought of the boyfriend with the stupid name?"

"I guess I would have thought he was a loser."

"Why?"

"Because he didn't do all he could to save Gordy."

"So you're saying you think a human life is more important than just words?" He glanced at Mom. "What do you think?"

For the first time Tedi could remember, Mom smiled at Dad. "I think you put it well."

Tedi sat in silent surprise for a moment. She had always wanted her parents to get along. It was something she had dreamed about, but why did it have to start right now?

"Is it Abby?" Mom asked.

Tedi couldn't keep her mouth from dropping open.

Dad laughed. "Face it, Tedi, you never were a good bluffer."

"Is she upset because her parents split up last weekend?" Mom pressed.

Tedi blinked at Mom. "How'd you know about that? They didn't want anybody to know."

"Get real, Tedi," Dad said. "Even I knew about that."

Mom sat back in her chair. "Tell us what's wrong with Abby."

Tedi picked up on the "us" word. She saw that Dad did, too, because he blinked and then shot Mom a surprised look across the table. They shared a very brief look of understanding, then turned back to their daughter.

Tedi sighed again. She might as well get this over with. Mom would drag it out of her sooner or later. "I'm just afraid she's going to hurt herself. Remember when she cut herself with barbed wire?"

"Barbed wire!" Dad exclaimed. "On purpose?"

"No, it was an accident," Mom told him. "Abby was proud of those stitches."

"Too proud," Tedi grumbled. "And she keeps talking about how that accident brought her parents back together for a little while. She talks about how Dad changed after he came out of detox. She thinks her parents will do the same thing."

Mom and Dad looked at each other again. Then Dad shook his head, and for a moment the smoky aroma of sizzling fajitas and onions and the chatter of the other diners filled the table.

"Tedi, that's wrong," Dad said at last. "I couldn't do it on my own. Only Christ could do that." He leaned forward and rubbed his hands across his face the way he always used to do when he was frustrated. "Maybe I should talk to Jason Cuendet. He might listen to me."

"No, Dad!"

"Why not?"

"I told you, nobody's supposed to know about this. Abby made me promise—"

"She *made* you promise?" Mom asked. "How could she do that?"

"Tedi, a promise has to come from a free will, or it isn't a promise," Dad said.

"But what if he gets mad when you talk to him?" Tedi asked.

Mom cleared her throat, leaning forward with her arms on the table. "Tedi, why don't you bring Abby home with you tomorrow after school, when I have some time to spend with you. Maybe I'll get her alone and talk to her. If that doesn't work I'll have to talk to Lindy."

"But Abby'll—"

Mom reached over and patted Tedi on the leg. "Maybe I'll talk to both of them. I *am* a doctor, you know. Maybe it wouldn't be so bad coming from me."

"But if Abby thinks I put you up to it—"

"She'll be mad," Dad said. "So what? Sounds to me like you're more worried about your friendship than you are your friend. Better get your priorities straight."

Mom nodded at him. "I couldn't have said it better. Thank you, Theo."

Tedi scowled at them. She felt like a traitor. "I guess you know Abby's going to kill me."

# CHAPTER 26

Thursday morning Estelle Pinkley walked past her secretary's desk and caught sight of the stack of data on the corner of the credenza next to the fax machine. It was data on one young man. The stack had been growing taller for the past three weeks, and Charlotte had remarked at least twice to Estelle that nobody could have that many legitimate emergencies.

Estelle picked up the top few sheets of copied medical charts. "Charlotte, how many area hospitals does this represent?"

The secretary turned from her computer. "Seven as of Tuesday, Mrs. Pinkley. The influx has finally slowed, thank goodness."

"Thank you. Would you collate the pages, putting information from each hospital into a separate file and putting all the charts into chronological order, please."

Charlotte looked at the stack and swallowed. "How soon do you need that?"

"Today. How soon can you have it?"

"I could try for noon, I guess, but—"

"Good." Estelle turned to leave, then turned back. "And, Charlotte, even more than usual, this is strictly confidential. This is sensitive material, and we don't want to take any chances." It might soon be a subject of conversation for the whole city of Knolls, but not if she could do something about it first.

"Yes, of course." Charlotte always took her lunch at the same time as Estelle, and she never failed to lock up. No one had been given the opportunity to sneak a peek.

"Thank you. Let me know if you need help with it, and I'll pitch in. I've got some free time this morning."

Under the weight of Charlotte's surprised stare, Estelle stepped into her office. She locked the door behind her and picked up the telephone.

Denise, Bailey Little's efficient legal secretary—and a recent, unobtrusive attender of Estelle's Lutheran church—had Bailey on the line within a minute.

"Yes, Estelle, what is it?" His words came through the line hard and tight.

Years of experience had honed Estelle's self-control to an art form. A hothead from birth, she had learned early in her practice to maintain a veneer of friendly control through the most trying of circumstances, and Bailey had always been one of the very most trying.

"Hello, Bailey," she said sweetly. "I trust you're having a good day. I have a sudden need to meet with you. Do you have some time this afternoon to fit me into your schedule?"

"This afternoon? Have you lost your mind? I have clients."

"I'm sure they'll be gracious enough to wait." Estelle's voice grew a little firmer. "We need to talk."

"Don't tell me your little COBRA investigator found something," he taunted.

Estelle smiled in order to retain a pleasant tone in her voice. "This hospital is clean. The meeting will be of utmost interest to you, however." She injected a fake sigh of sympathy. "I'm afraid you will also find it personally unpleasant."

There was a cold five-second silence on the line, then, "Why?"

"I'll just have to show you. There's too much material to fit into my briefcase, and I don't care to lug it all the way over to your office, so you'll have to come here. Let's say about two o'clock." She did not make it in the form of a question.

Bailey's typical aura of anger jolted through the line like a striking snake. "Is this a joke?"

"I'm sorry, is two o'clock not convenient for you?" Estelle drawled facetiously. "I could make it three, I suppose, but this information is melting the finish off the table. If it waits too much longer, I may have to call Harvey at the *Knolls Review* and see if he can take it for me."

There was another pause. "He wouldn't."

"Why, because you and Harvey are friends?" Estelle shook her head in silent reflection. "But do you know what makes you such good friends, counselor? The fact that for both of you business comes before personal relationships. When he sees this bounty his mouth will water. He won't be able to resist. If you were in his shoes, you would do the same."

There was a third shocked, furious silence, but before Bailey could snap a reply Estelle hung up. He would be here. He had too many dirty secrets that needed to be kept quiet.

She sighed. If Bailey Little weren't such a threat to this hospital, he would be nothing more than a man to be pitied.

She placed her palms flat against the desk to push herself to her feet, but the telephone rang again. She picked up and braced herself to hear another of Bailey's tirades.

It wasn't him.

The news from this voice brought a fresh, hopeful smile to her face.

————

The after-lunch ball game was already in the top of the second inning when Tedi stepped out of the school building and heard the shouts and laughter and screams of the kids on the playground. Maybe her team wouldn't call her to take her turn at bat. And if they did, when she struck out, maybe they wouldn't make her run out and take her place in right field. The balls didn't come out that way very often anyway, which was why they stuck her out there. Any time the ball did come toward her, the center fielder had to run over to her side and catch the ball or it didn't get caught.

Tedi hated baseball. The problem was, with only eighteen kids in her class, she had to play or they wouldn't have enough to practice.

Still, she hovered beside the building in the shadow of an evergreen tree and watched as Abby stepped up to the plate.

Abby was the best hitter in the sixth grade, and everybody knew it. She could place the ball wherever she wanted, and she could hit a home run just about every time. Some of the newer kids—kids who didn't value their lives—asked her how she got so good with such a scrawny body and skinny arms. They usually found out pretty fast how much muscle could hide inside a skinny arm. And her dad used to practice with her. He'd been a semipro ball player before she was born.

But even though Abby tried to teach Tedi how to catch and hit and pitch and throw, her efforts never worked. Tedi was hopeless.

The bat smacked the ball and shot it high into the air. Too high. It curved into the sky and got lost in the sun and dropped uselessly outside the right field foul line. Tedi could see the frustration in Abby's face from where she stood, and she also saw fresh determination as her best friend poised with the bat for the pitcher to throw her another one.

And something else touched Abby's expression as Tedi watched her. It was the same look she'd had in her eyes the day she cut herself, and the day she refused to call her parents to tell them where she was after the fire. It was the same look she had the day after her dad moved out of the house. Her mouth was set in a grim line, her chin jutting out, her gaze narrowed.

Abby's lips turned white as she pressed them together and watched for the right pitch. She placed her feet just right again and gripped the bat. When the ball reached the plate, she swung with the force of her whole body. A loud *thwack* reverberated across the playground, and the ball shot straight along the inside of the right foul line in probably the hardest, longest line drive in the history of the school. Everybody on the ball field shouted as Abby ran. She didn't limp or seem to feel the place on her leg where she'd had the stitches.

Tedi forgot she was lying low and shouted for her friend to round third. Then she caught her breath in disbelief when the ball bounced toward the school building and toward her. She scuttled backward, but the ball bounced again and flew at the basement window—the window where the protective screen had been removed for cafeteria repairs.

As Abby stomped third base on her way home, glass shattered into shards and flew from the impact of the ball like tiny icicles. The screaming and shouting across the field stopped in a combined awed gasp. Abby's foot slapped home plate, and she slowed her steps and glanced in the direction of the broken window.

"Look what you did, Cuendet!" outfielder Trent Pullman hollered. "Now what're we gonna do for a ball?"

Abby frowned and glanced back toward the dugout where her team had fallen silent. "We've got to go get it," she called to them. "It's the only one we have."

Nobody moved. They just sat staring at her.

Abby's frown turned to a scowl. "What are you scared of? It was an accident!"

Tedi knew she was a wimp, but she continued to wait behind the tree, hoping Abby didn't see her there. She wasn't about to get into trouble for something she hadn't done, especially something she hadn't wanted to do in the first place.

But then Abby turned and took a few steps toward the broken window. She hesitated, then glared at the others. Sighing, she broke into a trot, the old look back in her face, blazing from her eyes. She ran all the way to the window without glancing in Tedi's direction. She dropped to her knees at the broken window, bent down and peered inside, and hesitated.

Jagged shards of glass scattered across the grass around the outside of the window. Tedi saw Abby tense and lift her hand, then shift her attention back toward the field to see if anyone had followed her. They hadn't.

Even while Abby stuck her arm through the broken window close to the out-jutting slivers, Tedi knew what she was going to do.

Tedi jumped from behind the tree. "No! Abby, don't!"

Abby jerked and swung around, eyes wide, glasses falling down her nose. Her left forearm connected with the point of a shard, and the point dug in. Abby cried out and tried to jerk backward, but the shard dug more deeply. Blood spurted.

"Abby!" Tedi ran toward her. "Somebody call the nurse! Call Mr. Walters! Call for help!"

---

Lukas sat at his spot at the large ER desk and studied his marks on the T-sheet he had filled out on a man with a possible concussion—the patient had been showing off during his lunch break at work and attempted to break a board with his head. The CT would be back anytime, and Lukas would better know how to treat the man's self-inflicted injury.

Lukas looked up to see Buck leaning against the counter reading the *Knolls Review*, borrowed scrubs stretched tightly across his broad shoulders. "No apartments in here for rent," Buck muttered. "No job openings." He dropped the paper back where he'd found it. "Just some stupid pictures of the fire the other day." He gestured to the front page, which held an enlarged picture of a skinny young man with curly black hair standing by a fire engine. It was eighteen-year-old Explorer trainee, Kyle Alder, flexing his nonexistent muscles and smiling into the camera.

"How do you like that, Doc? Here I am suspended, and that wet-eared kid who can't even hold a fire hose with both hands is front-page news. It just doesn't figure." Buck shook his head and paced across the room and back.

Buck had come into work this morning as scheduled, with no word about where he'd been staying or what he'd been doing. They had been so busy, there had been little time to discuss it. Until now.

"Have you heard from Kendra?" Lukas asked, then braced himself for a storm. Buck turned to pace across the room again, and for a moment Lukas thought he wasn't going to answer.

"Heard *about* her," he said at last, turning back to face Lukas. He was silent for a moment, then said softly, "One of the guys from the station said she called looking for me there, and some idiot had to blurt the news that I was suspended."

"I'm surprised she didn't know it already," Lukas said.

Buck shook his head and turned for another lap around the room. "She might even call for me here, but I won't take the call. I've already told Carol not to bother me." He glanced over his shoulder at the secretary at the computer a few yards away, who was talking on the telephone and entering data in the computer at the same time, and had no time to eavesdrop on their conversation if she'd wanted to. "I heard Kendra got a job. She's working at the print shop for Jack. I don't think he needed the help, but he knew she would need the money."

"Maybe she needs more than just the money right now," Lukas said. "If she's busy, she won't have so much time to think about the past. Isn't that what has her so upset?"

"That's not the way I hear it," Buck said. "Sounds to me like I'm the only problem she's got." Buck stopped pacing and came over to lean once more against the central desk–counter. He sighed heavily and his shoulders slumped. He lowered his voice, even though Carol wasn't listening and no one else was in the room at the moment. "I went back down to the station and talked to some of the guys. They say the chief's been real sulled up lately."

"You would be too if you had a job like his," Lukas said. "Believe me, responsibility is no fun, and now his best man is out on suspension."

Buck nodded, then shot Lukas a brief smile at the compliment.

"Don't worry, Buck. I've talked to Personnel, and you can have more shifts here for a while. The reason they didn't want to switch you from part time to full time here at the hospital was because they didn't think the suspension would last long."

Buck raised his brows in surprise, and his expression lightened. "That's what they said?"

"That's what they said. It has nothing to do with your ability to do the job. You now have an excellent letter of recommendation from me in your file." Lukas didn't mention the fact that he also sent a copy of the letter to the fire department. "And you're still getting a paycheck from the department, aren't you?"

"Well . . . yeah." More of the tight worry eased from his face.

"Then why don't you just allow a little time to pass before you get all bent out of shape. You know, Buck, you might start practicing a little patience once in a while. It'll do you some good." The possibility occurred to Lukas that he might do well to take some of his own advice. "While you're practicing, though, do you have a place to stay? I've got an extra bedroom. You could bunk at my place until Kendra realizes what she's missing."

Buck's expression lightened further. "I could?"

"Sure. I'm never there anyway."

Buck looked at Lukas for a moment, then said in perfect seriousness, "But I would starve if I stayed with you."

Lukas sighed and shook his head. "You could raid my refrigerator for doggy bags."

"Guess I could bring my own doggy bags . . . start hanging out at the restaurants at night when they close and see if they have any leftovers."

"That's *not* what I do."

Buck gave him a teasing look. "I hear you don't even know where a grocery store is in this town."

"I do now."

"I guess I could move in with you for a while. Maybe I could mow your yard for you and clean out your gutters. Your place could sure use some work."

"I'm not looking for hired help, Buck. You don't have to—hey, my place isn't *that* bad."

A smile spread across the younger man's face from one oversized ear to the other. "Doc, you have trees growing in your gutters."

"Those are just little maple saplings." Lukas chuckled. "Okay, maybe my place could use some work."

"And maybe I'll take you up on your offer," Buck said. "It sure beats sleeping in my truck down at the lake."

The phone at the end of the desk shrilled, and Lukas grabbed it. It would be Radiology calling with the results. "How's the CT?"

"Actually, Lukas, I have better news than that." It wasn't Radiology. It was Estelle.

"Oh, sorry. I was waiting on a call about—"

"How would you like to have your day made?"

He could hear the excitement in her voice. "Sounds good to me."

"I got a call from Dr. Jarvis George this morning. Do you want to guess what he said?"

"He's coming back to work?" Lukas couldn't believe she would be this happy about that kind of news.

"Dr. George is in Kauai on an extended vacation–honeymoon, and his dear, wonderful new wife has convinced him to retire. Goodness knows he doesn't need the money, he's invested quite well over the years. Do you know what his retirement means?" Estelle demanded. "It means you now have the privilege of being the first on-site full-time director of Knolls Community Hospital Emergency Department."

Lukas nearly gasped aloud. That was *not* good news! "B-but, Estelle, you said—"

"Think of the power you have to make a difference, Lukas. Think of the policies you can improve, the lives you can influence, the—"

"The twenty-four-hour shifts I can work because I can't convince anyone to come in," he interrupted with alarm.

"No problem. We're going to hire four more full-timers plus a PRN, so you can work out a schedule to suit—"

"Please, Estelle, I'm not administrative material." Had he fallen asleep and drifted into some kind of nightmare? "You told me this morning that if Dr. George resigned his directorship you would . . ." What was that? Laughter? "Estelle. . . ?"

Yes, it definitely was laughter, and it grew louder, the deep tones of her voice raised to an unaccustomed level of obvious enjoyment at his expense. "Don't worry, Lukas, I have you covered. Three of the physicians applying for work in our ER have administrative experience. Surely we can find someone to take over your unwanted responsibilities and still be enough of a pushover to fall into line with my plans for this hospital."

Lukas gave a relieved sigh. "Where'd you learn how to bluff like that?"

"In the cradle. Sorry, I couldn't resist." She gave another deep chuckle, then she sighed, and the air grew serious over the line. "I needed that. Thanks for being the fall guy for me." She hesitated. "Lukas, I need your prayers this afternoon. I'm going to lock horns with Bailey, and it's going to get ugly."

"Ugly?"

"He can't win this fight. I've got all the ammunition I need to stop him, and when he realizes he's going to lose, he'll get nasty."

"What time is the meeting?"

"Two o'clock. He'll arrive late just to spite me, but not too late."

Lukas glanced at his watch. "You don't have much time to prepare."

"I'm prepared. Just pray."

"I'll do that."

He hung up, then turned around to find Cowboy Casey standing at the desk, a new gray hat shading his eyes from the glare of the overhead lights, a smile creasing his sun-worn face like a silver lining. Beside him, tucked against his side by his unhurt arm, stood Beverly with a glow in her eyes that seemed to reflect against her red hair like a sunrise.

Lukas didn't have to ask. He knew Beverly wouldn't be this happy about a new lion cub.

"Dr. Bower, we're getting married in a week," Cowboy announced in his deep Ozark drawl. "Want to come?"

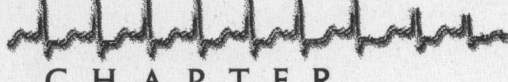

# CHAPTER 27

Lukas watched as Ken, the x-ray tech, wheeled a female patient out of exam room three into the Radiology department. The patient's left eye was angry red and purple, and her only explanation was that she had gotten clumsy and stumbled into a chair. Tears had filled her eyes since her arrival thirty minutes ago, but they never fell. It was as if the pain was too great for even a teardrop to touch.

Even in a small town like Knolls, the ER saw battered women with silent, unacknowledged tears. They came alone a lot of times because they didn't want anyone else to guess what was going on. And yet they kept going back to the men who continued to abuse them.

Buck stepped up beside Lukas with arms crossed over his chest, his face grim as he watched Ken wheel the patient out. "Guess she must have been clumsy six months ago when she bruised her jaw, too. Did you see her chart, Dr. Bower? She broke her wrist a year ago—or had it broken for her. Maybe she ought to do to her husband what Delphi did to Abner, then maybe he'd think twice when he flexes his muscles with his wife in the room."

"You know these people?" Lukas asked.

"Kendra used to work with Galen at Baker Metalworks before we got married. I doubt if he's changed. He was a real bully then." Buck uncrossed his arms and shook his head. "Makes you wonder, doesn't it?" Frustration edged every word. "Maybe Kendra'd go for somebody like that, somebody who'd knock her around and yell at her."

Lukas stifled a sigh. He'd managed to coax his friend into a better mood for a while, but he'd known it wouldn't last. Buck was obviously getting tired of the disappointment in his life right now. Lukas didn't blame him.

Buck nudged Lukas, and the gentle force of his muscular arm sent Lukas stepping sideways. "Look who's coming in, Doc." Buck pointed toward the entrance. "Just what I need to make my day complete."

Lukas saw Kyle Alder stepping into the waiting room.

Kyle caught sight of Buck, waved, and walked toward them. "Hi, Buck," he said. "Hi, Dr. Bower."

Buck straightened from the counter. "Aren't you on duty?"

Kyle shoved his hands into his pockets and shrugged. "Not until tonight. Some of the guys at the station said you had a shift here today." He sighed and looked down. "They don't want me over there."

"Join the club," Buck said bitterly.

"What's going on, anyway?" Kyle asked. "I mean, doesn't the chief know better than to suspect you? Anybody could've gotten that solvent. Everybody knew about it, and you never locked your locker."

Buck nodded and leaned back against the counter, arms crossed over his chest again. "Somebody should tell the chief that."

"I did as soon as I found out what happened."

"What did he say?"

Kyle swallowed and looked away. "Oh, you know the chief, never gives anything away. He . . . uh . . . asked me a few questions."

"Like what?"

"He wanted to know what kind of stuff you taught us, you know, how we spent our time on duty and . . . well, if we were with you when the calls came in for the fires . . . things like that."

Buck was silent for a few seconds. Lukas could almost feel the tension mounting once again, and he wished Kyle had opted to stay home today.

"What did you tell him?" Buck asked. His voice was soft. Controlled.

Kyle's eyes widened slightly, and his face flushed. "Buck, I had to tell him the truth. We weren't with you before those fires started, remember? You weren't even on duty most of those times."

"But I was at the station when we got the second and third calls," Buck snapped. "You knew that! Everybody knew I was staying there."

Kyle watched Buck for a moment. "You weren't with us every minute," he said, not breaking eye contact with Buck. "There were a couple of times I went looking for you and couldn't find you. Alex and I were working on your model, and we needed another piece, and we couldn't find it in your locker." His eyes widened, as if he'd just thought of something. "That was just about an hour before we got the call on the second fire, the one at that other convenience store down on Fourth."

"That's crazy," Buck said. "You all knew I was on a food run. I took your orders, remember? I went to get pizza, right down the street—"

"From the store on Fourth," Kyle finished for him. "And the chief reminded me that we were all here at the hospital for a fire drill just before Little Mary's caught fire—all except you."

"The *chief* told *you* that?" Buck exclaimed. "I don't believe it."

Kyle took a step backward. He drew his hands out of his pockets and spread them in front of him. "Look, I didn't do anything to get you in trouble, okay? The chief could've found that stuff out without asking me. He's asking everybody, and it would blow my future in fire fighting if I tried to lie to him."

"Your *future* . . . I didn't ask you to lie to him!" Buck glared at Kyle, then turned to Lukas incredulously. He shook his head. "I've got a patient to check on." He pivoted and stalked away. The squeak of his rubber-soled shoes shot through the ER after he disappeared from sight.

"Why's he so mad?" Kyle asked. "I didn't do anything. I thought he'd want to know what's going on at the station."

Lukas covered his own irritation at the teenager's insensitivity. He looked out into the parking lot and saw a car pulling in. "Kyle, it looks like we may be getting busy again, so . . ."

"Yeah, I guess maybe I should go now," Kyle said. "It doesn't look like I'm wanted here, either. But tell me, Dr. Bower. Doesn't it seem to you like Buck isn't happy unless he's the hero?" He shoved his hands back into his pockets and asked for directions to the rest room, then turned to leave.

Ken came back in from Radiology pushing the woman with the bruised face. He handed Lukas the plain film x-rays he'd taken. "Did you see Buck race through here a minute ago?"

"Yes, I thought he was going to help you," Lukas said. He took the films and mounted them on the light beside the desk.

"Nope, he sailed right by me." Ken took the patient back into her exam room, then came back out. "Anything broken there?" he asked, peering over Lukas's shoulder.

"I don't see anything."

Ken moved closer and lowered his voice. "Buck sure didn't look happy, Dr. Bower."

Before Lukas had time to reply, a car squealed into the ambulance entrance and jerked to a stop. A chubby man burst out of the door on the driver's side and yanked open the back door. He reached inside and half lifted, half dragged a limp and bleeding young girl from the vehicle.

"Carol, get me a nurse!" Lukas shouted as he rushed to grab a wheelchair. "And find Buck."

The front passenger door flew open, and another young girl stepped out. She, too, had bright streaks of blood over her clothes, face, and hands. She ran to the ambulance doors and pushed the automatic opener in time for Lukas to come out, and as she did so, he recognized Tedi through the streaks of blood. No!

"Tedi, what happened? Are you okay? What—"

"Lukas, Abby cut her arm on broken glass." She continued to depress the opener as Lukas pushed the wheelchair through the wide threshold. "The blood is all over the place, and it won't stop, and she's getting weaker."

"Has she lost consciousness?"

"Not yet. She's crying, and she's scared."

Lukas looked Tedi over as he rushed the wheelchair around to the other side of the car. "Go inside, Tedi. We need to check you out, too."

"But I didn't get hurt. It was just Abby. I watched her do it, Lukas, I was right there, and I tried to stop the blood, but it wouldn't stop. I can show you where she got cut." Tedi released the button and rushed over to walk beside Lukas. "They tried wrapping it when we got her to the nurse's office, but it kept bleeding."

By this time the man had Abby out of the car and was holding her in his arms. A woman stepped out of the car to join them. Lukas recognized her as the school nurse.

"Lead the way," the man said. "Tedi says she isn't hurt, but I'd like to get her looked at anyway, just in case. Abby looks bad." He nodded down toward Abby's gauze-wrapped left forearm. All the gauze was red. "We must be doing something wrong, because we can't get it to stop bleeding."

They loaded Abby quickly into the wheelchair, and Tedi once more depressed the button for automatic entry as the group of them filed inside.

Lukas aimed the chair toward the first trauma room. "Have the parents been called?" he asked the man.

"Yes, the school secretary should have already called them."

Claudia came running in just as Lukas bent to lift Abby onto the exam bed.

"Carol," Lukas called toward the central station, "call Arthur and Alma Collins, would you, please? The number for their cell phone is up on the bulletin board." Mrs. Pinkley had given permission for them to be called for patient counseling. It couldn't hurt to have them here for Abby's parents. "And, Carol, have you found Buck? I need him."

"Not yet, Dr. Bower. I'm still looking."

Abby opened her eyes as Lukas laid her down onto the bed. Tears had washed a course through the splotches of drying blood on her face. She struggled to sit back up, but Claudia stepped to her side and gently eased her back.

"It's going to be okay, honey. Dr. Bower's here now. He's the one who did your stitches, remember?"

As if too weak to fight it, Abby laid her head back against the pillow. "Are my parents coming? Have you called them? Do they know what happened?"

"I'm sure they'll be here," Lukas said.

———

"Dr. Mercy?" came the voice of a young woman over the phone. "This is Tiffany from Tedi's school. Mr. Walters asked me to call you and let you know that Tedi is on her way to the emergency room. In fact, she should be there by now."

Mercy felt a familiar grip of fear. Not again. "What happened?" She sank down onto the end of the sofa, glad Tiffany had known to call her at home on Thursday.

"There was an accident out on the playground when somebody hit a baseball through a window," Tiffany said. "I think Tedi's okay, but there was a lot of blood from the other girl. Mr. Walters and Mrs. Thomas want Tedi checked to make sure she didn't have any hidden cuts. Her friend doesn't look very good."

"Her friend?" Mercy asked. "Which friend?"

"Abby Cuendet. I just called her parents, and they're both on their way in."

"Thanks, Tiffany. I'm going in, too."

After hanging up, Mercy grabbed her jacket and stethoscope, then hesitated and glanced once more at the telephone. Tiffany said Tedi was probably okay.

But how would Theodore feel if he heard from someone that his daughter was rushed to the hospital?

She sighed and placed the jacket and stethoscope back onto the kitchen counter, then picked up the receiver once more.

———

Tedi sat quietly on the exam bed, wide-eyed and frightened, ignoring the nurse who cleaned the blood from her arms and legs. She couldn't tear her gaze from Abby, who lay on the exam bed across the ER, where Lukas and another nurse worked. Lukas had said something about an "arterial bleed" and "Von Willebrand's disease." He had ordered pressure dressings and two trauma IV's. They had left the curtains open.

"She needs blood," Lukas said, then took a step toward the desk. "Carol, did you call Dr. Wong for a surgical consult?"

"Yes. He was in his office, and he'll be right down."

Abby started to cry again, as she'd been doing off and on since she got cut. Her voice sounded weaker than it had when they first came in.

Tedi wanted to push the nurse away from her and jump down from the exam bed and go to Abby, but she knew she would just be in the way. Mr. Walters and Mrs. Thomas had already gone to the waiting room.

Lukas glanced in Tedi's direction. "How's our girl doing over there, Lauren?" he called to the blond-haired nurse with a ponytail, who was cleaning Tedi's arms and legs.

"Looking good, Dr. Bower. No cuts." Lauren patted Tedi's newly scrubbed knee and smiled at her. "That blood didn't bother you at all, did it, Tedi? You could be a doctor someday, just like your mom and your grandfather. Your parents will be so proud of you."

"What about Abby's mom and dad?" Tedi asked. "Have you heard if they're coming?" Now she recognized this lady. She went to Grandma Ivy's church.

"Is Abby going to be okay?" Tedi asked. "Is she losing too much blood? Do they need more? We're the same blood type, you know."

Lauren paused in her cleaning and cocked her head to one side, her green eyes studying Tedi's face. "You're really worried about your friend, aren't you? Well, you shouldn't be. Dr. Bower's going to take good care of her. We're well stocked with blood, and if Abby needs surgery, Dr. Wong will know just what to do. Did you know that Dr. Wong knows how to repair everything from bullet wounds to lion bites? He's great, and he's on his way here right now. How did you manage to get splattered with so much blood and not get a single cut?"

"I saw it happen, and I was the first one to reach her. What's that disease Dr. Bower's talking about? Is Abby sick?"

"No, sweetie, she'll be okay. Von Willebrand's disease just means she has a condition that makes her bleed a lot. When she cuts herself, the flow doesn't stop as easily as it does with you or other normal kids."

The shrill cry of an ambulance siren reached them, and Lauren glanced over her shoulder toward Lukas. "There's the man they called about, Dr. Bower. I can do the assessment. Tedi looks good, and I saw Buck just walk back into the ER, so he can take her from here."

A lot of things happened at the same time after that. Tedi saw the ambulance attendants wheel in a man who sounded like he was choking. His breaths came in short, wheezing gasps, and his eyes were wide with fear. When Lauren rushed up to him, he reached out and grabbed her arm.

"Help me!" he cried hoarsely. "Help!"

She reassured him and directed the attendants into an exam room. "Dr. Bower, we need you stat. Where's Dr. Wong?"

The ambulance attendant walked alongside the patient, pushing the gurney, giving his report to Lukas. ". . . dialysis patient who had the flu, so he missed his dialysis."

He jabbered some numbers to Lukas that Tedi didn't understand, and halfway through, the patient released Lauren and grabbed Lukas by the arm.

"Help me! I should've had dialysis, but I was sick and I didn't feel like . . ."

Right behind him came Abby's dad running through the double ambulance doors just before they closed. "I'm Jason Cuendet," he called to the secretary as he ran up to the central desk. "Where's my daughter? They said she was here. Is she okay? What happened?"

The secretary pointed him toward Abby as she turned and greeted a small dark-haired man, also in scrubs, who stepped in from the other door. "Dr. Wong, thank goodness! Your patient is in one. She needs you now."

————

Estelle Pinkley sat at her huge desk and stared out the large picture window of her office, kneading the painful hot joints and tips of her fingers. She didn't want to think about the stack of subpoenaed reports her secretary had just brought in and placed on her desk. She wanted to bask just for a moment in the golden-red autumn beauty of mature maple trees that graced the hospital lawn. She wanted to watch ninety-year-old Mrs. Robinson walk her elderly collie along the sidewalk across the street, as she had done every day at this time for as long as Estelle had been hospital administrator.

On the surface, Knolls County appeared to be the perfect community, where families could escape the crowded cities and raise their kids to be responsible adults who voted, worked for an honest living, and made enough money after taxes to send their own kids to college. Sadly, many people who moved here were disappointed. The county next door to theirs had the unenviable reputation of producing the most methamphetamine in the state. Knolls Community Hospital ER treated their share of addicts, to the point that Estelle had suggested to the long-range planning committee that they crunch the numbers for a future drug abuse treatment center.

The telephone intercom beeped, and the muted alto of her secretary's voice came through the speaker. "Mrs. Pinkley, Mr. Little is here."

Estelle sighed and dragged her attention from the natural outside beauty to the ugliness of the files before her. She pressed the button. "Please send him in." She glanced at her watch. It was 2:15.

She closed her eyes and recalled the earnest, intelligent face of Dwayne Little fifteen years ago. During his parents' nasty, lengthy divorce, Estelle had watched helplessly as the sweet little boy metamorphosed into a morose, angry teenager, and then a manipulative, drug-seeking adult. She'd shed tears over his death certificate this spring. She'd watched his father, Bailey, attempt to destroy this hospital and two doctors in an attempt to assuage the pain of his own guilt. Bailey Little was a very guilty man.

The office door opened, and as Bailey stepped through the threshold, Estelle felt an unaccustomed thrill of fear at the sight of his steel gray eyes set beneath a prominent brow. His features suggested the appearance of a bird of prey, and his combed-back hair, silver now, gave him an air of distinction. Refined danger.

But she would control this meeting.

He nodded coldly and took a seat across from her. "What are you hoping to gain from this summons?"

"Everything I need, Bailey, but it's going to cost both of us." Before he could reply, she continued. "Your COBRA investigator, Ms. Fellows, has refused to acknowledge that our records are excellent, and I'm tired of her wearying presence in this hospital, requesting confidential patient files and treating our secretarial staff like criminals who are trying to hide something. So the first thing I want is for you to call off your pit bull."

"I'm not—"

"Don't try to bluff me," Estelle snapped, fixing him with her own stiletto glare. She took a fax transmission from the top of her stack and shoved it across the smooth surface of her desk. It drifted to a stop in front of him. "This was from the investigator's home office a week ago, informing her that the material she had produced was not sufficient for her to continue her search." She didn't tell him that he had a snitch inside his own office, and that she knew about the faxed copies of that same confidential hospital material in his possession. "I also have data linking you to Ms. Fellows last year, when she was your client."

"That information is confidential!"

"Of course it is. Your previous association with her worried me, and so I had my own investigator dig a little deeper." She picked up copies of microfiched bank transactions. "Amazing what a subpoena will do. I found a few inconsistencies between her salary and her deposits. Cash deposits. Bribery is illegal, Bailey, whether you want to acknowledge that fact or not. She will lose her job as soon as I have enough evidence in my hands, because I've already spoken with her supervisor."

Anger darkened Bailey's eyes. His physical reaction to anger had always been his biggest weakness when he locked horns with her in court.

"Because Ms. Fellows has been so persistent in wasting federal money," Estelle continued, "and because you saw fit to advertise the investigation to the public, I decided it was time to do a little detective work of my own. You know how I love to research a good meaty case. Since Knolls Community Hospital is a not-for-profit enterprise, and the public supports us, how is it going to look when that same public finds out that the esteemed Bailey Little was the one who reported faulty information to COBRA about us in the first place?"

"Harvey won't print unsubstantiated rumors in the—"

"He'll print my open letter to the citizens of Knolls, or he'll have a lawsuit on his hands for printing yours," Estelle snapped. "And I'll be writing the grandmother of all letters to the editor, using some of the same sidestepping verbiage you used to stir up dissension against us. In that same letter, I will reveal the results of my research into RealCare, whom you advertised in your open letter as a strong, growing company with good ethical standards." She pushed another sheet toward him. "You probably aren't interested, but their employee turnover rate is three times higher than ours here at Knolls. My investigation has shown that the majority of employees are unhappy there, with concerns ranging from poor quality of patient care to overly regimented work hours to low pay and miserable employee benefits. Even more interesting, and more frightening, is the fact that the mortality rate for their patients is twice as high as the national average."

Bailey snorted. "What did you do, interview an ex-employee?"

"Would it surprise you to know that fifteen of our present employees, who are happy, dependable workers, came to us from RealCare facilities? I did not receive a single good report on RealCare from any of them."

"What did you expect, Estelle? Most ex-employees are unhappy with their previous place of employment."

Estelle slid another sheet across and waited for him to pick it up. He didn't. "This is a report from Dorothy Wild, our quality assurance director, who has been a proponent of yours many times in the past. I had her do a QA survey of our patients who have had experience with RealCare. The ratings that came back just yesterday were deplorable. In every health-care facility purchased by RealCare, the patients developed a lower perception of care over the period of a year. The doctor–patient ratio grew worse as physicians left the system and were not replaced. Don't you want to read the information, Bailey?" she asked as he refused to acknowledge the paper before him. "Afraid you'll see something you don't want to see?"

"No, actually, Estelle, I'm waiting for you to finish with the propaganda and get to your real agenda. What did you drag me here for?"

Estelle smiled pleasantly. She and Bailey had been opponents far too long. He knew her well. "Did you know that COBRA is investigating RealCare?"

He showed no surprise. "Welcome to the club. As you have seen here, that means nothing."

"Maybe in RealCare's case it does. Apparently the preliminary investigation uncovered some compromising information, because reinforcements have been called into the Springfield facility. They could be shut down."

Bailey held her gaze with the eagle-eyed stare for which he was famous. "You haven't answered my question yet. What am I doing here? If you expected me to buckle beneath these petty little threats . . ." He waved a hand dismissively at the sheets in front of him.

Fighting a wave of sorrow, Estelle met his stare and held it for several seconds, long enough for him to read what lay behind her eyes.

His face tightened, and he leaned back. "What is it?"

———

As people rushed from room to room and doctors worked and nurses helped and the telephones rang and more patients came in, Tedi knew that she would not want to be an ER doc. She watched Dr. Wong working over Abby in one exam room. Lukas was working on the man who'd come in by ambulance in the next room. Tedi was alone right now, but she knew Mom would be here any minute.

"What are you doing?" Mr. Cuendet cried to the doctor from the side of Abby's bed. "She's still bleeding! Can't you people—"

"Mr. Cuendet, if you can't control yourself, I will have to ask you to leave," Dr. Wong said as he turned toward the nurse who was helping him. "Claudia, we need to get her into surgery."

Mrs. Cuendet came racing through the ER door and saw her daughter immediately. "Abby, oh no, Abby," she whispered as she rushed forward.

Mr. Cuendet reached out and stopped her before she could get to the bed. "Lindy, they're taking her to surgery. They've had trouble getting the bleeding stopped and—"

"Let go of me!" She jerked from his grasp and rounded on him with fury in her eyes. "You didn't need me before, and I sure don't need you now." She turned her back on him and rushed to the bed. "Abby? Honey, I'm here. Everything's going to be okay."

"Tedi?" The calm, loving voice startled Tedi from the entrance to the exam room in which she sat. She looked up to find Mom standing there at the entrance to the room, her face pale. But she was smiling.

"Mom." Tedi couldn't help it. Everything became too much. Tears rushed to her eyes and spilled down her cheeks, and she reached up like a little kid for her mother's embrace.

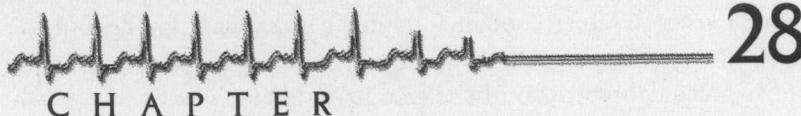

CHAPTER ——— **28**

Estelle picked up a file folder that contained copied sheets of medical charts. Labeled on the front was the name of their nearest ER neighbor to the south. She stood up and personally carried the file around the desk to Bailey.

She held it out to him and waited for him to take it. "I had hoped, Bailey, that it wouldn't come to this."

His eyes narrowed. "What are you trying to pull this time?"

"This is one of seven files from hospitals in this region. It's about Dwayne. Read it."

He took it at last, and Estelle walked back around her desk and sat down heavily. Dwayne had visited every hospital emergency department within a seventy-mile radius of Knolls. He did it in pursuit of pain medication—not just once or twice, but several times, until the personnel in each hospital grew suspicious.

As Bailey read, the color that had suffused his face now drained away.

"I could have done this sooner to protect the hospital," Estelle said softly. "Your son was a drug abuser, very likely an addict, and Dr. Bower picked up on that. He suggested that Dwayne needed to be in a drug rehab program. He offered alternative medication. He did everything according to COBRA protocol. Lukas Bower is above reproach." She stood up and scooted the remainder of the files across the desk. "It's all there. You can't hide from the truth any longer."

He did not look up or acknowledge her words in any way.

She sank down in her seat once more, feeling no satisfaction. Her sorrow increased. This was the right thing to do. She had to keep reminding herself of that.

She turned in her seat to stare out the window as Bailey read. Now she saw no beauty or comfort in the sky or trees or sculpted lawns of the neighborhood. She listened to Bailey's measured breathing, which grew louder as he read, then caught for a couple of seconds as if in wounded shock, then grew shallow, as if every breath caused deeper pain.

It had always struck Estelle as ironic that her chosen profession as an attorney was supposed to define the search for truth. She had spent her working days in just that manner, searching for the facts of a case, presenting those facts, and then allowing the impact of them to speak for her. It had saddened her early in her career that many of her colleagues, most notably Bailey, spent their time trying to coerce the facts to take on new meaning, as if the truth needed to be rewritten. But there was too much truth in these medical files to be manipulated, and this time Bailey could not threaten or bribe or blackmail his way out of it.

Estelle dragged her gaze from the window to look at Bailey again. That was when she caught it—a faint whiff of smoke. She frowned and glanced once more out the window. Someone could be burning leaves, but outside smells never reached her past the triple barrier of sealed windowpanes and granite and insulated wall. Besides, this was a smoke-free facility.

She shot another look at Bailey, his head still bent, his face pale as he read. He had given up cigars ten years ago after a judge caught him puffing on one in a courthouse and threatened to have him permanently removed from the premises.

With a deepening frown, she placed her hands on the leather armrests of her chair to raise herself. She heard the crunch of leather as the smell of smoke grew stronger.

Before she could stand up, a loud, intermittent *buzz-buzz-buzz* stridently burst through the room from overhead speakers.

At first she couldn't believe what she heard. The only time that obnoxious sound had come through this office was during fire drills. But there were none scheduled. And she definitely smelled the smoke.

"Bailey, that's the fire alarm. We need to—"

The sprinkler system spurted a few drips of water over the top of the desk in warning before it broke into a twisting spray, dousing Estelle and Bailey as they both scrambled out of their seats. But before they could reach the door in the downpour, they heard a clap of thunder so intense it shook the room.

The floor shifted, the window shattered, and Estelle's heavy desk jerked toward the back of the office as the floor beneath them buckled to the right. More smoke reached them, and they recognized the thunder for what it was—an explosion.

Bailey stumbled and fell hard against the wall. A heavy chair rolled toward him and struck him from behind, knocking him forward and pinning him. Estelle reached for him. The floor shifted again, and he slipped from her grasp as the desk crashed against her. The floor opened, and Bailey's legs fell through.

He turned terrified eyes toward Estelle. "Help me!" He reached for her, but the bucking floor knocked her sideways, forehead first into the desk. For her, everything went black.

———

The alarm on the ER dialysis unit beeped, went silent, and then beeped again as the floor rocked with the force of an earthquake and the atmosphere pulsed with a *BOOM!* from somewhere in the vicinity of the maintenance room below them.

Lukas grabbed at Mr. Weston, his emergency dialysis patient, to keep him from toppling out of the bed.

Patients screamed and staff shouted, and the faint smell of smoke was quickly overpowered by fear as the ceiling buckled and dropped two feet on the eastern side of the department, scattering debris over Lukas and his patient.

A voice reached Lukas over the frightened cries of his patient. It was a man shouting orders for evacuation to the staff. It was Buck. "Claudia, get the ambulatory patients out the front and into the far parking lot. Carol, empty the waiting room now! And take your cell phone. We may need it. Dr. Mercy, can we use your clinic? It's the closest, and these patients need a place—"

"I have the keys right here" came Mercy's suddenly strong, authoritative voice.

"But, Mom, what about Abby?" Tedi cried. "She's still in surgery."

"They'll get her out, Tedi. Let's go. Mrs. Lamberson, come with us. Come on, everybody. If you walked in here, you can walk out. We can take care of you over at the clinic." Her voice receded as she led others out.

Lukas felt a rush of relief. She and Tedi would be safe.

Mr. Weston gripped Lukas with his free hand. "It's going to collapse on us!"

Lukas reached down and squeezed his patient's shoulder. "It's okay. I'm not going to leave you. Please try not to panic, Mr. Weston. I need you to stay calm." He reached out toward the wall at the head of the bed and grabbed a nonrebreather mask, ripped it out of the package, and placed it on the patient's chest to use when he detached from the electricity to move him. He attached the mask to the oxygen tank on the chassis of the bed.

There was a sound of glass breaking, then Buck appeared in the doorway with a fire extinguisher in his hands. He had automatically switched to fireman mode. Lukas could see it in his eyes. "Dr. Bower, we've got to get you out of here."

Another rumble roared through the department, and someone called out, "Fire! I see fire!" Lights flickered and went out, plunging the ER into twilight as only the afternoon sun filtered in through the windows and entrance doors. Two battery-pack emergency floodlights came on in the department, but they barely reached the exam room. Lukas looked back toward the doorway, but Buck wasn't there. Seconds later came the blast of the extinguisher.

Mr. Weston cried out through the mask of his noninvasive ventilator. "What's happening? The machine went off! I can't see anything! I can't breathe."

"I know. I'll take care of it." Lukas pulled off the mask that covered the patient's face, then replaced it with the nonrebreather mask he had just hooked to the oxygen tank. He turned the oxygen tank wide open. "Keep breathing, Mr. Weston. Please try to stay calm." He grabbed the monitor from the top of the crash cart and set it on the foot of the bed.

The thin line of a light shot through the room. "Dr. Bower!" Lauren's frightened voice reached him from the dimly lit area of the hallway. "Here's a flashlight. Can I help?"

"Yes, we've got to get out of here. Have you evacuated the rest of the patients?"

"Yes, everybody's out."

Lukas choked on the smoke that gradually thickened the air. "Grab a crash cart and—"

Another rumble shook the floor, and plaster scattered on them from the ceiling. "Hurry, Lauren! I'll bring Mr. Weston." He kicked the brake on the wheeled bed and turned to push the patient out of the ER behind her. "If Carol has that cell phone, we need to use it. We need to airlift him."

"She's already calling. Rescue workers are on the way. Buck is afraid the main oxygen supply in respiratory therapy might be in trouble."

The front right wheel of the bed caught on fallen debris and jerked to a stop. Mr. Weston moaned while Lukas pulled backward, rerouted, and pushed forward again. If the main supply in respiratory therapy was affected, it could blow the whole side of this wing into the clouds. If they didn't get away from here in time, they could go with it.

Lauren rolled the crash cart forward and pushed open the double doors that led into the patient parking lot. "Do you want to take him to Dr. Mercy's clinic?" she asked as she pushed the cart out into the ambulance bay. "We're taking as many patients as we can get over there."

"Not if we can get a chopper to land at the end of the parking lot. This patient needs to fly now." As they stepped out into the parking lot away from the dust, smoke, and rubble, Lukas felt a wash of relief. They pushed their patient and equipment to the far end of the long lot and turned to find staff and patients filing from all the doors in the hospital. They were following evacuation procedure.

"What's the hospital census?" he asked Lauren.

"I think about thirty patients upstairs, two in ICU."

"Park the crash cart here." Lukas stopped at the helicopter landing site and turned back to his patient. "Lauren, we have to intubate."

She pushed the cart up beside the bed in the bright sunlight and nodded. She pulled a syringe and two medicine vials out of her pocket. "I already prepared."

As the screams of sirens converged on them from three different directions, Lukas thanked God silently for a good nurse.

———

Mercy raced through her waiting room and offices, pushing open exam room doors, switching on lights. Tedi followed close behind. A disaster had been called over the hospital intercom, and her clinic was closest. They were bringing the patients here, where the doctors and staff would do their triage. Carol, as well as every other able-bodied adult, was helping to transport patients.

"Tedi, call Josie's number and tell her we need her. Leave a message if she's not home. Then call Loretta. Her number's on the pad at the front desk." She turned to direct Claudia and Carol to wheel their patients toward the exam room at the far end of the clinic.

Claudia pushed through with a woman in her seventies who looked pale and frightened. "It'll be okay, Mrs. Davis. We'll get that stomachache taken care of over here." She stopped in front of Mercy. "We were just getting ready to give her a GI cocktail. If you want to tell me where your stash is, I'll see if I can't take over with the patients they bring over here."

"Thank you, Claudia." Mercy wanted to hug her. After giving the seasoned nurse the keys to the office and drug supply, Mercy gave the ER secretary instructions to get on the telephone in her office and call for backup physicians.

"Mom," Tedi yelled from her place at the front desk, "what about Abby? She's still in surgery! I've got to go find—"

"Oh no you don't! You sit right there and help out where Claudia needs you. They'll be bringing a lot more patients in here, and I want you here, out of the way of danger. I'll make sure Abby's okay, but knowing Dr. Wong, you'll see Abby anytime."

"But what if—"

The front door opened again, and respiratory and lab technicians came rushing in with more patients. "Dr. Mercy, where do you want these?" Carol asked from the hallway.

"Take them to Claudia. Is the outpatient area being evacuated?"

"Yes, just look at that mess out there." Carol gestured toward the large front windows, where the blinds had been pulled back to reveal the scene in vivid detail down the street. The patient and employee parking lot, which formed an L around two sides of the hospital structure, was rapidly filling with emergency vehicles, lights flashing, rescue workers running to their designated stations. In the center of the milieu, Mercy caught sight of Lukas and Lauren working over Mr. Weston. Lukas, at least, was safe.

Smoke that billowed from a collapsed section of outside wall between the respiratory department and ER was confined to that part of the hospital wing. Mercy felt the real problem would lie in getting all those sick patients down from the second floor. Rescue workers would have to carry the disabled ones down the stairs with stretchers, since they couldn't use the elevators.

"Look, Mom, there she is," Tedi said, pointing toward the side door closest to OR. Dr. Wong stepped out, accompanied by Abby's mother and father, and a nurse and a tech behind them, who pushed a gurney with Abby's skinny little body lying on top, draped in a sheet and still hooked to an IV.

Other staff members scurried out of the hospital helping patients, pushing some in wheelchairs and on beds, heading toward Mercy's office. She'd better prepare for a deluge.

And then she saw a car pull up alongside the curb in front. A red-headed man climbed from the driver's side and ran around to the trunk to pull out a folded wheelchair. Arthur and Alma Collins.

"Thank you, God," Mercy whispered as they hurried up the walk to join the throng headed to her door. "I owe you one."

———

Lukas barely heard the thunder of the chopper overhead before it landed, the noise and confusion were so thick on the ground. The fire chief had taken position in the center of the crowd of rescuers and was giving orders over a bullhorn to all of the fire fighters and anyone else who would listen. The landing pad had been left clear, and several cries and shouts accompanied the whoosh of air from the rotating blades as the huge flyer landed. Lukas and Lauren bent over to shield their patient, waited for the blades to slow and stop, and turned to help the flight team transfer Mr. Weston.

"Looks like you've got a bad situation here, Doc," the flight nurse shouted over the din. "You going to need us to call you any more help?"

"Yes. We have thirty patients from the floor and more from ER who'll need medical attention."

The nurse nodded and turned to load Mr. Weston into the chopper.

As they lifted with a rush of wind and a roar, Lukas heard a shout. He turned to see two more firemen come running from the building. One of them was Buck, his scrubs torn and covered with soot.

"Dr. Bower, we need your help." Blood dripped from a cut in his arm, and he wiped it on his side. "We've found Mrs. Pinkley and Bailey Little trapped in her office. They're hurt."

"How badly?"

"Rescue workers are getting Mrs. Pinkley out. She was knocked out, but she's conscious now and in pain. It looks like she might have cracked some ribs, maybe a broken leg and arm." He barely paused to catch his breath. "Bailey Little is trapped between the wall and the blown floor. He's unconscious and looks like he needs a needle decompression. I don't think we can free him soon enough to do it out here."

Lukas turned to grab the supplies he needed from the crash cart they had been using for Mr. Weston. "I'll come with you."

Buck laid a hand on his shoulder. "Dr. Bower, we're afraid the respiratory department is compromised. We've already had two explosions. If there's another one, the oxygen reservoirs could blow. This is dangerous."

"Then let's hurry."

---

Frightened patients and frantic nurses and techs scrambled for room in Mercy's clinic. The count had gone up to twenty-five patients, and more made their way down the street. All the beds and cots and chairs were full, and several people lay on the floor. Some moaned, some were silent with fear as the workers rushed to give aid and reassurance, their own voices frightened.

"Most of the hospital still has electricity, and the sprinklers are working in the patient rooms," someone informed Mercy as they walked by. "The fire fighters are worried about that whole wing, though. That's where the explosions hit. They think they came from down in maintenance."

Arthur Collins knelt on the floor, helping calm a woman having a panic attack, and his prayers were proving fruitful as the woman's breathing slowed. Alma sat in her wheelchair holding Lindy Cuendet's hand beside the cot where Abby lay, still pale but awake and mumbling incoherent words. Dr. Wong had gone back to help with the rescue effort in the main part of the hospital, which was undamaged. Ninety-year-old Mrs. Robinson from down the street had brought some cookies she had baked yesterday and was passing them around to the children.

Lauren McCaffrey came bursting into the office, her face flushed, eyes wide with fear. "Mrs. Pinkley and Bailey Little are hurt. Dr. Mercy, Dr. Bower's gone back inside, and they're afraid there will be another explosion."

Mercy gasped and ran to the window as the door opened again and more people stumbled into the clinic. Past the crowds of fire fighters and exiled patients, she saw the flash of royal blue—Lukas in his scrubs. He spoke for a moment with Buck, then nodded and went back through the opening of the shattered ER doors.

"No!" She watched in horror. "Lukas, no!"

———

Lukas followed Buck's broad shoulders through the gloom and destruction of the room he had left moments earlier. He was astonished to find large chunks of ceiling tile and plaster littering the floor and furniture. Tables, chairs, and cots lay overturned beneath the wreckage.

"Watch your step, Doc," Buck called over his shoulder. "The guys tried to clear a path, but we can't take for granted that anything's stable."

Breathing shallowly through the thick pall of smoke and ash, Lukas stepped over a fallen cot. "Where's the smoke coming from? Is there still a fire in the building?"

"I think it's all contained except for the hallway outside respiratory therapy." Buck led the way to the stairwell and opened the fire door, then looked back at Lukas. "Let's just hope it doesn't reach those oxygen tanks, or we'll go up with the rest of this wing."

"Thanks, Buck, you're a natural encourager," Lukas muttered. For a moment—just one stress-filled moment—Lukas found himself remembering Kyle's words about Buck less than an hour ago. Was he hoping to be a hero again? What measures was he willing to take to get there? And if these explosions were arson . . . no, he couldn't think like that.

The inside of Lukas's nose felt as if it was coated with smoke and plaster dust by the time they reached the second floor. Then Buck opened the second fire door, and they stepped into a different world. Here they found little damage as they made their way down the hall. The carpet had been tracked with black soot from the feet of fire fighters and other rescue workers, but the lights still burned from auxiliary power, computers still blinked, telephones still rang—there was just no one there to answer them.

Two soot-smeared uniformed rescuers wearing heavy fire-resistant jackets rushed out of the administration suite into the hallway with a stretcher carrying Estelle Pinkley. They had encapsulated her in full c-spine immobilization, and she could not move her head, but her eyes were alert. Blood and soot streaked the side of her face. She caught sight of Lukas and groaned, closing her eyes momentarily against the pain.

Lukas rushed to her side. "Estelle, can you talk? Where do you hurt?"

She tried to reach toward him, but her bleeding hand fell back to her side. "Get everybody out of here, Lukas. Take care of the hospital . . . and take care of Bailey. He's hurt."

She was talking, so her airway was probably out of danger. Lukas leaned forward to check for breath sounds and reached for a radial pulse, but the men moved on past.

"Sorry, we can't stay for a check," the front carrier told him as they took Estelle out of reach. "We've got to get her out."

"And get yourself out, Lukas!" she called back to him. "It's dangerous here!"

"Come on, Doc, we've got to hurry." Buck led the way into Mrs. Pinkley's private office. "The floor partially collapsed here, because it's situated directly above RT and ER, which are above maintenance, where we believe the blasts took place. Watch it here, Dr. Bower. As I said, nothing's stable. We think the first blast took out the main power, and then the second blast apparently took out the auxiliary power for the ER. The rest of the hospital retained power even when you lost yours because the backup generators for them are in separate areas."

Lukas paused at the entrance and stared around the administration suite. The floor slanted crazily toward the inside wall, and shards of glass riddled the carpet and furniture from the shattered plate-glass window. Two rescue workers huddled beside Bailey Little in the corner, attempting to free his legs from a prison of steel and mortar.

"He's barely responsive," one of the men called from the floor. "We're trying to get him out, but he's not going to last much longer at this rate."

More of the ceiling crumbled onto them as they worked, scattering powdered plaster over their heads and shoulders.

Lukas stepped forward, but when he reached the end of the upturned desk, the floor buckled further. He froze in position.

"Careful!" Buck called. "I told you that floor's not solid."

"Then somebody trade places with me for a moment so I can do a decompression," Lukas said. "Or you won't have a patient to rescue."

One of the men stood to his feet and took slow, careful steps toward Lukas. "Okay, Doc, switch places with me and make it quick. I don't know how much time we've got."

Lukas followed his orders. His feet slid on the crazily angled carpet, but he reached out and took another fireman's outstretched hand for support. He knelt beside Bailey's silent white form. At least the body wasn't blue yet.

Lukas pulled off Bailey's tie and popped the buttons to loosen the shirt and expose the chest. He pulled his stethoscope from his pocket and bent to listen to the side of Bailey's neck. He heard slight air exchange. There was no tracheal deviation. Good, that meant no tension pneumothorax. Next he felt for a pulse at the neck. It was there, but weak. Breath sounds were fast and a little shallow from shock. No telling how much blood the patient had lost.

"Doc, hurry!" Buck shouted. "That wall could give at any time."

The heart sounds were muffled. Reflexively, Lukas doublechecked the right side of the neck. It was not distended as he would expect, but Bailey had two out of three clinical signs: There was probably a collection of blood in the sac that surrounded the heart, secondary to trauma, which kept the heart from pumping. Cardiac tamponade. Lukas had to drain it.

The floor shook, and Buck shouted. Lukas caught his breath and braced himself against the wall. *God, let me be right. Help! I could kill this man with one stick of the needle! And if I don't hurry, we could all be killed.*

# CHAPTER 29

Three more physicians had come to the clinic in response to the calls, and the patients were being treated, transferred, and some of them released. Loretta had come in moments ago to take over co-ordination detail at the front desk. Tedi sat beside her friend, Abby, and held Lindy Cuendet's hand while Jason Cuendet paced and asked everyone who came in what was going on outside. Jason and Lindy were not speaking to each other.

Mercy knelt beside Alma Collins' wheelchair, fingers linked together so tightly they turned white, tears of frantic petition streaking her face. Her own internal dialogue of "Please, God, please, God, please" mingled with Alma's calm words and rich accent.

". . . and, Lord, we know you have all power, and that you care for your children in every way, and so we ask you to please take care of Dr. Lukas right now and see him safely out of the danger. Guide his steps and give him your healin' touch. Please help us care for these hurtin' people in this place and show us the best way to comfort them." There was a pause, a slight hesitation as the raucous noise of the cries and sirens and shouts threatened to invade the curious peace of Alma's words. But then she spoke again as her arm came around Mercy's shoulders. "And, Lord, touch this child here with your healin' love, too. Touch her spirit and her heart and shower her with your peace." The arm squeezed firmly. "Amen."

Then, as the tumult once more invaded, somehow Mercy felt anchored, at least for a moment, carried away by something more powerful than her fear. God's healing love . . . that was it. The sudden knowledge of it touched her with wonder. She'd never considered it before, but as a doctor it should have been obvious. Why hadn't she seen it? Many times she had to cause pain to her patients during treatment. A shot of antibiotics could burn like fire, but the long-term healing gave long-lasting relief. Was that what God had been doing with her?

But as she considered the possibilities, the sounds of the sirens outside and the noisy, frightened chatter inside came crashing through that temporary oasis once more. As it did so, she found herself wishing for a more permanent peace.

"Mom!" Tedi shouted, pointing out the window. "There's Dad."

Mercy pushed herself up from her knees as Theo shoved open the door and raced inside, eyes wide with fear, face dripping with perspiration, chest heaving as he tried to catch his breath.

He caught sight of Tedi and stopped. "Thank God," he breathed, rushing forward. Tedi stood to meet him, and he grabbed her in his arms and swung her off her feet. "Thank God!" He held her for a long moment, chin resting on the top of her head, eyes squeezed tightly shut, then he set her down gently. "Your mother? Where is she? Is she okay?"

"Sure, Dad, she's right over there." Tedi pointed.

Theo swung around and caught sight of Mercy and dropped his arms to his sides, still breathing heavily. "Mercy, thank you for calling me about Tedi." He paused for breath. "I know you said she'd be okay, but then a customer came into the shop and told us about the explosion. You wouldn't believe what was going through my mind. I just started running." He glanced out the window and across the street. "Are there more people in there? Do they need help?"

"There are more. They haven't completed the evacuation," Mercy said, trying to keep the quiver from her voice.

"Lukas is in there, Dad," Tedi said softly.

At those words, Mercy felt the panic rising within her again. Fear for Lukas held her captive, and she was no good to anyone like this. Her daughter needed her. Her patients needed her.

Theo stepped over and placed a hand on her arm. "I'll go check on him, Mercy." He turned and rushed back out the door.

Mercy felt the tears in her eyes once again.

Lukas pulled out the syringe from his pocket and one of the two needles he had brought with him. He attached the six-inch needle to the closed syringe and leaned over Bailey's chest. Pressing the needle against the left side just under the breastbone, he pointed the tip toward the heart and slowly advanced the needle as he pulled back the plunger on the syringe. The needle was about four inches in when blood spurted into the tube.

A voice shouted from out in the hallway. "Buck! Get everybody out of there. The oxygen is going to go!"

The floor shifted again, and the desk lurched toward them. The firemen braced against the wall, and Lukas scrambled to hold the needle in place. He pulled back on the syringe until it stopped flowing easily. Bailey moaned.

"That did it!" one of the men shouted. "We've got his legs free. Doctor, get back. Come on, we've got to get out of here."

Lukas took two seconds to pull out the needle, then scrambled backward as two of the firemen rushed to extricate Bailey. He leaned against the desk and let them go first. They were through the doorway and out in the hall when Bailey moaned again. It was a good sign. At least he was conscious enough to—

A cannon crash blasted through the room with sudden force that knocked Lukas sideways. The blow blinded him as the floor dropped from beneath his feet. He reached out for something to stop his fall and felt the grip of a hand on his arm, struggling to pull him out of the collapsing debris. He reached out with the other hand and kicked upward as the floor continued to collapse.

"Hang on, Doc!" came Buck's voice through the tumult.

The floor buckled again, but Buck grabbed with his other hand, too. He did not release his grip. "I've got you, Doc!" but he slipped, too. The whole floor gave way beneath both of them. The scream of metal and the rumble of concrete followed Lukas and Buck down into suffocating darkness.

Mercy's cry of anguish merged and blended with the others as fire and black smoke billowed into the sky with the impact of a bomb.

The entire end of the west wing seemed to erupt and crash into the lawn of Knolls Community Hospital in crumbling concrete and twisted rebar. Fire jutted angry fingers into the sky, and the fire fighters attacked the flames with bursts of water.

"Mom!" Tedi screamed from across the waiting room. "Dad's in there!" She jumped up from Abby's side and pushed her way through the people, her eyes wide with terror. "Dad and Lukas are both in there!"

Mercy couldn't speak. Her first instinct was to run into the building and find them herself. Those rescue workers didn't know the hospital the way she did. But she couldn't leave her daughter here alone. She grabbed Tedi close and held tight. She couldn't think, could barely breathe. She couldn't bear to look at the destruction, but she couldn't look away. Lukas was in there. And Theo. And others had still not made it safely out.

As she watched, two firemen came running out of a door from the main building, carrying a man between them with broken and bleeding legs. Bailey. . . ? It looked like Bailey Little. Wasn't that who Lukas was going in to rescue?

"Mom?" Tedi's fingers dug into the flesh of Mercy's shoulders.

Mercy turned to find those trusting eyes seeking hers for reassurance. But she couldn't give it.

Alma wheeled over beside them. She reached out and drew them toward her, and for a moment, she just held them close.

---

The shock of the explosion knocked Theo against the wall of the broad hallway on the first floor of the main hospital building. The pain in his shoulder knocked him breathless for a few seconds. He braced himself for a wave of heat and fire, but nothing came. He could smell smoke, but the fire walls and doors were apparently still working between the main building and the ER and outpatient departments. He continued his trek more swiftly now.

Theo knew this hospital well. Mercy's father's old office was just up this corridor . . . and there was a back way into the ER, a narrow concrete hallway near the front of the wing that had been closed off when they remodeled this section five and a half years ago. If he could get into the reinforced stairwell from there . . . he heard shouts coming from somewhere behind him. He hurried faster.

While rescue workers and fire fighters scoured the hallways in search of more people to evacuate, Theo avoided them and slipped through the deserted cafeteria and kitchen and into the cardiac rehab unit. If a fire fighter saw him, he would be evacuated with the rest.

The scent of smoke was heavier here, but not overwhelming. Part of one outer wall had crumbled enough to allow light in from outside, and Theo knew there would be worse to come. He had to keep trying. Lukas had saved his life.

He reached the staff entrance into Mercy's father's old office. Amazingly, there was power here, and he could see to push past the debris. The smoke thickened further as he entered the hallway between Radiology and the ER. A whole wall had fallen across the entrance, and he stopped, frustrated. He was so close! This was where the power ended, but battery-pack floodlights, plugged into a couple of the remaining electrical sockets, continued to give light.

He turned to backtrack and find another way in, but a faint sound stopped him. He paused and listened. Was it the fire fighters shouting in the distance? The crackle of flames?

----

Lukas choked and gagged on the smoke that surrounded him, and he felt the singeing heat and heard the popping, snapping bite of fire.

Someone grabbed him by the shoulder and shook him. "Doc, are you okay? I need your help," came Buck's firm voice. "We've got to find a way out of here. We've got to bust this wall down if we can."

Lukas turned around to find Buck kneeling beside him, the broad planes of his face lit by the orange glow of a curtain of fire. They were trapped against the wall in an area about the size of an ER exam room. And they were in the supply room. The worst possible place to be in a fire.

*Lord, save us! Help us out of here!*

"Don't get all the way up," Buck continued. "Stay down as low as you can. There's a draft behind the fire that seems to be taking care of most of the smoke. Probably means there's been a natural chimney created by one of the explosions, which is good for us. But that can change."

Lukas coughed again, glad there was no more smoke than this. His throat burned as he listened to Buck's calm, professional voice and tried not to panic. But how could he not panic? They were trapped in an inferno, surrounded by combustible linens and cotton balls and gauze. He knew this wall behind them was a fire wall. Brick beneath the Sheetrock. Solid. Even Buck couldn't break his way through that.

Buck reached toward the edge of the fire for a large cylindrical oxygen tank, and Lukas stiffened. Then he relaxed. They'd used that tank this morning. It was empty.

"Help me, Doc. Maybe we can use this as a ram against the wall."

Lukas crawled over beside Buck to help him lift the tank, and that was when he saw Buck's left arm. Something had gouged a deep gash through the flesh and into the muscle.

"Buck, you're hurt."

Buck grunted with pain as he tried to lift the tank with both arms. "Can't do anything about it right now. Help me!"

Together they heaved the tank up above their heads and slammed it at the wall behind them with all their might. The force of the impact jarred Lukas's hands and arms, and he heard Buck groan. Painted Sheetrock powdered and dropped onto their heads and shoulders.

"Again," Buck said.

And they tried again and again as Buck's arm bled and they choked on the smoke. As the fire continued to rage, Lukas sent up constant, silent prayers to God. The wall would not give way.

---

Theodore heard the men on the other side of the wall. He'd tried to get their attention, but they were making too much noise. For a moment he was torn. Would he have time to run back outside and alert the rescuers?

And what if he was too late?

He turned to look around the radiology department. He knew these machines. Was there anything heavy enough for him to use as a battering ram against this side of the wall? If they came at the brick from both sides, would it collapse?

And then in the glow of the battery-pack floodlight, Theo saw what he needed. A huge portable x-ray machine, battery powered, that must weigh half a ton—at least that was what it felt like years ago when one of the techs had let him push it. It worked along the same lines as a self-propelled lawn mower, but would it be powered up? He rushed over and tried the switch.

The motor started. He grabbed the handles and guided it forward. He would have to get a running start, but he could do this.

———

"Got some verses for you two." Alma's calming voice seemed to float across the waiting room, affecting not only Mercy and Tedi, but the others as well. "In the Bible, King David wrote in his psalms, 'What time I am afraid, I will trust in Thee.' He's talkin' to God, because at times like this, God's the only one who knows what's goin' on. But you've got to believe that He will do what's right, no matter what." She put a hand on Mercy's arm. "Do you believe that, honey? Hasn't He answered a lot of prayers lately? Didn't you tell us yourself that you think God's been workin'?"

Mercy nodded, her gaze still trained on the rubble of the west wing. Her heart clung more and more desperately to Alma's words. They were the only message that made sense, that gave any hope, and she had to accept them as her own.

"Our peace comes from God" came Alma's voice again. "It's the only place for any of us. I love the Bible verse, 'Thou wilt keep him in perfect peace whose mind is stayed on Thee: because he trusteth in Thee.' I memorized those words in the King James Version years ago, and I love the sound of it. I repeated it a lot while I was in Mexico on the mission field, and especially when I was in the hospital losin' this leg. God never let me down. Trust Him, honey. He's the only one big enough to put our faith in."

Mercy took a deep breath and let it out. The two men she watched for, the two they had been praying for, could be lost to her and Tedi for all time. They could be dead. She had come face-to-face with death many times in her life, and the finality of it had always been a shock. This time, though . . . this time she could remember Lukas telling her that physical death was never final. He believed it and revealed it in his life.

Maybe that was why he and Theo had both had been able to go back into that building to help others.

She looked down at Tedi, who continued to watch her with frightened eyes. "Yes. Tedi, we can both put our faith in Him."

———

*Lord, if you're going to take me now, I'm willing to go, but please don't take Buck. He doesn't know you yet.* Lukas's prayer continued as the fire licked closer, devouring linens and cotton supplies as it turned the dwindling space into an oven. Buck dropped the cylinder, breathless from the exertion, face dripping with perspiration, arm dripping with blood. It was a toss-up to see if the fire would get them first or if Buck would bleed out.

Lukas scrambled on his knees to a rack that held Ace wraps. He grabbed one, crawled back to Buck, and quickly wound the bandage around the gaping cut. Buck caught his breath and tried once more to lift the oxygen canister. Lukas took it from him. He had just lifted it to swing again at the section of badly chipped brick they had been working on, when a powerful thud shook the whole wall. Cement chinks fell from between several of the bricks. The impact knocked the remaining ceiling tile to the floor.

"They're breaking in from the other side," Buck said weakly. "We've got to get out of the way." He turned to look at the flames all around. "Grab those tiles, Doc, and shove them at the flames on this side. They're fireproof, and maybe they can smother enough of the flames—"

As Lukas rushed to comply, another thud shook the wall, louder than the last, and the wall buckled. A central brick loosened with a scattering of cement, and Lukas reached up to pull it free. They heard a motor then, and it sounded like a forklift.

He shoved the brick into the fire to their right while Buck threw the tile.

And there was another thud, and more brick fell. Lukas grabbed up the oxygen tank and hurled it once again against the wall with all the strength he had left. Mortar broke. Bricks scattered, and someone shouted from the other side.

"You've got it! There's room! Come on through!"

———

Lukas, Buck, and Theodore stumbled out into fresh daylight, gasping, choking, exclaiming with relief. A crowd from the parking lot cheered, accompanied by the roar of a chopper taking off with Bailey Little aboard. The squall of another ambulance breezed through the milieu toward them.

A young woman came running toward them. Kendra Oppenheimer stumbled on the cracked concrete sidewalk, righted herself, and kept running, even as others shouted at her to get back.

She didn't stop. "Buck!" she cried with a choked sob as she neared him. "You're alive! Oh, thank God you're alive!"

Lukas could hear his big friend's sudden gasp, could see the surprised joy flood his face as he held out his good arm to catch her in an iron grip.

"I'm so sorry, Buck, I was wrong, so wrong." Her soft voice broke as she buried her face against the bulk of his chest. "I don't care if you're a fireman or a tech or an astronaut. I can't stop loving you. I'll worry about you whether we're living together or not. I'm so sorry."

As the chopper lifted, Buck stumbled, righted himself with heroic effort, then stumbled again and fell to his knees.

Lukas grabbed him. "Would somebody get us a gurney or a wheelchair? I need to give this man some medical attention."

The crowd of rescue workers and hospital staff converged on Lukas and Buck and Theodore. Leading the group was the stout, muscular bulk of the fire chief, Todd Adams.

While Buck assured everyone, especially his wife, that he would be fine, they placed him in a wheelchair and pushed him toward the Richmond Clinic.

"Everyone's accounted for now," Adams shouted over the sound of the helicopter. He reached out to shake Buck's hand. "You done good, Buck. You kept your cool again. If you hadn't gotten Dr. Bower up there to Bailey in time, they don't think he'd have made it."

"What about Mrs. Pinkley?" Lukas asked. "Where did you take her?"

"They're taking her by ground to Cox South, same place the chopper's taking Mr. Little," Adams said. "Dr. Wong checked her out himself. Looks like she might have some cracked or broken ribs, maybe a concussion, a broken leg, but Estelle's tough as shoe leather. What'd you want to bet she tries to take over the hospital by the first of next week?"

"Dad! Lukas!" Tedi came running out of the front door of the clinic, and she didn't stop until she reached them. Theodore picked her up in a bear hug, and tears of relief flowed down both their faces.

And when he released her, she grabbed Lukas, smearing her face and clothing with streaks of soot and dirt. Lukas held her for a long moment in a strong embrace. That was when he saw Mercy.

She stood out in front of the clinic. Her long black hair was disheveled, and her hands were raised to her face as if she were in shock or crying. Her gaze did not leave him.

He took a step in her direction, but the crowd around him cut him off.

"Buck," the chief said as he walked beside the wheelchair, "you're back on the team."

Buck stared at his boss, his face black and red and dripping with soot and sweat and heat, his ears looking like singed doorknobs. "But I thought you'd be mad, Chief. I was suspended, and I played fireman anyway."

"You're not suspended anymore. We got our man, the same one we suspected all along." Todd grunted and shook his head with regret. "Sorry I couldn't let you in on it, but Kyle Alder was setting you up—or trying to."

"Kyle!" Buck turned and gazed at the destruction in amazement. "He did all this?"

"We have a confession. He even used a set of football pads when he torched the school cafeteria so it'd look more like you, and he used your jar of solvent. His Explorer buddy started to steer clear of him a couple of days ago, and we got suspicious, but you know how hard it is to catch an arsonist. So we let him think he had us fooled."

"How'd you catch him, Chief?"

"You know that picture on the front page in yesterday's paper? We did that on a hunch. We thought somebody might see it and place Kyle at the scene before the fire. It worked. One of the waitresses at Little Mary's recognized him and called us."

"He sure had me fooled," Buck said. "I didn't think he could pull off something like this." He gestured toward the wing of the hospital that lay in burning, steaming ruins.

The chief shook his head again. "Too bad we didn't catch him in time. He's confessed now, and he's been hauled off. He admitted he got mad at you for giving him a bad review and refusing to recommend him for further training, but he swears the torching just got out of hand. He used calcium carbide for this one." Todd jerked his head at the hospital. "Put it in the maintenance room. That's what caused the first explosion. He didn't realize the water from the sprinklers would make it so combustible. The generators exploded. That's what spread the fire."

Lukas couldn't keep his attention from wandering once more toward Mercy. She was walking to meet him, arms crossed over her chest now as if she were cold, but she stopped when she came to the edge of the crowd that surrounded Buck and Lukas. Her nose was red, and her eyes had makeup smudged in the wrong places. Even as he watched, more tears dripped down her cheeks, and she sniffed.

As Buck and his wife talked excitedly with the others, Lukas stepped back from the crowd, strolled around the perimeter, accepting an occasional pat on the back and inquiries about his well-being. He kept his attention on Mercy. He wanted to run to her, to take her in his arms and never let her go again. When he drew close enough to touch her, she spoke first.

"You're okay," she breathed. "When the building exploded I thought . . . I was so . . . ." Fresh tears filled her eyes, and she clamped her arms more tightly around her. "I prayed so hard, and those prayers were all answered. And I realized that God has answered so many of my prayers, and I've just ignored Him, blamed Him. I'm so sorry. Oh, Lukas, you're alive!"

He watched her for a couple of seconds in awe, then he grabbed her and pulled her to him, wrapping his arms tightly around her. She buried her face in the smoky front of his scrubs, and her shoulders shook with sobs.

"You're alive," she murmured. "Thank God." Another sob shook her. "Thank God."

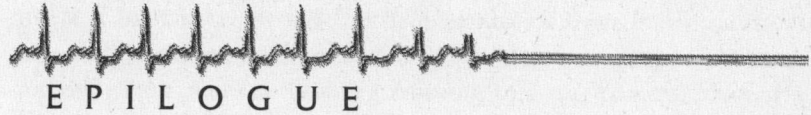

# EPILOGUE

Sunday morning came early in the patient rooms at Cox South Medical Center, earlier than Estelle Pinkley was used to awakening. It wasn't even daylight outside when she heard a nurse taking the vitals of the patient on the other side of the thin curtain. There had been no private rooms available, and Estelle longed for Knolls, where every room was private and nurses didn't have to disturb patients in the middle of the night in order to complete their duties.

The chair next to Estelle's bed was empty, and she gave a relieved sigh. Clyde, her husband of fifty-five years, had been beside her throughout this whole ordeal, red-eyed and droopy, dozing beside her day and night since they brought her in. She had ordered him out last night. It was the only way she was going to get any work done, and the only way he was going to get any sleep.

She waited for the nurse to walk out of the room, then pressed the button to move her bed into the sitting-up position, grimacing as her cracked ribs protested. It was a good thing her left wrist was just sprained and not broken. She pulled a note pad out from under the blanket beside her and reread what she'd written last night after Clyde and Ivy and Lukas and half the town of Knolls were forced to leave at the end of visiting hours. She changed a few words, wrote two more sentences, and nodded with satisfaction. It would work.

Slowly, gently, she reached for her bedside phone and punched the private home number for the editor of the *Knolls Review*, using her calling card. She noted with a nod of satisfaction that the call would wake him up.

Unfortunately, a female voice answered, that of Harvey's long-suffering wife, Barbara.

"Hello, Barb? Estelle here. Sorry to bother you so early in the morning, but I need to talk to Harvey, and the staff here is a little strict about patients working from their beds. Yes, yes, I'll be fine, just some cracked ribs and a broken leg and a concussion. The hospital will be okay, too, don't worry. Thanks, Barb." She checked her notes again, prepared to get tough if she had to.

The editor picked up an extension within ten seconds.

"Hi, Harvey. Listen, you got the information I sent you on RealCare, didn't you? Good. Those are publishable facts, and I want to see them in tomorrow's paper, and don't give me any argument, or I'll slap a libel charge on you and Bailey." Might as well let him know up front that he wasn't going to push her around in her weakened condition.

"Yes, Bailey's still alive to sue, bless his rotten soul." She didn't mention the fact that he was in bad shape right now and probably wouldn't walk for a long time. She wasn't going to walk for a while, either, but that wouldn't stop her. "I think I can convince him to retract his letter, but your paper did some major damage to the reputation of one of the best ER docs in the region, and you're going to do some scrambling to make up for it."

She listened with satisfaction while Harvey apologized and back-pedaled for a moment. She wouldn't be getting any bad press from him for a long time.

"First of all," she said, "you will print in the headline article that Knolls Community was cleared of all allegations by COBRA. Second, we were well insured. We'll have a bigger and better hospital than ever before, and I will be overseeing every aspect of the operations myself."

She didn't, after all, have to depend on her notes. It was all there in her head. When she got finished with Harvey, she would call some contractors in the area. Her hospital wouldn't be down for long. Neither would she.

---

Lukas sat nearer to the front of the pulpit than he usually did on Sunday mornings, but that was because he'd arrived late, and the church was nearly full. Many of the people here today probably only attended services at Christmas and Easter. Parking lots in churches all around town this morning overflowed out into the streets. It seemed as if everyone in the county was here. Except for Mercy.

Lukas couldn't deny his disappointment. After Thursday . . . after the look he'd seen in her eyes, the joy that seemed to suddenly flow out of her—and not just because she was relieved that he was safe— he'd expected something more.

It was all that had been on his mind aside from the shock of the explosions and fire and community outpouring of pain over the partial destruction of the hospital. He, too, was emotional. The destruction of the ER had devastated a part of him.

This morning's sermon was about new beginnings. Appropriate, since cleanup had already begun on the hospital, and the citizens of Knolls, always community minded, had taken part in the operation as much as they were allowed.

And Bailey Little had done his part. After giving Lukas an abject apology this morning for all he had done, he promised to call the *Knolls Review* and make a public apology, as well. There would be no more attempts to destroy what was left of Knolls Community Hospital.

Of course, since Bailey was feeling the effects of morphine at the time, Lukas knew he could only wait and see how sincere the man's words had been.

Shaking himself from the attack of cynicism, Lukas glanced across the auditorium and caught sight of slender, serene Darlene Knight sitting beside Ivy and Tedi. If Ivy had her way—and she usually did, except with her own daughter—Clarence would be sitting beside them as soon as he could get around better. Lukas had enjoyed several lively discussions with Clarence about God's unconditional love, God's power, God's grace. The big man's heart was changing, Lukas could tell. He was gradually releasing some of the pain he'd gone through in the past. Of course, Lukas had thought Mercy's heart was changing, too.

Theodore Zimmerman sat in the pew behind his daughter, his gaze straying to the back of Tedi's head every few moments with an expression of wonder, and Lukas felt a rush of joy for the new relationship being forged between father and daughter. And between Father and son.

In the pew in front of Lukas, Lauren McCaffrey sniffed and pressed a tissue to her eyes. Another woman sitting in the pew behind him sniffed and blew her nose, and he realized he had missed the past few minutes of the sermon, and that an emotional point had just been made. That wasn't like him. He usually listened. He often took notes on the backs of tithe envelopes if he forgot to tuck some loose notebook paper into his Bible.

The pastor concluded the message, and the organ slipped softly into a hymn of invitation. The congregation stood, and Lukas sighed. He had to get his mind off the could-have-beens. He was here to worship God, not scan the crowd for roll call or pine for a lost love.

He opened the *Baptist Hymnal* to "Just As I Am" and opened his mouth to join in the second verse when he detected movement in the aisle to his left. It was not polite to stare at someone walking down to the altar during invitation time, but everybody always did, sometimes out of curiosity, sometimes relief, oftentimes joy. An altar invitation was supposed to be a time of personal introspection and heartfelt prayer, but brotherly love was also allowed.

Lukas caught the amazing, beautiful sight of Mercy Richmond's dark hair streaming over her slender, erect shoulders—where did *she* come from? He'd done a thorough search for her at the beginning of the worship service.

As she reached the front, he wanted to shout a prayer of praise—he only did so in his heart. After all, this was a circumspect Baptist church. Mercy walked purposefully toward the pastor, who waited with hands outstretched in front of the pulpit.

She took those hands, spoke with the pastor, nodded eagerly, then bent her head in prayer while the congregation sang the third and fourth verses.

Lukas couldn't sing. He stared unabashedly toward Mercy, unable to see her clearly past the tears in his eyes. All his prayers over the summer were being answered right here in a church full of witnesses. All the words he thought had fallen on deaf ears, all the pleading and explaining and arguing that had ended in frustration, all the pain . . . everything was being answered. He felt a weightlessness so profound it made him dizzy.

Someone touched his arm, and he looked over to find Lauren holding a tissue for him. She, too, had tears in her eyes. He took the tissue and smiled at her and continued to smile as the pastor raised his hand for the music to stop.

"Ladies and gentlemen, I want to present to you a brand-new sister in Christ, Mercy Richmond."